I0710328

The Golden Needle

The Taiga, Book 1

T.J. Carroll

Cumberstone Press

For Brad, who always believed

CONTENTS

1. Chapter 1 — 1

2. Chapter 2 — 5

3. Chapter 3 — 13

4. Chapter 4 — 21

5. Chapter 5 — 24

6. Chapter 6 — 32

7. Chapter 7 — 42

8. Chapter 8 — 53

9. Chapter 9 — 66

10. Chapter 10 — 72

11. Chapter 11 — 80

12. Chapter 12 — 89

13. Chapter 13 — 98

14. Chapter 14 — 111

15. Chapter 15 — 123

16. Chapter 16 — 141

17. Chapter 17 — 149

18. Chapter 18 — 159

19. Chapter 19   176

20. Chapter 20   193

21. Chapter 21   210

22. Chapter 22   217

23. Chapter 23   229

24. Chapter 24   247

25. Chapter 25   252

26. Chapter 26   268

27. Chapter 27   274

28. Chapter 28   284

29. Chapter 29   291

30. Chapter 30   297

31. Chapter 31   310

To my readers...   327

Acknowledgments   328

Also By T.J. Carroll   330

About the Author   332

Chapter 1

Earth scuffed Dashi's palms as she moved, adding a fresh layer of filth. There hadn't been enough water to wash her hands in a fortnight. There hadn't been enough water to wash the rest of her in three months.

Outside, dawn was only hours away, but darkness would cling to her narrow world indefinitely. This was where it retreated when the sunlight declared victory, where it bivouacked before the next assault on the day. It was dusk and shadows here, always dusk and shadows.

Dashi turned at the corner, balancing on her hands and keeping her legs pointed to the ceiling. She was getting weaker—she'd only gone around two dozen times and already her arms were trembling—but she kept moving, letting the ache in her shoulders make up for the inaction of so many consecutive hours.

The guards were inattentive just before dawn: if you wanted to do something that was frowned upon, this was the best time to accomplish it. Not that there was much to choose from in terms of nefarious activity. Mostly, it consisted of a brisk trade in hand-rolled cigarettes, which Dashi didn't consume, and exhortations by her male neighbors to show them her "best parts," which she ignored.

Her perpetual restlessness wasn't even the type of behavior she'd thought a prisoner would need to hide. It wasn't dangerous. She wasn't trying to escape. *That* particular notion hadn't crossed her mind lately, not in any vehicle more serious than a daydream. She'd tried and failed at digging. The walls were made of enormous stone blocks, impossible to break. Beneath its patina of dirt, the floor was made from the same. She'd been stripped of any metal when she arrived and meals were served in wooden bowls with no utensils.

No, her compulsion to move stemmed from boredom and boredom alone. It was an unrelenting, painful kind of monotony and, like a horse that bites incessantly at the stall door when it's been stabled too long, she'd created her own methods of staying sane.

The guards didn't see it that way, naturally. They always paid closer attention to any prisoners who seemed overly energetic—"threatening," they termed it. Thus, Dashi confined her activities to the lifeless hours of early morning, when her only spectators were the flies from the offal bucket and the lice on her blanket.

The sharp creak of a door made her flip to her feet. In another breath, she was on her mat, curled up with every semblance of sleep. The tramp of footsteps reached her ears, growing louder as the guards approached. She thought there were three or four, though she couldn't be sure without opening her eyes.

"This the one?" The guard sounded like he was standing just outside her cell. No, that couldn't be right. They must have come for one of her neighbors; they'd been here longer than she had. Surely their judgment would come first, even if their crimes were less severe.

There was a murmur of assent, followed by the clank of the bolt being drawn and the protest of hinges.

They're not here for me. I have more time, she assured herself, but her pounding heart begged to differ.

The footsteps stopped just in front of her face and Dashi sat up quickly to forestall the inevitable kick.

"I'm up." Her voice croaked slightly, but she thought it was due to thirst, not nerves. That's probably why her hands were shaking too.

The guard grunted a laugh. "Knew you weren't sleeping." He turned back to the others, who, Dashi saw, weren't regular prison guards but men in military uniform. "Told you: criminals aren't made, they're born. Not one of the lot can be trusted, even over small things."

"You were born too," Dashi said, her voice still harsh. "To a hairy sow rolling in her own waste." Maybe it was nerves after all. Altan always said that's how she reacted to strain: by leaping from the precipice, lashing out in some way.

The guard's attention jerked back to Dashi and his hand fell to the cudgel hanging from his waist.

One of the soldiers cleared his throat. "We'll take the prisoner from here."

Nothing could have been worse than those words. Nothing could have better signaled her impending judgment. The khan wanted a clean show: no pre-bloodied prisoners for him. He let his executioners do that.

The guard peeled his fingers from the cudgel, instead nudging Dashi roughly with his boot. "You heard him. Get up."

Dashi got to her feet, moving in slow motion, as if she hadn't just been pacing the cell on her hands. Her eyes focused on the waiting men. Broad-shouldered military types, all of them. Not stupid either, if their sharp gazes were any indicator. One of them held out a metal cuff and, when Dashi took a step back at the sight, the guard grabbed her hair and shoved her forward so that she fell to her knees. The cuff closed around her neck with a snap.

This was it, then. *The end.*

The average prisoner didn't rate a trial. Not unless the public outcry was loud enough to make the khan take notice. Dashi couldn't remember the last time that had happened and she rather doubted it would be the case for her. More often, accused criminals were just executed. Publicly, on some occasions. With little fanfare, on others.

Even if, by some not-inconsequential miracle, she *was* being taken to trial, it would only delay the inevitable. There would be no escape from her fate.

She was guilty of murder, after all.

Chapter 2

The neck cuff was too big. It slid each time Dashi moved, pinching her skin and pulling at her hair in tiny bursts of pain. A small mercy that she wouldn't be alive long enough for it to truly chafe.

Her hands, also manacled, were attached to the cuff by a length of chain. A soldier held the other end. She tried to rub her neck, but he yanked her hands back down.

"Keep them at your waist. Where I can see them."

They trundled up the stone steps and into the empty guardroom. The soldier holding the chain halted next to the door and turned to one of the others. "Make sure they're ready outside."

It was to be a no-nonsense execution then, done on the prison grounds in the dark. Dashi twisted her sweating fingers together, her eyes jerking back and forth in search of an escape. None of the other prisoners who'd been executed had been taken at night, but perhaps their deaths had been public ones. She couldn't honestly say she would have preferred that. Public executions were long and drawn out and, though she appreciated every last second of oxygen, she'd just as soon get the ordeal over with.

Still, the idea of dying in the darkness was unpalatable. Whatever was coming, she wanted to see it.

The soldier who'd stuck his head outside glanced back, nodding at the one who held the chain. "All set."

Her feet turned to stone, but the soldiers propelled Dashi through the door anyway. Summer air flooded her lungs and she almost sobbed at the sweetness of it. She'd forgotten it would be summer by now. The snow had been thin and muddy when she'd been brought in three months ago. It had soaked her clothes when the prefects tackled her. She'd still been shivering when they'd turned her in.

The winter had been uncharacteristically easy. That's why Altan had suggested their last job. They'd take advantage of the early spring, he'd said. The wolves, sated from the mild weather, wouldn't be too bold and, besides, their buyer had offered double if they could deliver within the month—

Dashi shook the memories away. Her last thoughts should be good ones, *happy* ones, not stained with pain and regret. She would think of Altan and Zayaa, heads bent together over some old text; of Baris teasing her, his mouth tipped up in laughter. She would remember the way adventure tasted each time they left the city.

Slowly, resignedly, she lowered her eyes from the dark sky, bracing herself for the sight of executioners. But the courtyard was empty, save for a tall covered wagon. Between the moon and the torchlight, she could just make out a pair of yaks waiting placidly in front. Neither spared her a glance.

The soldier holding her chain motioned for Dashi to climb inside.

"Where are you taking me?"

He lifted her to the wagon without answering, pushing her head down at the last second so she didn't hit the crosspiece.

"Where are you taking me?" she asked again, though she could guess. Public executions were, of course, *public*, conducted on a platform near the center of the city where everyone could watch the show.

When no one answered, she began to curse: a foul stream of words gleaned from the streets and lovingly perfected by Baris over the years.

One of the soldiers grabbed her cuffed throat, while another wedged a cloth into her mouth, choking off her torrent. The fabric tasted rotten, a combination of animal fat and metal and dirt. Probably used to clean weapons and ancestors-knew-what-else.

"None of that," said the soldier who held the chain. It was dark, but she recognized his voice. She'd already pegged him as their leader. "If you make more noise we'll figure out another way to keep you quiet. Nod if you understand."

Slowly, Dashi nodded. He released her collar.

The wagon started forward, swaying clumsily from side to side as it hit potholes and rocks. After a while, Dashi began to hear the symphony of people preparing for the day: the squeak of passing carts, voices calling to one another, and the occasional dog barking. The wagon lurched forward suddenly as it gained traction on a well-maintained thoroughfare, leaving the rutted prison road behind. They'd reached the outskirts of Karak City, her home for the last ten years. It wouldn't be much longer now.

The inside of the wagon grew gradually lighter, illuminating the soldiers on either side of her. The lead soldier sat opposite. She shifted on the unforgiving bench; months of small prison meals had ensured her bones didn't have the luxury of extra cushioning. The men watched warily as she tried to get comfortable but made no move to stop her. Nor did they make any attempts at conversation, not with her and not amongst themselves.

They're nervous, she realized, though she couldn't figure out why. She jerked her hands suddenly and the chain rattled against the bench. All three soldiers jumped. The leader pulled the chain tight, making sure there was no slack with which to make further noise.

Despite the gag, Dashi grinned at him.

The wagon stopped suddenly. The driver spoke a few words and they lurched forward again, only to halt two minutes later. This time, the soldiers got to their feet, pulling Dashi up with them. She balked at the edge of the wagon, not because she didn't want to get out but because she couldn't comprehend what she was seeing.

The building before her was large, with a green tiled roof that sat up pertly at the corners. Like all houses in Karak City, the door faced east, welcoming the sun and the spirits of the ancestors. Mirrors over the doors and windows confused evil spirits. Gardens hugged the front of the house, curling in toward a ceramic altar, where someone had already lit the day's incense offering.

This wasn't the executioner's square. It was a noble's home.

The soldiers hustled her upstairs through an interior that screamed wealth. Dark wood panels, probably procured at an unholy expense, were outlined with bright molding. In the center of each, a piece of artwork was displayed: paintings, wall hangings, an unfurled scroll, and a few relief carvings. A cluster of delicate vases stood on a corner shelf. When she stopped to stare, the soldiers pushed her forward, but it didn't keep Dashi from mentally cataloging the opulence around her: a sixth-century tapestry here, a sculpture from the Latwan Kingdom there—too big for one person to move. She found herself taking in every detail, mentally enshrining each piece as if she could still relay the information to Altan, Zayaa and Baris.

She licked her lips. Even by a noble's standards, the collection was impressive.

"In here," the lead soldier said, indicating a door at the end of the hall.

Dashi stepped inside without arguing, curiosity beginning to temper her dread. The room was decorated with the same expensive taste. There were even, she noted with interest, a few truly ancient pieces, taken from the moldering Purek ruins that dotted Karakal's northern and eastern borders.

A bed stood in the center of the room, flanked by a silk dressing screen and a tub of water. Steam drifted lazily from its surface. A female servant waited nearby.

The lead soldier removed Dashi's gag and manacles but left the neck cuff. He nodded to the tub. "You'll bathe there."

Dashi crossed her newly liberated arms. "For what reason?"

"Because your stench is offensive."

"My stench has been offensive for months and no one thought to do anything about it. Who ordered you to bring me here? Am I to have a trial?"

"Of a sort. Get in the bath."

"I don't require an audience to clean myself."

"It's not safe for Gerel to be alone with you." He glanced at the dressing screen. "Or out of sight with you."

Dashi eyed the servant, who blushed and looked down at the bathwater. "There's no need for Gerel to stay either," she said, not bothering to argue the point. "I'm perfectly capable of washing myself." She tugged at the neck cuff. "Chain *this* to something, if it makes you feel better." She'd already seen the table of dressing accessories. There must be something there to help her shed this last encumbrance. A hairpin maybe, or even the tooth of a comb if she could break it right.

"I was instructed not to leave you alone."

"We're on the second floor. You can station your men outside the door."

"Get in the bath or I will put you in it myself."

Dashi's arms stayed crossed.

With a tight look on his face, the soldier grasped the hem of her ragged shirt. Dashi jerked away and stalked to the tub.

"You'll have to unhook the chain," she said sweetly. "Or I can't get my shirt over my head."

The lead soldier gripped her shoulder. "Don't move," he ordered, just before he slit the back of her shirt from top to bottom. She shucked off the rest quickly, eager to be in the water now.

Behind her, she heard the lead soldier step closer, though she wasn't sure whether it was to accommodate the length of chain or because he was afraid she'd drown Gerel in the bathwater. The water was so hot it hurt, but Dashi didn't complain. She curled into a ball and ducked beneath the surface, letting the heat seep into her face and scalp. When she came up, Gerel set to work on Dashi's matted hair, first washing it, then working out the tangles and lice with a fine comb.

Dashi's skin was red and smarting by the end, but instead of stopping, Gerel, who was either fastidious or sadistic, started the entire process over again. Dashi never looked at the soldiers, not wanting to know if they were watching. When she'd finally been washed and de-loused to Gerel's satisfaction, the servant offered her a dressing gown, holding it open to shield Dashi from the view of the men. By then, Dashi had made her peace with bathing in front of them, but the kindness in that one gesture made her forgive the servant for her abrasive scrubbing.

She stepped out of the tub feeling refreshed but wary; now that the bathing was done, she wasn't sure what came next. A trial of sorts, the lead soldier had said. What did that mean?

Dashi managed to don the undergarments without taking off the dressing gown, but when she went to pull on clothes, the lead soldier stopped her.

"Wait." He motioned to one of the others, who stepped forward and offered a cloth bundle. "Take off the dressing gown."

Dashi raised her chin but let the gown fall to the floor.

Without looking at her, the lead soldier removed a flexible metal band from the bundle, which he fit around her waist. Holding it in place with one hand, he gingerly unwrapped a second object—a thick disk made of the same metal—and used it to secure both ends of the band just over her belly button.

He continued squinting at Dashi's waist, turning the disk back and forth until finally he loosed a relieved-sounding breath and stepped back. Only then did he unlock the cuff around her neck.

Dashi looked down. The metal band was thin, with a whitish sheen to it, and fit her waist closely. She tugged it down, but the flare of her hips forestalled any hope of sliding it off completely. At least she could still breathe comfortably; the strange flexible metal seemed designed to move with her. The front of the disk, when she sucked in her stomach and tipped it up to face her, was glass, though it was unlike anything she'd seen before. She ran a fingernail across the surface: rough but still transparent. Beneath the glass, she could see two triangles, one balanced on top of the other. The top one was formed of tiny black circles and the other was plain white, but the symbol meant nothing to her.

"What is it?" she asked.

No one answered. *Fine.* She wasn't about to beg for information. Instead, she picked up the clothes Gerel had laid out—a plain *deel*, undershirt, sash and pants—and began putting them on. The clothing fit better than the prison uniform had, though the deel had extra room through the waist and chest, a legacy of the weight she'd lost. She wound the sash a little tighter to compensate.

The lead soldier stood against the wall, making no move to shackle her again. Gerel started for the door, followed by the other two soldiers.

"Better check your pockets," one of them murmured. "She's a thief."

"I'm an *art* thief, not a pickpocket," Dashi spat.

The door swung wide as another man entered the room. Like the soldiers, he looked fit and carried himself with confidence, though his deel was black, not the green and gold of a military uniform. The two exiting soldiers saluted him anyway.

"Art thief? Is that what they're calling tomb robbers these days?" the new man asked, striding toward her.

Dashi froze. No one knew about her trips to the ruins, not even the prefects who'd arrested her. No one *alive* anyway, except for her sister, but Dashi doubted Idree could even be persuaded to admit they were related these days.

"And let's not forget your other title," the man said, a smile sliding across his face as he caught her expression. "*Spy.*"

Chapter 3

The man slowed as he approached, but it was an ominous change of momentum, like a hawk just before it stoops. His hair, thick and black, was tied at his nape, but that was the only accommodation he made to current fashion. Everything else about him was unadorned. Dashi judged him to be fifteen years her senior, but his skin was already weathered, evidence of a man who wasn't content to watch life go by from the inside of his grand house.

"Any problems, Osol?" he asked the lead soldier.

"We had to gag her. Otherwise, smooth as cream, sir."

"Any damage?" He began to circle Dashi, his eyes moving up and down. Not in the way a man looks at a woman but in the way he might judge a horse.

"Underfed but not starving. Some bruising but no evidence of broken bones."

The presumption with which the noble spoke, with which he looked at her—Dashi could feel the familiar tide of her anger, rising higher and higher until it threatened to spill over. Anger was good; it prevented her from dwelling on the splinter of fear that had lodged in her mind.

"Why am I here?" She stepped to his right and began circling him in return, noting his height and build, the smooth way he moved. "There might be a Chertai vase in the hall and a servant to scrub me, but I've spent long enough in one prison to recognize another."

"I see your eye for art remains undamaged," he said in a dry voice.

Without examining it closely, Dashi hadn't been sure the vase in the hall *was* an original Chertai. Chertai was a popular artist and the market was full of imitations, but she'd guessed a man as wealthy as this one wouldn't display a fake.

"Aren't you worried I'll steal something?" she asked, forcing her feet to halt. She'd seen several Purek pieces that she and Altan *had* stolen...which made the noble's disdain for tomb-robbing more than a little hypocritical. She wondered if he knew where his artwork originated.

"A bit like letting the wolf bed down with the colts, isn't it?" he agreed. "But I think I've laid the groundwork for your cooperation."

"Oh?" Dashi raised an eyebrow. Did he want her to steal something? That seemed far-fetched; from all appearances, he had enough money to buy whatever he wanted. Anyway, there were plenty of other thieves to be bargained with. Or taken from prison, for that matter.

The noble didn't answer right away but turned to a piece of artwork hanging on the wall: a picture of the steppe in wintertime, painted in grays and browns. He ran a forefinger along the edge. "This was done by a Mori nomad."

"So?"

"You're Mori, aren't you?"

Dashi's skin prickled ominously. *Breath of the ancestors*, Baris called that feeling: a warning that something was about to go drastically wrong. She looked at the window over the man's shoulder. There was a lock on it.

"That's why your ring recruited you for their forays, isn't it?" he asked. "Because you speak Mori and the nomads are the only ones who know the northlands anymore. Altan, Zayaa and...what was the third one's name? Boris?"

Baris. She wanted badly to correct him—it felt like a betrayal to let Baris' name be mangled—but she kept her mouth closed.

"Boris," he continued. "He was closest to you in age, wasn't he? Such a shame that—"

"*What do you want?*" she roared. From the corner of her eye, she saw Osol jump. If the vase collection had been within reach, she would have thrown the prized Chertai at the noble's head.

He pursed his lips. "Altan said you had a combative streak. I trust it will see you through."

She took an involuntary step backward. This man had spoken to Altan?

"In his missives to the Tyvalaran crown, he mentioned you only twice: once as 'the combative girl-child who followed me before' and once as 'our brash interpreter.' That's why the consul's investigations into the spy ring skipped right over you: whether by accident or design, Altan made you sound like a piece of scenery, not an actor. I almost missed it too, but," he paused to seat himself in an upholstered chair, "I've found that necessity does funny things to the powers of observation. I started to wonder if maybe there'd been a fourth spy. Then one of my observant lieutenants," he nodded toward Osol, "remembered that he'd seen a girl being arrested for the murders of two men. Two men who just *happened* to have disposed of a spy ring a few days prior. He thought the girl looked like she might be part Mori."

Dashi felt light-headed. She hadn't eaten since yesterday afternoon and it was past time for breakfast.

"I read the prefecture report myself. The arresting officer said the murders were motivated by greed. But that didn't add up either. Both victims had full purses, yet you only stole a single item." The noble placed a small object on the arm of the chair, pinning it on its edge with one finger.

Dashi didn't move. She didn't need to. She could see the pendant clearly from where she stood: a gold disc made to look like a small, stylized sun. That's what Altan's name meant. *Golden sun.*

"Then I talked to the victims' comrades. They said the pendant originally belonged to a spy they'd been ordered to kill. I kept thinking: what were the chances that a ring of spies would be eliminated and that two of their executioners would also be killed...over something as small as this?" He tilted the pendant so it caught the light, eying it thoughtfully. "It still has blood on it, you know."

Dashi swallowed, caught in a maelstrom of emotions: grief for her friends; an increasing fear of this man and what he knew; anger at his insinuations. The idea of Altan, Baris and Zayaa having a separate identity, of them keeping something from her for *years*? She knew they'd spent time in Tyvalar, but *spies*? She couldn't credit it. They were the three people she'd known best in the world, the three people she had most idolized. She'd been closer to them than to her own sister.

"I don't know what you're talking about," she said finally. "Altan, Zayaa and Baris were killed by thieves, men who wanted the profit of selling artifacts from the ruins without the hardship of retrieving them."

"They weren't thieves. They were sent to eliminate your friends." He removed a piece of paper from his pocket and offered it to Dashi. The script was cramped and precise. *Altan's.*

She skimmed the contents. *"One of us nearly fell into a pit trap, but otherwise the tapestry was recovered with little trouble..."* The page went on to describe the tapestry in detail: an ancient ruler and his court, resplendent in their finery; the moon shining above; a woman holding needle and thread; a prone figure, without any clothes.

"Anyone could have written this," Dashi said, but she remembered the pit trap. It was Baris who'd almost fallen to his death. Her memory of the tapestry was a little hazier, but Altan's description brought it back. She looked away. "I would have known." *He would have told me.*

"This was recovered from a rider on the road to Tyvalar. Someone Altan met with." The noble took the paper back. "But you address precisely the question I've pondered most: *did* their brash interpreter know they were spies? I suppose you wouldn't admit it either way. A wise course of action under normal circumstances, but it won't make a difference today."

"Why not?"

"Because the skills I need from you have nothing to do with spying. As long as you were the fourth member of their group, as long as you were the one accompanying them to the ruins in the northlands—and I think you've just established that you were—then you could have shared a wet nurse with the Tyvalaran queen, for all I care."

"The skills you need from me," she repeated. "You got me out of prison because you think I'll go to the northlands for you?"

"Now we get to the crux of the matter!" His smile was sleek and fast. He folded his fingers around Altan's pendant. "You will be going to the northlands. And I need you to do it faster than anyone else."

Dashi bristled at the words "you will." She wanted to erase that confidence, to throw something at him—either figuratively or literally—that he hadn't anticipated. She glanced around the room for a suitable projectile.

"Faster than *who*?" Her leg jiggled with the need to move, with the urge to convert anxiety into action, but the noble got to his feet and began pacing before she could. There wasn't enough room for them both to pace, not without coming very close to each other, so she stayed where she was. Just as well. She didn't want to be like this man in any way.

"The khan has collected artifacts for a long time," the noble said. "He bought many of the antiquities that you and your fellow spies recovered.

It was the khan's chief adviser, the consul, who commissioned pieces of interest from Altan."

Dashi thought about their last trip, about Altan saying his buyer would pay double. Had it been the consul? She knew very little about the final destinations of the pieces they procured. Altan and Zayaa had always handled the business end of things, while Dashi and Baris shared a dislike for such details. Though different in temperament—Baris was laid back, while Dashi, in Altan's words, tended to be brash and combative—they'd both excelled at the physical demands of the job. *Leave the boring work to those two quill-holding scholars*, Baris always joked. *We're the muscle.*

And they had been, each in their way. Baris was a mountain of a man who excelled in every physical endeavor in which strength was imperative. Dashi's skills were particular to her early upbringing: in addition to being fluent in Mori, she was adept with a horse and a bow and had a proclivity for risky acrobatics, both on horseback and her own two feet.

The noble kept talking. "There's a special artifact the khan wants; he and the consul have been searching for it for years. Many of the pieces Altan retrieved were commissioned because the consul thought they could provide clues to its location." He paced to the end of the room and turned to face her. "The khan has announced a grand race...and a prize for whoever brings the artifact to him."

Dashi's mind whirled with questions, but the one that popped out first was, "What's the prize?"

"Two hundred thousand gold pieces."

Air hissed between her teeth. It was a fortune, more than twenty times what they'd made on their highest-grossing piece.

"The khan has plenty of men at his disposal," she said slowly. "Why not send them?"

"He has. Several times. A few returned. Most didn't." The noble paused and when he spoke again, there was a hint of bitterness in his voice. "The khan is a man who appreciates symbolism. A great race appeals to his sense of grandeur. It's the kind of thing that was done by the khagans of old."

Dashi didn't point out that, without an empire to rule, the khan was no more a khagan than she was. The last Purek khagan had perished, along with most of her subjects, when the veins of magic retreated into the earth. The survivors had trickled out of the taiga to settle in the tamer, flatter south. Only the Mori dared roam close these days. They'd existed before the rise of the Pureks and they continued to live, largely unchanged, centuries later.

"The khan's men who returned," Dashi said. "What did they say?"

"They spoke of many things: monstrous beasts, misty light which drove them to the brink of madness, traps and snares and a hostile land that seemed to conspire against them. But they most likely exaggerated to justify their failure."

Dashi nodded, but privately she had little doubt that the men spoke the truth, at least about the snares and traps. The ruins of the ancient Pureks were often rigged with devices designed to deter enemies. Or thieves. She'd never heard of insanity-inducing light, but the monstrous animals...

"Not one of the men reached their destination?" she pressed.

"The artifact is located in a temple. None of the men got that far, though one claimed to have glimpsed the temple before he turned around. The khan had him executed for cowardice."

Dashi's face twisted before she could stop it. *Cowardice.* This, from the man who sat safely in his city and sent others to die. "And he wonders why he lacks volunteers?"

The noble's smile was slower this time, and Dashi had the sense that she'd somehow given him information without meaning to.

"That was the most recent attempt," he said. "The khan could *order* more to go—an entire squad of soldiers was sent at one point—but instead he's resolved to open the endeavor to all-comers. Perhaps by pitting enough people against the northlands, someone will make it back to claim the purse."

And who cares about the ones who don't, right? Aloud, she said, "And the khan thinks a piece of art is worth that? That many lives? That much money?"

"The lives are of little import. The money...as I said, the khan means to emulate the lavishness of the khagans."

Dashi swallowed her retort. No one talked badly of the khan, especially among strangers. Brash was one thing. Stupid was another.

"I'm afraid you have the wrong person," she said. "I've been to the northlands, true, but my ventures were confined to the edges of the steppe. We never went into the taiga. Even the Mori don't go there. I doubt I'd be any more successful than the others who've tried."

"That is most unfortunate."

For a moment, Dashi thought he'd accepted her refusal. Her skin prickled a warning again. The noble wore a regretful look, but as she examined him closer, she realized it was only a token expression. His tone didn't quite match it. His gaze had sharpened.

"That is most unfortunate," he repeated, "because the belt around your waist is no ornament. It will explode in twenty-nine days unless you bring the artifact to me."

Chapter 4

Dashi touched the metal band through the fabric of her deel. Caught up in the story the noble had spun about Altan, Baris and Zayaa being spies, she'd momentarily forgotten it.

"It's not exactly made of fire powder," she scoffed.

"No, fire powder would be ineffective in such a small quantity. Like as not, it would leave you with an inconvenient burn but little else in the way of consequences. I wanted something more compelling: *your* belt contains pyrothrite."

"Oh?" Dashi's eyebrow rose skeptically. "I've never heard of such a thing."

"Pyrothrite is a Yassari invention. I'm told it has fifty times the explosive potential of fire powder and works even in small quantities."

The tiny island of Yassar was well-known for its advancements. Insulated by the ocean and a deep distrust of the continental nations, trade with the Yassaris was often stilted. When their wares did make it to the mainland, however, they easily eclipsed the local competition.

"The disc contains a timing device, which releases a nodule of pyrothrite each day," the noble continued. "Once the pyrothrite and saltpeter mix in the correct proportion, it becomes highly explosive. I hope you'll have returned by that point, but if you haven't, you'll know you're running out of time because the belt will become steadily warmer."

The metal band felt so thin. *If it's the disc that's the problem, then I'll have this band off as soon as he lets me out of his sight.*

The noble shook his head. "The other interesting thing about pyrothrite is that it can be used to artificially harden metal and glass. Blasted metal, they call it. The band cannot be cut by any normal means. The glass *could* be broken, but it would require either extreme heat or force, both of which would likely result in an explosion."

"You lie," Dashi said flatly. "A mysterious explosive anchored by an unbreakable metal? Do you think I'm stupid?"

"To the contrary, I think you're smart enough, stubborn enough and mean enough to succeed where the others have failed. If I believed otherwise, I would have left you to rot in prison until death relieved you of the tedium." He pulled another piece of paper from the pocket of his deel. "There are three days until the khan's race, counting today. The description of the artifact will be distributed then, but maps have been furnished in advance to allow for preparations. The map estimates eleven days for the outward journey, eleven for the return, and one to navigate the temple where the artifact is located. Including the three days from now until the start, that's twenty-six days total. I've given you twenty-nine: enough time to make up for small setbacks but not enough to sail to Yassar, where you might conceivably find someone to unlock the belt. If you deliver the artifact to me before day twenty-nine, I will free you."

Dashi had the urge to rip open her deel, to reexamine the disc tethering her to this man, but she remained motionless. The belt had seemed so innocuous that she'd forgotten about it almost immediately. Both the noble and Osol were watching her, waiting for a reaction.

"And you—what do you get out of this?" she asked, managing a lofty tone. She hadn't missed his earlier command to bring the artifact to him, not the khan.

"The khan will look favorably on whoever presents him with the artifact. I want that person to be me."

"You want to manipulate him. If you didn't, you'd let the race run its course, instead of selecting your own contestant and backing her against the wall."

The noble inclined his head.

Dashi could hardly believe his audacity. And he'd called *her* brash.

"And then what?" she demanded. "What happens to me after I deliver the artifact? You expect me to believe I can just walk away?"

"Believe what you want, but you would indeed be allowed to 'walk away.'" The noble stood to leave, Osol on his heels. "I expect you to rest in preparation for race day. Osol will collect your list of supplies tomorrow." He paused at the door. "I wouldn't recommend attempting to remove the belt yourself. It's not the same as picking the lock on a door, you know."

The door snapped shut after him, leaving Dashi to fight the sinking feeling in her stomach.

Chapter 5

Dashi went straight to the window: eight rectangular panes of glass joined by lead came; a lock but no bars. She wondered if the man entertained prisoners here often, or if the security precautions had been undertaken solely for her benefit. No matter. This place would be a memory soon.

Unfortunately, Gerel had taken the comb and other dressing accessories with her. Dashi's gaze skipped over the furnishings, touching on and rejecting possibilities. Wooden plate and cup. Not helpful. The wood frame of the dressing screen held some potential. Perhaps it would splinter nicely.

She was stepping toward it when she glimpsed the Mori painting on the opposite wall. *There.* Something better than splinters: wire. The Mori used braided horsehair to hang paintings; the idea was that their art should move with the wind, just like the Mori did. However, once a painting was acquired by someone who was not of Mori descent—a rich collector in Karak City, for instance—thin filaments of wire were added to keep the fabric stiff. Dashi pulled the piece down and ripped the seam apart with her teeth. Two thin wires slid into her hand.

She spent the remainder of the day resting and trying to make up for the weight she'd lost in prison. Both were enjoyable tasks. Thoughts of the pyrothrite belt were put away for later; mentally compartmentalizing risks was something at which she was well-practiced.

Osol delivered food within the hour: *buuz*, steamed dumplings filled with salted mutton, cabbage and curds of mare's milk. There was even *boortsog,* fried pieces of dough topped with sugar, for dessert. It was hearty fare but not so rich or in large enough quantities that she could eat herself sick, which she surely would have done if she'd been able. She wondered if the noble had anticipated her weaknesses and compensated for them. The thought was unnerving.

Finally sated, she fell into a deep sleep, waking just before midnight. She stretched and got to her feet, ignoring the race map, which sat where the noble had left it. She didn't intend to cooperate with him, nor was she convinced it was her only option. The belt could be removed somehow.

Zayaa had been the best with locks, but Dashi knew the basics and the window lock was a simple one, with only a single tumbler. She had it open in seconds.

A dark figure was positioned at the front gate. Another stood by the compound's outer wall. *Where are the others?* She squinted into the darkness, her eyes and ears alert. There, stalking the edge of the wall like caged animals, were two more. Another rounded the corner of the house, his footsteps crunching on the gravel path.

The moon gawked down at her. Not exactly ideal conditions. Keeping an eye on the guards, Dashi settled back against the wall, still and focused. Altan had claimed it was the only time she was actually patient: when she was anticipating something risky. She waited as the moon crept across the sky and the muscles in her back grew tight. She waited until the guards' patrols took them far from her, each at the same time, their orbits lining up like planets preparing for an eclipse.

Dashi swung the window wide and stepped onto the sill, the painted wood scratching against her bare soles as she felt for each step. She stretched out over open space, reaching for the next sill. This window looked in on the upstairs hall, which was now empty. Osol must have resigned his post for the night, trusting the bolted door to hold her until morning. *Fool, fool, fool.*

A slow smile crept over her face as she remembered her conversation with the noble. Perhaps her friends' spirits were nearby; she could almost sense their reactions as she turned toward the hall window and reached into her sash for the wire. Altan would be hissing at her to follow directions for once in her life while Zayaa chewed nervously on her lip. Baris would shake his head as if in agreement with Altan, but his eyes would be laughing.

This window was even easier to open than the other had been. It was latched, not locked, and opening it was simply a matter of inserting the wire at the jamb and easing the latch forward. Anticipation bubbled up inside Dashi, making her want to laugh. Only long practice allowed her to clamp down on her glee as she stepped from the sill and onto the thick rug that ran down the center of the hall. She grinned down at the blue Chertai vase before wrapping it securely in the sash of her deel.

Her exit from the grounds was relatively simple. When the guards were far enough away, she pulled herself into a fruit tree, then sprang toward the wall, throwing the blanket she'd taken from the noble's house before her as she went. It landed neatly on top of the wall, its fabric protecting her from the shards of broken glass she'd seen winking in the moonlight.

There was a narrow alley on the other side, the kind of shortcut Dashi liked to memorize in case she needed to avoid prefects. She hadn't stolen from Karak City's nobles in a while, but at one time she and Altan had done it regularly. It had been right after Altan had taken her in, before Zayaa and Baris came along. Altan had justified it by saying he needed the money. Not that Dashi, who was nine at the time and whose conscience had always been somewhat fluid, had demanded an explanation.

Altan refused to allow her to come with him. Instead, he'd confined her to the role of lookout, an injustice that had rankled until she decided to do something about it. After she'd single-handedly robbed a wealthy noble, he'd taken her seriously.

Even as a child, she'd thought Altan's professed poverty was a bit overblown. He'd arrived in Karak City just after her own grief-stricken family, but he'd seemed to have money from the very beginning. Not a lot, but enough for an extra set of clothing and boots that were always in good repair. Enough that he could afford to take in his neighbor's two children.

Dashi had always assumed the money was inherited, though Altan certainly hadn't come from delicate noble stock. He was hearty enough to endure weeks-long trips to the northlands and practical enough to learn from anyone who had something to teach. Now she wondered if the money had come from the Tyvalaran crown.

Dashi shook her head, angry at herself for letting the noble's words gain purchase. She couldn't let him color her memories.

She picked her way steadily through the city until she reached a place she recognized: the public fountain that divided the jade circle, where the nobility resided, from the silver circle, where the merchant class lived. She turned right, taking the quickest route to the blacksmith shops of the leather circle. No smiths would be awake at this hour, of course, but Dashi was rarely in the mood to wait. She pulled the wire filament from her sash and rolled it between her fingers as she walked.

The smith and his wife slept at the very back of the shop, but their room still smelled of sweat and metal. Even though the coals were banked for the night, the heat of the forge slipped over Dashi, a pleasant sort of thrall that quickly became stifling.

Dashi nudged the smith cautiously, poking the broad slab of his back with one finger while also trying to stand out of reach, in case he didn't appreciate being awakened early. He roused quickly, a mountain of bedding that transformed into a snarling beast.

"Who are you? What are you doing here?" he roared, brandishing his meaty arms like other men do swords. Beside him, his wife sat up, her hair a confused halo.

"I have a job for you," Dashi said. "Come into the smithy. There's no need to bother your wife."

"I don't need jobs. I'm up to my ears in work and I get precious few hours of sleep as it is." He swung his legs over the bed ominously. "Leave now, while you can still walk."

Dashi held up a placating hand. "I can pay. It won't take long."

He stood up suddenly and Dashi leaped back, positioning herself closer to the door. *Cursed ancestors, he moved fast.*

"Girl, don't push me."

"Twenty minutes."

"Get out."

"Ten minutes," she said, then quoted the price she thought the Cher-tai vase would fetch, though it was really just a guess since she had little experience selling art. The smith's wife, still clutching the sheets to her chest like she thought Dashi intended to ravage her, gave an exclamation of surprise.

The smith was silent. "Ten minutes," he said finally.

He followed her out a moment later, an enormous deel belted sloppily at his waist. Dashi had already unwound her sash and slid her own deel off her shoulders.

The smith held up a hand, his eyes sliding away from her thin under-shirt. "I don't know what you think you're doing. And with my wife in the other room."

Dashi plucked impatiently at the metal band around her stomach. "This is what I need you to look at. I want it removed. Can you do it?"

An incredulous expression came over his face. "You want *what*?" Without waiting for an answer, he turned to the worktable and cleared a place. "Lay down."

She climbed up and eased back onto the unfinished wood. The black-smith loomed over her, holding the lantern close enough that its warmth lapped against her skin.

He tapped the metal appraisingly, tilting it back and forth. Then he reached beneath the worktable and withdrew an immense pair of metal cutters. "You'll have to suck in your gut. What little you have."

Dashi drew a breath and held it, staring at the ceiling while the smith fit the cold cutters around the band.

He closed them decisively.

Silence.

Dashi raised her head. The smith was looking down with a puzzled expression. Without warning his arms came together again, straining over the handles of the cutters until the veins stood out in his forearms. There was a whine, like a begging cur, and the handles of the cutters bent inward. The blacksmith stopped immediately.

"What's this made of?" he asked, looking Dashi in the face for the first time since seeing the belt.

"I was told it's called 'blasted metal.'"

"Never heard of it, but it's burred my damned cutters." He held up the tool for her to see. Sure enough, there was a dent in the metal blades, exactly as wide as the belt.

The smith squinted at her stomach, all trace of sleepiness gone as he scrutinized the puzzle before him. "What about the disk holding the band in place? Can it be removed?" He leaned closer with the lantern and tapped the black triangle. "What is it?"

"Something called pyrothrite."

The smith jerked his hand back. "Are you mad?" He shot an apprehensive glance at the forge. "Get out!"

Dashi sat up. "What?"

"Out!"

"But I need help!"

"I'll talk to you in the courtyard. Just get out of my smithy with that thing."

He looked ready to throw her over his shoulder, so Dashi jumped up from the table, grabbing her deel on the way out.

"Pyrothrite," she heard him mutter as she left. "Of all the reckless—"

Dashi dressed hurriedly in the courtyard, pacing back and forth while she waited. She could try another smithy, she assured herself, but her worry metastasized anyway. What if no one could help her?

The blacksmith appeared before she came to a conclusion. He was visibly calmer, though he kept running one hand over his scraggly beard. He stopped a few feet away.

"I don't know about the metal," he said without preamble, "but the pyrothrite I've heard of. And I know it's not to be messed with." He jerked his thumb toward the smithy. "Or placed near heat."

"It's really that explosive?"

"A Yassari delegation came through a while back, hawking some new wares to the khan and his ilk. Some of the merchants and tradesmen were invited to see their demonstrations too. They put pyrothrite on top of a boulder, mixed something up with it—they wouldn't say what or how much—and proceeded to blow the thing to dust." He ruffled his beard again. "I don't mean it cracked the boulder, either. I mean *there was nothing left*. Just a flash of fire and a big hole where the boulder had been and gravel raining down on our heads."

A flash of fire. Would it be quick or would she feel the bite of the flames like her mother had, screaming from her burning bedroom?

"They use pyrothrite to make the metal too," Dashi said hollowly. "I don't know how exactly, but that's what I was told."

"Wish I knew." The smith glanced at her waist regretfully. "There wasn't even a scratch on that metal. Would make me a fortune."

"There's no way to break it?"

"I didn't say that."

Dashi's eyebrows rose hopefully.

"I mean, *theoretically*. Anything can be broken with enough force and leverage. Or melted with enough heat. But with pyrothrite, heat is out of the question and I don't know where you'd find cutters big enough to give you the correct amount of leverage." He squinted at her. "How did you find yourself with pyrothrite locked around your waist?"

Dashi winced at the word *locked*. That sounded permanent. It was the word the noble had used too. "There's a man...he'll only remove the belt once I've done something for him." She didn't dare breathe anything more specific than that. If a whiff of conspiracy reached the ears of the khan or his consul, soldiers would be on her before she could blink. At least the noble would go down with her, she thought grimly.

The smith stared at her for a long moment, his face craggy with shadow. "Well," he said finally, "I'm an honest man. I've an honest trade and I don't like the thought of getting crossways with anyone, least of all the people with power. If I were you, and I had a way of doing what this man wants, I'd do it. Better that than ending up like the boulder."

Chapter 6

In the end, the blacksmith wouldn't take any payment. Dashi showed him the vase and explained its value, but he just sighed. "I had the feeling you didn't have that much money."

"It's worth that much," Dashi insisted. "It's an original. My word on it."

"I'm not saying it isn't. Anyone who pays with vases and has pyrothrite belted to them...no offense, girl, but I don't want anything to do with you." He turned back to the smithy. "Keep the money. Maybe it'll help you get that thing off."

Dashi let her feet decide where to go after that. In the wild seed of her hopes, sown when she'd laid in the impossibly soft bed in the noble's house and nourished as she dreamt, she'd thought she would be free by now: of prison, of the belt, of the noble who'd put it on her. Not free of her grief—she still felt her friends' loss keenly—but perhaps free to finish the business of finding those who'd caused it.

She thought again about the noble's assertion that Altan spied for Tyvalar. She thought of how Zayaa and Baris had shown up: first Zayaa and, six months later, Baris. Friends from childhood, Altan said, and he'd welcomed them so warmly that Dashi believed him. Now she wondered: had they been close because they'd grown up together, or because they were bound by a secret? Dashi clenched her fists, hating the noble for making her question whether Altan had kept something from her.

Her steps took her to a well-kept section of the leather circle. Without thinking, Dashi stopped next to a boot shop, slipping into its shadow so she had a good view of the bakery opposite. Already the smell of frying dumplings drifted across the street, though the sun wasn't up yet. Soon the shop would open its counter and begin selling dumplings, barley porridge and *suutei tsai*—tea with milk, salt and butter—to the hungry passersby. Dashi's mouth watered at the thought.

As she watched, a girl came from behind the bakery and began sweeping. She was dressed simply, but her hair was neatly plaited down her back and her features were full and healthy. She was nearly twelve, though, like Dashi, her small size made people assume she was younger.

No, Dashi corrected herself, her sister *was* twelve. Her twelfth birthday, along with Dashi's eighteenth, had come and gone while Dashi was in prison.

Like Dashi, Idree had the high, wide cheekbones, narrow forehead and full lips common to the Mori nomads. But Idree's face was a perfect oval, lovely and soft like their Karak mother's, while Dashi's had changed in recent years, becoming harder and square-jawed in the image of their Mori father.

A second girl, a shop worker on an errand, stopped to talk to her sister and Idree's laugh, low and reserved, sounded in the early morning. Idree returned to her sweeping with a faint smile, then began wiping the counter, moving efficiently and with an attention to the mundane that Dashi could never have mustered. No wonder Auntie Nima, the woman who owned the bakery, loved her.

Having completed her morning chores, Idree picked up the broom and started for the rear of the building. Dashi's mouth opened, her sister's name waiting on her tongue. But no sound emerged and Idree disappeared inside. There was a click as she latched the door behind her.

Dashi stayed in the shadows, her head leaning against the wall of the boot shop while she stared at her sister's home. They hadn't lived together in seven years. With Dashi immersed in Altan's affairs, which often required lengthy trips away from Karak City, he'd arranged for Auntie Nima to take care of Idree. It would be a better environment for a little girl, he'd said, with a significant glance in Dashi's direction. He'd always regretted Dashi's involvement in his lifestyle. Whenever she spoke with too much alacrity about exploring ruins, he'd get a hangdog look and say that maybe she would have been better off without him. Which was a pile of dung, of course.

He needn't have worried about Idree following in Dashi's footsteps. Idree was meek and fainthearted. She hadn't been able to sleep alone until she was nearly nine and most of Dashi's early memories involved trying to pry her crying baby of a sister from her leg so that she could go somewhere.

Idree had seemed composed just a moment ago, true, but who knew how she'd take Dashi's news: that a scheming noble had broken Dashi out of prison and forced her to enter the khan's race by shackling her with an explosive. Probably with a lot of hand-holding and a runny nose, Dashi thought acidly. Anyway, they hadn't parted on the best of terms. She could almost hear Idree's voice now, drippy with emotion, saying she never wanted to see Dashi again.

Dashi stood up. She didn't need to deal with her overwrought sister on top of everything else. Besides, she reminded herself, Idree had looked content. It would be worse to upset her. Maybe she would try again with Idree when the race was behind her.

And what if you don't survive, a wheedling part of her mind asked. *Shouldn't you make amends now, while you still can?* Dashi frowned. She didn't make a habit of examining the odds too closely. Nor did the idea of a guilt-driven reunion with her sister sound remotely appealing. But the thought was there now, hard and uncomfortable.

If I don't make it...well, Idree will go on being content, right? Her sister valued stability and safety above all else and the opposite sort of words seemed to follow Dashi wherever she went. And, Dashi thought in a flash of inspiration, maybe she *could* help her sister, regardless of the race's outcome. What would make her sister feel safer than a nest egg, just in case something happened to Auntie Nima? She felt for the vase, still tucked against the small of her back, and started walking in the direction of the market, ducking behind the boot shop just in case Idree happened to look out the window.

She had a few more stops to make before dawn. After that, she would be able to concentrate on surviving the khan's race—and the noble's pyrothrite belt—without any burdensome thoughts of her sister.

Dashi's toes curled against the sill, seeking traction as she pried at the window. She had approximately thirty seconds to get inside the noble's house before the next guard appeared. The window swung open and Dashi ducked inside, closing it behind her as the guard's footsteps became audible. She winced as her feet hit the floor. They were filthy and sore from walking so far without shoes.

"Welcome back," a voice said from the shadows.

Dashi leaped into the air, spinning to face the speaker at the same time. The noble sat in the upholstered chair, one foot propped unconcernedly on his knee. Osol stood behind him, awaiting orders.

"Now that you've finished second-guessing me, I trust you're ready to focus on the race." The noble leaned forward to light a candle. It flared brightly, then faded, leaving the room in a mellow half-light that should have been soothing.

"What are you talking about?" She was still stiff-legged in front of the window, annoyed at the way her heart pounded from the surprise of finding him here.

"Just what I said. I hope you've been able to verify what I told you. That's why I let you go: because I knew you'd be back, and that, this time, your mind would be focused on what you need to accomplish."

"You didn't let me go."

"No?" He looked pointedly at the Mori painting, which Dashi had rehung. "Very well. Let's say you escaped against my wishes. If your pride needs further assuaging, it should please you to know that none of my guards saw you leave and only one saw you return."

Dashi gritted her teeth. "Where?"

The noble looked amused. "He saw you cross the wall, but he came directly inside to alert me, so he didn't see how you got upstairs. I assume you climbed the vine on the corner?"

Dashi relaxed a fraction. No one had seen her go through the hall window before climbing back into her own. The noble didn't know about the missing Chertai vase...or the imitation that now graced his halls. Even *he* couldn't anticipate everything.

"I went up the column," she said, not bothering to hide her smugness.

"Ah. Well...I hope you're ready to work together now."

"Oh, I am. Like an exhibition bear works for its owner." *And waits for the chance to tear the owner's face off.*

"A fighting bear?" He laughed. "A miniature one, perhaps. Nonetheless, I'm happy to hear it. We have an interest or two in common, I think, even after this race is concluded."

"We have nothing in common," she said flatly.

"We have the same goal. That's everything."

"My goal is to survive. You've chained an explosive to me."

The noble smiled again, that same silky movement that set Dashi's teeth on edge. "They say in order to get out of the fire sometimes you have to jump through the flames. Consider this one of those circumstances."

"I will. If I live that long."

"You will, I think. And when it's over, we'll see what else we can accomplish together."

"You said you'd unlock the pyrothrite if I brought the artifact to you." Not that she'd entirely believed him. The more she thought about it, in fact, the less probable it sounded. In breaking her out of prison, he'd found someone vulnerable to manipulation and blackmail—and someone who was utterly disposable.

"And I will. But I will also offer you the two things you value nearly as much as your freedom: revenge for your friends' deaths, and respect."

"I don't want respect."

"We all want respect. It's endemic to mankind. And you...a half-Mori orphan?" He stood up and began pacing and Dashi was again seized with annoyance at the similarity to herself. "Before I got you out of prison, I went to the leather circle. I wanted to make sure you were involved in Altan's trips to the ruins and not a mere acquaintance, as his missives suggested. I talked to neighbors, to shopkeepers. I heard about how you were an orphan; about how, even though the four of you were rarely seen together publicly, you would all disappear for long stretches of time; about how you would spar with a giant named Baris in the middle of the night when you thought no one was watching."

Dashi's jaw clenched. He'd known Baris' name all along.

"All of which supported my hypothesis: that you knew more than Altan let on. But do you know what really convinced me that you had a chance of succeeding in the khan's race? The other things I heard. I heard about a girl with a chip on her shoulder. Someone who would always accept a dare...and a fight. I heard about a fearsome goathead player: agile and quick and able to knock opponents from their horses, yet never satisfied with scoring. Someone who never stopped running her mouth even after she'd won."

He turned toward her suddenly. "When I mentioned the race, your first question was about the prize, but it's not money you want. By all accounts you've never lacked food or other necessities; Altan looked after you like a sister. But respect? Maybe even power—something that can't be taken away, something no one can look down on? I think *that* appeals to you greatly." He paused, challenging her to contradict him. "It's the *idea of winning* that attracts you. If you hadn't been in prison, I think this race is *exactly* the kind of thing you would have done, just to prove yourself."

"*I* need respect?" Dashi started moving rapidly across the room. She couldn't help it; if she didn't find something to do with her body, she would flip upside-down and walk on her hands, and she wanted to preserve *some* sense of dignity in front of the noble. She gestured expansively with one arm. "You don't want for money either. Yet you're still seeking *something*, aren't you?"

The noble ceded the floor, seating himself gracefully in the upholstered chair. He didn't argue, but neither did he seem bothered by her accusations. She realized she hadn't denied what he said. Doing so now would only sound desperate.

He was wrong about one thing: she wouldn't have entered the race. Altan would never have let her. As much as she liked to push him, to remind him—as forcefully as possible—that she should be taken seriously, it was *his* approval she'd desired the most. Altan might've allowed her to take risks at the ruins, but he had lines she wouldn't cross, and avoiding official attention was one of them. Not being seen in public with him,

Zayaa and Baris was another. Her stomach twisted and suddenly she was sure: Altan had been a spy. And, though she'd known him since she was a young child, he hadn't trusted her enough to tell her.

"You say I want prestige," she said finally, "but even if I win, no one will know."

"True. That's why it would behoove you to work with me afterward: if I obtain the artifact instead of the consul, my influence will grow. Yours could grow too."

"What do you mean *instead of the consul*?" The consul was the khan's right hand, the man who managed his affairs. Like the khan, Dashi had only glimpsed him once, and from a considerable distance, but everyone knew his reputation as a cruel, capricious enforcer of the khan's dictates.

"The consul will also be in the race," the noble said.

Dashi raised an eyebrow. "Does he have pyrothrite strapped to him as well?"

The noble gave a short laugh. "Something else just as threatening: the angry khan at his back."

"The *khan* wants him in the race?" That didn't make any sense. Why not send the consul alone, or with a contingent of soldiers to retrieve the artifact? Why make the consul compete against ancestors-only-knew how many others? *Unless...*

"Does the khan want him to die?"

The noble leaned back in his chair, his eyes narrowed on her face.

"The consul's failure to recover the artifact has angered the khan," he said after a long moment. "*Deeply*. The consul promised it to the khan years ago and has yet to deliver. The race is sure to be...eventful and there will almost certainly be casualties, but the general consensus in the jade circle is this: if the consul is not the one to deliver the artifact to the khan, he would be better off not returning to Karak City at all."

Dashi frowned. That would make things difficult indeed. It was one thing to compete against someone motivated by greed. It was something else entirely to face someone who feared his own death. Especially someone like the consul.

"I would never advise underestimating the other racers," the noble said, following her thoughts, "but it is the consul who will be your biggest competition."

"Your concern warms my heart."

He ignored her sarcasm, instead reaching into his deel. There was a flash of gold as he withdrew Altan's pendant. "Somehow the consul became suspicious of your friends. He decided to have them watched. He didn't investigate as thoroughly as I did: he didn't interview half the leather circle and he didn't find you. But he did realize Altan was a Tyvalaran spy. So, you see, we *do* have a common goal. You"—he flipped the pendant high in the air and Dashi caught it without thinking—"want revenge, or you wouldn't have killed twice already. I would like to see the khan, and his allies weakened."

The pendant was warm in her hand. She knew it was only because the noble had been holding it, but that didn't stop her next thought: that once Altan had warmed it too. And that he never would again. Dashi clenched her fist so tightly that the pendant bit into her palm.

The noble rose to leave. "It's been an enlightening chat, for both of us, I think." He tapped the folded map on the table, an admonishment to give her list of supplies to Osol. "Your primary goal may be, as you put it, survival, but you should use the days ahead to think about what I said...and about whether the man who ordered your friends' deaths should go unpunished."

His exit felt like a great exhalation, like his presence had held her underwater and only the closing of the door allowed her to breathe freely.

How could he pack so much unsettling information into such a short period?

She wished she'd been able to refute what he said—both about wanting respect and about wanting revenge. She could hardly deny that she wanted revenge—she *had* sought out her friends' killers. *Wanting respect*. She cringed at how weak that sounded. Altan used to say she had fight in every step. She'd always been proud of that. It made her sound tough. But now she wondered if he'd been saying something else. Had he thought she was insecure too?

Dashi started to flop on the bed, but a sudden thought held her upright. She tore off her sash and ripped her deel open, sucking in her stomach and bending nearly in half to see the front of the belt. The disc looked the same, except for one tiny detail: a black sphere—a single nodule of pyrothrite—had dropped from the black triangle into the white one.

Chapter 7

Race day dawned gray and sullen, an anomaly for the end of June, which usually saw Karakal drying out from snow melt and spring rains. The knock on the door didn't wake Dashi; she'd been pacing for so long that she was surprised there wasn't a path worn into the floor.

"Come in."

The door opened, revealing Osol with an armful of packages.

She smiled sweetly. "Presents?"

"Supplies." He dropped them in front of her with a thump, then turned to retrieve the rest: an assortment of leather saddlebags and a lightweight saddle studded with silver ornaments.

"Where did you get that?" she asked sharply. She reached out one finger but drew back before she touched the side, where blood still coated the leather in a black-red crust.

"The belongings of arrested criminals are auctioned off unless their family claims them. I can have it cleaned if you like."

"No!" She couldn't tell if Osol was being intentionally inscrutable or if he really didn't know the saddle had belonged to her. "No, I'd rather...ready my gear myself."

He turned to go. "I'll have rags and water sent up. The starting ceremony is in five hours."

She nodded, still surveying the assembled supplies. "This isn't everything I asked for."

"You'll get your weapons at the starting line, not before," he said over one shoulder, not needing her to elaborate.

She laid out the supplies she'd requested, taking special care with the food. She'd have to ration carefully to make sure she didn't run out. She couldn't waste precious time on hunting, but neither did she want to overload the horses with more food than she needed.

With nothing left to do, she turned her attention to the saddle. It was custom-made, given to her by Altan on her thirteenth birthday. Its low cantle allowed her to swing one leg over the seat easily, enabling the kind of reckless trick riding that had prompted Altan to say he regretted giving her the saddle in the first place. She smiled and touched the silver ornaments, each engraved with a different symbol to bring her luck. Perhaps they'd done their job, she thought; she *was* still alive.

The stain started on the side and swept back toward the cantle. The blood wasn't hers, though it had been transferred from her deel when the prefects dragged her from her horse. She knew it couldn't be a coincidence that the noble had procured her old saddle for the race, but she had a harder time parsing the meaning. Was he emphasizing what the consul, their common enemy, had taken from her? Or was he trying to remind her of the freedom he'd returned to her...and of what she had to lose if she didn't win?

Dashi plunged her hand into the soapy solution, not letting herself dwell further on the saddle or the blood—she had no desire to conjure those particular memories. The stain came off easily enough, turning the water pink with each wring of the washcloth. Mud and blood had dried so thickly along the back edge of the seat that at first she couldn't find the hidden seam. She dragged her thumbnail along the leather until it caught, then ran her finger sideways, using her nail to scrape away coagulated blood. After several applications of soapy water, she managed to pry the little door open.

It was a small space, a rectangle about the size of her palm. She'd been delighted when Altan showed it to her: her own hidden place, just like the hidden places they were always combing through. Mostly, she'd used it for collecting trinkets from the ruins, little things that no one else cared to take: bronze buttons; ancient coins, each with the face of a different khagan; a fragment of parchment—a perfectly preserved image of a hand holding a silver cup—that she'd found beneath a skeleton; a thimble, one edge slightly bent. She'd socked them away in her nook at Altan's house. *A mouse's collection of treasures*, Zayaa had teased. *What will you save next? Kernels of wheat?*

The compartment was empty now. She'd traded her trinkets from the last trip, a pair of earrings, for information about the location of her friends' murderers. The rest were gone, along with everything else in Altan's suite of rooms.

She washed the tiny door carefully, opening and shutting it several times to make sure no sticky residue remained. Then she dried it with her sleeve and, placing Altan's pendant inside, closed it once more.

The compartment had been sealed with blood. No one had found it. Not the prefects who'd arrested her, not Osol, and not his boss, despite all their thoroughness. The thought made her smile.

Osol escorted her to the starting ceremony, followed at a discreet distance by the two other men who'd taken her from jail. Like Osol, they wore plain clothes today instead of a soldier's uniform.

"Are you really a soldier?" Dashi asked, her voice muffled. Like most everyone else, her nose and mouth were covered with a scarf to keep out the billowing summer dust.

Osol didn't look at her.

"What's your boss' name, anyway?"

More silence.

"I know how to get to his estate. I could lead someone there."

"It would be unfortunate if he had to go into hiding before he could remove the pyrothrite. He said to remind you of that."

Dashi didn't bother to answer. She'd figured as much.

The khan had declared a holiday to mark the race's start and already the streets of Karak City were choked with people. Vendors sold fried delicacies on every corner and children raced back and forth, their shouting caretakers on their heels. A bookmaker read off the names of racers in a stentorian voice, pausing to accept bets on everything from who would win to how many racers would fall before they'd left the city.

The atmosphere should have been contagious—*would* have been, under any other circumstances. Dashi wasn't tense exactly, but neither was she relaxed. Her muscles were loose and her breath came easily, but her awareness was heightened, automatically cataloging the people and things around her.

"Is my name on that list?" she asked, with a nod at the bookmaker.

"You're registered as Togzan Khunbish, from the dirt circle."

Dashi shot him an incredulous look.

"Many racers are from the dirt circle," he said, misinterpreting her glance. "They have the most to gain. And it will be more difficult for someone to follow up on you among the masses of poor."

"*Delicate soul*? You gave me a name that means *delicate soul*?"

Osol looked straight ahead, but Dashi saw the corners of his eyes crinkle.

Her head turned as they passed an empty lot where a goathead match had just begun. Horses thundered past, riders crouched low over their withers. One rider veered to the side, hanging perilously from his saddle to grab a four-handled leather ball from the ground. A second rider bore down, hitting the ball carrier with a padded bat to make him fumble. The ball carrier wheeled his horse, cutting off his assailant's mount as he galloped toward the goal.

Dashi craned her neck. This was when the match would turn interesting. The other team would swoop in with their bats—

"Hurry up," Osol snapped.

Dashi shot him an annoyed glance, casting one last look at the game.

"You play?" he said after they'd left the field behind.

"You already know I do. You heard what your boss said."

Osol shrugged. "Do you miss it?"

Dashi didn't answer for several strides. "I miss a lot of things."

She'd thought about goathead in prison. It had been one of the few things she could dwell on that didn't remind her of her friends. They'd come to watch her matches on occasion, but goathead had been hers. The game—named because it had originally been played with a goat's severed, still-warm head—was something of an obsession in Karakal. It was a harsh sport that rewarded the aggressive and, to a certain extent, the unethical. Dashi excelled at it.

"I still play quite a bit," Osol volunteered. "Whenever I get the time."

Ah, so that was it. He was no different than any of the players she knew: constantly sizing each other up, jockeying for standing, both on the field and in their own minds.

She grinned viciously. "Well, Osol, when I come back I'd be happy to teach you how to sling a goal or two."

He slanted a look in her direction. "In my experience, the poorer circles like to think of themselves as grittier, when in fact they're just poor."

Dashi threw back her head and laughed. "By all means, test your theory on me. I hope your boss plays too. I would enjoy meeting him on the field." The very idea made her step jaunty, any trace of nerves gone.

She was still sailing on a wind of bravado when they reached the gates of the khan's fortress.

"Your race registration," Osol said, handing her a paper. "Your supplies and mounts are inside. From this point, you go on alone, but remember that we'll be watching. If you attempt to signal anyone in any way, we'll put an arrow through your throat."

Dashi matched his stare, her lip curling. She hated to be ordered around, especially if she had no choice but to obey.

"Good luck then."

She gave a mock salute. "See you on the goathead field."

The gold circle, the innermost point of Karak City and the location of the khan's palatial home, was actually octagonal, not circular. Towers sprouted from the parapet at regular intervals and Dashi could see the shadows of the guards in the nearest crenels. A large fountain stood in front of the main gate: four silver wolves, each facing a different direction. Normally water flowed from the fountain, but today a different beverage poured from the mouth of each wolf, landing in the troughs at their feet: *airag*—fermented mares' milk—from one; mead from another; beer and wine from the final two. People packed against the fountain, emerging only after their cups were full.

Dashi walked up to the line of guards standing near the fortress entrance. "I'm signed up to race today," she said, tugging her scarf down from her face.

"Name and papers?"

"Togzan Khunbish." She handed him the registration.

He glanced at the paper in his hand. "How many mounts?"

"Three for riding. One for packing supplies," she said, quoting the specifics she'd given Osol.

He nodded, seemingly satisfied, and ushered Dashi through the door. The fortress walls were impossibly thick, as wide as the boulevards that cut through the jade circle. The mere act of stepping through the doorway made the air turn cool and damp, even in the summer.

She heard the commotion of the palace yard before she reached it: a cacophony of animal noises and the slap of saddles being thrown over horses' backs, overlaid with voices made harsh by urgency. Dashi stepped out of the walkway and gazed around. She'd emerged next to the stables: a long stone building with a tile roof. Beyond the stableyard, she glimpsed the green symmetry of gardens, laid out like a table setting in front of the khan's palace. Like most homes in Karak City, the roof of the palace was green and sloped so that each corner curved upward. The palace, however, was easily fifty times larger than any other building in the city.

Roughly three dozen racers had assembled in front of the stables, each with a string of horses in various stages of readiness. They were mostly men, but Dashi noticed a few other women scattered throughout. A bevy of servants rushed back and forth, delivering supplies and checking last-minute requests from the racers. A peacock raced across the yard, chased by a dog and a pair of desperate-looking servant boys.

The other racers milled around her, but Dashi had eyes only for her string of horses, which she found beneath a placard bearing her fake name. They were exactly as she'd requested: four mounts of Mori breeding, with their characteristic jug heads and legs that were strong, but so short that the animals straddled the line between horse and pony. Dashi checked them over, lifting each hoof, feeling each leg and peering into each mouth. They all appeared healthy and bright-eyed. So Osol knew good horseflesh when he saw it, she mused, even if it was disguised in rough Mori packaging.

When she got to the last horse, she froze. She *knew* this horse. She'd ridden him for the last four years. She'd been pulled from his back the night she was arrested. The animal, an unattractive shade of gray, raised its head and whickered in greeting.

"*Spit*," she breathed. "What are you doing here?"

Spit butted his forehead against her chest by way of an answer, knocking her back a step. Osol must have procured him at the auction along with her saddle. Maybe she'd been wrong about the noble's motivation. In procuring a familiar mount, maybe he was trying to give her an advantage, not a warning. She ran her hand from Spit's thick neck to his front leg, feeling his knee and fetlock. Like the others, he looked to be in excellent shape.

"I'm glad you're here," she whispered, rubbing his neck. His forelock was already affixed in a top knot, which stuck into the air like a flag, the traditional ornamentation for a racehorse. Someone—either Osol or the noble—had guessed Spit would be the mount she chose to ride out of Karak City and had designated him as such.

The supplies she'd packed that morning were piled in front of Spit. Beside them was an unfamiliar bundle, wrapped in a blanket. She unrolled it carefully. The smile she gave the contents was usually reserved for old friends, but then, what could be friendlier than the assortment before her: a collection of knives and several quivers of arrows, carefully fletched with crane feathers. Beneath the arrows was a short sword, made for someone of small stature, and a recurve bow. The bow was also short, designed for use on horseback. Dashi stroked the wood and bone reverently. It wasn't her bow—that one had broken during her arrest—but it was just as nice. The sword, however, was familiar. Baris had given it to her.

She shoved two knives into her sash and another into her boot, buckled the sword belt, then returned the bow to its oil cloth. She would examine it later when she had more time. Right now most of the racers were waiting for the signal to mount, and her horses weren't even saddled or packed yet.

Dashi placed the saddle high on Spit's withers, sliding it backward to make sure it wasn't pushing his coat the wrong way. Beside her, a racer who looked like he might be younger than she was, was attempting to make conversation with the man on his other side.

"Two hundred thousand gold pieces! That's enough money to take me all the way up to the jade circle if I'm careful with it. And I will be. Been saving to get out of the dirt circle."

He talked so freely that Dashi had a hard time believing he wouldn't be as free with his money. She flipped the stirrup over the saddle seat to tighten the girth while covertly studying the two men. She would have known the young man was from the dirt circle even if she hadn't been eavesdropping. His face and neck were already dark from the summer sun and his hands were chapped. Probably a road laborer. Harsh winters made road maintenance an annual necessity and the constant digging and shifting of rocks tended to wear at the workers' hands.

The other man was harder to read. Like most of the other racers, he wore a scarf against the dust, and it covered the lower half of his face. He was tall but moved easily between his horses, not lumbering the way that most big men did.

"Wonder when they'll give us the details on how to win," the young man continued. "I thought they would've done it by now, but I guess they're waiting until just before the race starts. Don't you want to know what it is?"

The man with the black scarf shrugged. "Does it matter? As long as the khan pays for it."

"True," the younger man agreed. "It must be something extraordinary if the khan wants it. Probably jewels. Or maybe an ancient crown."

"The khagans didn't wear crowns," the man said, throwing a pack onto one of his horses. "They wore headdresses."

Dashi glanced up, surprised that someone else knew that fact. Maybe it wasn't so surprising though: everyone knew the khan favored the styles of the ancient Pureks and he'd recently done away with his father's crown in favor of a more ostentatious headdress.

"A headdress. Maybe that's what we're after," the young man said agreeably, as if he hadn't yet realized they'd be competing against one another.

Dashi finished tacking Spit and moved to the packhorse. Like the man with the mask, she hadn't bothered to wonder what she would be retrieving from the northlands. She'd been too busy thinking about pyrothrite and why the people she'd cared about most had hidden their true identities from her. She hoped the artifact was small, whatever it was. A headdress wouldn't be too bad, but anything bigger would be difficult to conceal, and she didn't relish the idea of openly carrying something worth two hundred thousand gold pieces. Other than that, Dashi was inclined to agree with the masked racer: it didn't matter what the artifact was, as long as she was the one to retrieve it.

Somewhere nearby, the servant boys were still trying to corral the errant peacock. Dashi could hear the bird's shrill call, followed by a flurry of cursing as one of the boys crashed into a nearby racer. The other boy dove for the peacock, which clumsily launched itself at Dashi. Startled by the peacock, one of her horses reared, pulling free. Dashi's arms closed automatically around the bird, catching it and then shoving it at one of the servant boys.

Her escaped horse, a bright chestnut, was already on the other side of the stableyard, busily making friends with another racer's horses. Their owner, a dark-haired man with a well-coiffed beard, was of a different mind, however.

"Get your nag away from my string!" he barked, looking around wildly for the owner of the chestnut, who was now helping himself to a portion of oats. The man glanced down, saw the chestnut's opportunistic gorging, and smacked the horse's muzzle with a leather quirt.

Dashi darted around the chestnut, catching the quirt in her hand as it began to descend again.

"There's no need for that," she snapped, yanking it from the man's hand.

"There's every need," he sputtered, glaring at her, "when I'm surrounded by people who don't know how to control their animals."

"You're the only animal who needs to be controlled here." She tucked the quirt under her arm and grabbed her horse's rope. The chestnut was still agitated, eying the man warily.

"Give me the quirt, you mongrel whelp."

Dashi's shoulders jerked back, a puppet whose master had just pinched the strings. Without another thought, she hurled the quirt as far as she could. It bounced off the inside of the fortress wall, landing just in front of the main gate.

The racer's jaw tightened and he took a step toward her. The cloud cover broke apart just then, and something about the changing light made Dashi take a second look at the man: his beard, the sharp cheekbones, the thick nose. They were familiar. She'd seen them over and over for the last three months, as she relived the events that led to her imprisonment. They were the features of the man she'd killed.

Chapter 8

Dashi staggered backward as memories invaded her mind, overlaying with the face before her: a similar-looking man, younger and with slightly heavier features, lying on a bed. Flush with blood money, he'd spent that day and the preceding one at the brothel. But prostitutes talk as much as everyone else—perhaps more so—and the offer of a pair of earrings sealed the deal. The prostitute would let Dashi know when her work was finished.

She'd waited in the dark, as the sleet slid down her neck and the river of chamber pot discards slowly dampened her feet. By the time the woman cracked the door and waved her inside, her body felt wooden, but her feet moved anyway, driven forward by some unspeakable impulse.

"Where is he?" The air eddied around her, thick with sweat and the clash of perfumes.

"Upstairs," the woman murmured. "Second door on the right."

"He's asleep?"

The prostitute hesitated. "You said there wouldn't be any trouble. I don't want trouble."

Dashi tilted her head, looking up at the woman through her eyelashes. "What could I do to a grown man? I just want to ask him a few questions."

"Alright," the prostitute said, eager to be mollified. "He's sleeping. See that you don't mention me."

The front staircase of the brothel was wide and showy, adorned with metal sconces fashioned to look like women's nude torsos. The back stairs, however, were dark, their only decoration a single lantern and the smoke-darkened ceiling above. She'd been here before—Baris was a favorite with women everywhere, regardless of their profession, and sometimes needed retrieving. *Was. Baris was.* The grief hit Dashi anew, heavy because of its freshness. *Baris.* She wanted him back. She wanted all of them back. If she could have journeyed to the spirit world and reclaimed them like some epic hero of yore, she would have. But she didn't know how, didn't know the way. Instead, she was here, following a different path.

Stop procrastinating and do what needs to be done. The thought propelled her from the top stair, where she'd temporarily stalled.

Dashi drew her knife as she approached the room. The door squeaked as it opened, but the man in the bed was oblivious. He was also naked. He lay on his stomach, the bedding twisted over one leg to reveal the side of his buttocks. A tray of half-consumed food sat beside the bed, along with two clay bottles. One bottle was tipped over, the last few drops of wine making a dark pool on the floor.

Maybe he's drunk, she thought. *Maybe that will make it easier.*

His clothes, discarded in a passionate frenzy, had shed coins and something else that glowed in the light of the fireplace. Dashi knelt to pick up the golden disc: a pendant in the image of a stylized sun.

Her fingernails ground into her skin for a moment, then she pocketed the pendant and walked to the bed. She stared down at the man, studying his face in sleep. He didn't look evil now. His lips were parted slightly, his cheek a little smashed from where the pillow pushed against it. Maybe she should stop here. She knew Altan would want her to. But...she'd seen that face alert. She'd seen those eyes narrowed with greed as he rolled Altan's limp body over and began rummaging through his pockets.

There was no stopping here.

With a small cry, Dashi leapt onto the bed, straddling the man's back and grabbing a fistful of his hair. She pressed the knife against his throat. To his credit, he didn't cry out or beg. He went from peaceful slumber to the edge of death with nary a shudder.

"I want to know about the people you killed," she said. Anguish made her voice come out low, almost masculine.

"Alright." The man's voice was calm. Much calmer than Dashi's. She wondered if it was the alcohol or if, like her, he was able to act in the face of danger. "What do you want to know?"

"Why did you kill them?"

"Money."

Her fist tightened in his hair. "They weren't *carrying* money."

"I meant I was paid."

"By who?"

He made a strangled noise and she wasn't sure if it was because of the pain or if he was laughing at her. "Don't you know? They made a lot of enemies doing what they did."

Dashi's anger was a fire, scorching her from the inside, begging to be loosed into the world. "You're lying. You're *lying*." She sucked in her cheeks, trying to think through the heat. Altan had no enemies.

"You have a knife at my throat. Why would I lie?"

The fire was spreading down her arm, moving to claim the hand that held the knife. *Press harder*, it whispered. *Just a little harder.*

"*Stop it!*" she growled, not sure whether she was talking to the man or herself. She swallowed, trying to steady her thoughts. "Stop stalling and tell me who." She pressed the blade a little harder against his skin. *Not enough. Press harder.*

"My brother," he said.

"Your brother paid you or he knows who did?"

"Yes."

"Was he with you when you killed them?"

"No."

"Where is he now?"

"If I tell you, you'll kill me."

Dashi didn't answer.

"I'll take you to him. We can come to an agreement. I'll take you to him and you can let me go."

What a shameless coward, she thought. *I would never sell out Altan or Baris or Zayaa.* "There were more of you. I want to know who else was involved."

"My brother knows."

It could be a trap. *I'm not Baris; I can't fight that many at once.* Again, she thought of Altan. He'd tell her not to be stupid, not to put herself at risk. *I should honor his wishes.* The thought was brief, but the fire inside her burned hotter, turning Altan's imagined protests to ash.

"Let me take you to Negan," the man said, wheedling. "He knows—

With a sudden jerk, he bent Dashi's wrist backward, forcing the knife away from his throat. Dashi slid her other arm forward, crooking her elbow over his windpipe the way she'd practiced with Baris, but she wasn't heavy enough to hold him down. He bucked against her shoulder, rolling them both onto the floor. The knife skidded out of reach.

The man picked up one of the bottles. It was the full one; one hit would knock her out cold. Dashi pulled a second knife from her sash. He *was* drunk; she saw it in the slight delay in his movements.

"I wouldn't," she warned. "You're clumsy and drunk. Take me to your brother and I'll let you go."

The man cursed, still in that unhurried voice. "I may be drunk, but I can still beat a little girl. And I'll never take you to my brother."

He stepped closer, rocking the bottle back and forth in his right hand. An old trick, one Baris always used. Baris was ambidextrous and—

Dashi ducked the man's left-handed punch. The bottle came just after, aimed at her knees. She sprang into the air and lashed out with her feet, catching his jaw with the heel of her boot. His head flew back and his body followed, toppling into the fireplace. There was a great crash as the bottle, still clutched in his hand, broke upon the brick hearth. Wine sprayed everywhere, splattering Dashi's boots and making the coals hiss and dim.

She landed on the balls of her feet. When the man didn't move, she sighed and wiped her cheek with the back of her hand. Wine had landed there as well. *Wonderful*, she thought, *now he's unconscious*. She would never be able to move someone so big and she doubted she had much time. They must have made a terrible racket, even in a place accustomed to raucous noises.

Dashi retrieved her knife and approached the man cautiously, in case he was faking. No, his head was right next to the coals; that was too uncomfortable to fake.

She nudged his side. "Get up. I need answers."

There was no response.

She kicked a little harder. "Get up."

Nothing.

Dashi's skin prickled with alarm. She didn't have time for this. Avoiding the puddle of wine near the man's shoulders, she stepped closer. "Hey! Get—"

Her head finally registered what her eyes had seen: the red pooled near the man's head wasn't wine. It was blood. And his head wasn't just lying against the fireplace. It had broken on the sharp brick corner, split like a piece of fruit.

She took a step back. Then another. *This is what you wanted. This is why you came here.* She'd told herself she *needed* blood on her hands, that she needed to avenge her friends, but when the man had given her a reason not to kill him, she'd felt...well, relieved. Now her hands were shaking. Her whole *body* was shaking. Even the inner fire that had urged her onward, goading her toward violence, was gone, extinguished like the coals.

The door flew open, hitting the wall with such force that a crack formed in the plaster. Dashi whirled around, her hand finding a knife on instinct, as a second man crashed into the room holding a sword. She recognized him immediately: she'd seen him riding beside Baris' body. *Great ancestors, are* all *of them at the brothel tonight?*

The swordsman took one look at the body in the fireplace and raised his weapon. Dashi yanked a chair up, blocking his swing just in time. Her ankle twisted as she flung herself away, but she felt no pain, just the thrumming desire to stay alive. He stepped closer, swaying slightly, and she skittered away again, rolling to retrieve a piece of firewood with which to parry. *Should have brought a sword.* But she hadn't wanted to alarm the prostitute. Hadn't thought she'd need one.

His blade glanced off the firewood and grazed her forearm, leaving a shallow trail of blood. The man was strong as a yak but slow. He was no Baris. Or, very possibly, he was a decent swordsman who was very drunk.

"Who are you?" he growled, advancing. She smelled wine, but she couldn't say whether it was from his breath or the wine-soaked floor. "What do you want?"

"I want you to tell me," she grunted, blocking another slow but forceful swing, "why you killed my friends."

He paused, looking confused, as if he'd killed so many people he couldn't place the victims specific to her.

She cursed. "Two nights ago, you ox." She was nearly backed against the wall, but the fire inside her had returned, stoked by the dance of survival.

Then, unforgivably, he laughed. "How do you know about that?" He slurred the ends of the words, not even caring enough to pronounce them fully. His sword moved in an arc, cutting through the air on her left side. She dropped flat, letting it embed in the plaster, then darted in with her knife to slice open his sword hand.

He cursed and drew his own knife, but Dashi struck first. Her knife found a home at the base of his throat, sending blood in a slow wave down her arm.

"Because," she said, twisting the knife a little, "I was there."

She didn't look at the second body. Already, rushing feet sounded in the hallway. She went straight to the window, rolling into the landing as she dropped. *Dead. Two men. Escape.* That was the only thing that mattered now: getting away. Sorting through her feelings was always uncomfortable and time-consuming. This would be no exception. Best to do it later.

She'd left Spit in the care of a street boy. Now she jogged in that direction, limping a little. Tossing a coin at the boy, Dashi flung herself into the saddle and turned toward the city gates. Idree was out of the question. Altan, Zayaa and Baris were dead and their rooms had been destroyed while they were gone. Karak City had no place for her.

"There!"

Dashi threw a glance over her shoulder. The street boy was pointing straight at her. He was talking to three prefects, their deels made bright as stars by the light of their torches. She could outmaneuver three men on horseback; she did it all the time on the goathead field. She leaned forward as Spit flew around corners, his hooves sounding their own alarm on the quiet streets.

Hooves beat behind her, but they weren't close enough to be an immediate threat. It wasn't far to the city gates. She hadn't brought any provisions—she could almost see Altan shaking his head; *lack of forethought*, he'd say—but she had her bow. The next closest town was only a day away. Of course, they might anticipate that—

A flare of light. There, atop the wall, a torch had been lit. She glanced over her shoulder. More torches, a whole line of them. The prefects had raised the alarm. The gates would be closing. Dashi jerked Spit down a side street, but there, riding straight at her, was a fourth prefect. Another prefect on her right. He raised his voice, hailing his comrades.

Her breath was coming hard now. *No place to go.* The wall loomed on one side, cutting off all exits. She aimed Spit at one of the prefects, kicking hard with her heels. If she could squeeze between him and the building—

Hands were on her waist, pulling her sideways. Someone wrenched her arms back, pushing her face into the freezing mud until there was grit in her mouth, grit clogging her nostrils—

Dashi caught her breath, pushing away the memories that had sucked her three months into the past. The past was...the past. What was important was the man before her now. This was him, she was sure of it: Negan, the brother of the man she'd killed in the brothel.

Impossibly, the man seemed to recognize her too, though she knew they'd never met. His eyes widened and he stepped toward her, one hand balled, the other reaching for the long dagger at his waist. "*You!* You killed—You're supposed to be dead."

The world fell away as he spoke. She searched for the flame of anger inside herself and found it, ready and waiting.

Across the stableyard, a guard moved to the edge of the wall. Like the other royal guardsmen, he wore green and gold and carried a long bow, but when he turned his head toward her and nocked an arrow, she recognized one of the men who'd taken her from prison. She wasn't sure if the arrow was meant for her, because she hadn't gone unnoticed, or for the man, because he'd recognized her.

Dashi shifted to the left, putting the man between her and the arrow. Then she smiled and slid a hand to her knife. "Maybe I've come back for you."

His mouth twisted. "I hope you have."

"Consul Negan," someone said in an urgent voice.

The man turned his head, listening without taking his eyes off Dashi.

A lanky woman with dark hair stood nearby. "The race will start soon. His Most High awaits you."

He nodded stiffly. "See to my mounts."

"Of course." The woman's eyes flicked to Dashi. "Any...other orders, Consul?"

"No. I'll take care of it myself this time." He smiled grimly at Dashi, even as he released his dagger. "Ride hard, mongrel. I'll be coming for you."

She held his gaze, unwilling to let him see her shock. The brother of the man she'd murdered and the khan's consul were one and the same? *Ancestors above, what have I* done?

Negan turned in the direction of the palace, barking directions at attendants as he went. Dashi watched him go. She didn't take her hand off her knife or return to her preparations until he'd disappeared behind a wall of racers and horses.

The khan arrived just before the noon hour, riding on a shaded litter balanced on the shoulders of glistening servants. Musicians followed, bearing lutes, gongs and boxy Karakalese fiddles with scrolls carved to resemble the royal standard: a wolf's head. The musicians continued through the main gate to entertain the spectators waiting outside, but the khan's litter turned, crossing in front of the line of waiting racers.

Along with the rest of the racers, Dashi's head had been bowed since the khan's litter first appeared.

In a voice that filled the stable yard, one of the litter carriers called, "The Great Khan of Karakal." Still, no one moved or spoke, save for an occasional stamp from an impatient horse. The litter moved slowly down the line of racers, stopping here and there at the khan's command. He didn't speak to any of the racers, just slowly ran his eyes over each one, measuring them against the task he'd set.

Unexpectedly, the litter paused in front of Dashi. It felt like the top of her bowed head was emblazoned with her guilt, an admission that she'd been instructed to bring the artifact to someone else. Dashi willed her hands and legs to stay still, lest her nerves cause Spit to fidget. She'd already pulled her scarf over her face in anticipation of the race's start and now she was fiercely glad to have her expression hidden.

Shadowed by the canopy of his litter, the khan was only a vague shape at the periphery of Dashi's vision, but she saw him lean forward with interest.

"I remember you. I remember your copious weeping." His voice was cool and authoritative. "You think to save what's left of your family?"

Copious weeping? What was left of her family? Dashi's eyes darted from side to side, trying to gather clues without raising her head.

"I think only to serve, Most High." The person beside her—the talkative young man from the dirt circle—answered before she could.

On the other side of him, the man with the black scarf relaxed ever so slightly, relieved the khan was not speaking to him.

There was a long silence. Finally, the khan said. "See that you do. You do not want to meet the same end as others who've disappointed me."

The litter moved slowly forward, taking the khan past the remaining racers, and then up a ramp that led to the top of the wall. One of the litter carriers announced the khan in bellowing tones, this time aimed at the crowd in front of the gate. Again, there was no response. Like the racers still hidden behind the wall, the crowd would remain silent until the khan spoke or chose to release them.

Flags whipped in the eerie silence. A rooster crowed from behind the stable. The khan stepped out from the shadow of his canopy. He was a narrow man who wore his dark hair pulled back at the nape of his neck, just like the ancient khagans. The style had metastasized throughout Karak City, particularly among those who wished to curry the khan's favor. He turned to the waiting crowd, raising his hands. As one, thousands of heads rose to look at him.

"This has always been a land of strength and greatness," the khan cried, his voice ringing into the silence. "Before it was Karakal, it was part of the Purek Empire, the greatest power ever known. Now it is our turn. Karakal stands poised to take its place in history. Our military has never been stronger. Our future, never brighter. We stand on the edge, ready to brave what lesser men shrink from." He paused, waiting for his words to take effect.

"To commemorate our destiny, I have declared a day of feasting and sport. The racers you are about to see will face untold dangers to explore the northlands. The winner will receive a purse of two hundred thousand gold pieces and a place of honor in my court."

There was no mention of the artifact, Dashi noticed. Where did the spectators think the race ended? At some random point in the taiga's trees?

"Karak City, here are your racers!"

The crowd roared, whether because they were actually excited or because that's what the khan expected, Dashi didn't know. Most likely they were eager to see the racers gone so their access to the wolf fountain could resume uninterrupted.

Dashi hadn't seen Negan, the khan's consul, since his summons from the khan, but at the last moment, he reappeared and rode to the front of the line, a dark smile on his face. The gates opened and the racers began to ride through, one by one. Dashi sat quietly on Spit's back as she waited, each of her senses working in concert to absorb the moment. She breathed in the aroma of dust and horses, felt the leather reins between her thumb and forefinger. Her mind felt clear.

At last, it was Dashi's turn. She shifted in the saddle and Spit moved forward without any other cues. *That's why it's nice to have a familiar mount*, she thought, satisfied. It was like working with an old friend. You could finish their sentences, anticipate their laugh, predict their triggers. Dashi patted Spit's neck. Spit, the last partner she had left. *May you fare better than the others.*

The noise of the crowd hit her like a physical force, attacking from all sides. One of her extra mounts—the same flighty chestnut who'd led her to Negan—danced sideways in alarm. She thought she heard someone shout her name, but when she looked, she saw only a sea of unfamiliar faces.

Dashi halted at the starting line, edging between two racers and their tall, expensive horses. Spit snorted in disgust. Dashi didn't blame him. Starting like this, arrayed in a long line with the wolf fountain at their backs, was showy and pointless. The expensive horses on either side of her would surge ahead, their slender legs making short work of the city streets. No matter. This race lasted for weeks, not minutes, and she'd wager that the racer who led on day one wouldn't be the same one leading on day twenty-three.

A servant walked the length of the starting line, handing each racer a folded piece of paper: a description of the artifact they were supposed to deliver to the khan. Or to a scheming noble who'd promised to unlock an explosive belt.

Dashi flicked the paper open, curious to see what could possibly be important enough to necessitate a journey into the taiga. The paper showed a bare sketch of a woman, a statuette, plus a few lines of extra descriptors. The statuette would probably be made from gold and her hands might be holding any number of items, or nothing at all. There was little else in terms of concrete description.

Behind Dashi, a gong sounded five times: a final warning to clear the streets. She could hear the crowd shifting in anticipation, but as she shoved the paper into her deel, she didn't look to either side, just at the open road ahead. She tightened her grip on the reins, leaning forward ever so slightly to tell Spit they were about to go. One of his ears flicked backward in acknowledgment.

The khan's voice rang out. "Karakal! Let the race begin!"

The gong sounded again, a single note that hovered in the air around the racers as they leaned forward, gouging with their heels, raising their quirts and urging their horses forward.

Chapter 9

Spit surged forward, muscles bunching and lengthening as he stretched out into a gallop, the string of extra mounts trailing behind him like tail feathers. Already the bigger horses had rocketed to the front, just as Dashi had predicted. They clustered so tightly that she could barely see past them, much less ride there.

The road snaked from the jade circle into the silver circle. People flashed by in a blur of screaming faces, but Dashi heard only the howl of the wind and the beat of hooves. She was part of her horse, part of the sunlight streaming down, part of the breeze itself. She let out a whoop that was immediately lost in the rushing air.

The street widened temporarily as they flew into the leather circle, just enough to accommodate the public fountain in the middle of the road. When it whisked past, she saw its rim was crowded with children, intent on proving their bravery by standing in the midst of the race. Dashi grinned appreciatively; she could easily picture herself doing that a few years ago...and just as easily picture Altan yelling at her for it.

Suddenly, the horse in front of her cut hard to one side, crashing into another racer. Thrown off balance, both horses stumbled and fell. Spit swerved to avoid the wreckage, but a thundering sound behind her, followed by the shrill scream of an animal in distress, made Dashi glance under her arm. A third horse had gone down. Its rider sprawled, motionless, beside it.

The crowd cheered wildly, driven to a foam-mouthed fervor by the unfolding action. The children standing on the fountain yelled the loudest.

Dashi turned her attention forward. Somewhere in Karak City, she thought, someone had just made a lot of money by betting that three racers would fall before they'd reached the city gates.

The dirt circle passed in a whir of felt and wood lean-tos, a shantytown that few rose above. Even at a gallop, Dashi could smell the stench of garbage and human waste. The crowd was loudest here. Free entertainment and a day off work were celebrated to the fullest extent.

The city gates stood open, spilling the racers onto the steppe in a fast-moving river. It was a far cry from the night of her arrest, when the gates had dammed her in, leaving no escape. Ahead, the frontrunners were nearly obscured by dust. She glanced behind her: several other racers had gotten past the wreckage near the fountain and were coming into sight around a corner. All the distances were relative, she reminded herself. The field of racers would shift positions constantly. *And I'll make sure the shifts are in my favor.*

Dashi kept pace with the two closest racers: the tanned laborer from the dirt circle, whose horses had been tied next to hers, and an older man with a braid of fair hair. Both men had pulled scarves over their noses and mouths to ward off the lingering cloud left by the frontrunners.

The steppe spread out before them, a vast table of green and gold that formed the bulk of Karakal's territory. Karak City had been built on a strategic jumble of hills, which reigned over the surrounding plains. Other hills were sprinkled in the distance, but most of the steppe was rolling grassland, its reaches bullied by the wind and, except for the nomadic Mori people, largely empty.

A broad river creased the plains to the north of Karak City and the map pointed the racers to one of the few crossings: a canyon, where a bridge had been built over the river's thinnest point. The fair-haired racer snuck glances at Dashi as they approached the bridge. He was bigger than her and stronger. She was sure she was better on a horse—that statement was usually true no matter who she compared herself to—but the bridge would curtail her advantages while doing nothing to hamper his. She pulled Spit back, letting the fair-haired man go first over the bridge. If he was thinking of eliminating competition, she didn't want him at her back anyway.

Sweat already coated Spit's neck, but Dashi wasn't worried as they clattered off the bridge. If she paced him well, he could keep going for much, much longer. The canyon stretched high and long on either side, its walls lined with skinny, erosion-made ledges and pocked with shallow caves that housed swallows and hoopoes. Already the shadows along the western side were lengthening, bringing coolness with each incremental shift.

The changing light nearly obscured the danger ahead, but she spotted it at the last moment: a cord strung across the path. Dashi hauled on Spit's reins, ignoring his neigh of protest as she scanned the rugged canyon for other anomalies. She opened her mouth, but the fair-haired racer was already plowing through the cord, snapping it in two.

Above them, boulders shuddered and began to turn, slowly at first, then rapidly as gravity took hold. As they fell, Dashi saw they weren't boulders at all, but piles of smaller rocks held together by nets. She had a split second to pull Spit toward the side of the canyon, hoping to protect his legs if the rocks came bouncing this far.

The fair-haired racer didn't notice the rocks at first. By the time he did, it was too late. One rock hit his mount in the head. Another struck him in the side. Dust and noise obscured everything after that and Dashi had to concentrate on calming her own mounts. Her extra horses tried to turn and run. Spit reared. She clung tightly, leaning forward to keep her seat.

"Don't be afraid, don't be afraid," she soothed in a singsong voice. After a few minutes, the crashing ended and Spit's ears, which had been flattened against his skull, rose cautiously.

The dust cleared in stages. She saw the shape of a horse first, twisted on the ground. Dashi rode forward, swiping dirt from her shoulders and face. The fair-haired racer didn't get to his feet until she approached, like it took the sound of Spit's hooves to convince him the worst was over. He cradled his right arm to his chest.

"It's dead," he said, sounding incredulous. He eyed the horse lying in front of him. Its skull had been split wide. Dust temporarily colored the exposed brain matter, but blood had started to reassert itself. Dashi saw the body lying in the brothel fireplace and looked away.

"It's dead and the rest of them," he paused to kick the dead animal, "ran off."

Sure enough, the end of the canyon was choked with dust as the man's extra mounts made their getaway.

"Karak City isn't far," Dashi said, her mind already on the rest of the race.

The racer came at her all at once, with a knife in his hand and no pretense of innocent intentions. Dashi wheeled Spit away, simultaneously grabbing for the quiver belted to her thigh. She swung the bow up just as the racer raised his blade. He froze.

"Drop it." Spit pranced beneath her, picking up on her tension.

The racer hesitated a moment, then the knife hit the ground in a muted plume.

"Now walk back to the bridge."

He stared.

"*Walk back to the bridge*, or I'll put this arrow through your chest."

Muttering something under his breath, the fair-haired man turned toward the bridge. Dashi swiveled in her saddle, keeping the arrow trained on his back as he walked. When he was far enough away that she felt safe, she dismounted, wanting to check her packs and her mounts' lead ropes.

She'd just finished when hoofbeats made her head jerk up. The laborer from the dirt circle was riding toward her.

He slowed his horse, glancing back at the fair-haired racer, now a small figure standing on the bridge. "He's as good as dead, with a broken arm and no mount."

Dashi snorted. "If he walks fast, he'll be in Karak City tonight. What would you do, give him a horse so he can keep pace and kill you in your sleep? He was dangerous before; now he's desperate."

"I know. He swung at me when we were riding." The laborer shifted in his seat. "But he's injured."

"And I'm not playing nursemaid to someone who attacked me," she said, retying her pack horse. "We're lucky that trap didn't take us down with him."

"Trap?"

She turned to give him a disbelieving look.

"I...I thought it was a rock slide."

"There was a tripwire. One of the frontrunners must have rigged it after the map was distributed, then set the wire after they passed through today." She studied him for a moment. "You didn't really grow up in the dirt circle, did you?"

"Why?"

"Because I spent most of my life in the leather circle and you don't seem like you grew up poorer than I did."

He looked at his reins. "Jade circle," he muttered. "But it invites fewer questions if I say dirt circle. My father...fell out of favor with the khan. We thought we might stay with friends while we—" He shook his head. "We ended up in the dirt circle and I found work maintaining the roads. They'll take anyone, skilled or not."

"And now you're risking your life to please the man who ruined you?" She didn't ask about the "we" in his story: either he'd entered the race in some vain hope of saving his family or he'd already lost them. Either way, she didn't want to know.

"Something like that," he said.

Dashi glanced at the sleeve of his deel, now darkened by blood.

He pulled up the fabric. "The other racer. It's fine though. He didn't get me too badly."

Dashi shrugged. *Just as well.* She wasn't offering her bandages and ointments. With this many casualties on the first day of the race, there was no telling what else awaited her.

"Be careful," she said, turning Spit. "If there were traps here, there might be more farther along."

"Wait! We could ride together. You know...help each other." He smiled warmly. "I'm Aizhan."

She laughed. *I could help you, is more like it.* She couldn't see what help he could offer her, especially now that she knew he was from the jade circle. "I don't want to know your name and I don't want to help you. I want to *beat* you, whatever it takes. Trust me when I say that goes for everyone else out here too."

She trotted off down the canyon, scanning for more traps and putting as much distance between herself and the hapless laborer as possible.

Chapter 10

The laborer made no more attempts to befriend her, though he kept pace in the distance behind her. Not far from the canyon, Dashi passed the fair-haired racer's escaped mounts, now grazing contentedly in the deep grass. She hoped the laborer didn't do something stupid, like try to return them to their owner. Not so much because he would probably end up dead, but because she didn't relish the idea of having the fair-haired man behind her.

According to the map, the racers would turn east in a few days, when the hills of the taiga were so close that even the Mori grew uneasy. For now, the steppe was as flat as a table. Hares and bustards sprang up underfoot, fleeing the horses' hooves on their stilt-like legs. In the distance, she could see the dark shapes of the frontrunners, but she made no effort to catch them. There were so many of them and she had no way to conceal herself. Better to bide her time. She knew the land just south of the taiga. She could pull ahead there, when the hills would hide her and their pampered horses began to tire.

She didn't stop until the sun sank into the steppe and the grasses seemed to bend with the burden of their shadows. There was no trail to speak of, but she knew most of the racers would continue straight north, as the map advised. She turned west, riding until she felt reasonably sure no one would stumble upon her by accident.

Dashi's knees almost buckled when she swung off of Spit. It had been a long time since she'd ridden all day and the muscles it required were different from the ones she'd exercised in prison. She leaned against him for a moment, collecting herself, then stumbled away to stake and hobble the horses for the night.

There would be no fire. Its light would only lead other racers straight to her if they were looking. Even if they weren't, she was too tired for it to be worth the effort. Instead, she lay against her saddle in the sweet-smelling grass, eating dried meat and staring at the stars. The night insects, temporarily quieted by her arrival, renewed their frenetic courtship songs, intent on summer's fleeting bacchanalia.

Dashi sighed. The stars, the grass, the night songs: she hadn't thought she'd live to see them again. She dozed in the twilight, her eyelids made heavy by the long day and the quiet night, her hand resting against the saddle compartment that hid Altan's pendant.

She couldn't say how long she lay there, only that her rest was fitful. She awoke after midnight. Spit had abandoned his grazing and stood with his ears pricked toward the east. The insects had halted their songs once again. Their silence moved closer and closer, matching the soft tread of boots on the grass. Dashi remained sprawled against the saddle, unmoving except for the slide of her right arm over her hip. There was a soft *whuff* as Spit processed the intruder's scent.

The boots stopped beside her. Dashi kept her breathing deep, marshaling every last nerve to make her feigned sleep appear genuine. She felt rather than heard the person squat down, sensed the hand stretching out toward her.

Dashi sprang up, knocking the racer's hand away with one thrust of her arm and aiming her next punch between his legs. The racer gasped, but instead of falling to the ground, he staggered to his feet. He was short, she saw, even shorter than she was. She adjusted her tackle at the last moment, hitting low to account for her target's center of gravity.

The racer went down with absurd ease, too surprised to react at first and too small to do anything once they hit the ground. Dashi straddled his midsection, pressing her knife against his pale throat. Her shadow darkened the stranger's face so that she couldn't see who had come after her, but she could feel the slightness of the rider's body, the narrow hips and the stem-like wrists that she contained with one hand.

"Who are you?" she hissed. Why would a person this frail enter the race? Dashi was small too, but at least she was muscular. This person would be vulnerable alone—Dashi glanced around, her senses suddenly on alert. Maybe this was a decoy, meant to distract her while someone else came from behind.

The thoughts raced through her head so quickly that the other rider hadn't even responded yet. Dashi rocked forward, placing her knee on one wrist, while she bent the other backward. "Who are you working with?"

"D—Dashi, it's me," a voice gasped. "Don't hurt me. I—I'm alone."

Dashi dropped her sister's wrist like it had become a live serpent. "Idree! Why are you here?"

"I came to find you. I—you're hurting me."

Dashi stood up, feet braced, looming over her sister. Idree pushed herself into a sitting position, rubbing her wrist and then her stomach, as if Dashi's weight alone had injured her. Maybe it had, Dashi thought; her sister had never been particularly tough.

"How did you find me?" Dashi asked.

"I knew you'd be at the front." Idree said it matter-of-factly, without the usual tremors of accusation and envy. "Once I stopped passing racers I let Bat decide where to go. I figured he'd want company and would find Spit."

"I'm not at the front. There's a whole group of riders ahead of me."

Idree shrugged. "You will be."

Dashi glanced at Idree's horse, a piebald Mori mare. "Auntie Nima let you take her horse?"

Idree ducked her head.

"You *stole* from her?" She grabbed Idree by the arm and shoved her toward the mare. "You're leaving. Maybe she'll take you back if you apologize."

What will I do if Auntie Nima refuses? Altan's not here to deal with it.

Idree stopped next to the mare and Dashi held the stirrup out impatiently. When Idree didn't move, Dashi sighed and cupped her hands together; her sister probably still couldn't mount without a block.

Stealing from her employer to join the khan's race? Against people who are willing to kill? She can barely ride, *let alone—*

"I'm not going back, Dashi."

"Well, you're not staying here. Get on the horse, Idree."

"You don't understand. I *can't* go back. Men came to Auntie Nima's looking for me. They were—I think they wanted to hurt me. They—"

"Why would they be looking for you? What did you do?"

"I didn't do anything! They were looking for me because of *you*! I—"

"What are you talking about?"

Idree stamped her foot. "Blessed ancestors, Dashi, let me finish talking!"

Dashi crossed her arms.

"I was in the kitchen when a group of men burst through the front door. We have a refuse chute in the corner. It goes into a trough out back. The opening is below the counter, so it's not that easy to see, especially if you don't know where to look."

Dashi nodded impatiently. Trust her sister to go through every last detail before moving on to the crucial parts.

"When I heard them come in, I—I don't know why, but I ducked beneath the counter. They were shouting at Auntie Nima; one of them hit her, I think. They asked where you were and whether I was your sister." Idree's voice broke. "If they hurt Auntie Nima because of me, I don't know how I'll—" Her sobs started falling, thick and fast like summer rain.

Five minutes, Dashi thought. That's how long Idree had lasted without rinsing her tear ducts.

Idree kept crying. Five more minutes. Then ten. Finally, Dashi couldn't take it any longer. "Finish the story, Idree."

Idree nodded but didn't stop crying. *How do people keep that many tears inside,* Dashi wondered. Her own mind didn't function that way. She skipped straight over sadness to anger. If ever she found herself wallowing in sorrow she searched her mind for the cause, searched for soil in which the seed of anger could germinate. It was more useful that way. Even in prison, she hadn't cried. True, she'd indulged in lengthy fantasies about murder and about what she could have done differently, neither of which necessarily qualified as "useful," but at least it had given her thoughts purpose.

Finally, Idree dragged the heel of her hand over her eyes, pushing back the heavy fringe of hair that fell onto her forehead. "They checked the upstairs first. I think they thought I might climb out a window, like you would have. But I got into the refuse chute and slid into the scrap trough. I found Bat's saddle and I...I left. I wanted to check on Auntie, but they were so—it sounded like my being there would get her into more trouble."

Dashi's mind juggled the possibilities rapidly. No one knew she was out of prison but Osol and the noble. And Negan, the khan's consul.

She glanced at Idree and mentally added her sister to the list. She'd ask about that later. Would the noble have sent Osol to look for Idree? He would use every available leverage to get what he wanted—she knew *that* firsthand—but to what end? If he was hoping to motivate Dashi further, wouldn't he have mentioned Idree *before* the race? Or was Idree to be insurance of some sort, in case Dashi decided to take the artifact to the khan?

She'd started walking at some point, pacing between Idree and the horses. "This happened when?"

"A little after the start of the race. I was making up the dough for tomorrow's dumplings." Idree sniffled.

Dashi hated that sound.

The consul certainly wouldn't hesitate to go after her sister—he'd probably see it as justice, even though Idree was a child and his brother was a murderer who deserved a slower death than the one he'd gotten. He'd been in front of Dashi once the race started, in the fastest group of horses. She hadn't seen anyone double back toward the city, but he could have given the order before he left. She thought of the dark smile he'd worn when he rejoined the other racers, how his gaze had swept back and forth, searching for her. She wasn't sure how much, if anything, he knew about her connection to Altan, Zayaa and Baris, but he knew she'd killed his brother. After that, the rest would probably follow. As the noble had pointed out, what were the chances that she'd go after the killers if she *hadn't* known the victims?

Dashi glanced at her sister. Idree was standing next to Auntie Nima's mare, nervously plaiting its mane. "How did you know I was in the race?" Dashi asked.

"I saw you at the starting line. I went to the wolf fountain with one of the girls who works down the street. We were supposed to meet some boys but—well, I got distracted when I saw you."

"You're too young to meet boys." It came out sharper than Dashi intended, but she didn't backtrack. "Did anyone else recognize me?"

Idree's lips thinned. "I don't think so. At least, no one mentioned it when I got back to the leather circle. Your face was mostly covered."

The steppe was silent, undisturbed except for the insects, who were only too happy to fill the air once more.

Undisturbed. Minutes ago, *she'd* been undisturbed. Even the pyrothrite belt couldn't ruffle her continuously. When she thought of it, it bothered her. Or when she remembered the noble's casual arrogance. But lying on the steppe beneath the stars, her problems had seemed far away.

But this? *This* disturbed her. How was she supposed to win while dragging her sister along? The khan's race was dangerous. Hadn't today proven that? It was no place for a child, especially one as weak as her sister. Then there were the logistics of it. The food she'd packed wouldn't be enough for two people. Her extra mounts would have to rotate between two riders instead of being able to rest fully when they weren't being ridden. Her sister didn't even have warm clothes and the northlands could get cold at night, even in summer.

But what else could she do? Sending Idree back was dangerous. Her sister had been lucky to skirt the other racers without incident, most likely because they were sleeping. Could she do it a second time? Some of them might leave a lone girl to herself, but others...

Even if Idree *did* make it back, then what? If the consul's men were looking for her, then no place in Karak City was safe. Maybe no place outside the city either.

Dashi stopped pacing abruptly, her mind made up. Idree's head was bowed, her fingers still buried in the mare's mane.

"I only have one bedroll. But there's a saddle blanket. That will have to do. Maybe we'll pass a Mori clan we can trade with."

Idree nodded solemnly.

"I don't want to see any tears, Idree." Dashi settled back against her saddle once more. "Do you understand? Not one. This isn't the place for them."

There was no answer. Even if Idree had agreed, Dashi wouldn't have believed her. The crying, the weakness: it wasn't something her sister could control.

Dashi closed her eyes and waited in vain for sleep to take her.

Chapter 11

Dashi startled awake just before dawn. Idree, used to rising early at the bakery, was already up. She'd gone through one of the packs in search of breakfast, which she handed to Dashi. Dashi broke the hard bread in half and, without a word, swapped it for the whole piece Idree had been about to eat. They would still consume the day's allotted provisions, each girl getting half of what Dashi had originally planned for herself.

Idree looked at her portion doubtfully. "Is this all?"

"Next time bring food with you." The words came out of their own accord. Dashi knew she was being unfair—of course Idree hadn't gathered food before she fled—but she was still put out by her sister's presence.

The night had been a tiring one. When she finally drifted off, she'd been awakened by a far-off scream. She couldn't tell what made it—sometimes animals could sound disturbingly like humans, especially from a distance—but she thought about the trap in the canyon and didn't close her eyes again.

The sleepless night had given her time to mull another complication caused by Idree's presence: it would make them a target. At least some of the racers would be willing to use violence. Not that she blamed them: you shouldn't embark on something dangerous unless you were willing to become that way yourself. But strength responded to strength and traveling with a child was a sign of weakness.

She'd come up with a tentative plan to work around this liability. She would stay to the west of the mapped route—and far away from the other racers—for as long as possible. Idree was small, but from a distance she would look like any other racer.

Dashi gobbled her bread as she moved between the horses, readying them for the day. Idree sat in the grass next to her saddle—Auntie Nima's saddle, actually—pinching the last few crumbs from her palm and placing them on her tongue. A small recurve bow, wrapped in oiled leather, was tied to the back of the saddle. It was a child's bow; the same one Dashi had learned to shoot with. She could still remember her father handing it to her. She'd been six. Idree had been a baby. He'd gotten sick the following year.

"Hurry up, Idree. We need to leave."

"Are you going to tell me why you aren't in prison?"

Dashi slung the saddlebags over the packhorse. "How did you manage to bring the bow if you left in such a rush?"

"Auntie Nima said it couldn't stay in the house. I grabbed it when I was saddling Bat." Idree's gaze darted to the bow, but she didn't touch it. "I thought it might be useful."

Food is useful. A bow you don't know how to shoot is the opposite. "Who said I was in prison?" Dashi asked aloud.

Idree rolled her eyes. "I'm not stupid, Dashi. Just because the prefects don't tell us anything doesn't mean people don't talk."

"I was let out. The winning racer has to retrieve an artifact for the khan. Apparently, some people think I have a good chance of succeeding."

Idree got to her feet, lifting her saddle with an effort. "Why would the khan need you when he has all those other racers?"

There were no more mentions of the past: not about the fight they'd had on the last night they'd seen each other, or about what, exactly, had transpired after they'd parted.

Dashi shrugged, the lie coming easily. "He wants all the help he can get. He's been trying to get this particular artifact for a while."

"What is it?"

"A statuette of a woman. Supposedly it's made of gold."

"And they're going to let you keep the purse money if you bring it back?" Idree asked, eyebrows rising. It was one of the only features they had in common: straight, un-arched eyebrows that gave their faces an air of intensity even when they were laughing.

"I'd be surprised."

Idree cocked her head, eyes sharp in her soft face. "They promised you freedom."

Dashi nodded.

"Why wait? You *have* freedom; you could be halfway out of Karakal by now."

"The people who killed Altan, Zayaa and Baris are still out there. If I leave Karakal, I lose my chance at finding them." Dashi wasn't sure why, but she didn't want to tell Idree about the pyrothrite belt. *Why would I,* she thought as she mounted. *She'll only nag at me.*

Idree's eyebrows sank and she lowered her head, a bull prepared to charge.

"Are you ready yet? I can't sit here any longer."

Idree winced as she pulled herself onto Bat. She was tall enough to mount by herself, Dashi noted with surprise. Dashi waited for the whining to begin, but Idree only pressed her lips together, letting Dashi take the lead.

The next four days fit the same mold as the first: a few words exchanged here and there, but mostly Dashi continued as she had before Idree appeared: pushing northward from dawn until dusk, switching horses when necessary. For her part, Idree stayed quiet, fatigue informing every movement. Dashi caught a few glimpses of that particular blend of clever and stubborn her sister wore when she wanted to ask a question—or complain about something—but her mouth stayed shut.

It was a pleasant surprise. Dashi had expected a barrage of whining and chatter, but there was none. True, the hours might have passed faster if she'd had someone to talk to, but she and her sister had never had that kind of relationship. If Baris had been there, he would've had Dashi laughing so hard she couldn't stay on her horse. Or maybe Zayaa would have regaled her with an ancient tale that she'd dredged from some crumbling text. Either way, it would have been preferable to silence, which was, in turn, preferable to Idree's blather.

They kept to the west for four days, avoiding the other racers. When Dashi finally turned east, the steppe's gentle undulations had become more marked, turning into real hills that gave her a brief glimpse of the receding racers at each crest, and left her riding sightless at each trough. To the northeast, a dark swell of land rose, like a temple built to bridge the gap between earth and sky. *The taiga.*

They began to pass the frontrunners' horses, abandoned as they succumbed to overexertion and poor food. One had lamed, its delicate foreleg still swollen in death. Another's throat had been slit for no apparent reason. In Karak City, they'd been worth a small fortune. On the steppe, they rotted beneath the tender ministrations of scavengers and the sun.

On the sixth night of the race, Dashi checked the noble's pyrothrite belt—she refused to call it "hers"—for the first time since the race began. Its presence had been weighing on her, growing increasingly irritating with each rider who grew more distant. She waited until Idree went to relieve herself before hurriedly unwrapping her deel. Six nodules of pyrothrite had fallen since the beginning of the race, their shapes silhouetted against the white background of the lower triangle. In total, there were eight nodules there now, biding their time until they could reduce her to fleshy splinters. That gave her twenty-one days until the pyrothrite became explosive.

Her fingers retied her sash methodically. Yes, more nodules had moved from one section of the disc to the other. So what? She'd known that would happen. *I'm doing fine*, she told herself. *A little farther back than I wanted to be, but I'll make it up. I'm doing fine.*

Idree returned a few minutes later, her face pale and drawn. The reduced rations were taking their toll on Dashi as well. At least their horses were eating well, their hearty stomachs making short work of the tough grass that the more expensive racehorses found unpalatable. They gleaned moisture from it too, she knew, and though they would drink their fill if they happened upon a river, they could last many days without such a luxury.

The land was different here: hillier and rockier, with shrubs and brush congregating in the low-lying areas. The near-taiga, the Mori called it. For their camp, she'd selected a depression between two hills, which shielded them from the wind and the other racers. She was tempted to light a fire, if only to break up the monotony of the nights, but decided the cover was too sparse. Her sister didn't complain, though Dashi knew she probably wanted to.

Idree was snoring gently when the killing began. She jolted upright at the sound of the screams, but Dashi was ready, a hand over her sister's mouth before she could cry out. When she was sure Idree had herself under control—or as sure as she could be with her sister—Dashi cautiously removed her hand.

"What is it?" Idree whispered.

"The other racers, I think. I'm going to ride closer. If there's a threat, I need to know what it is."

"I'm coming too."

Dashi shook her head. She knew her sister would be afraid to stay alone, but she needed to be as quiet as possible. "I'll be quicker by myself."

Idree's eyebrows pushed downward. "I'm not—"

"Not the time for arguments, Idree. See that hill over there? Take a blanket, if you want, and one of the saddlebags of food. If someone does come they'll look near the horses first, then walk down the depression searching the bushes. It'll take them a while before they look on the other hills. I'll be back by then."

I hope. She didn't want to think about what would happen if the other racers found the horses. They'd either kill them or steal them. They would certainly take the supplies. *She* would, if the tables were turned. Either way, she and Idree would have only one mount and one saddlebag of food between them. There would be no way to win the race then. She might as well charge straight at Negan with her sword out and, if she pulled *that* off, she'd head back to Karak City to find the noble—*Quit it,* she told herself. *Don't borrow defeat before it's even happened. The same goes for revenge.*

Dashi handed a knife to Idree. "Mind you don't fall on it in the dark."

Idree opened her mouth to retort, but Dashi was already walking toward Spit. Her extra mounts—the chestnut and a dun horse, who she'd dubbed Dirt and Dust, respectively—were fresher, but she trusted Spit more. She wouldn't be taking a saddle or a bridle—nothing to creak or jangle or catch the light.

She slung her bow over her shoulder, strapped on her quiver, and leapt to Spit's back. "Whatever happens, Idree, you can't fall apart. You have to keep thinking."

Idree's head wobbled up and down, but she didn't tell Dashi not to go. Didn't tell Dashi she never wanted to see her again, the way she had when Dashi left three months ago.

"I'll meet you on the hill." Dashi squeezed her knees against Spit's ribs and took off. She stuck to the sides of the hills, avoiding any areas where she might be silhouetted. Spit's warmth was comforting in the cool night. She tried not to think of the last time she'd ridden ahead like this, or what she'd found when she came back. *Idree will be fine.* Whoever had been screaming had stopped now. Somehow, Dashi didn't think that was a good thing.

There was a particularly high hill to the east. She'd glimpsed light as she rode toward it—either a fire or a torch—so she left Spit stripping leaves in a thicket at the bottom. The western face of the hill was dotted with rocks and scrubby plants, and Dashi ascended it on all fours, slowing as she neared the top. *Voices.* The speakers were just on the other side.

Dashi flattened herself into a shallow drainage gully, pressing her cheek against the ground. The grass was thin here, on account of the washed-out soil, and she could feel dirt sticking to her face.

"Finished?"

Negan's voice. She recognized his sneering tone even in the dark.

"There were two camped to the southeast, maybe an hour away," a second man replied. "I got both, one right after the other."

"Men or women?" There was a muffled crunching as they stepped closer. They stopped on the very backbone of the hill, able to look down either side. Dashi could see their shadows without moving her head.

"Men. Barely put up a fight."

Negan swore in a harsh voice.

"Maybe someone else took care of the girl," the second man said.

"They've all reported back. Three women, none of them young and none of them half-Mori."

More footsteps approached. "We got eighteen tonight." A woman's voice.

"We're still missing a few," Negan said. "One in particular who might be a threat."

Eighteen dead racers in one night! How many are left? She thought there'd been three dozen to begin with, but in her shock at seeing Negan and the rush to get ready, she hadn't counted.

"Go through the bodies for supplies and valuables," Negan said. "Burn everything else."

"What about the one you're looking for?" the woman asked.

"She must be close by; she hasn't passed us." Negan bit off the words like they were something bitter he wanted to flush out of his mouth. "I'll find her before the race is over."

If only he knew how *close*, Dashi thought. The thought made her heart jump. Altan was right: there was something wrong with her. She should be scared. Or appalled at the casual way they dealt death. Not excited.

"What about the canyon?" the other man asked. "The trap could've taken her out."

"Aren reported no bodies."

"Even if she gets to the artifact first, she'll never get it back to Karak City," the woman said. "We've ten to her one."

"Exactly," the other man said, turning down the hill.

For a moment Dashi thought she was alone, but then came a soft exhalation. Someone was still there, looking out over the hills.

She didn't dare look up—he was too close—but she caught a glimpse of his profile from where she lay. *Negan.*

Her bow was beside her. Dashi's fingers flexed involuntarily, feeling the smooth wood that could give her what she wanted. She could kill him, this man who was responsible for the deaths of her friends. She could send an arrow through his heart before he realized what was happening.

Her hand hesitated. How far could she get before his comrades came after her? What if they caught her? Without her, Idree would—

Muttering, Negan started back down the slope and Dashi let her fingers go slack around the bow. She'd missed her chance at revenge.

Chapter 12

Dashi slid down the hillside, her heart beating erratically. Now that the sky-high feeling of danger was wearing off, her brain grappled with what she'd learned. Negan—along with nine others apparently—had just killed off eighteen other racers. They were also responsible for the trap near the bridge.

Negan was looking for her. Normally she might have welcomed that. Let him obsess over killing her. For months, *she'd* obsessed over killing *him*, though she hadn't known who he was. But with Idree here, things were different. She was hampered, riding with a visible weak spot that was just waiting to be exploited.

As she neared the hill where Idree should be waiting, fear suddenly gripped her, cold and unreasoning. Idree wouldn't be there. Or worse, she *would* be there, lying on the ground, watering the summer grass with her blood. Dashi swung her leg over Spit's back before he'd come to a stop. She half ran, half fell up the hillside, banging her shins on rocks and ignoring any need for caution.

"Idree?" she called in a whisper.

Silence.

"*Idree!*"

"Dashi!" A shadow detached from the ground. "Sorry, I—I think I fell asleep."

Dashi let out a breath. "Oh."

"Did you see the other racers?"

Dashi hesitated. If she told Idree the truth, would her sister crack under her fear? "I did see some racers," she said finally. She needed her sister to understand the need for caution. "They've...allied. They killed off eighteen other racers. That was the screaming we heard."

Idree inhaled sharply. "What if they come after us?"

"They won't." Dashi started down the hill.

Idree trotted after. "What will we do?"

"We'll move farther away and we'll stay there for as long as possible. And we'll take turns keeping watch."

"But...what will I do when it's my turn? What if I hear something?"

"You'll wake me up."

They collected the horses and moved farther west. Dashi tried not to think about how the other racers were riding east, getting closer to the artifact, while she was heading in the opposite direction.

Dashi took the first watch figuring that, if Negan's men were coming for them, it would be sooner, rather than later. She sat cross-legged, waiting, but the night was quiet now. Even the wind, which had been brisk only hours ago, had gone still. Eventually, her nerves loosened and her eyelids grew heavy; she had to stand to keep herself awake for the last few hours. When it was Idree's turn, Dashi was asleep almost as soon as she touched her bedroll.

Her dreams were old things, ragged from overuse and tinged with blood and grief. Once again she was riding ahead to scout—no bridle, no saddle, no light except for where the moon pressed its face against the clouds. Dashi pulled her fox-lined hat over her ears and readjusted her scarf so it covered her mouth and nose. She was cold, even in her furs. It had been a mild winter in Karakal, but now a storm was bearing down with a vengeance, girding its loins for one final barrage against the spring.

Ahead, Dashi saw the glow of the campfire. Not many people came out here. Not this far north. *Especially* not this time of year. On the other hand, how dangerous could they be? They'd made no effort to conceal their presence.

Why am I out here? That's the real question. She couldn't understand Altan's rush, even when he'd mentioned the buyer who would pay double if they delivered a particular scroll within the next few weeks. But Zayaa and Baris shared his eagerness; it was only Dashi who wondered why they were so willing to bow to the buyer's timetable. Still, it *had* been a mild winter. And she wasn't one to shy away from risk, especially when she would be the only one expressing reluctance.

They'd found the archive that held the scroll easily enough, in a crumbling foundation half-covered with earth. The specific scroll, which was supposed to detail the training of elite Purek soldiers, had taken more time to discover. Dashi helped as best she could, but her knowledge of ancient Purek wasn't as strong as Altan's and Zayaa's. She handed them anything having to do with military history for closer inspection.

The weather had deteriorated by the time Altan finally located the scroll. He'd been jumpy ever since, a tension that seemed to infect everyone else. Case in point: sending her off to scout something as innocuous as a campfire.

Dashi shook her head, then immediately tugged her hat down again. *If I lose a toe to frostbite,* she grumbled mentally. *I'll throttle Altan the next time he suggests going out before spring.*

She slid to the ground, her feet sinking into the ankle-deep snow. Spit shoved his bewhiskered muzzle against her chest, echoing her desire to be home. Dashi laughed softly and pushed his head away. His winter coat was white-gray and thick, almost hand-length. If he lay down, he'd be mistaken for a snowdrift.

"Weren't you born out here? You've gone soft, old man." She glanced toward the strangers' fire, burning merrily in the distance. "I'll be back soon." Spit hung his head and lipped the snow listlessly. He wouldn't wander far unless coerced.

Dashi moved toward the fire, weaving between small trees, their skeletal branches outlined in white. Trees: yet another sign that she was on the edge of the taiga. A cold blast of air seemed to go right down her spine and she hugged her furs closer. Her coat was the same color as Spit's, letting her blend in with the frozen landscape. *Like two winter spirits*, Altan said. He meant it as a joke since the taiga—or all of the land north of Karak City, depending on who you asked—was supposed to be cursed. *Stories and superstition*, Altan insisted. *All the ruins we've been to along the taiga's edge and has anything ever bothered us?* Dashi always agreed with him, mostly because she didn't want him to think she was superstitious. But she still remembered bits and pieces of her Mori childhood: tales of voices in the fog, of the giant beasts said to stalk the thick forest. Now and then, these stories percolated up from her subconscious, rising to the top of her mind like bad water. Tonight was one of those nights.

She crouched low as she neared the fire. She'd originally thought it might be from a Mori camp, perhaps a funeral pyre. But as Dashi studied the small clearing, she could see there was no pyre. There was no camp. There were no *people*. The fire was starting to die, but *someone* had piled it high with wood, their tracks already obliterated by the snow. Where were they now?

Unease washed over her, a chill so real she almost mistook it for the wind. Still squatting, Dashi turned slowly, her eyes searching the shadows for clues. Her immediate urge was to bolt, not stopping until her friends were arrayed at her back, but she squashed the impulse. If the makers of the fire were dangerous, a sloppy flight would only play into their hands. Haste created noise, which would cover any sounds from her pursuers. The dark, coupled with the driving wind and snow made her nearly blind; there was no need to shutter her other senses as well.

Dashi crept back to Spit, periodically searching the ground for tracks. There were none. The snow reached the bottom of her calves now. It piled against the windward side of the rocks and clotted in low-hanging branches. She was in real danger of frostbite now, especially her fingers, but burying them in her pockets would only leave her defenseless. She kept her bow out, an arrow nocked.

There was a sudden movement to her right, a glimpse of a dark coat. She loosed an arrow without thinking, striking the furred shoulder of—Dashi started. She'd taken it for a man's back at first, but it was an animal. A *beast*. Not a bear, though it was as large as one. It had a long hairless tail and—

The animal whirled and bared its teeth: four long, rectangular incisors, two upper and two lower. They were topped by a pointed nose and framed on either side by a spray of whiskers. The beast hunched its back and then it was gone, melting into the shadows as if it had been one all along.

Dashi stood there for a long minute, her hand frozen on her quiver, ready to pull another arrow. When she was sure the animal, whatever it was, wasn't coming back, she continued toward Spit, checking over her shoulder for predators—of all kinds—as she went.

Spit was where she'd left him, looking miserable and hang-dog in the snow. Dashi's whole body was shaking with the cold and it took her two tries before she could pull herself onto his back. Several hours had passed since she'd left; the others would be worried. She hoped Zayaa would yell at Altan for making her go, then wondered if he would believe her when she described the strange animal. He thought like a historian, interested only in what had been documented and vetted by the ages.

He'd probably say the cold was making her imagine things. But *she* knew what she'd seen.

In her shock over seeing the beast, she'd nearly forgotten the strangers she was supposed to be scouting, but she remembered when she heard their voices. She shrank into a copse of pines as they passed: a dozen figures with a few extra mounts sprinkled between.

No, Dashi saw with horror, those were *her* extra mounts. Her friends' mounts. Tied cross-ways over the backs of the last horses were bodies, their backs dusted with fresh snow. Altan was closest. His body was motionless except for the gentle sway of limbs and the flop of golden hair, a silent accompaniment to his horse's strides. Blood, still too warm to freeze, slid over the side of his face, dappling the snow with red. Baris lay over his horse in the opposite direction. Like Altan, he didn't move.

Dashi was absolutely still, staring at Altan until her eyes began to burn from not blinking. By some miracle, she stayed quiet. The men's passing released her, however, and her breaths started coming fast and shallow, making moisture condense inside her scarf. Her lungs felt rigid, unable to accommodate the air she needed. She lay down, as well as she could on Spit's back, her cheek against his mane. Ice had become threaded through the long hairs there and it bit her cheekbone where the scarf didn't cover.

Baris' irreverent laugh, bound to encourage all kinds of reckless be-havior. Zayaa's sharp tongue and burning intelligence, the wise eyes that could see exactly what others were thinking. And Altan...Altan who'd been a steady presence in her life since she was eight years old. Before Zayaa and Baris, it had been just the two of them. He'd taught her to read, bought her a grown-up saddle and bow, and awkwardly instructed her on how to handle her monthly bleeding. He'd let her tag along on his adventures even as he found a more stable home for her quiet, nervous sister.

She knew he'd wondered whether it was wrong to involve her, had questioned whether his influence had cost her a normal life. But the truth was, she never would've excelled at mending clothes or transcribing messages, or spending endless days in a dim shop. She'd been born with an aversion to the stationary, to the boring and safe. The truth was Altan had cost her nothing and he'd given her everything in return: a home when she had none; a mother and father when hers were gone; and perhaps just as important, a purpose, however seamy, at which she excelled.

She wasn't sure how long she lay there, only that when she sat up the men were gone and she was no longer thinking about the cold. Spit was still looking in their direction, his instincts undoubtedly telling him it would be safest to join the closest herd. It wasn't a conscious plan that prompted her to go after them. It was the thought that she didn't want Altan to leave her behind and that, after so many years at his side, she wasn't ready to be on her own.

The sparse trees provided cover as she followed them. Her mind had gone numb, like the icy wind had somehow worked its way into her skull. But it was a good numbness; it let her be patient. Calculating. It let her follow from a distance, never pressing too close, letting Spit's coat and her own furs meld with the winter landscape. *Like two winter spirits.*

The men were tense. At first, she thought their darted looks and hushed voices were because they expected a counterattack. Gradually, however, she realized they knew nothing of her presence. They were scared, not of retribution, but of the taiga. They stopped briefly at their fire—a decoy, she realized now—to regroup and warm themselves before they put out the flames.

Most of them stayed bundled up, but one, a young man with a beard and a broad nose, pulled his scarf down while he ran his hands over Altan's body, removing anything of value: a small knife from Altan's boot, the flint he always carried. Dashi felt a heat sweep her from the inside out, a deep unreasonable anger that left her teetering on the brink of a suicidally reckless act. She clenched Spit's mane in both fists to keep herself from plunging into the open and trying to fight a dozen men at once.

A second man, his face covered by a thick red scarf caught sight of the young man. "No time to go through belongings, Onan. We're moving on."

"I did the work with this one. I get the spoils," Onan retorted.

"We're not waiting on evil's doorstep while you roll the bodies, Onan," a third man said. "I got a good look at those tracks and I didn't like them. Unnatural. And they're following us."

There was a mutter of agreement. Several of the men had already remounted and they jiggled nervously up and down, setting their horses on edge. *They're talking about the same animal I saw earlier*, Dashi realized.

Onan was still arguing. "We got what we came for. Anything extra fits just as well in my pocket as it does in yours."

"After we've met up with the others—and they've found the missing girl—*then* we'll divide everything up," the bundled man said. "Fairly."

"The *fighting* wasn't divided fairly. This one stuck my arm good and —"

"Onan, leave it," someone barked. He was bundled too, but his authority was unmistakable.

Onan sighed and made a show of stuffing the items back into Altan's deel, but with his other hand, he snapped the cord of Altan's necklace, pocketing the golden pendant for himself. Dashi forced her gaze away, searching for Zayaa's body among the lumpy bundles piled onto the unridden horses, but the darkness made it impossible to see clearly.

The men rode quickly, in a hurry to put the creepy northlands behind them. *Wishful thinking.* They would never escape what they'd done here. They thought the spirits were tied to the land, but they were wrong. She would follow them all the way to Karak City—beyond, if she had to—a winter spirit on an endless ride. She would follow them until they relaxed, until they ate their fill and dreamt deeply, until they no longer suspected that death dogged their heels.

Dashi awoke to a hand on her shoulder and a face hovering much too close to hers. *Idree.* She blinked rapidly, her mind assimilating to the change of time and place.

Idree's face shone white in the night. Her grip on Dashi was hard with fear.

"What is it?" Dashi whispered.

Idree licked her lips nervously. "Someone's coming. I think they've found us."

Chapter 13

Dashi was out of her bedroll in seconds, snatching her bow and quiver and belting her sword over her deel.

"Where?" she asked, keeping her voice low.

"Over there, I think." Her sister pointed north. "I don't know how many," she said, anticipating Dashi's next question, "but the birds stopped and I thought I heard a branch snap."

Dashi glanced at the horses. They didn't seem perturbed. Then again, horses made imperfect watchdogs.

"I want you to hide," she said to Idree. "Stay in this thicket—you'll be too conspicuous if you leave. Do you still have the knife I gave you?"

Idree nodded.

"Good."

"W-what will you do?"

"Don't know yet." It depended on how many of Negan's men had found them.

The thicket she'd chosen for a camp stretched north and south in the crease between some hills. None of the trees were full-sized—not like they would be a day's ride to the northeast, in the taiga—but they were large enough to hide the camp from view. Which also meant they would hide attackers.

Dashi started through the thicket, stepping carefully in the thin light. Dawn lingered just below the horizon, already painting the sky opaline. Three hours of sleep had left her bleary-eyed and stiff, but she pushed her discomfort away, focusing on the problem at hand. How many men were there? There was no thud of hooves, no swing of branches as they were pushed aside by a large animal. Whoever was here was on foot, not horseback.

Dashi moved a little higher up the slope, stopping when she found a window in the leaves where she could see the trickle of water that sustained the thicket. The footing was rocky and unstable, but the vantage point was perfect. Animals always tried to conserve energy, instinctively choosing the easiest paths along gullies and ridges and beside stream beds like this one. Humans were no different.

The crunch of a twig. The brush of leaves. Not loud things, but definitive nonetheless. There was someone nearby. Were there more men on Idree's side of the thicket? *If only it was fully dark.* She and Idree could have slipped away without being seen. The loose earth shifted a little under her feet. *Damn.* She'd chosen a bad spot to stand, but she couldn't move now without being overheard.

It was silent for a few moments and then a sliver of a figure appeared through the leaves, half-protected by an interceding tree. Dashi recognized him instantly: the racer who'd been talking to the laborer, still wearing his black scarf. She drew her bow in one slow pull.

The man took two steps and stopped, still partially hidden. He was tall, but the way he held his head, unmoving and high, made him look even taller: a stag scenting his territory, alone and wary.

She tensed, waiting for him to cross into an open space. *Just like any other shot.* But the resemblance to a stag had unnerved her. It wasn't a deer that she was about to shoot; it was a man. She'd never killed anyone like this. The men in the brothel were different. They'd been trying to kill *her*, for one thing. And they'd been murderers, for another. She wished she knew if this man had helped Negan ambush her friends.

Wallowing, she thought disgustedly. That's what she was doing, when the situation should have been clear-cut. *If he's so innocent, what's he doing here?* Whether he'd murdered her friends or not, he was here *now*, to kill her and her sister. *He's a future murderer. That's the same thing.*

The man stepped cautiously, following the little stream like she'd known he would. This was it: a clear shot. Dashi's fingers twitched against the bowstring. *Just do it. Waiting won't make it any easier.*

She swallowed, downing her discomfort with an effort, then pulled the bowstring a little farther and—her heel slid sideways in the loose footing. Somehow the arrow still flew clean; it was the target that moved. Forewarned by the grind of her heel, the man threw himself to one side just as the arrow plunked into the tree next to him.

He came up quickly, rolling to his feet before Dashi could reach for another arrow. His next move was to charge, hand stretching for his sword, any resemblance to a nervous deer long gone. Dashi drew a second arrow, but he was nearly upon her, lunging with his raised sword. It was a sloppy swing—he'd barely freed the sword from its scabbard—but he managed to hit the bow with the flat of it, knocking her shot sideways, where it skewered the soil. In the moment before he smashed into her, Dashi dropped the bow, rolling to the ground and down the slight incline to the clearing below.

She slid her sword free as she got to her feet, cursing inwardly. She'd been trained in swordsmanship—by Baris, no less—but it wasn't her best skill. The sword was unforgiving of reckless behavior, which was what Dashi was best at producing. She vastly preferred the bow and she was good enough to back up whatever boasts she made.

She'd never beaten Baris with a sword. Not once. Not even close. He'd been bigger and faster and stronger and no amount of practice ever seemed to make up for that.

The man came down the bank after her, his huge strides eating up the ground. He wasn't as heavily built as Baris, but he was broad-shouldered and his long arms would give him more reach. *Her* sword was short and light, made for a person with those same characteristics.

I hope you're happy now, she snarled to herself. *You didn't want to shoot him and now look! Go ahead; bask in the fairness of a one-on-one fight...for the remaining two minutes of your life.*

Thoroughly furious, both with herself for wallowing, and with the man for dodging her arrow, Dashi attacked as soon as he'd reached the bottom. The sound of crashing metal bounced between the hills as their swords met. If he'd brought any friends, they'd be here shortly. There was no time in which to study him; her only hope was to finish this quickly before more of Negan's men arrived. But his parries seemed unruffled. He was toying with her. *Not good. Not good at all.* She renewed her attack, pushing him deeper into the low thicket where his height and the reach of his sword might be a disadvantage.

"Put down your sword," he said. "I'm not here to hurt you." His voice was smooth; his words clipped and precise. She thought of the fine horse she'd seen him saddling at the start of the race. A noble for sure.

Dashi snorted. "Was that what you told the other racers?" Did he think she'd just surrender, to be slaughtered like a lamb for dinner?

She jumped onto a fallen log, trying to use the added height to get past his guard. The man sidestepped and swept his blade toward her legs instead. Dashi cleared the flashing steel, landing lightly on the log once more.

The man switched abruptly to the offensive, his blows falling so fast that Dashi could barely keep up. She was forced off the log and into a hasty retreat, but she made sure to pull him deeper into the tangle of branches, jumping backward over logs and curving around trees to trip him up. She only needed one chance, one little opening. The footing was good here, and the thicket was dense, its branches coming to the top of her head, which was shoulder-height on her adversary. Unfortunately, he seemed to have an uncanny awareness of where the next branch was and how much room he had for each swing, and he ducked and wove without ceasing his assault. Her arms, weakened by their three-month hiatus in prison, burned.

"You're not wearing that scarf for the dust anymore," she panted, trying to distract him. "Hiding something ugly?"

"You're traveling away from everyone else. Maybe you're the one hiding."

His sword nicked the branch of an alder tree overhead, sticking there for a second. It was the opportunity Dashi had been waiting for. She swept her sword across, aiming for his exposed side, but the man turned, lightning quick, and pulled a dagger, swiveling to deflect her blade into the same tree. She was trapped right next to him now, her shoulder hard against his chest, her hip pressed into his thigh. Worse, her entire side was exposed and her sword was pinned, unable to protect her.

Dashi's free hand went to her knife, intending to finish him the same way she'd killed the man in the brothel, but he anticipated her move, grabbing her arm and wrenching it back. She followed the momentum instead of fighting it, letting him assist her in rolling out of reach. Her sword fell to the ground, abandoned. He could pick it up and come after her with two swords—Baris would have—but Dashi bolted before he had the chance. Her knives would be no match for his sword. Her *sword* hadn't been a match.

She needed the bow.

It wasn't far, just a few strides past the clearing and up the little incline. She hurtled through the underbrush, the man crashing somewhere close behind. Jumping off a stump, she landed in the clearing, her legs already churning. *Almost there.* She could see her quiver, leaning against the tree where she'd left it.

The man hit her from behind, his shoulder ramming into the small of her back. The ground flew into her from below, the man from above. It felt like falling from a horse mid-gallop.

Dashi grunted and rolled over, blinking to clear her rattled brain. Beside her, the man was pushing himself to his knees. For some reason, he didn't have his sword; it must still be lodged in the tree. Dashi kicked him in the ribs, then flipped to her feet and swung at his face, catching the outside of his eye with her fist.

He caught her next punch, pushing her back to the ground. Dashi brought her elbow up, hitting his jaw.

He ducked the next blow. "Will you stop—"

She got in one last hit before he pinned her arm above her head. His weight was crushing, nearly unbreathable. The pyrothrite belt pressed into her back.

Her left arm was clamped against her side, held there by one of his knees. Her fingers inched closer to her waist. Closer to what she needed.

She pushed against the ground with her feet, bucking her hips against his, and then she had it: a cool bone handle and one last chance at salvation.

"Stop it," he growled, "so I can—"

"I'm not interested in anything that ends with me dead." She turned her wrist, letting the blade of the small knife press against his stomach. "But I have something to tell *you*: stay very still or I'll open you from gut to groin."

She could feel his stomach tense momentarily through his deel, as if he might deflect the blade by sheer force of will, then he relaxed and let go of her arm. Dashi ran her fingers along his side and his waist, front and back, and as far as she could reach along his legs, searching for weapons. She found two knives: one, she stuffed into her sash; the other, she rested against his throat.

"Now get off me."

He gingerly levered himself off the ground, his eyes on her face. She stared right back, trying to gauge something—anything—about him.

"Stay on your knees." Dashi moved behind him, one blade to the side of his neck, the other pushed against his back.

"Take off the scarf. Slowly."

He removed it, tossing it to the ground. She couldn't see his face from where she stood, but she felt a perverse satisfaction in knowing that it wasn't covered anymore.

"How many of you are there?" she asked.

"Just one."

"Where?"

"You're looking at him."

"Horseshit. Where's Negan?"

The man seemed to give this some thought. "Man with a beard? Wide nose? With the remaining racers, I suppose."

Dashi clenched her jaw. "Where. Are. They. The ones you brought with you."

The man held up one hand and Dashi tensed. "There's no one else with me. I came to talk to you, not kill you."

"We're opponents. Why would you want to talk to me?"

"I don't know. You're not making a good case for yourself."

She pushed the knife against his neck until a tiny trickle of blood spilled over the blade and onto her finger.

"Still not," he muttered. Louder he said, "I was going to offer an alliance."

She spat on the ground. She didn't have time for this. If he was lying about being alone, then his men could be closing in on Idree at this very second. Even if he *had* come alone, she still didn't have time: she was hours behind the other racers as it was. "If you don't tell me the real reason by the time I count to three, I'm going to bury these knives and be done with you altogether. One, two—"

"That *is* the reason," he said firmly. Dashi noticed with annoyance that he didn't sound afraid. "A group of racers is killing off the competition, but it sounds like you know that already."

"Go on."

"I came to offer an alliance. We can take turns keeping watch. If it comes down to a fight, our odds will be better than they would be alone."

Dashi wondered how good Negan's men were with their swords. From what she'd seen, this stranger was very good. She was lucky she hadn't ended up on the ground with a gaping hole in her chest.

"An alliance," she said. "Why would I trust you to watch over me while I slept? You could slit my throat."

"And you, me. But that's a chance I'll have to take. I was close enough to hear what they did to the others and they'll be looking for those of us who are still alive. I can't keep watch all night and ride all day."

He had a point. Already she was dragging from reduced rations. What would it be like after a few days of reduced sleep as well? "How do I know you're not making this up just because I have a knife to your throat?"

"Because—"

Dashi's head jerked up. She'd heard something. Something close. She'd been so intent on the enemy in front of her...what if—

He struck faster than a steppe adder, grabbing the knife she held to his throat and jerking her arm forward, so that she hurtled over his shoulder and landed with a thud on her back. Then he was grasping her under the arm and dragging her upright, pinning her against his chest with one arm. The knife he'd taken from her was against her own throat now. He pried the other knife out of her hand and tossed it aside.

"Come out!" he called at the trees.

Dashi saw nothing in the thicket, but she could hear the crunch of dried leaves as someone shifted their weight from one foot to the other.

"You accused *me* of being part of their group," he growled next to Dashi's ear.

"I'm not with them." She could feel him behind her, rigid with tension. He must be telling the truth, at least about not bringing Negan's men with him. He wouldn't be so jumpy otherwise.

"You knew Negan by name," he said.

"*You* knew plenty about them too."

There was still no movement from the trees. "Show yourself or she dies!" he bellowed, nearly deafening her.

The sound of footsteps, dragging and reluctant, reached the clearing. A small figure emerged, long black hair in disarray after a slog through the undergrowth. *Idree.* Well, Dashi thought, it was better than the alternative: Negan's men. Still, she'd been hoping to keep Idree a secret for longer than this.

Dashi felt the surprise go through him: a sudden clenching of the arm that crossed her chest, then a loosening as he realized the threat was, in fact, a child.

"What is this?" he asked Dashi. His voice was still suspicious, like maybe her sister's presence was evidence of some cunning race strategy: use children to distract, then sprint for the artifact while the competition is looking the other way.

"My sister," Dashi said.

"Your *sister*? You brought a *child* with you?"

"I don't know you," Dashi said flatly, "and I'm not in the habit of justifying myself to anyone, let alone the person holding a knife to my throat." There was no way she was admitting that Idree, with no practical skills to speak of, had tracked her down on the steppe. That her little sister had forced her hand and Dashi had caved.

"I would think you'd be *especially* keen to answer the person holding a knife to your throat."

"Well, I'm not. Either use it or put it away." She'd felt his answer before she spoke. His arm had gone comparatively slack in front of her. He'd already dismissed her as weak.

He dropped his arm and she pushed away, turning around to face him. He had dark hair and light eyes and a long scar that ran from ear to chin, making his mouth turn down savagely on the left side. Something about his voice had left her with the impression that he was much older, but with his face uncovered she could see that he was in his twenties, close to Altan's age, she suspected.

He stared back at her, waiting for her to say something, but she turned away and picked up her knife instead. It was bloody. She must have gotten his back when he'd flipped her over his shoulder. *Well, good.* That had been her intention.

"He looks like he got the worst of it," Idree whispered, sidling up next to her. The man stood a little apart from them, fingering his jaw and cheekbone. Both were livid from their fight. "Are you alright?"

Dashi glared at her. She *was* alright, but it had nothing to do with her skill and everything to do with the fact that the scarred man hadn't wanted to hurt her. He hadn't been proposing an alliance because she held a knife to his throat; the knife had never been a threat to him in the first place. Knowing that his offer wasn't fueled by self-preservation should have made her happy—with her sister tagging along and Negan looking for her, an alliance would be to her benefit—but Dashi only felt more annoyed.

"You're supposed to be hiding," Dashi said.

"I heard fighting."

"You knew there was going to be fighting. You were supposed to stay hidden."

For the first time, Dashi noticed Idree was carrying her own little bow. *Ancestors help me if she'd used it*, Dashi thought. Altan had insisted that she try to teach Idree how to shoot a few years back. He'd given her some line about Idree understanding the Mori side of herself, but Dashi had seen right through him: he felt guilty because she and her sister weren't close. *He'd* arranged for Idree to live separately, since she was too small to accompany them on their trips. *He'd* become Dashi's sibling, not Idree. Altan felt so much guilt over her—and for so many needless reasons—that it made *Dashi* feel guilty. She'd agreed to teach Idree.

They'd started on the ground with stationary targets. Idree was nervous around horses anyway. Dashi tried to remember the way her father had taught her, but it had been so long ago. Her own marksmanship had been perfected mainly through trial and error and an almost pathological desire for competition, even with herself. But if this trait was present in Idree, Dashi hadn't seen it. Instead, Idree, who'd been eight at the time, had flopped to the ground after a half dozen attempts, complaining that the bowstring was blistering her fingers and that the sun was making her scalp hot. Dashi, ever impatient, had snapped that it was fine with her if Idree never learned to shoot and ride because then they'd never have to bring her along.

And that was it. Idree ran home crying and Dashi stomped off to a goathead match, hoping to assuage her anger. Idree became Auntie Nima's apprentice a few weeks later. There were no more shooting lessons. Now that Dashi thought about it, she couldn't believe Idree had kept the bow.

Now, Idree hunched her neck. "I know. I just—"

"I need you to do what I tell you, Idree. I can't be distracted when it's most dangerous."

"I thought maybe I could help you."

Dashi would have loved to retort that she hadn't needed help. The fact that the *opposite* was true was like a burr stuck in her boot. "You couldn't."

The man walked into the trees, returning a few minutes later with both swords.

He held Dashi's up to the sunlight, which was just now making an appearance, to examine the place where her initials were engraved. *So your enemies will know who stabbed them*, Baris had joked.

"Finely made," he said, offering it to her.

She took the sword without answering.

"Well?" he asked.

Idree looked back and forth between them, confusion on her round face.

"What happens at the end of the race?" Dashi asked. She couldn't split the purse money, if that's what the man was proposing. There would be no money for her, only a pyrothrite-free waist and a chance to go her own way.

Not that she planned to tell *him* that. She'd already decided she needed his help. He was right when he said it was impossible to keep watch all night and ride all day and she needed someone who could fight if it came down to it.

"We split when we get to the temple. Every racer for himself—or herself."

That was dangerous. He already knew too much: that he could beat her in a sword fight; that Idree was with her; that Dashi had chosen to keep her sister hidden instead of having her join the fight. By the time they got to the temple there was no telling what he might have gleaned.

But what choice did she have? Somewhere out there Negan was looking for her and if he saw Idree he'd kill her for sure. In the meantime, she still had a race to win and only twenty-one—*no, twenty*—days to do it.

If she had to double-cross this man later to get his help now, then so be it.

Dashi nodded once. "Until we get to the temple."

Chapter 14

The man's name was Sevlin. It was Idree who told her that; Dashi hadn't bothered with formal introductions. When she returned from collecting the horses, Sevlin was naked from the waist up. His chest was crisscrossed with scars and, even this early in the summer, burnished by the sun.

Dashi stopped, still as a snake. Her eyes darted to Idree, squatting next to one of the packs.

Sevlin caught her glance and held up a hand as he reached for his deel. "I needed someone to look at my back and your sister obliged." He paused. "I had a long knife wound."

"If you're looking for an apology, you'll be waiting a long time."

"I wasn't."

Idree straightened and handed him a small jar of wound ointment, which Dashi didn't remember giving her leave to distribute. She turned back to the horses.

"Is she always this surly?" Sevlin asked. Idree's response was smothered by the stamping of hooves, but whatever she said made him huff with amusement.

They spent the day hurrying between the hills of the near-taiga, moving steadily northward. Around mid-afternoon, when Dashi was nearly dead from lack of sleep, she spotted a circle of white domes blooming like strange mushrooms on the land: the *gers* of a Mori camp.

Halting the chestnut, she waited until Sevlin and Idree drew abreast of her. "You're going to need more than one horse," she said to Sevlin, looking down at the gers. They were the first words she'd exchanged with him since that morning.

"I lost my extra mounts the night of the attacks." He was on her left side, so she couldn't see his scar, just the barest of indentations in his silhouette, below his mouth. "They're probably in someone else's string of mounts now."

"If it's any consolation, those horses won't be much good where we're going." She nodded at his mount. "Not if they're in the same condition as that one."

"These are the best horses money can buy."

"They are...if you're racing around in a circle. They might make it out here if they had good grass and oats. And if they didn't break one of their long beautiful legs in a ground squirrel's burrow. The Mori horses might be ugly, but they'll eat anything: dry steppe grass, leaves, bark, green twigs. And they're better over uneven ground."

She hated to give Sevlin an advantage he could use against her later, but after six days of constant movement with unsatisfactory food, his horse was visibly flagging. Its head drooped and foam flecked its muzzle, even though the day was only half over. What would it look like in a few more days, with no other mounts to relieve it?

"Do you have money?" she asked. Judging by his horse, she assumed he did, but she needed to be certain before they reached the Mori camp. "You can use your horse for part of the trade, but it's not worth much out here. You'll have to make up the difference."

He gave her horses a dubious glance. "I do."

"Good." She started down the slope. Osol had given her a small pouch of money. She could use it to get more food and another horse for Idree.

As they neared the camp, Dashi could see a knot of Mori gathered around a practice range: a serpentine course of rawhide targets, interspersed with obstacles. Young men and women spent their free time honing their skills with horse and bow, competing fiercely for nothing more than bragging rights. She angled toward the gers instead; their business required an elder.

A woman came out of the nearest ger. Its white felt exterior was decorated with geometric symbols in brown, red and black: the markings of the family and the clan. Dashi recognized the latter; she'd been to this clan years ago, translating for Altan.

"Greetings to you and your ancestors," Dashi said in Mori. "I wish to speak to Elder Gansuh."

"I'm afraid you cannot," the woman said. "But Little Gansuh, his son, is at the archery course."

Dashi nodded. "My thanks."

She translated for Idree and Sevlin as they rode to the outside of the encampment.

"Why do we need to talk to Gansuh or his son?" Idree asked.

"Because we're outsiders. The head elder makes sure nothing is sold that the clan might need in the future. It protects them from being taken advantage of by outsiders." She didn't look directly at her sister when she spoke. Idree should have known that. She should have been able to follow Dashi's conversation with the woman. Dashi should have taught her.

"Communal property rights trump individual ones," Sevlin mused. It was a scholarly comment, like something that would have come from Altan or Zayaa.

"When they have to," she said, glancing at him.

A woman was completing the archery course as they approached. She rode with no hands, guiding the horse with her knees and shooting at each target she passed. She sent her horse over an obstacle, turning to aim as he jumped. Her shot went wide and the crowd of onlookers groaned sympathetically. As she crossed the finish line scratched into the dirt, a group of children dashed from the sidelines, racing to see who could retrieve the most arrows.

One by one, the Mori turned toward Dashi and her companions, their voices hushing when they noticed the strangers. Men and women stood together, ranging in age from young teenagers, the sides of their heads shaved to denote their unmarried status, to fifty-year-olds, their hair gray but their bodies still fit and muscular. Instead of cloth sashes, they wore thick belts of leather and bronze. Their deels were accented by brightly colored ribbons and bangles. *Ceremonial dress.* It was rude to interrupt a clan ceremony, but Dashi had little choice. She couldn't wait until tomorrow.

"Greetings to you and your ancestors," Dashi said, scanning the group. She didn't remember a Little Gansuh from her last visit, but it had been a while ago. "And an apology for interrupting. I'm looking for Little Gansuh, son of Elder Gansuh."

"I am Little Gansuh," a man said, pushing himself up from where he leaned against his horse. He was older than Dashi and tall by Mori standards, with straight black hair that was tied back to show the shaved line above his ears.

Dashi repeated her greeting, managing not to blink at the coolness that suddenly emanated from the group. Idree huddled closer, alarmed. Sevlin kept his horse back. She wasn't sure what he was doing. Probably preparing to flee if things went bad.

"We seek permission to trade for extra mounts," Dashi finished.

"You have come on an inauspicious day," a thin man standing next to Little Gansuh said. "Elder Gansuh has gone to join our ancestors."

That explained the ceremonial dress. Dashi cursed internally. She remembered Elder Gansuh as a reasonable man; she didn't know about his son. Though he hardly qualified for the word elder, they were probably in the midst of deciding whether Little Gansuh would succeed his father. Leadership among the Mori was both a matter of heredity and support. A candidate had to be related to the previous leader *and* earn the votes of the clan. That also explained the archery course; it was a way for Little Gansuh to demonstrate his prowess as a hunter.

She bowed her head. "My apologies again. However, we are in desperate need of horses. As your sister, I call on you in my time of need."

"*Sister?*" The thin man again.

Dashi ignored him, focusing on Little Gansuh. "I'm half-Mori, of the Sagan clan, by my father's line. I sought help here four years ago. I remember your father. He was a fair man."

"I do not remember you," Little Gansuh said, his voice heavy with sorrow. "But my father sent me away often, to learn from the other clans. Why are you not with the Sagan clan?"

"My father died when I was young. My mother was from Karak City. She returned there with us—my sister and me—after his death."

"So you are not really Mori then. Your mother did not think so or she would not have separated you from your people."

"I am both," Dashi said.

"And which did you marry, Mori or Karakalese?"

"Neither. I am unmarried."

"Her head is not shaved," the thin man pointed out. "She speaks our language and rides our horses, but she is not Mori. She is a pretender. Let us return to our mourning. It is a sacrilege to be interrupted by an outsider today."

This was the opposite of the taunts Dashi had gotten in Karak City. There, her face had been too square, too hard, never quite enough like the other Karakalese to avoid notice. Here, it was the Mori side that was lacking.

While the Mori were nominally citizens of Karakal, their customs and language remained their own. They still spoke of a time before their incorporation, when they'd been completely independent. Dashi had encountered animosity from them before, but usually she had time to talk her way out of it, to tell stories of her childhood in the Sagan clan.

"Only a pretender would know Karak City," someone scoffed.

"This girl is not Mori," the thin man said louder. "We cannot offend the ancestors as they come to gather Elder Gansuh."

There were mutters of agreement from the crowd. Someone called for her to leave. Little Gansuh had half-turned away, listening to those around him. In another moment, she would need to leave or risk being driven away.

She couldn't go without more horses and food, nor did she have time to listen to the clan debate the issue. Not while Negan and the remaining racers were riding toward the artifact.

Dashi wheeled her horse, simultaneously drawing her bow as she galloped toward the archery course. The chestnut was faster than Spit; she'd ascertained that the first time she rode him. Probably why Osol had included him on her string, despite the horse's flighty nature.

Dashi let her arrow fly before she got to the first target, grabbing another right away. A tall pile of brush sat between her and the next target, with a narrow chute cutting through the center. The chestnut was exactly the type of horse who would balk at such an obstacle, but Dashi didn't give him the chance. She reached back with her hand and slapped his rump, goading him with her heels at the same time. Sticks scratched against her pants as she shot through the opening and loosed another shot.

The next dozen targets went by quickly. They were spaced one right after the other but on alternating sides, so that Dashi hardly had time to think: reach, turn, fire; reach, turn, fire. Her arrow found its mark each time, making a muffled thump of approval as she rode past. Then came another series of obstacles: a jump, a second brush chute and a wide, shallow pit someone had dug across the course. Each needed to be negotiated while aiming and firing. The chestnut shortened his stride, preparing to execute an outright refusal. Dashi forced him through, but her arrow flew slightly ahead of its mark, embedding on the edge of the target instead of the center.

The end of the course consisted of three jumps with barely a stride between and multiple targets on each side. This was the part of the course she'd seen the female rider struggle with. Dashi began firing as soon as she was within range, hitting as many targets as she could before she reached the obstacles. The course had doubled back toward the crowd of onlookers, but their yells were lost in the beat of hooves and the slide of wood off the arrow rest.

Her horse gathered himself for the first jump, muscles tightening as he pushed off the ground. She felt the landing in her legs and seat: a hard bump, followed by another stride, and then he was taking off again, hurling himself over the second jump. Dashi clung with her legs, shooting as they hung in the air.

The chestnut landed hard, stumbling when his rear hooves clipped the pole. Dashi steadied herself and reached for an arrow, but it was already too late: he was sailing over the final jump, putting the last target behind them.

As soon as he landed she dropped her stirrups and swung her leg over the saddle, lowering herself toward the rushing ground and letting it bounce her back into the air. She swung her leg over his back, settling into the saddle again, albeit facing the wrong direction. Now she had a clear view of the receding target. She let one arrow fly, then another for good measure. Both lodged in the back of the rawhide target just as she whisked across the finish line.

On her right, Little Gansuh covered the bottom of a clay funnel to stop the time. It was a Mori timing device, like an hourglass but without the glass. Sand fell through the funnel until someone stopped it, then the sand was weighed to determine who was the fastest.

Dashi pulled the chestnut to one side, letting him catch his wind while Idree and Sevlin rode up.

"What was that?" Sevlin demanded.

"Proof," Dashi said, a little out of breath. She switched her position in the saddle so she was facing forward once again. "Elder Gansuh just died and it's bad luck to deal with outsiders before the pyre."

"And that's proof you aren't an outsider?"

"Hope so."

"You've done the course before."

"No."

He fingered his reins with one hand, watching her. "You could have turned to shoot the last target. Without getting out of your saddle."

Her pride, dented by their earlier sword fight, had been mollified by the archery course. She found herself grinning. "*Could* have."

"What if it wasn't enough?" Idree asked. "What if they still think you're an outsider?"

Dashi looked back at the cluster of watching Mori. "Then we should leave. Quickly."

"I think they're waiting for you," Sevlin said. His tone was neutral, but his lips were stretched thin.

Little Gansuh was weighing the sand when she trotted up. A gaggle of children surrounded him, describing the accuracy of her shots. Two of them approached her, staring boldly, to return her arrows.

"You get a time penalty for missing the last target," Little Gansuh said in a brusque tone. "Shooting it through the back does not count."

"It would in real life."

He crossed his arms, eyes roaming over her. "Even with the penalty, you finished third."

"Who were the first two?"

"There is a tie, between my cousin," he nodded toward an older man, "and myself." He pulled out a horsehide flask of airag and took a sip before handing it to her. "I do not believe the ancestors will be affronted by your presence today. You are Mori. Join us for our feast later."

"I am half-Mori. Just like I was before," she said, but she took a drink, wiping the warm liquid from her lips with the back of her hand before returning the flask. "I would be honored to attend your feast, but I have no time to spare." She sketched a brief explanation of the race and how some of the racers had banded together to eliminate competition.

"The taiga is a dark place," Little Gansuh said, lowering his voice. "There are things there that are more dangerous than the greed of other men. It is not meant for humans anymore, not since the veins of magic withdrew."

"I think the khan is trying to change that with this race."

"Then he will find himself disappointed. This is folly. You would do well to abandon it."

"You're probably right," Dashi said, thinking of the previous men the khan had sent. Even the ones who'd made it out of the taiga hadn't lived long. "But I have no choice."

"And your companions?" He looked past her at Idree and Sevlin. "Even the girl?"

"I will pass on your message, but the man will probably want to continue. The girl...the girl is my sister." She hesitated, suddenly struck by an idea and unsure how to politely phrase it. "I could compensate you for her food and safety."

"She is half-Mori as well?"

Dashi nodded.

"Then we would take her in."

Dashi smiled gratefully. Maybe she'd found an alternative to dragging Idree through the taiga after all. After she'd explained their other needs, Little Gansuh called over a handful of men and women holding *uurgas*, the pole-and-rope tools used for catching horses.

"It will only take a few minutes," he promised Dashi. "I told them to get four horses, but I will only trade one horse for the man's mount. I know what that horse is worth to the Karakalese," he said quickly, anticipating an argument, "but it will be a long time before we head south. We will have to baby it just to keep it alive until then."

"He can pay for the other mounts," Dashi promised. She went back to Sevlin and Idree.

"What did he say?" Sevlin asked before she could open her mouth. He sat with his shoulders back, one hand near his sword. His eyes darted between her and Little Gansuh.

"That's a healthy case of paranoia you're nursing," Dashi said dryly. "He said we shouldn't go into the taiga. He wanted me to tell you it's dangerous. He said to reconsider."

Sevlin's response was every bit as immediate as Dashi's had been. "I can't."

"Right." She'd known the purse money would override any abstract warnings. *Now, on to the next task.* She turned to her sister. "Idree, he also agreed to take you in while I finish the race. You'll be safe here and—"

"No."

Dashi plowed on. "—I can come get you after it's over."

"No."

"Why not? They'd welcome you. I explained you were my sister and I offered to pay for your food—"

"You're going to pay them to take me?" Her sister's face was set: eyebrows beetling together, delicate chin jutting out.

"To take *care* of you, Idree. I want to make sure you're safe."

"Then make sure I'm safe! Don't pay someone else to do it!" Idree's voice had reached a dangerous pitch: the one that preceded tears.

Why did it always go this way, Dashi wondered. Idree never responded well to anything she said. She glanced around helplessly. Why wasn't Altan here to reason with her? The Mori were all staring at them, though she doubted they could understand what was being said. Sevlin had stepped away, probably to give them privacy. *Or*, Dashi thought, *because, unlike me, he could tell where this conversation was headed and he wanted to get far, far away.*

"Idree," Dashi said, striving for a calm tone. "You heard what I told Sevlin. No one knows what the taiga holds. But here, you might like it." She cast about desperately for things her sister enjoyed. "It's...quiet. And you could cook."

"There are things I like besides the quiet. And I only liked cooking because of Auntie Nima. If you leave me here, I'll...I'll steal a horse and come after you like I did before. They can't keep me tied up."

"Why do you *care*?" Dashi asked a little desperately. "You hate riding. You hate shooting. You hate being scared and sore and uncomfortable." She threw up her hands. "Why won't you listen to me for once? I'm trying to help you."

"You're trying to help *yourself*." Idree turned and stalked to where Sevlin was untacking his horse. He glanced up and said something to her and she gave him a watery smile in return. He turned to look at Dashi, one eyebrow raised.

Dashi turned her back on him. *Interloper.* Trust Idree to seek solace from someone they barely knew—someone who would turn against them in a few days—instead of Dashi, who was *trying* to help her.

So what if she was also trying to help herself? Idree acted like that was a bad thing, but *she'd* done the same thing when she invited herself along on the race. She hadn't stopped to consider what *Dashi* wanted.

Gansuh returned with the horses: three for Sevlin and one for Idree. Her sister was so light that she only needed one extra mount. He also brought food, enough to replace what Sevlin had lost and enough for Dashi to feed both herself and her sister. Money exchanged hands, as did Sevlin's horse. He seemed genuinely sorry to see it go, like he couldn't believe he had to trade such an elegant—if recently haggard—animal for one with such clumsy conformation.

He *did* look slightly comical on his new horse, his long limbs a contrast to its stubby ones. But the thought was a fleeting ray of sunshine in Dashi's otherwise black mood. She'd suddenly realized what the Mori timing device resembled: the pyrothrite disk. Two triangles, one facing up, one facing down. It was an hourglass, trickling away the remaining hours of her life.

She pulled herself into the saddle without a word to either of her companions. Little Gansuh laid a hand on her horse's coppery neck. "Go like the wind, come like the wind," he said, the traditional farewell of a plains people buffeted on all sides.

If only, Dashi thought, as she galloped away. The wind was fast and free. The wind was unencumbered, with no need for interlopers, especially the kind who worked to turn her sister against her.

The wind would have been to the taiga and back by now.

Chapter 15

The taiga rose to meet them at nightfall, a looming shadow that Dashi knew would prove all too solid. They'd pushed hard for the rest of the day. Idree looked ready to topple out of her saddle, but Dashi didn't let up until they reached the ruins that marked, in her mind anyway, the true beginning of the taiga.

If Idree wanted things easy, she should have stayed behind, Dashi thought as she slid from her horse.

The land before them was steeper and higher than the hills they'd just traveled through. But it was the trees that really defined the taiga: a dense, black forest of larch, spruce and pine that was impenetrable to the eye. Without the steppe's thick carpet of grass even the ground felt inhospitable, Dashi thought, scuffing the soil experimentally. The ruins in front of her—and the others that dotted the taiga's southern boundaries—marked the limits of her explorations. Despite his insistence that the tales about the taiga were rumors and superstition, Altan had never pushed farther north.

Sevlin dismounted and walked to the edge of the ruins. They jutted out of the ground, low and uneven, like the teeth of an old man. There were twenty-four buildings, or what was left of them: twenty-three arranged in a precise square with a larger, circular building in the center. In most places, only the foundations and dilapidated walls remained, but the round building in the center still had its roof. Dashi had visited it—raided it—years ago. It was the first ruin Altan had taken her to, back when it was just the two of them. They hadn't found much: low-grade artwork and a collection of scrolls that Altan had perused with great enthusiasm before ultimately declaring them worthless.

They'd returned often, mostly using the round building as a landmark and a shelter in bad weather. The pitted bronze door was still the way they'd left it: braced closed with a pile of rocks to keep out animals. There were no windows. Altan said it was because sunlight was damaging to artwork and the ancient Pureks knew it. Most of their buildings, especially the ones that housed the best artifacts, were like this. They'd been centers of learning once, open to anyone with an appetite for knowledge. *Libraries*, Altan called them. He'd said some still existed outside of Karakal.

Sevlin crouched next to a foundation wall, examining the stones. He'd seemed content to let Dashi take the lead during the day, though several times she'd seen him consulting his map and the sun, double-checking their course.

"Must've been a small village," he said.

"Mmm," Dashi said. "Or a large village that sank into the earth. Maybe this is all we can see. A single coil of a snake." That had been Zayaa's and Altan's theory anyway: that there were more buildings, hidden under layers of soil and rock. They'd talked enthusiastically about digging for them. Baris had been horrified. She could almost hear his baritone now: "*The brains come up with these great ideas all the time, but it's the brawn who ends up doing the work.*"

"What?" Idree asked. She stood a little distance away, gazing around with wide eyes.

It was the first thing she'd said to Dashi since they'd left the Mori camp. Not that they'd had much cause to talk—they were all exhausted—but Idree had still managed a few words to Sevlin.

"A single coil of a snake," Dashi said. "It's like how a snake will curl under something. You know it's there, but you don't know how long it is; you can only see a single coil because the rest is hidden."

"You might be right," Sevlin said, with a thoughtful glance in her direction. "Buildings settle over time; that would be especially true for something this old. And out here wind and erosion would hasten the effect."

"Why didn't these ones disappear?" Idree asked.

He shrugged. "Maybe they were on higher ground to begin with."

"We can camp here," Dashi suggested like she hadn't already made up her mind to do just that.

"You don't believe the stories about the ancient Pureks?" Sevlin asked. "About them having never left the ruins?"

Oh, she believed them alright. She'd seen enough skeleton-filled buildings to attest to the fact that most of the ancient Pureks hadn't made it out alive when the veins of magic burst, first flooding and then retreating from the surrounding land.

"I believe the people *telling* those stories believe them," she said.

A thin mist was curling through the forest, catching in the treetops like ribbons in long hair. It moved quickly. *Hungrily,* Dashi thought, like it wouldn't be satisfied until it claimed every tree.

Idree stepped closer, hugging her arms to her chest. "It seems...wrong to stay here, sleeping on top of buried...things."

"That was just a theory of—" Dashi stopped before she said Altan's name. She didn't want to answer any questions if Sevlin asked them. "That was just a theory. And it might seem eerie, but that's what makes it ideal. Everyone steers clear of these places. We'll be safest from the other racers here."

"Sounds like you've already decided," Sevlin said.

"You have a better idea?" Dashi asked.

He shrugged, declining the chance to argue. "There's water here. We can't go much farther today anyway. It's almost dark and we need to eat."

"Can we have a fire tonight?" Idree asked in a small voice.

Dashi glanced at Sevlin. "Negan is at least half a day ahead of us. We haven't seen anyone since the Mori camp, so the remaining racers must be pretty well scattered." *Or else they're way ahead too and we're running dead last.* Her fingers touched the pyrothrite belt beneath her deel.

"I'll get wood," Sevlin said.

Dashi nodded. "We'll unpack the food."

She watched Sevlin walk to the tree line, showing no hesitation in approaching the taiga. Maybe he was like Altan, a believer of facts who put no stock in rumors until they were proven true. Her gaze shifted higher. The fog had finally stilled in the trees.

"Sevlin's from Tyvalar," Idree announced.

Tyvalar. Where Altan, Zayaa and Baris were really from, according to the noble in Karak City. She almost said it aloud. Her sister had known them too. Not as well as Dashi, but she'd certainly be interested in knowing that they'd lied about everything. But if Dashi told her that, then Idree would want to know how Dashi knew and that would lead them back to the real reason she was in the race.

"How do you know that?" she asked Idree instead.

"I asked. He wanted to know about us, so I asked why he didn't like the taste of airag. Everyone in Karak City drinks it, but when we were in the Mori camp I saw him grimace when he took a sip."

"What did you tell him?" Dashi asked sharply. She didn't want Sevlin to know she'd explored any ruins before. True, she'd never been to the temple that was their destination, but the ancient Pureks tended to incorporate certain trends into their buildings and she didn't want Sevlin to know she had experience navigating them. If he thought she was too much of a threat he might end their alliance early...with his sword.

"I didn't tell him anything, really," Idree said. "Mostly just about mother and father and what happened after they died."

"Did you mention that I've been to any ruins?"

"No, just that you stayed with Altan and I went to live with Auntie Nima."

Dashi let out a breath. That didn't sound too incriminating. *Still...* "You have to be more careful, Idree. Don't talk to him unless you have to. Don't tell him anything he doesn't need to know. He's still the competition."

"Ancestors protect me, I haven't forgotten," Idree snapped. "I *got* information from him and I didn't give him anything important in return. I *know* he's the competition; that's why I thought you'd want to know he was from Tyvalar. And I'll talk to him if I want to!"

Dashi pulled out the provisions they'd purchased from the Mori. "Fine. Do what you want. Just don't forget he's not your friend. If he's talking to you, he's got a reason. He thinks you're useful to him in some way." She said the last part quietly; Sevlin was on his way back.

"Then he's the opposite of you, isn't he?" Idree muttered and snatched the provisions from Dashi's hands.

Dashi balanced on her hands, watching her breath drift upward toward her feet, the only disturbance in the still night. It was much cooler here than in Karak City. She'd used the last of her money to purchase warm clothes from the Mori for Idree and she was glad now.

The fire was down to a few doomed coals, with just enough life to illuminate the sleeping forms of her sister and Sevlin. She couldn't see the dark bulk of the library building, but she knew it was there. Waiting for her.

It was second watch. She'd given Idree the first watch—the earlier it was, the less scary the night would seem—but Dashi had woken before her turn and wordlessly sent Idree to bed.

Sevlin turned over in his sleep. She'd given him third watch, the worst one, just to see if he said anything. He hadn't. Just like he hadn't said a word when she'd taken the lead on horseback. She knew he couldn't be that easygoing—no one who entered the khan's race and made it this far could be—but he was always quiet, watching, seemingly content to flow with events as they came. His reticence made Dashi more uneasy than if he'd been argumentative; at least then she'd know the lay of his mind. As it was, he remained as murky as the taiga. Maybe she should have encouraged Idree to keep talking to him.

Flipping right-side up, she resumed pacing, this time on her feet. She wondered what Zayaa would make of Sevlin. Zayaa had been uncannily skilled at deciphering other people: their goals and plans, their motivations and fears. As her thoughts strayed to her friends, her feet turned, taking her outside the fire's dying light and in the direction of the library.

There was no need to go inside. She knew what was there. Anyway, she should stay near the camp and keep watch. *But it will only take a few minutes. And I haven't seen anything more alarming than a cockroach all night. I'll just check the door and make sure it's tight against animals.* She moved toward the packs to unwrap her lantern, knowing even as she did so that she wouldn't stop at the door.

The library entrance was indeed secure, but she removed the stone cairn anyway, carefully placing the rocks to one side. Time had made the door recalcitrant and she had to jam her shoulder into it to get it to open. The sound from the ancient hinges—high-pitched at first, before dropping to a protracted, guttural groan—gave Dashi goosebumps, even though she knew exactly what caused it. It would have terrified Idree, had she been awake. Dashi glanced over her shoulder, but neither Idree nor Sevlin stirred. She picked up the lantern and scooted through the doorway without further noise.

Cabinets lined the library's walls from floor to ceiling and marched in rows to the center of the room, where they created shadowy alcoves that the lantern refused to penetrate. Inside the cabinets were scrolls, all that remained of the ancient Purek's thoughts and words. Some were purely informational. Those were the ones Zayaa and Altan preferred: reams of facts and descriptions about ancient cities, military and culture. Others were literary works: ballads and poems and stories filled with hyperbole and feats of daring. When Dashi could sit still long enough to translate the texts, those were the ones she chose.

Half of the cabinets still had doors, although many of the documents preserved inside were gone, having been sold to wealthy collectors by Dashi and her friends. Other cabinets had been shattered by age and neglect, their doors listing drunkenly to one side, while their guts disgorged onto the floor in moldering piles. Those scrolls were largely illegible, unless you happened upon a cabinet that had only recently fallen apart. She'd once plucked a wonderfully preserved painting fragment—a picture of a hand holding a silver cup—from such a pile, but she'd never seen anything else of value.

Dashi walked to the center of the library, her feet crunching over leaves and paper and other things too decayed to identify. The room was filled with tokens of the past: pieces of carved wood and carefully contorted metal that used to form furniture; paintings, both frescoed and on canvas, all fading.

And skeletons. There were skeletons galore.

She'd been scared the first time she saw one. At age nine, she was still young enough that Altan's lectures on history and factual observation hadn't eclipsed the Mori tales on which she was raised. Because of those tales, she already distrusted their proximity to the taiga. The presence of human bones seemed alarmingly portentous in that context.

It wasn't her first dead body, of course—she'd seen her father, laid out for his pyre, and found her mother's charred remains—but there was nothing ominous about the bodies of her parents. Tragic, yes, and terrifying for what they represented: both the all-consuming pervasiveness of death, and a tipping point in her young life, beyond which everything would change. The bodies themselves, however, weren't frightening.

The ruins' skeletons, conceived in a horrible magical cataclysm, were something else entirely. It was easy to imagine their spirits, eternally restless and angered by the presence of intruders, hovering nearby. Altan had sat her down next to one and painstakingly detailed the skeleton's anatomy to show Dashi that it was indeed lifeless.

"That's the tibia. And that slender one is the fibula," he'd said, pointing out the individual bones. *"A skeleton is an object, Dashi, able to be categorized like any other."* He twitched a finger bone in her direction. *"I'm Karli."* He used a high-pitched voice that sounded awfully similar to a neighborhood girl who'd called Dashi names once.

After that, they'd made a game of it. They named one skeleton at each ruin, greeting the skeletons by name anytime they returned. For years, Dashi had secretly turned this into a superstition of her own making: the named skeleton was a gatekeeper. If she greeted the skeleton when she entered the ruin, it would keep all the others at bay.

Dashi held up her lantern, facing a skeleton that sat beneath a fraying tapestry. It was smaller and more delicate than the others. A woman's, Altan had said.

"Hello, Karli. It's been a long time." The bones were silent. Dashi glanced around. "I see you've done a lot with the place."

The roof had begun leaking. The building was still protected from the elements for now, but one day soon the section would collapse, spelling the end for the small library. The cabinets beneath the leak had fallen apart, the scrolls already beginning the transformation to dirt.

She shone her light on one of the skeletons near the ruined cabinets. The skull was blackened with mold, which grew in an archipelago down the cheekbones and onto the shoulders. It looked like a creeping sickness. Flesh rot, maybe, if the thing had had flesh. She shook off the image.

Many of the skeletons still held the positions they'd taken at death. The molded skeleton, obviously a guard of some sort, slouched against the wall beside a spear. Another lay in front of a cabinet, its emaciated fingers stretching toward the door.

The library was a monument to what had passed and to what might have been. This was why she'd been drawn here tonight. Her friends had walked this floor, looked at these same walls. Their bones might not keep company with the skeletons, but their spirits did. She glanced at the cabinets and she could see Zayaa sitting cross-legged in front, chin resting on her palm, while she flipped through the scrolls. Baris would be over there, near the debris at the center of the room, where he would have plenty of ammunition to lob at Zayaa. If she managed to ignore him, he'd wander outside to do some sort of physical fitness drill, probably cajoling Dashi to join him whenever Altan said she'd done enough work. And that elaborate fresco of a festival? Altan was standing in front of it, hands clasped behind him, face tilted up as if to sunlight.

The pain hit her again, more powerful than it had been on the day she'd seen their bodies. On that day she'd seen what had been done, had known with her head that they were gone, but she hadn't felt their absence yet. Hadn't known the joy of seeing a familiar figure, only to have it transform to hollowness as she realized she'd mistaken a stranger for a friend. She hadn't felt the disorientation of turning to relate a joke only to find that the intended audience had vanished, never to reappear.

She stood there without moving, feeling the finality of it all, the hopelessness that came from the knowledge that she would never see them again, except like this: in snatches of dreams, in her fragmented consciousness.

A tear ran down her cheek. Then another. What was she supposed to do without them? Never mind the race, never mind the belt. Never mind revenge, even. What was she supposed to *do*—

CREAAAAK. Her thoughts broke off at the sound of the library door.

Dashi jerked around, holding the lantern higher, but it was too weak to illuminate the doorway from where she stood. *The lantern.* Its light made her an easy target. She placed it on the floor and darted to a shadowy alcove, then to another. There was a flicker of motion across from her and she saw a shadow, its proportions grossly distorted, splay across the wall: a man, not an animal.

"It's me," a voice said from the darkness. There was a thud, followed by a muffled curse, and a second later Sevlin appeared at the edge of the light. His gaze swung to each of the alcoves, looking for her. Had he decided to finish her off here? Why hadn't she brought something besides a knife?

"What are you doing here?" Her voice sounded low and harsh and she saw with a sliver of satisfaction that she'd startled him.

"I saw you going inside and I thought maybe you'd seen something." He waited a beat. "I wasn't trying to sneak up on you. I just didn't want to start shouting your name before I knew what was going on."

Dashi edged forward and his eyes caught the movement immediately. She glanced at his side, where his sword belt dangled in a loose grip.

He followed her eyes and leaned the sword carefully against the cabinet. "I only brought it in case there was trouble. You can put the knife down."

Dashi let out a breath. "No, keep it. I was stupid not to have brought mine." She returned the knife to her sash.

"What *are* you doing in here?"

She motioned vaguely at the walls. "I wanted to see what was inside."

He didn't answer, but his eyes dropped to her cheeks and then he turned away, staring intently at the tapestry hanging above Karli's bones.

Dashi hastily scrubbed away her tears with the heel of her hand. Had he overheard her greeting the skeleton? She hadn't been loud, but if he was standing right outside...

Always catching me at a disadvantage, she thought at his back. It made her want to fight him again.

"It's a coronation," he said.

"What?"

"The tapestry." He looked over his shoulder, his expression one of excitement. "The ancient Pureks believed the new moon was the most auspicious time to begin an endeavor," he said, misinterpreting her silence as ignorance, "so state ceremonies took place then. New khagans ascended the throne at midnight on the night of a new moon."

How dare he lecture *her* about the ancient Pureks? "That's Khagan Nuray," she said. "One of the only female khagans." *There. You're not the only one who knows something.*

He turned around fully. "How do you know that?"

"Not only did she forge an empire, but she also accomplished the infinitely more laborious task of keeping it happy," Dashi said, folding her hands behind her back and gazing upward, just as she'd pictured Altan doing. "She was known as Nuray the Just or Nuray the Generous. She's always pictured holding scales or a bountiful offering of some kind, usually on a platter or in a basket." She pointed at the woman in the tapestry, who held both. "Also, look how short she is. Nuray was known for her short stature."

"No, I mean, how do you *know* that? Karak City has no public colleges and it's hardly common knowledge." His eyes narrowed. "I've heard the khan holds a great enthusiasm for the ancient Pureks. Are you from his court?"

"No. I—" She thought quickly, cursing her need to show off. "She's rumored to be of Mori descent. They hold her in high regard." Not a total lie. She knew of two Mori clans who claimed Khagan Nuray as an ancestor, but she doubted those clans knew Khagan Nuray was usually shown holding scales and food platters. That knowledge was peculiar to Dashi's trade.

"Ah. An ancestral affection, then," he said, not taking his eyes off her. "Yet your sister says you were raised in Karak City."

"I spent the first part of my life with the Mori."

"And your sister...?"

"Was too young to remember any of it." *And I never taught her.* "We moved to Karak City when she was two."

"How old were you?"

"Eight."

"But you still remember how to shoot and ride in the Mori style."

"The Mori learn to ride and shoot right after they learn to walk. And I've had a lot of time on my hands since then." *In fact, over the last three months, I've had nothing* but *time,* she thought wryly. Not that she'd been able to practice much besides walking on her hands and counting fleas.

"Well, thank you for using your skills to get the horses. I apologize for my paranoia, as you put it. I accepted your word in our deal; I should have accepted that you would keep it, even if you were speaking another language. I'm not often kept in the dark and I don't enjoy the feeling."

Does anyone, she wondered, thinking of the lies Altan had spun over the years. Perhaps that desire to understand his surroundings explained why Sevlin was content to sit quietly and observe, but it still spoke of someone who cared deeply. She'd been right: he wasn't as easygoing as he seemed.

"I wasn't *keeping you in the dark*," she said.

He waved a hand. "Bad phrasing."

Neither one of them said anything for a minute. Sevlin's gaze wandered around the room, stopping here and there on items of interest. He'd picked up her lantern and the light flickered against his face, making his scar look like a canyon cutting across the muscle of his cheek.

"Did you look at any of these?" he asked, motioning toward the scrolls.

"No." *Not this time.* "I was still looking around when you came in."

He squatted next to the skeleton that was reaching for the door, holding the light so he could examine it at close range. He was a peculiar sort, she decided, rather like Altan in his clinical interest of things. But Altan had been to dozens of ruins. Assuming he was telling the truth about being from Tyvalar, this would be Sevlin's first. Karakal was the nation closest to the old Purek empire, and the only one that bordered the taiga and its string of ruins.

Dashi's eyes drifted over him, taking the chance to study him while his focus was elsewhere. His hair was several shades darker than his skin and closely cropped, much shorter than was fashionable in Karakal. Only Baris had worn his hair that short—better in a fight, he'd said—though he always lamented not being able to let women run their fingers through it. The lantern flickered, setting Sevlin's irises aglow with reflected light, and Dashi's gaze was dragged back to his face. Everyone in Karakal had dark eyes. Except for the odd horse or dog, Dashi didn't recall ever seeing eyes that weren't some shade of black or brown. Even Altan, Baris and Zayaa, though they hailed from Sevlin's homeland, had dark eyes. Dashi hadn't noticed Sevlin's eyes when she'd first seen him at the start of the race. He'd been gathering his gear, and the angle of his face and his dark lashes had combined to hide their color. It was difficult not to be arrested by the gleam of gray-green at close range, however.

Sevlin tilted his head to study the skeleton from a different angle and Dashi's gaze skittered away, lest she be caught staring.

"It's a good thing you don't believe the stories of restless spirits," he said.

"Don't suppose I would've come inside if I did." She focused on the tapestry. "You don't believe them either."

"Don't suppose I would've come inside if I did," he murmured without looking up. "I would've left you to whatever fate awaited."

"I'm certain I would have handled it just fine."

"I'm certain." His tone was neutral. She couldn't tell whether he was serious or making fun of her.

"What's a Tyvalaran doing in a race organized by Karakal's khan?" she asked, switching instinctively to the offensive.

"The same thing as you, I suspect: trying to win." He didn't look up or sound surprised that Dashi knew where he was from. "Your khan hardly tried to keep it a secret." He cocked his head at the skeleton. "Do you think they had any idea what was coming?"

"With the cataclysm? No. They didn't even have a chance to move." She pointed to the skeleton with the spear. "That one is still at his post."

"Ever faithful," Sevlin murmured.

Dashi's skin prickled. "The Pureks were almost compulsive in the way they chronicled things," she said after a moment, seeking to distract herself from the thought of the guard's spirit, still on duty. "They collected knowledge the way people today collect..." she paused, searching for an appropriate analogy.

"The way people today collect artifacts from the ruins," Sevlin supplied in an ironic voice.

She looked at him sharply, but he was examining the scrolls now. *The khan's artifact. Of course. That's what he's referring to. Not me.*

"Exactly. We know there were some survivors. The fact that they left no record of what happened shows that the cataclysm occurred with so little warning that there wasn't time to investigate it."

"And you know all of this from Mori tradition as well?"

"The Mori have passed down stories of survivors trickling southward out the taiga, on their way to found Karak City," she said evasively.

"No records," he paused, "that we know of. But they left behind rumors about what caused the cataclysm. Those still circulate to this day."

"There are rumors about every aspect of the Pureks," she countered.

She wasn't sure why she was arguing. He was right; there were so many rumors that their variations were innumerable. The pious, for instance, said the ancient Pureks were punished for not honoring their ancestors. She'd heard others say that the cataclysm was driven by chance—the geomagical equivalent of a dice roll—and then they would raise a flask to enjoying every minute of life. The khan even mentioned the cataclysm in proclamations, claiming that it was his great-great-something-or-other who'd led the surviving Pureks, which formed the basis for his right to rule.

One of Altan's crusades had been to locate a definitive account of the cataclysm, but there had been nothing. Plenty of vague references to magic existed but nothing about its end. The exact mechanism of the magic was similarly vague. Altan had speculated that the veins of magic were only used by a small group—the ruling elite, perhaps, or warriors—who guarded the details fiercely, which would explain their scarcity in the old records. The specifics of magic hadn't been of much interest to Dashi—Why would they be? Magic was gone—but there

were one or two fictional pieces that, once translated, had been enter-
taining.

"I've always found rumors to be a good place to start looking for the
truth," Sevlin said. He stretched up to reach a scroll and made a face.

"What?"

"My back. The cut you gave me," he added when she looked confused.
"Check to make sure I haven't ripped the stitches, will you?" Without
waiting for a response, he unwrapped his sash and shucked off his deel,
raising his undershirt with one hand. His back was long and leanly
muscled: a tan canvas marked by dark scars, evidence of a long history
of weapons training. There were a lot of them, some small, some large,
though none looked as severe as the one on his face.

Dashi took the lantern and held it closer to his skin. The cut was about
the length of her forearm, shallow at the bottom and wider at the top
where she must have twisted the knife as he threw her over his shoulder.
A row of stitches paraded upward, neat and orderly as a column of
soldiers.

"My sister did this?" she blurted. She'd have pegged Idree as the type
to turn limp and impotent at the sight of blood.

"Depends on which part you're looking at. You gave me the wound.
She patched it up. A family effort, I'd say."

"I didn't know I'd gotten you good enough to require stitches." That
took some of the sting out of her defeat but only a little. She may have
wounded him, but he could have killed her.

"'Good' is in the eye of the beholder," he said dryly.

Dashi laughed. "I suppose it is. The stitches look fine. Nothing torn."
She picked up his sash from where it had fallen to the floor. "It'll scar,
but at least it's on your back where no one—"

Where no one can see it. She froze halfway through the act of handing him the sash, as she realized what she'd just said. "I'm sorry. I didn't mean that like it sounded."

He took the sash from her. "It's just something people say when you're wounded." He motioned toward his face with one hand, while he pulled the deel closed over his chest with the other. The left side of his mouth was slightly lower than the right, where it had to fight to overcome the pull of the scar. "Unless of course the wound is actually on your face."

She opened her mouth to tell him it didn't look bad or to say that at least it hadn't gotten his eye, but then closed it. He must know how it looked, just as he knew he was lucky not to have lost an eye.

"How did you come by it?" she asked instead. He was obviously a fighter of some skill and, in her experience, those were the ones who didn't mind telling the stories of their scars. Baris never had anyway.

"When I was fifteen, thieves attacked my home. I got it protecting my sister."

Dashi was quiet, not sure what response should follow such a statement. "It would be difficult to think of a better way to get a scar," she said finally, "than fighting for someone you love." Is that what prison was to her? A scar?

His mouth twitched. "I have scars from stupid things I've done—mistakes I've made, hastily made judgments, poorly executed parries. And I have scars from times when I did the right thing, however difficult, and it cost me. I never regret the latter."

"How old is your sister?"

He nodded in the direction of the library door. "A few years older than Idree."

"Hopefully *your* sister acts her age."

"Idree acts hers. She's not as naive as you think."

Dashi's head jerked back a little. "You've known her for one day. I've known her my whole life."

Sevlin shrugged. "Sometimes that's when it's hardest to see someone."

And what is it, exactly, that you think I'm not seeing clearly, she wanted to ask. Granted, Idree had managed not to have an emotional blowup for the first few days, but she'd gotten to it eventually, at the Mori camp.

"I should go," Dashi said. "I'm supposed to be on watch and the closer we are to the taiga..." She trailed off, not sure what she wanted to say. She'd just declared that she didn't believe the tales of restless spirits, but she also remembered the beast she'd seen that night in the snow.

Sevlin followed her outside, where Dashi cajoled the door into closing and rebuilt the cairn that kept it in place. She knew the war against time and weather would one day be lost, that the place where her friends had tread would be swallowed up by the land eventually. Yet she couldn't help fighting the battle, stacking rock after rock, scraping her knuckles as she went, and then, when she'd run out of rocks, gathering extras to add to the pile. Anything to stave off the day when the monument to what had passed, passed away itself.

Chapter 16

At dawn they headed northwest from the ruin, going straight for a gap in the otherwise featureless wall of trees. The race map had the spot marked clearly, indicating it as the path used by the khan's men months prior. The gap turned out to be a ravine, with steep slopes that penned them in on both sides and a looming roof of trees that blocked out the sky. The morning sunlight was a pale specter of itself, hardly strong enough to push through the canopy.

The ravine was currently dry, but all it would take was a summer storm higher up in the taiga for it to become a seething torrent. Judging by the swaths of washed-out soil and the branches that lay marooned at irregular intervals, such an occurrence wasn't unusual. The sides were so steep that it would be difficult to escape a flash flood. It reminded Dashi of galloping through the city, the prefects on her heels and the stone wall barring her escape. She stroked the neck of the dun horse she rode like he was the one who needed soothing.

She kept their pace moderate; it wouldn't pay to charge ahead one day, only to have weary mounts the next. They ate their noon meal on horseback, chewing on *borts*, dried meat procured from the Mori, and washing it down with a few swallows of water.

Dashi's eyes darted back and forth, searching for a trap like the one near the canyon bridge. The whole ravine was one long ambush point, as far as she was concerned. Tracks crisscrossed the sandy soil, weaving a story that was easy to read if you knew the language.

"At least a dozen other racers," Sevlin said, pulling his horse close to hers so they could ride abreast in the narrow ravine. "Not that long ago either."

"I figure a day," Dashi said.

He nodded without looking at her. "For the biggest group of them, yes." He pointed to a set of tracks along one side of the ravine, the edges crisp and still wet with dew. "There were a few stragglers."

She squinted at the land in front of them, hoping to read some clue there. "I don't like them being in front of us," she said finally. "Too easy for an ambush. They set one just past the bridge. You were ahead of me, so maybe you didn't see it, but it took out another racer."

"We should take turns leading then. Whoever is in front needs to have fresh eyes."

A great idea if she'd been with her friends, but how could she trust someone who was trying to beat her? Her squint deepened. He might let danger go unheralded, hoping to take her out without having to lift his sword.

"I'll go first," she said. "We can switch when I'm tired." *Which will be never.*

His eyes swung up to hers. "If I wanted to kill you, I would have already."

"Never know when you'll change your mind."

"I won't, unless you give me a reason."

"And getting the khan's purse isn't reason enough?"

"No."

Dashi shrugged. "It would be for most people."

"You include yourself in that statement?"

"I wouldn't kill for the purse." *But to get this belt off? Probably.* "Anyway, I agreed to travel with you, didn't I?" she asked. Like him, she knew that didn't necessarily mean anything. Else, she wouldn't have balked at the idea of him leading.

His pale eyes, light gray with a hint of green, were unnervingly fixed on her, and Dashi was reminded of an albino horse she'd seen once. He gestured in front of them. "Lead on."

It occurred to her, as she felt his gaze on her shoulder blades, that maybe she shouldn't have been so quick to leave him at her back. Which was the greater danger: Sevlin, a companion she hardly knew, in her blind spot, or Negan, with his traps and deep-seated grudge, lying in wait?

The animal tracks appeared a short while later, following the ones left by the racers like a pack of faithful hounds. The prints were strange though, and not made by anything as mundane as a dog.

The hind foot had an elongated heel with five widely-spaced toes. The outline of the front foot resembled a thumbless hand. Each toe ended at a point that suggested a sharp claw. Dashi straightened in her saddle and ran a hand over her face, trying to wipe away any trace of fear.

"Do you see those?" Sevlin called a few minutes later. The ravine was so narrow here that he could no longer draw his horse beside hers.

"See what?" Idree asked. Sevlin had dropped to the rear, letting Idree ride in the middle. Dashi wasn't sure if it was because he wanted to keep them both in his sight or if he wanted to protect Idree.

"Animal tracks following the racers in front of us," he said.

"Following them? Like...wolves?" Like everyone else in Karak City, Idree knew how bold the steppe wolves could be, especially during winter. "But it's summertime."

"Whatever left those tracks is bigger than a wolf," Sevlin said.

"What do you think it is? A bear?"

There was a long pause. "They look like rodents," he said finally. "Huge rodents."

Dashi stifled a sigh. She didn't need to turn around to see the fear on Idree's face. She ran a finger over her bow, thinking of the last time she'd seen tracks like these.

Sevlin drew abreast of her the next time the ravine widened. "It defeats the purpose of having someone ride point if that person doesn't alert anyone else to dangers."

"I didn't see any dangers," Dashi said, "only tracks that were hours old."

The right side of Sevlin's mouth pinched inward in annoyance. The left side rarely moved, she'd noticed. She wondered if the scar had severed some necessary muscle, or if it was a learned trait.

"If we're not going to help each other, we might as well go our separate ways," he said. "At least I'll know who I can trust if I'm alone."

She'd had the same thought herself...and had to keep convincing herself that it was a fallacy. Deep down, she knew she hadn't seen the last of Negan. When she faced him again, she wanted Sevlin's sword on her side. She needed an ally, whether or not she could fully trust him.

"Fine." She glanced over her shoulder to where Idree trailed them. "I knew you'd notice them. I didn't say anything because I didn't want to scare Idree."

"Won't she be more scared if she's surprised by the animal that made those prints?"

"We might not even see it. She doesn't need to know everything, especially if it's something that might not come to pass."

"Is that what you prefer, to have information hidden beneath sugary words and sweet assurances?"

"No!" she said angrily, thinking of Altan's deceptions. "But Idree and I aren't the same. She's a child."

"My sister is young and I've seen her bear news more stoically than many adults."

"How wonderful for your sister," Dashi said acidly, "but Idree is different. She cries when she's frustrated, is constantly frightened. You've only known her—"

"I haven't seen many tears from her so far. When she thought you were being attacked by Negan's men, she didn't cry. She came after you with her bow."

"She doesn't even know how to use it."

He shrugged one shoulder. "We were talking about fear. Skill is a different matter. She's going to become an adult whether you believe it's possible or not. If you teach her tracking and shooting you can at least ensure she becomes a capable one."

Sensing that she was the topic of conversation, Idree maneuvered her horse closer. "What are you talking about?"

"The race," Dashi said.

"The strange tracks," Idree guessed. "The ones that look like rodents."

Dashi locked eyes with Sevlin. What was the point in keeping it to herself now? Idree already knew half of it.

"Rats," she said, her gaze shifting to her sister. "I've seen them before. When I was following—when I was out this spring. I came upon a body, or what was left of one, and several sets of tracks just like these. The tracks were in snow and there was blood everywhere but," she shrugged, "I recognize them."

"How can you be sure it was a rat?" Sevlin asked.

"I saw it. It was enormous. A giant. Something that..." She paused, searching for the right word. "I've never seen anything like it on the steppe before. I think it was pushed down from the taiga by the storm that night."

"*How* giant?" Idree asked.

"Only a hand or two shorter than the horses." *Big enough to make facing Negan seem preferable.*

They were silent after that, each absorbed in their thoughts. Dashi didn't know if Sevlin believed her, but she could tell Idree did.

When they finally saw a taiga creature, however, it wasn't a rat. Her first clue was her horse, which began snorting and throwing his head up and down. Dashi scanned the ravine in front of them, looking for the cause of his nervousness. Finding nothing, she raised her eyes to the upper edge, where the trees crowded close to the precipice, daring each other to jump. *There.* More tracks, but they were different than the ones left by the taiga rats. These flowed along the sides of the ravine at an angle that defied belief—and gravity.

She jerked her horse to a halt. The tracks were strange: ovals that were slightly pointed at one end. She turned in her saddle, looking over Idree's head at Sevlin.

"What do you think made those?" she asked.

He shook his head. "They don't look like hooves, but they don't have toes either. I've never seen anything like them."

"Maybe we should get out of this ravine," Idree said softly.

"Whatever made them, it seems plenty able to climb out of the ravine too," Sevlin said. "At least here we can see where we're going."

Dashi glanced up at the dark trees. Already, they grew closer together than they had at the edge of the taiga, near the ruined library. It was as if the forest was crowding toward them, preparing to swallow them whole.

"Sevlin's right," Dashi said. "And even if we wanted to, we'd have to find a place where the horses could climb out. For right now, we have no choice but to keep going this way."

She kept an arrow loosely nocked after that, but even that didn't calm her. The dun horse, picking up on her mood, grew progressively more restless, until finally, he started to balk outright. Floodwaters had carved the ravine wider here, littering the ground with a maze of boulders that seemed to alarm her horse further. It wasn't until she was nearly upon the creatures that she realized what they were. To be fair, the brownish ovals that made up their heads and the segments of their bodies looked like the nearby boulders, but the similarities ended there. The delicate, jointed legs; the wobbling antennae; the enormous serrated jaws that looked like they could snap a log in half: all belonged to an animal she'd seen before. In the city. On the steppe. Virtually every place she could imagine. An insect as common as the dirt itself, though every other time she'd seen them they'd been much, *much* smaller.

The ants—if that name still applied—were gigantic, monstrous specimens. Their height was similar to that of a yak, and they were slightly longer than they were tall. Their hard outer skeletons, a shade darker than copper, were shiny, almost wet-looking, and contrasted starkly with the black bulbous eyes that protruded from either side of their heads. A few of the ants carried things in their jaws: objects wrapped in bloodied scraps of cloth. It took Dashi a moment to realize that she was looking at the dismembered body of a racer. Or maybe several racers.

Idree, riding just behind Dashi, saw the creature a moment later. "What is...?"

"Get back," Dashi whispered, but the ants had already seen them. Dozens of inhuman heads topped with waving antennae swiveled in their direction. Their eyes were huge and pupil-less and their faces lacked the familiar characteristics of mammals. You could guess what a fox or a wolf was thinking, Dashi thought. They might not be human, but they had ways of conveying their mood. A snarl was aggression. A lowered head meant submission. But the ants were still, in body and expression. Only their antennae moved. Even without facial cues, however, she thought it was a good bet not to come between a wild animal and its meal.

"Back," Dashi whispered again. She looked over her shoulder. Sevlin had already managed to turn his horses around in the narrow space between the boulders, but Idree was having trouble.

When she glanced back at the ants, they were on the move. The ones carrying the human remains trudged up the sides of the ravine, seeming to have no trouble with the slope. A vanguard of others advanced toward her.

Idree managed—*finally*—to turn around and Dashi wheeled her horse after her sister's. They thundered back the way they'd come, flashing by one towering tree after another: dark sentinels, warning them not to return. A white mist had begun to curl through the forest again, stroking the treetops with long fingers.

Dashi shuddered.

Chapter 17

Dashi wasn't sure how long they backtracked, but the pyrothrite belt seemed to grow heavier with each stride. She tried not to think of how much time they were losing, of how much closer Negan was getting to the artifact. They couldn't risk pushing farther up the ravine: there was no way of knowing how aggressive the ants were and a narrow ravine littered with boulders wasn't a good place to find out.

When they finally stopped for the night, she threw herself from her horse and, on the pretext of needing a moment of privacy, retreated to check the belt. Ten nodules of pyrothrite had fallen. It was the end of the eighth day of the race; she was supposed to be three days from the temple at this point. She pulled her deel back on. At least the noble had built in some time for "small setbacks," as he'd had called it, but it was difficult to muster any gratitude toward someone who'd chained her to explosives in the first place.

She heard Idree's laugh before she got back to camp.

"Think of the odds the local bookmakers would have given you if they'd seen your scar," Idree said. "Although my friend and I saw you at the starting line and we thought you looked intimidating even with your face half covered."

"Almost everyone wore dust masks," Sevlin protested.

Idree shrugged, smiling.

"I would have worn it at the start of the race even if it wasn't dusty," he said, "because of the crowd. I don't relish the stares." Idree made a sympathetic noise. "I wore it the night I found you and your sister because it made it easier to hide from Negan's men in the dark."

Strange, Dashi thought. He spoke like he was embarrassed of the scar, as if he would be hurt by people gaping, but when he'd spoken of it in the library he hadn't seemed self-conscious at all.

"You still stood out," Idree said. "At least to me."

"Ah, well, I'm lucky that didn't make me more of a target for the consul and his men."

Now there was amusement in his voice, an upturn to the right side of his mouth. While neither characteristic could truthfully be called expressive, they were a far cry from his normal coolness. Is this how he acted when he was relaxed, or was it only a show to lull Idree into chattiness? Not that she needed much lulling. Dashi glanced at her sister, taking in her glowing eyes and the way she was fully turned toward Sevlin. *Wonderful.* As if having a twelve-year-old along wasn't bad enough. Now she had a twelve-year-old who thought she was falling in love with the competition.

"Dashi says looking intimidating makes people leave you alone," Idree said.

"And does that advice seem to work?"

Idree dimpled. "Oh, not for me. Being intimidating isn't helpful in my line of work. I work at a bakery," she clarified. "I'm supposed to seem nice, not mean."

"What about your sister? Is that why she walks around looking so dangerous? She wants to be left alone?"

"She doesn't always act like that. I mean, a lot of the time she does, especially with me, but with her friends she laughed a lot. And when she walks around looking mad..." Idree shrugged. "Well, that usually means she *is* mad, not trying to be intimidating. Dashi isn't bothered with consequences or complicated strategies. If she's angry with someone, you'll know it. There'll be violence. If there's no violence, then she's not angry."

Dashi pursed her lips, but even if she'd been part of the conversation she didn't know what she would have said. She knew what Idree was referring to when she spoke about a lack of concern for consequences—the night Dashi had tracked down the murderers—but she didn't want to replay that fight with her sister. Especially in front of Sevlin.

She'd heard enough though. If she didn't put a stop to this conversation now, Idree would spill everything she could recall. *And she said she'd be careful when she talked to him. Ha!*

Sevlin looked up, directly at where she stood in the shadows. "A sure recipe for an interesting life," he said, his tone slipping back to neutral.

"Perhaps you've never been truly angry if you've never fought like that," Dashi said, stepping into the light of the small fire he'd kindled. They'd decided the benefits of a fire, namely keeping the taiga's denizens at bay, outweighed the risks of attracting Negan's attention.

"I didn't say I hadn't," Sevlin said, before turning his questions on her instead of Idree. "Is that what's between you and Negan?"

Dashi almost laughed. *Blood*, that's what was between her and Negan. Lots of it and a thirst for more. Killing the men in the brothel had been a shock, but she'd had three months to think about it, to realize that she wasn't sorry, only unaccustomed to the sight of a person dead at her hand. She doubted Negan felt regret over his role in her friends' deaths, and neither would she.

Dashi made a pretense of selecting a spot by the fire. "Who said there's anything between us?"

She didn't want to get into her history with Negan. Even Idree didn't know that he'd been involved in killing Altan, Zayaa and Baris—or why—and the subject of how her friends had kept everything from her was still a tender one.

"You call the consul by his first name," Sevlin said, "and when you say it, I can hear the venom in your voice."

"I know his name because I got close enough to listen to his plans. And if I'm venomous maybe it has something to do with riding through a trap left by his men and waking up to the screams of other racers."

Idree made a face. "Did they come after you?" she asked Sevlin.

"Not directly. I happened to be riding behind one of the victims. He had a blazing fire going every night. It drew them right to him."

"Did you try to help him?"

"I rode in that direction, but I was too late," Sevlin replied with such gravity that Dashi thought he actually might be telling the truth.

Idree beamed at him. "Even though there were so many of them?"

"I'd be lying if I said I relished the idea of that fight," Sevlin said, "but a long time ago I decided I would raise my sword to help whoever needs it, wherever duty has called me."

And you came all the way from Tyvalar for noble ideals? Horseshit. Sevlin might say he fought for duty, but to Dashi, it was far from clear where that duty lay.

Somehow the ride back to the place where they'd seen the ants took longer than Dashi remembered. Had they really lost all this ground in their flight? She clamped down on her frustration, forcing herself to maintain a steady pace. Galloping headlong through the ravine would only end in disaster—whether because of Negan's traps or because of a giant taiga animal. She squinted at the dust, sullen with dew. The rat tracks were still visible, as were the odd oval tracks left by the ants.

The boulder-strewn section where the ants had been yesterday was empty. Other than the mishmash of tracks, there was no sign that they'd been there at all. Whatever—*whoever*—the ants had been eating was gone as well. Lines in the dirt showed where the bodies had been dragged for a short distance, but even those marks ended abruptly.

"Lifted," Sevlin said in a low voice. "Just the way ants lift breadcrumbs to carry them out of the kitchen."

It was nearing midday, but Dashi no longer wanted to eat. "Let's push on," she said, not even trying to hide her unease.

An hour later, she still hadn't relaxed fully. The rat tracks hovered nearby. Now and then more ant tracks appeared around the rim of the ravine. Both were constant reminders that they were still in the taiga, still in danger.

The sun was beginning its descent when Dashi saw the horse, its saddle deserted and one leg dragging slightly. The dark shape of a body lay nearby.

"Do you think the rider is still alive?" Idree asked when she and Sevlin had drawn close to Dashi.

"Maybe." Dashi shrugged. "A trap?" She glanced at Sevlin.

"Could be." He ran a hand across his chin. "I'll go." He paused and fixed his pale eyes on Dashi. "*If* you'll cover me with that bow of yours."

In answer, Dashi pulled an arrow from her quiver. "They strung a line across the canyon near the bridge. Watch for that."

Sevlin dismounted and handed his reins to Idree, then unsheathed his sword and crept forward, hugging the edge of the ravine.

Dashi stayed where she was, scanning for movement. From the corner of her eye, she could see Idree biting her lip nervously. Sevlin made it to the motionless body and squatted by it for a moment. Then he straightened, gave the area around him another long look, and waved Dashi and Idree forward.

The body in the ravine was a woman's, her back red with blood. Sevlin was leaning over a second body, a man's, which hadn't been immediately visible. The shaft of an arrow protruded from the man's stomach.

"Is she...?" Idree asked, glancing back toward the woman.

Sevlin shook his head. "She's dead, but she was killed with a sword, not by animals. Negan is already in the lead," he said half to himself. "Why keep worrying about who's behind him?"

Dashi shrugged. "Maybe she was right on his heels."

"Maybe he's afraid he'll be ambushed after he recovers the artifact," Idree said.

Dashi glanced up in surprise. She'd been contemplating that exact thing, though she hadn't mentioned it to her sister.

A groan from the second body made them all jump.

"He's alive," Idree gasped, slithering from her horse in a rush.

Dashi took a closer look at the man sprawled on the ground. His hair was matted with blood and his skin was paler than when she'd last seen him, but there was no mistaking him: it was the sun-tanned laborer from the dirt circle.

"We have to help him," Idree said. She reached for the arrow shaft. The laborer's hand twitched in a feeble attempt to stop her.

"Idree..." Dashi began, swinging off her horse. "I don't think we can. He's already lost so much blood. If we remove the arrow, he'll lose what little he has left."

"But he'll die if he stays like this!"

"He's dead either way," Sevlin said gently. "Is there anything we can do for you?" he asked the man. "Water? A message we could take back to Karak City?"

Dashi cast about, searching the corners of her mind for the man's name. "Aizhan." He'd asked for her help. Would she have been able to help him, or would it be her body lying on the other side of the ravine instead of the nameless woman's?

At the sound of his name, Aizhan's eyelids fluttered open. His eyes moved over their faces, passing over Dashi's, then coming back to rest there.

"Girl," he said. His voice had a thick, almost viscous quality to it.

"Yes?" Dashi leaned closer. So did Idree, her face stark with horror.

"Mori girl," he croaked again. Blood flew from his lips and landed on her cheek. "He's looking for you."

Dashi straightened abruptly, trying to physically distance herself from his words, but he grabbed her wrist with a sticky hand.

"What do you mean?" Idree asked. "Who's looking for us?"

"He...asked about her. He—" The words stopped, replaced by a gurgling sound. Then, silence.

Idree looked up, stricken. "He's..."

Dashi could only nod. She forced her eyes away from the laborer's face. Idree looked ghastly, like she couldn't decide whether to vomit or pass out.

"Idree, come away," Dashi said. "Don't look anymore."

Idree ignored her, busily tending to the dead man, placing his hands on his chest, careful not to bump the arrow shaft, though it could no longer hurt him.

"Idree..."

Her sister stood up without saying anything and walked a little farther down the ravine, hugging her arms around herself.

Dashi put a hand to her forehead and squeezed. This was no place for her sister. She'd tried to dissuade her, and then tried to accommodate her with a second mount and warmer clothes, but the fact remained that Idree shouldn't be here. She was too fragile, too emotional.

"You lied," Sevlin said from behind her.

She didn't answer, watching Idree's bowed back.

"You said there was no history between you and Negan, but there is. He's looking for you."

"He's looking for us all," Dashi said wearily. "He wants the artifact and that means getting rid of everyone who's a threat."

"But he wants you in particular. Why?"

There was an ominous note in his voice, an implied threat of some degree. Dashi turned to find him standing a few strides away, one hand on his sword.

"Were you about to attack me?" she asked mockingly. "With my back turned? I thought you fought for duty, not anger."

"You've been dishonest. I can't trust you." He was staring at the bow in her hands, watching it, weighing who would be faster.

"Oh, and I'm supposed to believe you've been nothing but forthcoming? Anyone who could hear about the khan's race and leave almost immediately—which you would have to do to get from Tyvalar to Karak City in time—probably doesn't need the purse money, but you know too much about ancient Purek history to have entered on a whim. And you're certainly not in the race to win a place at court or to earn the khan's favor because you're not even Karakalese. You didn't cover your face at the starting line because you're afraid of being stared at; you're proud of your scar." She made her next words a statement, not a question. "You were hiding from someone."

"I want to know why Negan wants *you*, why he thinks you're a particular threat."

Dashi gave a sharp laugh. "And I want to know the answers to the questions I just asked, but I doubt I'll get them. You're not my confidant, Sevlin, you're my competition. What I have against Negan and what he has against me is none of your business."

"It is if it endangers me."

"Being in the *race* endangers you. If you want to—where's Idree?"

The ravine to the north of them was empty.

Sevlin turned. "She was right behind me."

"No, she started walking—" Dashi swore and dashed to her horses, hastily grabbing the reins of Idree's horses on her way. Sevlin mounted just as fast as she did.

To the north, the sides of the ravine dipped lower, becoming, for a brief span, less steep. Sevlin jerked his horse to a halt, pointing to the scrapes in the dirt where someone had scrambled up the side. Leaping from her horse, Dashi looped the reins once around a fallen limb and started up the slope. Sevlin passed her a moment later, his long legs covering the ground faster than hers could.

At the top he paused, looking right and left. "Idree?"

A muffled voice answered. Sevlin ran into the trees without waiting. Dashi followed, dodging the black trunks and trying to duck the branches that lashed at her face. She skidded to a stop, nearly running into Sevlin, who was towering over Idree, one hand on each of her shoulders. He was talking to her in a voice so quiet that Dashi couldn't hear what he said. She ducked under his arm so she could face her sister.

"What were you *thinking*, Idree? Why would you go into the trees by yourself?"

Idree's mouth and eyes were pinched. "His horse is hurt. I wanted to—"

"Of all the ridiculous—You could have been—wandering off after a horse!"

Sevlin moved his hand from Idree's shoulder to hers. "Lower your voice."

"Shut it, Sevlin," she growled, but she stopped yelling.

A horse snorted behind Idree, drawing Dashi's attention. It had been an elegant animal once, one of the expensive racehorses. Now its head hung low and its coat was dull and stretched tight in places where it shouldn't be. It must have belonged to the female racer, not the laborer. He hadn't been riding anything half so fine.

Sevlin held out his hand, approaching the horse slowly. The animal took a few steps away, its head lurching up and down as it limped. Sevlin cursed softly. The horse's leg was broken.

"It's hurt," Idree said again. "Maybe we could—"

The horse gave a panicked snort as Sevlin drew his sword across its throat. "There's no saving it," he said in the same quiet, even voice he'd used when he first reached Idree. "It's kinder to kill it now than to let it wander through the forest where it will be torn apart by ants or rats."

Idree nodded, chin trembling. She turned back to the ravine and Dashi followed. The metallic tang of blood went with them and Dashi wasn't sure if it was from her wrist, tattooed with the laborer's bloody handprint, or from Sevlin's sword.

Chapter 18

"We're not stopping for anything else," Dashi said, her heels striking the ground in time with each word. She turned and started back the way she'd come. "I don't care if we find the khan himself lying in the ravine. *We keep going.*"

Idree tossed a twig at the fire without answering.

"Ask Sevlin," Dashi continued, "if you'd rather talk to him—"

"I would." Idree's voice was low, sullen.

"He'll agree with me. We're going to lose the artifact if we keep this up." Granted, one of them was going to lose the artifact no matter what, but she'd worry about that later. "Can you at least see that?"

"I was only trying to help something that was hurt. It didn't even take that long."

"You're missing the point; we don't have *time* to help every hurt racer and animal we come across! You have to keep your emotions in check, Idree."

"You're not exactly in control of your emotions, you know! You get angry all the time. You were angry when you found me with the horse. You're angry right now."

"Anger is a useful emotion," Dashi retorted. "Feeling sorry for everything you come across is not. Especially when it makes you do something dangerous like wander off into the forest alone."

"You're not angry because it was dangerous. You're angry because you want to win," Idree said, her tone thick with disgust.

"So? Your precious Sevlin wants to win too. Why aren't you disgusted with him?"

Idree turned her face away, officially lapsing back into silence.

Dashi sank to the ground opposite her sister, her hand automatically going to the pyrothrite belt beneath her clothes. She knew Idree was right: they hadn't actually lost that much time following the horse and they'd ridden until night to make up for it. Taken with all the other delays, however, it seemed intolerable. She sighed and picked up a handful of dirt, letting it fall through her fingers. Maybe Idree just made an easy scapegoat; she could hardly berate the ants, after all.

She pulled the race map from the inside pocket of her deel and unfolded it, angling it toward the fire. The map only showed a fraction of Karakal's border with the taiga, the portion most relevant to the khan's goal. In reality, the taiga stretched farther to both the east and the west, and for an untold distance to the north. Most of the ruins Dashi had explored with Altan had been just below the taiga's southern border, in the hills of the near-taiga. Always within sight of the dark trees, but never among them.

Her finger snaked along the wrinkled paper, tracing their route. There was the mouth of the ravine and the ruined library. *Here,* she thought, halting her finger. *This is about where we are right now.* Her eyes traveled north. *And* that's *where we'd be if we hadn't lost time on the ants and resupplying and avoiding Negan on the steppe.*

"What's that?" Idree leaned forward, curious despite herself.

"A map of the taiga."

"I *know* it's a map. I meant that." Idree picked up a second piece of paper that had fallen when Dashi opened the map.

"A sketch of the artifact we're supposed to be retrieving." Dashi held out her hand for the paper.

Idree ignored her, flattening the sketch against one knee. "A solid gold statuette," she murmured. "No one knows what she'll be holding?" Although the sketch showed the figure holding a pitcher, a line of script at the bottom advised racers that the statuette might instead be holding a globe, a cloth or a flame, any of which could be seen to represent the earth's magic.

"Guess not," Dashi said.

"How does the khan know she'll be holding *anything* if no one has seen her before?"

Dashi's lips twisted. She had a pretty good idea of how the khan knew. To her knowledge, there was only one group of people who'd ventured into the ruins and trafficked in its relics. If the khan had information about a specific piece of artwork at a specific ruin, then the knowledge had come from something she and her friends had retrieved. And if the noble from Karak City was correct, then the consul had ordered Altan's murder only after taking the pertinent information. Her friends' lives, as well as their deaths, were inextricably linked to the khan's race.

The thing that Dashi found strange was that the consul would have them killed *before* the statuette was retrieved. Why not ask Altan to find the artifact first, then kill him? Dashi wasn't sure if he would've agreed to it; a ruin in the inner taiga was much harder to access than a ruin on the edge.

"Figures in Purek art are always holding *something*," Dashi said. "It's part of their symbolism. Different khagans are represented by different items. I suspect the sketch is based on scrolls and artwork taken from the ruins over the last few years." She let the sentence hang in the air until Idree's eyes widened.

"By you and Altan?"

Dashi nodded.

"Do you think that's why they were—"

"I don't know, Idree." Dashi ran a finger along the edge of the map. It stung and she pulled her hand away to find a single drop of blood suspended against the skin. "I don't know." *But I'll find out. Somehow.* She returned the paper to her deel just as Sevlin's footsteps approached the fire.

She didn't look up from her map, but she heard the smile in Idree's voice as she gave Sevlin food and asked after the wound on his back. Her sister's infatuation was growing more apparent every day. She wondered if Sevlin was oblivious or if he planned to manipulate it somehow.

The map stared up at her mockingly. They were supposed to follow the ravine north before turning east at a rock formation that resembled a man's hand. From there, they would continue along a wide river valley until they reached the foothills on the eastern end. That's where the khan's men claimed to have glimpsed the temple that held the artifact. Dashi's eyes shifted to the right of their present location where, in a fit of understatement, a half dozen trees had been drawn to delineate the unknown reaches of the taiga. Cutting through the forest would be shorter in terms of distance, but it would be more dangerous. There was no telling what lay there.

A shadow moved across the page. "Discover anything you missed before?" Sevlin asked.

"No."

"We're more than a day behind now."

Behind him, Idree looked at the ground. Oh, she felt bad for disappointing *Sevlin*.

Dashi nodded her agreement. "Barring a major mishap to Negan, I don't think we'll be able to get to the temple first."

He tilted his head. "A major mishap is a real possibility out here."

"For us as well."

"True. It's still anyone's race."

Dashi sighed and refolded the map. "Maybe they'll run into giant ants or something."

She thought she saw a flicker of amusement in his eyes but he didn't smile. "Maybe. But we need to consider what we'll do if they reach the artifact first."

Dashi felt her eyebrows rise. "You're suggesting an ambush?" It was something she'd been mulling herself, though she couldn't decide whether to involve Sevlin or not. She didn't want to steal the artifact from Negan only to have to fight Sevlin for it moments later. On the other hand, Negan and his men greatly outnumbered her; Sevlin would be useful in a fight.

Sevlin sat down, close enough that she had to turn her head to look at him. Shadows danced across his face, even as the firelight tipped the stubble that had grown along his jaw with gold. His eyes swept over her once, finally fastening on her own, demanding and firm, and she had to fight the urge to squirm.

"We may have no other choice," he said, levelly. "They cannot be allowed to keep the artifact."

They cannot be allowed. Not, "Let's take the artifact from them." Not, "I want two hundred thousand pieces of gold." There was something absolute in his statement, an unstated consequence that Dashi wasn't seeing.

Idree asked the question before Dashi did. "Why not?"

Sevlin rubbed his scar before answering. "However valuable it might be in artistic terms, the statuette is more than an artifact."

"The race does seem like an extravagant way to add to an art collection," Dashi conceded. "But it's the khan. He can throw away two hundred thousand gold pieces if he wants."

"No, I mean it's not the statuette he wants at all. He's after something more." Sevlin paused and looked deliberately at Dashi. "You were right: I don't need the purse money. I don't want to be introduced in the khan's court. You wanted to know the real reason I came from Tyvalar for this race: the khan is after a magical artifact and I've been ordered to bring it to the Tyvalaran queen."

Dashi stiffened. There were two remarkable things about that statement. The first was the word "magical." The second was that they'd been riding with an agent of the Tyvalaran crown. She was an escaped murderer, her best friends had been executed for spying and she suspected that Negan had sent men after Idree because of it. She didn't need one more thing to make her return to Karak City more dangerous.

Idree seemed undeterred. "The queen? You know the queen of Tyvalar?"

"I've met her, yes." Again, that amused quirk of his lips.

"Have you been to the inner circle?"

"We just call it a palace, but yes."

"What's she like?"

"Young," he said. "Young, but determined. Intelligent. Gifted at music—she could be quite good if she had more time to practice. I think she will make a good leader."

"Is she pretty?"

"I think she will grow into her looks," he answered diplomatically.

Idree, also diplomatic, nodded sagely, but Dashi could tell she was relieved. As if she had a chance with someone over a decade her senior. Or he had a chance with a queen, for that matter.

"What's the palace like? Is it as large as the khan's fortress?"

Dashi stood up before Sevlin could answer. "You accused *me* of putting *you* in danger. I can't think of many things that are more dangerous than for *us* to be caught riding with an agent of the Tyvalaran crown."

Sevlin eyed her warily. "I agree. That's one of the reasons I'm telling you."

"And the other reason?"

"The other is to offer you a safe haven in Tyvalar. *If* you help me bring the artifact there."

"And lose two hundred thousand gold pieces? I could go wherever I want with that much money," she retorted, stalling for time. *Safe haven?* What could she possibly say to that offer? To say no would be to declare a de facto war with Sevlin. He might decide to leave now and she still needed him, especially if it came to wresting the artifact from Negan's grasp.

"I'm sure the Tyvalaran crown could compensate you for the lost purse," he said.

"*You're sure.* Are you authorized to speak for the queen of Tyvalar? How do I know you're not lying just to get my help?"

"*Dashi,*" Idree admonished. "You don't have to call him a liar."

Dashi rolled her eyes.

"I am authorized to speak for Queen Lyazzat on this," Sevlin said. "The artifact is very important to her. She will make sure you're...comfortable in Tyvalar."

Idree clasped her hands in excitement.

"Why now?" Dashi asked. "Why not tell us this last night or the night before? You've had ample opportunity."

"It appears I might need more help in acquiring the artifact than I'd originally thought. You've been to Purek ruins before. I haven't, but I understand they're often rigged with traps and other hidden dangers. Your experience could mean the difference between success and failure."

How did he know about— "You eavesdropped on us!"

"Eavesdropping isn't the same as overhearing," he said in his carefully enunciated way. "And I already had my suspicions. The ruins we camped in, that library...I could tell you'd been there before."

"You eavesdrop on us, decide I might be useful, and *then* offer a safe haven. That's not exactly a recipe for trust."

"I'll admit the timing isn't the best," he said. "But whether I try to steal the artifact from Negan or beat him to the temple in the first place, I need to know you won't put an arrow in my back as soon as I succeed."

The words had been pulled practically verbatim from her head. "Why?" Dashi asked again. "What is so precious about this statuette that the khan of Karakal and the queen of Tyvalar both want it?"

"It's not a statuette. It's a container, a vessel designed to conceal a magical object used by the ancient Pureks: the golden needle."

"What's that?" Idree asked.

Sevlin's gaze moved to Idree. "The golden needle is said to be able to draw magic from the veins of the earth and suture it to a person."

Idree made a soft "oh."

"Where did you hear that story?" Dashi's anger drained away, replaced by something else: disbelief. Not because she doubted his explanation, but because she couldn't believe she was hearing it again. Here, of all places.

She'd been the one to *find* that story, to reclaim its details from the fog of time. It had been a beautiful scroll, illuminated with hand-painted pictures and so engrossing that she'd hardly bemoaned the work of translating it. She'd only understood a fraction of the words on the page—it was far beyond her skills in Purek—but she hardly cared. Altan had praised her find. They all had.

She'd asked Altan if she could keep it. She hadn't meant to—she'd never asked for anything before—but the idea of selling it had suddenly seemed crass and the words popped out before she could stop them.

"*No,*" he said. "*No, this is in such good shape. It will pay our expenses for months.*" She nodded. She understood. Their expeditions were for business, not pleasure, and if they kept every pretty thing they found, there would be nothing left to sell. A custom-made saddle was waiting on her bed several weeks later, a birthday gift from Altan with some of the proceeds from the scroll. He'd even had the saddlemaker include a concealed space for keepsakes from the ruins, but she never found anything she wanted half as much as that scroll.

"What story?" Idree asked.

"You knew them," Dashi said a little breathlessly. "Altan, Baris and Zayaa. You had to. They were Tyvalaran and so are you. They were spies for your queen and she's the one who sent you here."

"You and Altan were spying for the Tyvalaran crown?" Idree asked, staring at Dashi. "You said they were killed because of something they found for the khan!"

"*They* were spies," Dashi said. "I didn't know." *They didn't tell me.* To Sevlin she said, "I'm right, aren't I? You knew them."

"The queen has spies in Karakal," he said, "just like your khan has spies in Tyvalar. By necessity, their identities are known only to a few."

"Oh," she murmured, deflated. "I was..." *I was hoping someone else knew them too.* Idree hardly knew Zayaa and Baris at all. She knew Altan better, though not as well as Dashi had. He'd made an effort, but he was often busy, trekking to ruins or negotiating with buyers. *Or sending information to rival countries.*

"You think you know some Tyvalaran spies?" Sevlin asked.

"Knew them," she corrected in a leaden voice. "Like Idree said, they were killed."

"Ah."

That was it. He would report it to his queen and they would bemoan the loss of information for their country, she thought bitterly.

"I don't know exactly why they were killed. I think maybe they wouldn't bring the artifact—and the golden needle too, I guess—back to the consul," Dashi said before he could ask. "I only found out that they were spies recently."

"How did you find out if Altan didn't tell you?" Idree demanded. "Did you—*oh*."

Dashi knew what her sister was thinking—that she'd learned the information from the men she'd murdered—but she didn't bother to correct her.

Sevlin cleared his throat. "And how do you know about the golden needle if they didn't share anything else with you? It would have been highly secret."

"They shared plenty," she retorted. "Altan was like my older brother." As soon as she said it she realized how delusional she sounded. After all, how close could they possibly have been if he hadn't revealed who he really was? She kept talking. "As for the golden needle, I was the one who found the scroll. Have you seen it?"

"Not the original, no."

"It was beautiful work," she said. "And a good story." She put a slight emphasis on the word story. The ancient Pureks could access magic; that much was common knowledge. But the golden needle story was so fantastical that she could hardly credit it. Altan had said it was fiction.

"*What story?*" Idree asked again.

"The story of how the golden needle was found," Sevlin said. "The Pureks knew about the veins of magic in the ground but they thought they were the province of the ancestors, impossible for the living to access. Then one day a young man stumbled across a vein and fell unconscious. When he awoke, there was a golden needle in his hand."

Sevlin had a good voice for story-telling, Dashi thought absently: the words were precise, but somehow the tone still flowed, rising and falling in measured cadences. Any other time it would have been enough to pull her into the story, but she was having a hard time concentrating.

"Amazed, the young man took the needle back to his village. He was a healer's apprentice and he began using it when he stitched wounds. The results were...chaotic. Many of his patients sickened and died inexplicably, even from small wounds. But the ones who lived became powerful. *Magical.* The healer's apprentice became the first seamstress. That's what the Pureks called someone who could hold the golden needle and use it to manipulate magic."

"That does sound like a good story," Idree said.

The right side of Sevlin's mouth twisted. "It doesn't end happily. At first, the young man achieved fame and fortune. People came from far away, even if they weren't wounded, just to have him stitch the magic into their skin. But the process was very painful—much, *much* worse than regular sutures—and, like I said, many of his patients died. Eventually, an angry mob burned his home, forcing him to flee into the wilderness, taking his sweetheart with him. They lived there for years, hunting and harvesting and living peacefully, until one day his sweetheart became pregnant. It was a difficult pregnancy and the man decided to venture into town to purchase some medicines for her. While he was there, someone recognized him. He fled back to the wilderness, but men from the village followed and captured the seamstress and his sweetheart and took them to the khagan.

"The khagan was a rapacious man, whose only interest was obtaining more power. He tried to forcibly take the golden needle, but it burned everyone but the seamstress. Even with gloves, the needle still would not yield its magic. The khagan brought the seamstress before him and forced him to sew magic into the skin of the imperial warriors. If the seamstress tried to refuse, the khagan would threaten the man's sweetheart and his baby daughter. Many of the khagan's warriors died, but some survived the procedure and became very powerful. The khagan grew jealous and, despite the risks, demanded that the seamstress give him magic too. But the khagan was an old man and he never recovered from the stitches. His son, the heir, accused the seamstress of treachery and had him and his sweetheart put to death." Sevlin spread his hands to show the story was at an end. "For all his power, the seamstress couldn't save himself."

Idree looked shocked. "No," she said faintly. "That's not a happy ending."

"It's not real," Dashi said. "Altan said it was a parable to show the cost of power and greed."

"A memorable lesson," Sevlin agreed. "But not a parable. The story is true, a historical recounting."

"The Pureks left behind scroll after scroll of ballads and stories and poems. How can you be so sure the story of the golden needle is true, while the others aren't?"

"I don't necessarily think the others are untrue," Sevlin said. "And I think the golden needle is real because there is plenty to corroborate it. Tapestries, paintings and scrolls: all refer to a golden needle and the seamstress."

"I went to dozens of ruins with Altan and Baris and Zayaa. *We* found those tapestries and paintings and scrolls. I've never seen anything to make me think the needle was an actual thing."

"Then it was concealed from you. Queen Lyazzat received ample proof. Enough that she sent me here."

"They couldn't have," Dashi protested. "I would have noticed."

"You were young. Perhaps they misled you when you came close to discovering the truth. You never saw mention of the seamstresses?"

"Yes." She drew out the word reluctantly. "But that was a ceremonial title, a figurehead. The seamstress kept the rites to remember the spirits of the ancestors."

"Over time it became that too, because the magic was seen as a gift from the ancestors. But the seamstress' real job was to wield the golden needle. How else do you think the ancient Pureks controlled magic?"

"Altan said..." She faltered, then regained her mental footing. "Altan said it was done through secret rites, like prayers and sacrifices to the spirits. He said they were so secret that they hadn't been written down, that no one alive could replicate them."

Sevlin's squint looked sympathetic.

Dashi turned her head, staring at the fire as anger and hurt heated her skin. *Lies. Years of lies. Over stupid things too, like ancient customs and long-dead magic.* Except Sevlin didn't believe it was dead, which meant Altan hadn't either. That meant...so many things. Their trips to the ruins hadn't been about finding art to sell. They'd been looking for clues that would lead them to magic.

To the golden needle.

From the sound of it, the ancient Purek's military and their magic were closely linked. She thought of how Altan had instructed her to hand over anything of military significance to him or Zayaa for translation. How she'd done it, eager to have more time to explore and play around with Baris. And Baris...he'd been in on it too. She thought of all the fun they'd had together—fighting, riding, daring each other to jump off high things—while Altan and Zayaa continued translating. Had he only been distracting her so she didn't overhear anything important?

It was obvious they hadn't trusted her. Had they even *liked* her? Or had they only been using her: accepting the locations of Purek ruins, information she'd translated from the Mori, and giving nothing of their own in return? She thought of how the noble in Karak City had assessed her as craving respect. Maybe, on some level, she'd suspected that she didn't belong with Altan and the others. Maybe that's why she needed respect. Maybe she'd worked hard to make herself competent because, somewhere inside, she knew Altan needed a reason to keep her around.

"So then what happened?" Idree asked. "The seamstress was dead. Who used the golden needle?"

Dashi didn't answer. She was finished with this conversation. The story, once enthralling, was now tainted by the thought that maybe her friends hadn't been friends at all.

"At first, no one," Sevlin said. "The new khagan tried to get the seamstress' daughter to use the needle, but it was obvious she had no proclivity for it. The ability of a seamstress isn't passed from parent to child, though the relatives of a seamstress do tend to survive the stitching a little better than others—a later khagan found that out after he forced a seamstress to sew magic into his own family. Ultimately though, the magic chooses who will wield it."

"How can the magic choose anything?" Idree asked, her eyebrows drawn low.

"The new khagan decreed that a census be taken. Every person, young and old, rich and poor, was to be counted. But it was really a ploy to find a new seamstress. When a villager came forward to be added to the census, he or she also had to touch the golden needle. One by one, each person was tested and each person drew their hand back in pain, until a young man—a boy, really—stepped up. He didn't even have a chance to touch the needle. It shot forward and fastened itself to his hand, almost as if it was held there magnetically. Just the way it had done when it chose the first seamstress.

"The new khagan took the second seamstress from his village and treated him as his father had treated the previous seamstress. And that's how it was for many years. The needle would betray the identity of the new seamstress and then he or she would be manipulated for the rest of their lives. By many measures they lived well—materially, they lacked nothing—but they never had freedom. Never free will."

"And I'm to believe the khan is secretly searching for this?" Dashi asked, breaking her silence. "That he believes this story?" If it was true, then why hadn't the noble mentioned it? *Why would he*, her mind shot back. He'd barely told her anything, beyond what was necessary to make her enter the race.

"Believe what you want," Sevlin said, "but it's true. Your khan seeks to recreate the magic of the ancient Pureks. Like his father before him, he has eyes for Tyvalar's fertile valleys and trade agreements. He is already building his army. Once the needle is in his possession, he will search for a seamstress to wield it. From there, Queen Lyazzat believes he will forge a group of magical warriors to help him take over Tyvalar."

Dashi pursed her lips. That was supposedly how the later khagans expanded their empire. *Magic*. What was she to believe?

"Surely your sword skills could stand up against a little magic?" she asked, stalling.

His eyes glinted with amusement, but his mouth was serious. "I would do my duty, naturally."

His duty. That's what he said he fought for. That's why he was here.

"The consul must know about this too," Dashi said slowly.

"Yes," Sevlin said. He was waiting for her to answer his earlier question—why she and Negan hated each other—but Idree spoke up.

"Why wouldn't the khan just send his consul after the needle?" she asked. "Why hold a race at all?"

"A good question," Sevlin agreed.

Dashi glanced at her sister, who was flushed from his praise. "I think Negan has fallen into some trouble with the khan," she said, choosing her words carefully to avoid the appearance of knowing too much. "I saw him get a message from the khan before the start of the race. I don't know what it said, but when Negan returned he didn't look happy." *Of course, that could also be because he'd just discovered his brother's murderer was alive and free.* "That's the only reason I can think of why the khan would make him fight his way through dozens of other racers. It's a comeuppance for Negan, a trial set by the khan."

"At least he gets a purse for encouragement," Idree said.

The purse, Dashi thought regretfully. *What horrible luck. To have reward money offered on all sides and not be able to claim any of it.* Even if Sevlin was right, the story of the golden needle did nothing to change her predicament.

"So," Sevlin said, his eyes on Dashi. "I've answered your questions and I've offered you gold and a place in my country. Can we work together, not just to reach the temple, but to bring the artifact back to Tyvalar?"

She could hear Idree, who'd scooted closer during the discussion, catch her breath.

No, Dashi thought, *we* can't *work together. A safe haven and all the Tyvalaran gold in the world won't help me if I'm incinerated by pyrothrite. The only person who can save me from that is in Karak City.*

She looked at the fire. "I believe that my friends were killed on the orders of the consul. I have no reason to help him. Or the khan, for that matter." And yet she would still be bringing the golden needle to Karak City. She wondered if the noble actually planned to give the needle to the khan, or keep it for himself. Which would be worse?

"That explains why you hate Negan but not why he hates you." Sevlin's voice was level. He hadn't missed her half-answer.

"My friends were killed near one of the ruins." She spoke plainly. The unspooling memories inside her head allowed no room for embellishment. "Far to the west of where the ravine began. I followed the murderers back to Karak City. They were celebrating—drinking and whoring, not at all worried about the blood on their hands. I killed two of them and I—it wasn't hard." She didn't mention prison; she didn't think Sevlin would buy her line about the khan letting her out to compete in the race. Hopefully, Idree would take the hint and not mention it either.

"And Negan?"

"One of the men I killed was Negan's younger brother. I mean to kill Negan too."

She didn't know Sevlin well enough to read his expression. There was a twitch along his split cheek muscle which could have been dismay, and that might have been a flicker of surprise around his eyes, but otherwise he kept himself under tight control.

Idree was wide-eyed. It was the first time she'd heard Dashi recount the events of that night.

"I have no reason to help the khan," Dashi said again.

"So you'll aid Tyvalar in keeping the golden needle out of Karakal?" Sevlin pressed. Again, her omission hadn't escaped him.

She looked into his eyes, at the fire reflected in those light irises.

And lied.

"I will."

Chapter 19

Morning came hard, the way a headache follows a night of too much airag and mead. Dashi awoke feeling anxious, knowing there was something momentous that needed remembering. She had it a second later: the golden needle and the conversation with Sevlin the night before. Not only had she been confronted—again—with the fact that Altan had lied to her repeatedly, but she'd promised to help Sevlin take the needle to Tyvalar.

Sevlin was in a fine mood, humming under his breath while he saddled his horse. Idree was just as delusional, though her cheer was probably due to daydreams about moving to Tyvalar and growing up to marry Sevlin or something equally nonsensical. She'd had the final watch last night and had already assembled breakfast by the time Dashi awoke. She gave Dashi an extra half-portion with a smile.

The more Dashi noticed their moods, the worse her own became. She was farther behind Negan than ever. Even if they managed to get the needle from him, she would end up disappointing her sister and betraying Sevlin.

Suddenly, despite—or maybe *because* of—the fact that it could never happen, she wanted to go to Tyvalar. It would be nice to start over there, she thought: a miraculous salvation from the trouble that undoubtedly awaited her in Karak City. Tyvalar was known for its clean cities and bucolic countryside. There would be no ambitious nobles with pyrothrite belts, nor would anyone hunt her and Idree because of their association with spies. She wondered what Sevlin meant when he said they'd be comfortable there. Their own set of rooms, maybe. Idree could find another apprenticeship. Were there any ruins in Tyvalar that needed to be explored? Did they play goathead?

She stood up abruptly and hefted her saddle, carrying it over to Spit. *You're as bad as Idree*, she told herself savagely. *It doesn't matter what Tyvalar is like.* You *won't be going there. You'll be lucky if you survive*—she calculated the days left on the pyrothrite belt—*the next seventeen days.*

"You don't seem as excited about going to Tyvalar as your sister," Sevlin said, squatting nearby as he unhobbled one of his mounts.

"My sister has no concept of what it will take to get the needle there." She settled the saddle on Spit before looking at Sevlin. He was running his hands over his horse's forelegs, checking for swelling. His knuckles were scarred, as were the backs of his wrists. Nothing major, just small lines here and there, like the ones on his back. Being at the queen's beck and call must necessitate quite a bit of sword practice.

"What do you do when you're not off searching for magic in rival countries?" she asked.

"I'm a soldier."

"You must be fairly high ranking if you're known to the queen."

"Yet still unimportant enough to be dispensable." He moved to unhobble his second mount. "What do you do when *you're* not searching for magic?"

"Eat too much *boortsog*. Shoot things. Play goathead." That's what she'd done before prison, anyway.

"All admirable pursuits. Rather innocuous for someone who hunts down murderers, though."

Dashi stiffened.

He leaned his elbows on his horse's back, studying her. "Which did you enter the race for, the purse or Negan?"

"Both." *Neither.*

He kept watching her, not saying anything, and for some reason, she kept talking.

"My friends, they were outnumbered four to one. Never had a chance. And then, when I found the men, one of them laughed about it." She rubbed her thumb along the pommel of her saddle, thinking about Altan's hair, pointing toward the ground and swaying with each stride of his horse.

"Negan's brother?"

"No. The other man was the one who laughed. Negan's brother...I was trying to make him tell me who was behind the ambush, but he attacked me and..." She trailed off, not sure if she wanted to admit that she'd killed him by accident. It probably didn't matter. You were supposed to feel sorry after an accident happened. She didn't. "Then the second man burst into the room before I could leave."

He was silent, waiting for her to finish, so she shrugged. "When I was finished with him, I climbed out the window."

Let him think she'd escaped. Anything else would make him suspicious. She'd have to ask Idree not to mention the fact that she'd been in prison. That wasn't all, either. She'd have to tell Idree about the belt too, sooner rather than later.

Sevlin was absently scratching his scar, but his eyes were sharp on her. "Where were you when they were killed?"

"Scouting. Altan saw their fire and sent me ahead to see who it was. When I got back—" She shook her head. "The fire was a decoy. No one was even there. I should have been there to help them and I wasn't."

"One person wouldn't have made a difference with those odds."

"One person can make all the difference," she said tightly, "and now I'll always wonder."

He didn't answer and she turned her attention to tacking Spit.

"The men who gave me this scar also killed my mother," he said with no warning. She looked up. He was staring past her shoulder. "I was in the garden when we heard them. She told me to go to my sister. So I did. But I wonder—I don't regret saving my sister, but I used to wonder if there was a way I could have saved them both."

"You don't wonder anymore?"

"It gets pushed to the back of your mind over time."

"I don't know how far back I'll be able to push it. Not until I find the killers. Altan...maybe all he did was lie to me, but he was still like my brother. He saved my life."

"Idree told me how he looked out for you after your mother died."

Dashi shook her head. "No, I mean he actually saved our lives. There was a plague in Karakal when we were little. That's what took our father and then, after we'd moved to Karak City, our mother caught it too. Maybe she would have gotten better, I don't know. One day a mob marched through the dirt circle, setting the homes of plague victims on fire. Altan was our neighbor. He got us out just before the roof caved."

The right side of Sevlin's mouth twitched. She could see that he'd read between the lines—her mother hadn't made it out—but she appreciated the way he didn't overreact. There were no pitying looks, no murmurs of sympathy to strangle her. It made it easier to get out what had happened. Maybe that's why she'd kept talking this whole time.

"Maybe Altan had a real family back in Tyvalar," she said. "I have no idea. But he was mine, blood or not."

"We could find out. I don't know if you'd want to meet them, but if you did, it could be arranged."

Dashi looked at him. *Really* looked. His expression was serious and measured, and she caught no hint of pity. But something must be there—an empathy born of mutual tragedy, perhaps—to make him offer to find Altan's family. She took a deep breath. Did she *want* to do that? Would she say something to them or would her tongue rebel, leaving her to watch silently from afar, the way she'd watched Idree before the race?

It took a moment for reality to catch her. It didn't matter if Altan was related to the queen herself, she wouldn't be meeting his family and she wouldn't be going to Tyvalar.

"How's your back?" she asked abruptly.

His eyebrows rose. "Worried about me, now that I'm the one who'll make sure you get a reward?" The right side of his mouth turned up and she knew he meant it as a joke.

"Nothing more, nothing less," Dashi said lightly as she reached under Spit's belly and grabbed the girth.

"Well, don't be. Your sister checked first thing this morning. Said it looks fine."

I'll bet she did. When had Idree become so crazy about the opposite sex? And how was Dashi going to tell her they wouldn't be going to Tyvalar?

"Good," Dashi said. She swung onto Spit's back, ignoring both her apprehension and Idree, who'd stopped braiding flowers into her hair to call out another question about Tyvalar.

Dawn was breaking. They had a lot of ground to cover.

There were fresh tracks—both ant and rat—nearby, though Dashi had noticed nothing during her watch. Neither had Idree or Sevlin. It was unnerving, to think of the beasts coming so close in the night without being noticed.

"Why didn't they attack?" Idree asked.

Dashi shook her head, but it was a gesture of confusion, not disagreement. "Maybe it was the fire. Maybe they're just biding their time. Either way, we need to picket the horses closer. Make sure the fire is going all night." She looked at Idree. "No gathering wood after dark."

Idree nodded, for once not arguing.

"Sooner or later the fire will attract other unwanted attention," Sevlin said. "Right now the ravine hides the light, but when we get to the valley it'll be a beacon for trouble."

Dashi nodded unhappily and started forward. "We'll have to decide which we fear most: giant ants and rats or Negan."

Not long after the midday meal, Dashi saw the mist again. It glided toward them, traveling in tendrils instead of a solid bank, braiding itself through the trees as it went. It shone bright white, almost sunlit, but when Dashi glanced at the sky, it was overcast. The hair on her arms and neck tingled. *Breath of the ancestors*, she thought. A warning, perhaps, but of what?

"Dashi?" It was Idree.

Her sister looked puzzled. Sevlin leaned to one side, trying to see past Idree. His eyebrows rose in a question when he caught Dashi's gaze.

Didn't they notice the strange mist? The unnatural way it moved? It was sliding down the banks of the ravine now, spilling over the rim like floodwater.

"This way," Dashi said, pushing her horse a little faster without taking her eyes off the mist to their right. *You're running from fog*, her mind taunted. *The breeze is making it move, nothing more. Altan would tell you to stop being a superstitious fool and focus on reality.*

Altan is dead, she snapped back, *and why would I listen to him anyway? He lied about everything.*

She saw with dismay that the mist was creeping down the entire length of the ravine. They were going to have to go through it.

Just fog. Just fog. Spit snorted as they approached the gleaming white air but didn't shy away. Behind her, the chestnut whinnied nervously.

The tendrils reached Dashi, one after another, sliding over her skin like waves of clammy hands. She shook herself, trying to detach the mist, but if anything, she felt more tangled in the stuff. *That's impossible. How can you become tangled in vapor?*

In only a few moments the mist had obscured her view, surrounding her all at once. It was so bright that her eyes hurt and she waved one arm in an attempt to fan the moist air aside. The ravine walls and the trees along the rim, towering though they were, were barely visible now. She turned in her saddle, but Idree and Sevlin were out of sight as well. Even her extra mounts were only vague shadows trailing behind her.

"Idree?" she called, slowing Spit. Her voice bounced back in her face like she was in a small room instead of outdoors.

No answer.

"Idree? Sevlin?" She yelled again, louder this time.

Her heart thudded in her chest and she fought to keep it under control. *They're still behind you. Where else would they be? The fog is just doing strange things to the sound of your voice, that's all. They probably couldn't hear you.*

She turned forward in time to see a figure approaching through the pearly haze. Dashi pulled Spit's head hard to avoid a collision, but she needn't have worried: the figure evaporated before her eyes, becoming another swirl in the vapor. She blinked rapidly, her breath feeling a little choked. Her imagination must be playing tricks on her.

"Idree? Sevlin? Are you there?"

The voice that answered didn't belong to her sister or Sevlin. It was like the wind, except it didn't come from one direction but flew at her from all sides. "Dasssshhhi. Dasssshhhiii."

She'd nocked an arrow before the voice finished speaking. "Who's there?"

Spit had come to a stop. His head drooped and his sides filled with deep, restful breaths. Dashi kicked him. He jerked, his sleep disturbed, but didn't move.

"Lazy nag," she muttered. If only she could see where to aim. Or at least move to one side of the ravine, where she could put something solid at her back. She couldn't stand the feeling of the cold mist on all sides, waiting to attack.

No. Fog doesn't attack. A *person* had spoken her name, not vapor.

She kicked Spit again, but he didn't react. *Fine.* If he wanted to sleep in the middle of the ravine, she'd let him.

Dashi started to dismount just as another figure appeared. She watched, waiting for him to turn out to be nothing more than her imagination, but he stayed solid, right up to the point where he touched Spit's nose with an outstretched hand.

The man's head was bowed and when he looked up Dashi felt the air solidify, lodging like clay in her throat. She stared at him, while her voice unfolded, slowly stretching its wings.

"Father?" she croaked. Her eyes bounced over him, memorizing the hard angles of his face, the wide cheekbones, the full lips. *Impossible.* Impossible for him to be moving, breathing, *being*. She'd sat the vigil for his emaciated, plague-ridden body. Seen the flames leaping over his funeral pyre. Yet now his face was healthy. *Alive.*

Her father grinned, an expression that simultaneously made him look less harsh and more feral. "You were always one to court trouble. It doesn't surprise me to find you here."

He let go of Spit's muzzle and began to move off, smoothly, as if the floor of the ravine was flat and free of impediments, which Dashi knew was not the case.

"Father? Wait! *Father*!" She choked on the words she hadn't said in so long. It had been years since she'd cried for him. Years during which she'd said goodbye to the steppe and his Mori kin and started over in a strange, loud city...and then started over again when her mother died. Dashi had been left clinging to the new family she'd created with such a vengeance that she couldn't afford to look back at the family that had come before.

She'd forgotten how strong and daring her father looked. She'd forgotten how much she missed him.

Her father kept walking. Well, not walking, exactly. Dashi's gaze dropped to where his feet should be. Mist swirled below his knees.

"It's good to see you, Dashi."

Dashi whirled around. Her mother stood on Spit's other side, far enough away that the mist made her features soft and gauzy, but Dashi could see that her face was whole once more, not blackened by fire.

"Mother...I...where—"

Another figure appeared behind her mother: an older woman who kept walking, her only acknowledgment a smile in Dashi's direction. It looked like her Mori grandmother, but that couldn't be. She'd been dead for—*they're* all *dead*, Dashi corrected herself.

None of this was real. She knew that, but her hand stretched out to compel her mother to stay. Her mother shook her head sadly and turned away, disappearing into the bright white just like her father.

More figures passed, appearing suddenly out of the incandescence, solidifying from vague silhouettes into definable *people* with different clothes and hairstyles and mannerisms. She recognized some of them—a late uncle here, a dead cousin there—but as more came, they grew less familiar. Some stopped next to her, though none but her father came close enough to touch. Others walked past without a glance, ignoring her completely. None of them seemed malicious, but Dashi was acutely aware of the strangeness of the sight and it filled her with unease. It was unnatural to be standing among the dead. True, every house in Karak City had a shrine to the ancestors, but you weren't supposed to *see* them.

The flow of figures began to slacken, a deluge wearing itself thin. Dashi swayed in the saddle, partly from relief and partly from fear and partly because her head felt disconnected from her body. Her thoughts were like fish in a stream, taunting her with flashes of silver but scattering before they could be caught.

She tried to kick Spit again—if he would just *move*, they would be free of the mist—but she lost her balance instead. She grasped the pommel with both hands, listing precariously to the right. She was dizzy. Maybe she should get down. Less distance to fall. She swung a leg clumsily over the saddle and poured herself to the ground, clinging to Spit's side like he was the only real thing left in the world. *He might be*, she thought dazedly. The mist grew steadily brighter until she was squinting from behind the cover of one hand. *Move forward,* she told herself. *Get out of the mist.* But she stayed rooted at Spit's side.

Abruptly, the light dimmed and when she pulled her hand away there was another figure in front of her: a woman, compact but powerfully built, her shining black hair coiled around her head in a coronet of braids. She wore a headdress too, a mass of golden feathers and beads which overlay her hair and forehead and cascaded onto her shoulders. Her deel was made from a material Dashi had never seen, an ornate fabric of purple and blue and gold that shimmered like metal. A sword was belted at her waist.

Dashi leaned her head back, trying to take in the woman's appearance. The ground was hard against her knees, but at least it was solid. Unlike her body, which had become jellied with no warning whatsoever. No, that wasn't right. Why were her knees on the ground? When had she fallen?

The woman was staring down at Dashi with a severe expression. She looked, if not disdainful, then like she was accustomed to getting her own way and Dashi was guilty of disappointing her.

"I am not sure you have what it takes," she said in a husky voice. "*I* was not knocked to my knees when I first encountered magic."

Dashi reached back blindly. The stirrup knocked against her hand and she grabbed it, pulling herself into a crouch and from there into a standing position. *There*. Now she didn't have to look up at the woman.

"What do you want?" Dashi asked irritably. "Go float away like the others."

"No."

The mist grew brighter for a second, forcing Dashi to shut her eyes again. When she reopened them, the woman was glaring at her. "The others are nothing. They cannot swim against the stream of the spiritworld; they can only float in it. *I* am a wielder, and what is the spiritworld but another kind of magic?"

Dashi's chin hit her chest and her eyelids fluttered downward. *No, stay awake. Get out of the mist. Things will be normal out of the mist.* She raised her head and took a step forward, then another, leaning heavily against Spit.

"You're not real," she muttered. "Leave me alone." *Good, that's it. One step at a time.* She'd reached Spit's head now. She'd have to walk the rest of the way on her own.

A hand closed around Dashi's throat and the ground disappeared beneath her feet. She was lifted backward, legs kicking feebly, until her shoulder blades slammed into Spit's side. He didn't even stir, the worthless beast.

"I am as real as you are," the woman said, "and the more you resist, the longer this will take."

Her face was only inches away. Dashi could see each eyelash that framed her glittering black eyes, had time to notice the light spattering of freckles over her prominent nose.

"The spiritworld is hard on the living. The more time they spend in its proximity, the looser their grip on sanity becomes. Your companion cannot last forever. Magic does not flow in his veins."

Dashi clawed at the hand around her throat. She tried to say Sevlin's name, to ask where the woman had put him, but no sounds emerged. The woman released her suddenly and Dashi sagged against Spit, her back scraping against the saddle before she caught herself.

"What do you want?" she gasped.

"Do you know who I am?" the woman countered.

Dashi's chin jutted out. "Why would I?"

"My given name was Nuray."

"*Khagan* Nuray?"

The woman neither confirmed nor denied the title, only stood there, silently watching. Dashi still felt the urge to leave the mist—somehow she was sure that would eliminate the visions and return her to a normal state of mind—but how to do that with this woman standing menacingly in front of her? In any case, Dashi was growing less certain that this was all merely a bubble from her subconscious. The hand around her throat had felt solid enough.

"I've seen portraits of you," Dashi protested. "Paintings, tapestries...in the ruins." Her eyelids felt like they'd been cast in iron. "You look...different in them."

"More docile, you mean," the woman said in a dry voice.

"I...don't know," Dashi lied, watching the woman warily. *Yes,* she wanted to say, *a thousand times more docile,* but she could tell from the way that Nuray had spat the word 'docile' that it was an insult.

"You said you were a wielder," Dashi said in a thick voice. "You mean...the golden needle? But...you were the khagan..." The words were difficult to keep track of. Had she said them aloud, or only thought them?

"I was unlucky enough to be chosen as the seamstress. I *made* myself the khagan."

"Nuray...the Wise..." Dashi's head slumped forward again. "Nuray...the..."

She'd meant it as a compliment, a peace offering of sorts, in the hopes that Nuray would step aside and let her leave. Those *were* her titles, after all. But Nuray stabbed two fingers between Dashi's eyebrows, pushing her head back against Spit until their eyes met.

"Nuray the Generous," she finished, her expression bitter. "Nuray the Bountiful, the Good, the Harmonious. All very beautiful, very *docile* names. But before I was Nuray the Generous, I was Nuray the Fierce and Nuray the Bloody. History has forgotten that."

"Why?"

"It was easier for people to accept a woman who seized power out of noble impulse—because of her wisdom and love of her people—instead of revenge. People were uncomfortable with that, even after my death. Grasping, they called me. A bitch with no love for anyone but herself. Historians and scribes like a good story as much as the next person, maybe more so, and my advisors worried about the continual challenges to my authority. So they made me more noble, more *docile.* My predecessor is called 'the Bold' and his father was called 'the Relentless.' But what did they do? Start the grand temple that *I* finished? I *tripled* the size of our territory and I am called 'bountiful,' as if the land sprang from my kitchen garden and added *itself* to the empire." Her eyes were like twin drills, boring into Dashi. She poked Dashi's forehead again, hard, for emphasis. "Deception is easy," she said in her gravelly voice. "It is the truth that can be difficult to swallow."

Dashi blinked stupidly. Were they discussing titles right now?

But Nuray was only getting started. "Before me, the seamstresses were glorified slaves. A seamstress stitched magic day in, and day out, adding to the ranks of elite warriors when she succeeded, and to the ranks of the dead when she didn't. She had nothing of her own. She ate and drank and slept in luxury but anything she enjoyed, anyone she loved, was held apart, used as leverage if she ever stepped against the khagan."

Dimly, Dashi remembered a similar conversation, but it felt like a lifetime ago.

"Until *me*," Nuray said. "Until *I* strode into the khagan's chambers and started warming his bed." She made a noise that might have been a laugh, had there been any humor in it. "It was not an enviable task, I can tell you, but I made him believe it was. And then, when I was ready, after I had made promises and threats and accrued allies, I cut his throat and let him bleed out in his own sheets. I became khagan the same day, the only khagan to also wield the golden needle. The first seamstress not to be manipulated for her affinity with the land's magic."

Despite the miasma that was slowly overtaking her brain, Dashi's eyes widened. All she'd ever heard about Nuray was what a magnanimous ruler she'd been, how she'd allowed conquered people to keep their lands and expanded legal rights. Harvests had doubled. Discord evaporated.

"But...the harvest platter..."

Nuray snorted. "Do you know what my official seal was? A needle crossed with a sword! A *sword*, not a scale or a platter." She shook her head. "I rooted out my enemies and squashed the rebels who thought they could do better. The countries on our western and southern borders were weak, so I conquered them, commanding the magical warriors *I* had made." She paused, seeming to assess how closely Dashi was paying attention. "They call me generous because I met with my subjects, wise because I adjudicated their grievances. Because I grew an empire, I'm called Nuray the Bountiful. But my land was not peaceful when I became khagan, nor was it an empire. *I made it one.* Through generosity and wisdom, yes, sometimes. But also through vengeance and blood. I worked both sets of qualities in tandem."

"I'm sure you...did...what...you had to," Dashi ground out, striving for something diplomatic. Her body was starting to ache. Little pinpricks of pain, like her blood was pooling instead of circulating.

Nuray frowned and pushed Dashi's head, which had begun slouching, upright again. "Are you thick or are you confounding my point on purpose?" When Dashi didn't answer, she went on. "There is a time for power, for vengeance and aggression and ferocity. Like me, you have grasped that easily enough. But there is also a time for generosity and selflessness, for using your victories to protect the weak and seeing that they thrive. It took me a long time to see that, but when I finally did, *that* is what secured my goals for the realm: selflessness *and* ruthlessness, together. You prize your ability to fight for yourself, but you should cultivate giving as well. It is only with both that you can stave off destruction."

"That's...it?" Dashi blurted. "You came all the way...from the spiritworld...to tell me...to be more generous?"

"The spiritworld is not the distant journey you seem to think it is," Nuray said dryly, "and one would think the manner of delivery would elevate the advice in your esteem. However, you are free to take it or cast it aside. It is only a word of guidance. The living do as they will while the dead can only watch. But know this," she said, her hand rising to point at Dashi's waist. Mist billowed outward from the movement, clinging like frost to the front of Dashi's deel. "There is more at stake in this race than your life. The veins of magic are resurfacing and they will either bring with them great good or great pain. Perhaps you will succeed, I do not know, but the key lies with the seamstress." She leaned closer, close enough that Dashi should have felt breath on her face, had there been any. "The seamstress must be protected."

She turned and started gliding away from Dashi, her strides as smooth and unreal as Dashi's father's had been.

"Remember," the khagan said, her voice floating back to Dashi before she was consumed by the white mist, "be ruthless and selfless in equal measure. One without the other is a pathway for evil."

Dashi came to, flat on her back in the dark. She noticed the gravel first. It pushed through her deel, making dents in her spine and hips. She rolled to her side with a groan. Only then did she realize it wasn't dark. Her arm had been flung over her face, the crook of her elbow tenting her eyes.

She pushed herself up, blinking in confusion. She was still in the ravine. Sevlin and Idree lay a short distance behind her. Their horses stood placidly, eyes closed.

Dreaming. The creeping mist. Images of people who somehow felt familiar. Dashi pressed the heels of her hands to her eyes. What had happened? Why was she on the ground? Her body felt stiff and cold, but not bruised, the way it would if she'd fallen from Spit's back. What was the alternative though, that she'd dismounted to take a nap in the middle of the ravine?

Her deel was twisted around her. She unwound the sash distractedly as she stood up, looking around for some signpost to tell her what had occurred. But this was the taiga: signposts, if there had ever been any, had vanished with the Pureks.

Her sash had come unwound and, when her deel flapped open, the sudden influx of cool air refocused her. She looked down at the pyrothrite belt.

Everything else fell away—the ravine, the mist, her confusion, all of it. She stared at the belt, first in bewilderment, then in growing horror. *No. No, that can't be right.* It was the tenth day of the race. Only twelve pyrothrite nodules should have fallen by now.

Twelve, not *nineteen*.

Chapter 20

PYROTHRITE REMAINING: 10

Dashi spun around. Had *days* passed while she lay in the ravine? No, that was impossible. There were the tracks they'd made, still crisp. There was Idree, the flowers in her hair rumpled, but unwilted. Dashi's relief withered almost as quickly as it had bloomed. Even if she hadn't slept for days, the belt *thought* she had.

She'd been worried about the pyrothrite before, true, but she'd been able to reassure herself. By her reckoning, there was a better than even chance of returning to Karak City, artifact in hand, with enough time to have the belt removed. But now, the pyrothrite loomed before her, refusing to be put off.

Why were seven more nodules of pyrothrite crouched at the bottom of the disk? She looked at the belt expectantly, but it didn't answer.

Hastily rewrapping her deel, Dashi ran to Idree, shoving her sister awake.

"What—*ow!* Dashi? What'd you do that for?" Idree sounded as confused as Dashi, but she woke immediately.

Dashi sprinted to Sevlin's prone form without stopping to explain. His face looked paler than normal. Sweat had turned his hair stiff.

"Sevlin!" When he didn't respond, she shook his shoulder.

He groaned and rolled over. She kept shoving.

"Get off me," he growled. His words were slurred with sleep, no longer carefully pronounced.

"Wake up! We have to go!"

"I just—what?" He sat up abruptly, bringing his face close to hers without seeing her. His eyes swept the ravine over her shoulder, taking in the horses and Idree, as she stifled a yawn. "What happened?" he asked, finally fastening on Dashi's face.

"I'm not sure, but we need to get moving." She sounded like Idree, all shrill with emotion, but she couldn't keep the panic out of her voice. "We have to go," she said again.

"I had the strangest dreams," Idree said, rubbing her eyes. "I dreamed of our parents. I don't even remember them, but I suddenly could see them so clearly."

Sevlin looked perplexed. "I don't remember anything. What happened?" His skin was so pale it nearly matched his eyes.

"As soon we started riding through that fog, I felt funny," Idree said.

Sevlin's forehead was lined in thought. He glanced at Dashi. "Do you think...?"

"I don't know," Dashi said impatiently.

"What?" Idree asked.

"Magic," Sevlin said, his voice still groggy. He seemed to be taking longer to get over the mist than Idree and Dashi.

"But the magic veins were," Idree waved a hand downward, "sucked back into the earth."

White mist. Nuray's husky voice. *The veins of magic are resurfacing.* Dashi blinked. *What is the spiritworld but another kind of magic*? If the mist was magic, was that what had affected the pyrothrite? Would the nodules continue to drop too quickly, or would they resume their normal pace now that she was away from the mist?

The thought slammed into Dashi. It didn't matter what the mist was or what she'd seen in her dreams. *She'd* lost seven days, even if no one else had.

"We need to go," Dashi said. She strode toward Spit without waiting for an answer. When she looked back, Sevlin was still sitting, a hand over his ashen face. She hoped he could keep up.

Their pace was blistering for the rest of the day and Dashi pushed them until nightfall. Idree muttered a few complaints and for the first few hours Sevlin looked so sickly she thought he might topple out of his saddle, but otherwise the day was a blur of green-clad treetops and serpentining hoofprints which marked where the other racers had gone before them. The following day was the same, and dusk found them with barely enough energy to eat. They'd seen no more ant or rat tracks since the mist. Perhaps the animals were afraid of the stuff, Dashi thought. That would explain why nothing had mauled them while they lay in the ravine dreaming.

"We must be getting close to the river valley where we turn east," Sevlin said, eying the sides of the ravine, which had transformed in the last two days. It was rockier now and stone outcroppings sprouted intermittently, abandoned by the water that had carved them. So far none of the formations looked like a man's hand, however.

Dashi could only nod. No matter how close they were to the river valley, it wasn't close enough.

Terrified that the belt was damaged somehow and that the pyrothrite would continue its free fall, she'd snuck off to look at it a second time. The good news was that the pyrothrite seemed to have resumed its steady descent. The bad news was there were still nineteen nodules at the bottom of the disk. That meant only ten days until it became explosive. If she could get to the temple in two days, that would leave one day to navigate it and seize the needle from the other racers, including Sevlin. Then seven days for the return trip—*no, that wouldn't work*. She closed her eyes briefly, willing the numbers to work in her favor. Her mind had already raced to the temple and back to Karak City at least a dozen times, playing with the timeline, trying to anticipate problems, worrying through her plan to snatch the needle from Sevlin. She leaned against the chestnut for a long moment, trying to collect the energy to move.

"We haven't seen any rats," Sevlin said, echoing her earlier thoughts. "Maybe they're not as bold as you thought."

"They are," Dashi said, stifling a yawn. She was so tired she could barely think. Sleep. That's what she needed. They'd have to leave before dawn—

"I know what you said before, about one attacking during the snowstorm, but maybe it was wolves and their tracks overlapped."

"It wasn't."

"You don't think it's possible you missed something?"

"No."

"What's not possible?" Idree asked.

"That Dashi is wrong," Sevlin said. Idree laughed. "I'm not saying a giant rat *couldn't* hunt humans," he said to Dashi, "but I don't know if I'd jump to that conclusion either."

"I didn't jump to conclusions," Dashi snapped. "I saw a rat and then I saw its tracks leading through the bloody snow. There were no other prints. I'm not wrong."

Idree gave Sevlin a conspiratorial shrug. Dashi clenched her jaw and set to work unsaddling the chestnut.

Suddenly, one of Sevlin's horses reared, neighing shrilly. They'd camped in a crevice along the side of the ravine. Something was moving on the other side, lifting its head and sniffing the air with a fleshy, pink-brown snout. Through the spiky branches, a dark, liquid eye blinked. *Not branches. Quills.*

The porcupine was as big as a ram, its quills easily the length of Dashi's forearm. It stood closest to Idree, only a half dozen strides at most, its nose twitching in a nearsighted way. Dashi's hand automatically reached for her bow, only to realize she'd set it on the other side of the stream, next to her saddle. The porcupine went rigid, its quills drifting upward until they were perpendicular to its body.

Idree had also gone rigid. Moving slowly, Dashi stuffed her reins into Idree's motionless hand and drew her sword.

"Go!" Dashi shouted at it. "Get out of here!" When the porcupine only sniffed again, she added curses and threats to her rant, waving the sword wildly.

The porcupine twitched its nose one last time and lumbered through the brush and out into the main ravine.

Beside her, Sevlin lowered his crossbow, releasing his breath as he did so. "I think what finally convinced it," he said, "was when you threatened to pickle its snout."

Dashi cracked a smile but didn't look away from the direction the animal had gone. "That usually does the trick."

"They're herbivores. At least, I think they are when they're of normal size."

Herbivore or not, the thing's quills were big enough to do serious damage, depending on where they became lodged.

"Do you think everything is extra large here?" Idree whispered.

"Not everything," Dashi said. "We've seen squirrels and chipmunks and birds that were all normal-sized. Insects, too."

"I think," Sevlin said slowly, "that only the animals that were here when the cataclysm occurred became giants."

Dashi glanced at him. "Why do you say that?"

"You're better acquainted with the Purek's records than most. Have you ever seen any mention of giant animals?"

She shook her head.

"The ancient Pureks recorded everything that wasn't a state or military secret. If they didn't mention any giant animals, then I don't think they were present before the cataclysm. And what have we seen? Ants, a porcupine, rats—or evidence of rats." He ticked them off on his fingers. "We haven't seen anything that was big to begin with. No deer or wolves or bears. All the giant animals are things that would normally be small."

"Ancestors be thanked," Idree said gravely. "Can you imagine facing a giant wolf or bear?"

Dashi resisted the urge to point out that maybe there *were* giant wolves and bears and they just didn't know it yet.

"No," Sevlin said, just as seriously, "but I don't think we have to worry about that. I think when the cataclysm occurred, the larger animals fared the same as the humans: they either fled or died. The smaller animals—insects, rodents and the like—would've been too slow to escape, but maybe some of them still managed to survive."

"And what, got turned into giants?" Dashi asked. "There's no record of that ever happening with the magic."

Sevlin shrugged. "The cataclysm itself was unusual. Maybe it had unusual results as well. The veins of magic caused dramatic changes in humans. That was the point of the golden needle, to manage those changes in a way that could be useful. Without the needle, who knows how the magic would affect living things."

Dashi drummed her fingers along her thigh, not caring how the animals had gotten to their present size as long as they left her alone long enough to collect the needle. Her eyes snagged on Idree's saddle, taking in its proximity for the first time. Idree's small bow and quiver leaned against it, both well within her sister's reach. When the porcupine came Idree hadn't even raised them to defend herself.

"We need to collect wood," Dashi said, ending the discussion.

"You two can carry more than I can," Idree said, shooting a nervous glance at the shrubs that grew in the crevice. "I'll hobble and stake the horses if you want."

Dashi and Sevlin handed over their reins, then walked deeper into the crevice to collect dead wood. Dashi grabbed dry pieces of wood with one hand, loading them into the crook of her other arm. A few steps away, Sevlin was doing the same, but his face was angled away from her so that only the side of his head was visible. His scar bisected his ear lobe, carving a wedge-shaped piece of meat from the circle of his ear.

He was fifteen, she thought and tried to picture herself at that age, compared to how she was now.

"How old are you?" she asked, realizing she didn't know.

Still crouched down, Sevlin turned his head, studying her. "Twenty-four," he said. "Idree asked me that the first day I rode with you. I assumed she would have told you."

Dashi shrugged and reached for another branch. "Maybe she didn't think it was important."

"But you do?"

She glanced at his scar, gesturing at her own cheek. "Only because I wondered how long it had been."

"Nine years. A long time," he said, gazing unseeing at the leaf litter in front of him, "but sometimes not long at all."

"I know."

He glanced up, startled.

"My mother died nine years ago." She relinquished the branch she was holding, nestling it with the others balanced across her arm. Her mother's face, so recently glimpsed in the mist, burned cleanly in her mind for once, without the haze of time and distance. "Late summer," she said softly, to herself.

Sevlin stood up and, without knowing why she did it, Dashi copied him, facing him over an armful of firewood.

"Dashi," he said, "I think you—"

Something crashed in the underbrush and Idree appeared, panting slightly. "Did you hear anything?" she asked. "I thought I heard...a rat, maybe?"

Dashi shifted her load of wood and cocked her head, listening. "I don't hear anything. I'm sure the horses would be skittish if there was something close by. If you're finished hobbling them, can you start on the food?"

Idree nodded, but stayed where she was, her eyes darting at the wilderness around them.

"We're coming too," Sevlin said after a moment, taking pity on her. "We have enough wood for now."

Dashi could feel Sevlin's eyes on her as the three of them emerged from the crevice, but she kept her gaze—and her thoughts—facing forward. Impromptu moments of intimacy were not something she could afford.

She remained silent as they ate, too preoccupied with her problems to do anything but chew. The small blaze radiated warmth and light, masking the dark ravine, as Idree chattered about Tyvalar and her apprenticeship in Karak City.

"I think I could help you find something at another baker," Sevlin said. "Although our food is a little different than yours. No airag or...what is that tea and butter drink you have?"

"Suutei tsai," Idree said, dimpling.

He wrinkled his nose. "None of that either."

"Maybe I could start a little stand selling Karak food."

The conversation grated on Dashi. There would be no stand of Karak food, and no apprenticeship in Tyvalar. She longed to be up and pacing, except that would look strange right now. Still seated, she ground the heel of her boot against the rocks instead.

Idree's face grew serious. "I'd like to try something else. If it's not too much trouble, I mean." She glanced at Dashi and then back at Sevlin. "Perhaps boot-making? I'd like an apprenticeship in that."

He shrugged one shoulder. "I don't see why not. I'm no expert on the trade, but Tyvalarans need boots just as much as they need baked goods and Karak butter tea."

"I'm sure styles are a little different there, but I've repaired several pairs for Auntie Nima—she said I was good enough to charge money. I don't know how to do the actual design part, but I've always wanted—"

"Why didn't you ever say anything about a different apprenticeship?" Dashi interjected. "Altan could have found something for you."

"Auntie Nima was very kind to me. I didn't want to leave her." Idree looked at her hands and then at Dashi, her expression suddenly fierce. "And *Altan* was always busy."

Dashi heard the words left unsaid. *You were busy too.* "He wasn't too busy to make sure you were settled," she said, trying not to sound defensive. She'd always thought Altan had tried very hard to make sure Idree was taken care of.

"Settled isn't the same as happy," Idree said so quietly that Dashi almost missed it.

"Well," Sevlin said into the silence, "I'm sure we can find something suitable in Tyvalar. The final say will be up to you, of course," he said to Idree.

Dashi shoved her heel harder into the ground.

"The horses," Sevlin said abruptly.

Dashi had been so tired, her limited attention fixed on the conversation in front of her, that she'd missed the subtle signs of unrest among the animals. Now, they were obvious: shifting hooves, nervous snorts, raised heads and pricked ears. Idree's horse reared, an action that was repeated immediately by Dashi's packhorse. With the sound of a cracking whip, the lead rope broke and the packhorse took off, running headlong through the shadows of the ravine, its packs slapping rhythmically.

Sevlin leaped to his feet, grabbing a flaming branch from the fire and holding it aloft. Dashi followed, her bow ready. Rocks shifted as something fled their approach. They were silent for several long moments, squinting into the darkness and trying to hear past the horses' snorting.

"I think the fire scared it away," Sevlin said finally. "Whatever it was."

"The packhorse," Dashi turned to Idree, "why wasn't it hobbled? And why were its packs still on?" She should have noticed, should have checked over Idree's work, but she'd been so tired.

"I...I heard a sound, the one I asked you about. I was about to fix the hobbles, but I...was scared and I wanted to make sure it wasn't a rat." Idree hung her head. "I guess I forgot to go back and do it."

"We *needed* those provisions, Idree!" Dashi put a hand on her forehead and squeezed. Without any provisions, how would she be able to get back to Karak City fast enough? She already had to find a way to shorten the return trip; she wouldn't have time to hunt.

"I meant to do it," Idree said again. "I'm sorry."

"That won't bring our food back."

"I said I was sorry!" Idree's voice rose a little. "You don't have to be mean."

"You're right. I'm out of line," Dashi said, her voice heavy with sarcasm. "Usually I'm pleased as a hog in a wallow when the person I'm depending on lets the packhorse run off into the taiga."

"You weren't *depending* on me! You didn't even want me to *come*!"

"Of *course* I didn't want you to come! It's a dangerous race, not a parade, and no place for someone who's afraid of noises."

"That's got nothing to do with it. You've never wanted me to come anywhere." Idree was nearly shouting now. Tears stood out in her eyes, catching the light from the flames. "Not on your trips with Altan, not to ride on the steppe, not even on a trip to the market. That's what I was talking about earlier. Too *busy*. You, Altan, Zayaa. I barely even *met* Baris. None of you wanted me around. *That's* why I got sent to Auntie Nima's, not because Altan wanted me to learn a trade. Because he wanted me out of the way! Because he already had you and I was only a tagalong!"

How had an argument about their rapidly disappearing provisions morphed into something about their childhood, Dashi wondered. "That's not true!" she said. "It wasn't—you were young and Altan spent a lot of time out of the city. He did a lot for us that he didn't have to do."

"All he did for me was take away my sister."

"He didn't take me away," Dashi said, glancing in Sevlin's direction. Why did Idree have to dredge this up in front of him? "Our trips from Karak City never lasted more than—"

"*Trips* aren't what I'm talking about, Dashi. After you got involved with Altan, you had no time for me. Suddenly I was the kid you rolled your eyes at, the one who was always in the way. I was young, but I still remember that."

"*Involved with?* Our parents were *dead*, Idree. Altan was the only person looking out for us. You make it sound like he was this sinister influence—"

"Wasn't he? You started stealing from graves—"

"They're not graves, they're ruins—"

"People died there! I don't care what you call it, that's what it is!" She paused just long enough to draw a breath. "After Altan, everything changed."

"If it's so abhorrent, then why are you angry you didn't get to come?"

"I just *said* why! You weren't listening!"

"I did listen! You were blaming everything on Altan, when he's the only reason we didn't burn to death or end up living in the cesspits like the other plague orphans. He took care of us—fed us, housed us. We were only his neighbor's brats; he could easily have looked the other way. Honestly, Idree, don't you realize how *lucky* we were? Things might not have gone perfectly for you, but without Altan we might not be here at all."

Idree jutted her chin out aggressively. "You're right: without Altan, we'd be home in Karak City, not in the taiga. He's the only reason you came. Because even *dead* you'd rather do something for him than for me."

Dashi crossed her arms, so angry now that she didn't care what Sevlin thought. "You know it's not that simple. You can't blame Altan—"

"You're right. I blame you. *You're* my sister and *you* let us get separated. *You* killed those men. I begged you not to go and you went anyway. You chose Altan—avenging someone who was already dead—over staying with me. I needed you, Dashi, and you ran straight—"

Dashi interrupted before Idree could mention prison. "Needed me? I didn't leave you on the street! You had Auntie Nima! "

"Auntie Nima was *paid* to take care of me. Just like you wanted to pay the Mori. I'm your *family*! And you chose—"

"What was I supposed to do? Stop because I was afraid? Let them get away with it?"

"*Yes!*" Idree stamped her foot. "Let them get away with it! No matter what you do, Altan, Zayaa and Baris aren't coming back."

"You're glad they're dead," Dashi said, digging her fists into her thighs.

Idree smiled humorlessly. "I would be if it changed things. But you're the same as you always were. We could've left Karak City together.

Instead, you entered this stupid race just for another chance to avenge them. You didn't even tell me! Why does it matter how they died or why? It's not like they were innocent bystanders—*you're* the one who said they were all spies! Whatever the risks were, they knew them, and they didn't even warn you! What else do you need to know?"

Dashi gritted her teeth. She'd thought about that herself and, like a rotten tooth, it was painful every time it was prodded. Even more so when Idree was the one doing the prodding.

"You wouldn't understand," Dashi said. She couldn't tell Idree about the belt. Not with Sevlin standing there. She wondered if it would make a difference, or if her sister would see her as the villain regardless of the circumstances.

"That's always your answer," Idree spat. "I'm too young. I wouldn't understand." She threw up her hands. "I don't know why I came chasing after you. I should've just *gone,* left Karak City for somewhere else. You probably wouldn't have even noticed." Her parting shot complete, she stomped off, leaving Dashi next to Sevlin and the remaining horses.

"I can't believe her," Dashi muttered. "First, she forgets to hobble the packhorse because she's jumpy over a little noise, then blames *me* because she followed me on this race. This is what I meant when I said she's still a child. Children don't take responsibility." Dashi gave in and started to pace, just a little, going between Sevlin and the nearest horse. "I should have made her stay with the Mori. Or made her go back to Karak City," she added, even though she knew she couldn't have, not with Negan after them both. Maybe Idree had a point: *that* part was her fault.

"She *did* say she was sorry," Sevlin said. "Anyone could have done it."

"No," she said. "You and I wouldn't have."

"Not now maybe. But you never made mistakes when you were her age?"

"You were just lecturing me about how she was nearly grown up. Now you want to use her age as an excuse?"

"There's no excuse needed. It was an accident."

"An accident that cost us half of our provisions!" She was getting worked up again. *The packhorse, the needle, Negan, the pyrothrite belt, Idree.* She could feel her heart starting to beat faster.

Sevlin put the burning branch back in the fire. "It must have been nice coming into the world as a fully-formed adult, with no fears and no faults."

"This isn't about me."

He crossed his arms. "It *is* about you. You talk about taking responsibility. She's jumpy because instead of teaching her how to do anything, your instructions are to keep still and leave everything to you. And then when something goes wrong, you're angry that she didn't act exactly like you would have."

"I'm not her parent, Sevlin, and you're not mine." Cursed ancestors, she could see the logic to his words. Why couldn't she stop arguing?

"No, you're her sister. Start with acting like that instead of like someone who's got a stray dog nipping at her heels."

Dashi's hands balled into fists and she took a step closer, glaring up at him. She wasn't far from throwing a punch, however disastrously that would end. "This isn't your business, Sevlin. *So stay out of it.*"

Abruptly, Sevlin's posture shifted. He shrugged and unfolded his arms as if he didn't care at all. "Just an idea."

Dashi sighed, trying to release her anger into that one breath. "I'll go after the packhorse. Can you...?" She glanced at Idree's back.

"Don't you think *you* should do that?" he asked pointedly.

She looked away. She hated when Idree was like this. Always had. "I'll deal with it later."

Sevlin pursed his lips, somehow managing to do it with just one side of his mouth. "We don't *need* that packhorse. I have medical supplies in my packs. Once we get the needle, we can take time to hunt on the way to Tyvalar."

Dashi shook her head. "We should have extra provisions in case something happens to our other packs or we aren't able to hunt right away."

Or we go our separate ways. She needed that packhorse for the return trip. She supposed she could always take *his* packhorse, but that seemed especially coldhearted. *Oh, and double-crossing him isn't?*

"It's getting dark," Sevlin said, a warning in his voice.

She brushed past him and vaulted onto Spit's bare back. "It can't have gotten far," she said, putting her heels to Spit's sides.

The packhorse had galloped off to the north, straight up the center of the ravine. The light was fading fast, but there was enough to see what had spooked it in the first place: rats, their tracks leading over the side of the ravine.

She hurried along, squinting at the shadows. What would she do if she couldn't find the packhorse? Would she really steal Sevlin's and leave him in the middle of the taiga with no supplies? She thought about the way he'd lectured her about Idree, making her head boil until it almost burst. But even that wasn't enough to justify leaving him in such a way. When he wasn't being self-righteous about her sister, she liked him well enough. She certainly didn't want him to starve, or injure himself and not have any medical supplies. But she had to admit to two realities: one, the idea of Sevlin pursuing her was not appealing; and two, without provisions, Sevlin would be much slower.

Darkness was falling quickly, forcing her to slow Spit. Stone spires and outcroppings stood out like dark statues. She should stop. Though the rat tracks had disappeared, they could still be lurking nearby and she was alone, with only her bow and a quiver of arrows.

A nearby whinny changed her mind. *The packhorse. The supplies she'd need to return to Karak City.*

It sounded close. *Just a little farther*, she thought, kneeing Spit forward.

An opening appeared in the rock wall to her right and another whinny sounded from that direction. The sides of the ravine had nearly been washed away here. She dismounted and slung her bow over her shoulder so she could scramble up the low rise. Spit snorted and stayed where he was.

She halted at the top. In front of her was a swath of bare land, a tan scar that cut through the trees crowding on either side. The ground was unstable here and she saw several places where the banks had given way completely, taking the trees with them. Deep cracks split the earth, visible only because they were slightly darker than everything else. Rocky formations clustered intermittently. Silhouetted against the fuchsia remnants of the sunset, one formation caught her attention: an oval of rock with five points jutting from it like fingers. *A rock shaped like a man's hand.*

The packhorse stood at the edge of the unstable earth, ears twitching uncertainly. In the distance, she could see a wide valley laid out on a perfect east-west axis. Unlike the scarred, collapsing land in front of her, the valley had gently tilted sides and a shimmering river cutting through the center. Squinting eastward in the worsening light, she made out the bald knobs of foothills and the snow-capped behemoths beyond.

Just like the map described, she thought giddily. *We're almost there.*

The yoke of tension that had pressed down on her since the pyrothrite nodules accelerated began to ease. *The valley!* She'd found it! She couldn't wait to tell Idree and Sevlin. A pang of dread shot through her: if they were this close to the temple it wouldn't be long before she had to betray Sevlin. No longer smiling, she picked up the packhorse's dragging lead rope.

She'd have to tell Idree about the belt beforehand though, about how her life depended on betraying Sevlin and getting the needle back to Karak City. Otherwise, there was no way her sister would cooperate—she liked Sevlin too much. Dashi grimaced, thinking of the words her sister had just flung at her. Would Idree even *want* to help her after everything she'd said?

It was Sevlin who'd argued that Idree was mature enough to stand bad news, but given her most recent outburst, Dashi wasn't so sure. She couldn't just pull Idree aside and whisper that they wouldn't be going to Tyvalar. Her sister might react badly or speak without thinking. Sevlin might overhear. No, she'd have to find a way to get Idree alone, to give her time to run her emotional course.

She was so deep in thought that it took her a full heartbeat to notice the man standing at the edge of the rock formations. Even when she did, her first thought was that Sevlin had somehow learned of her treachery and followed her. That would explain the crossbow pointed at her chest. But of course, her thoughts were still secret. And the man holding the crossbow wasn't Sevlin.

It was Negan.

Chapter 21

Negan's crossbow didn't waver as he stepped toward her. A second, burlier man stood nearby. He also held a crossbow.

"I don't believe it," Negan said, a sneer splitting his beard. It was no longer carefully trimmed but stuck out in tufts like an animal preparing to shed its winter fur.

Dashi's hands flexed, itching to move for the bow she'd foolishly slung over her shoulder.

Even though the movement was slight, Negan noticed it. He shook his head. "Throw it on the ground."

She hesitated.

"The bow. *Now.*"

She tossed the bow to one side.

"And the quiver."

Her fingers floundered with the buckles, trying to tell her that throwing away perfectly good weapons was a horrible idea, but she had no choice. She still had two knives: a small one inside her boot and another hidden under her sash, but they wouldn't do much good at this range.

Dashi looked up as a third man emerged from the tree line. It wasn't until Negan nodded to him that she realized she'd been hoping it was Sevlin. But no, Sevlin was back with Idree. He might come looking for her eventually, but by then it would be too late.

Stupid. Stupid. Stupid. Why had she assumed she was far enough away from the other racers to not be in any danger?

"Good," Negan said. "Aren, tie her up."

Aren, the burly man, wrenched her arms behind her back and lashed her wrists together with a piece of rope, then searched her for weapons. He found the bone-handled knife in her sash—the same one she'd surprised Sevlin with when she'd tussled with him—and then the one in her boot. Now she was truly weaponless. He also removed the map and the description of the statuette and handed them to Negan, who examined the papers eagerly before crumpling them in disgust.

Dashi was trying to remember how many men Negan had with him when he took his first swing. He caught her on the side of the jaw, splitting the corner of her lip and warming her mouth with the taste of iron and salt.

"I've been wanting to do that since I saw the prefects drag you from your horse."

She knew she should feel fear—and she did—but it was tempered with so much anger that it was nearly nonexistent. At Negan, for the blood on his hands. And at herself, for being in this position. *She* was supposed to get revenge against him, not the other way around.

She spit blood onto his boots. "What took you so long?"

He hit her again. The blow landed on her cheekbone, snapping her head back against Aren's shoulder. More punches followed, striking her in the ribs and shoulders and jaw, leaving her doubled over and gasping.

"I was on my way to meet Onan that night." Another punch landed in her gut. His breath was coming fast now, sawing in and out of his lungs with each swing of his fist. "Did you know that? I saw you arrested, but I didn't think anything of it. Just another mongrel whelp too stupid to live. Then I went inside and saw Onan and I knew, I *knew*—" He hit her in the mouth again. "—that I'd just seen his murderer. If I'd had my way

I would have killed you that same night, but when I came back outside they'd already taken you away." He examined his knuckles. "Luckily, you're not in prison anymore. Now, why don't you tell me how you got out?"

Dashi smiled, the movement pulling at her bloodied lip. "I escaped."

Negan leaned closer. "*How?*"

She shrugged one shoulder. The movement hurt. "Raw talent?" At least, that's what she meant to say, but the words came out thick and slurred with blood. Negan seemed to understand the sentiment though. He hit her again.

"No one escapes that prison. And even if they did, *you* shouldn't have. I sent a summons to the captain in charge of the prison, requesting that you be turned over to my custody. Do you know what I received instead?" He didn't wait for her answer. "A body!" He was yelling now. "A body! He said you were already dead. Why would he do that?" Negan's knuckles were bleeding, sending thin rivulets over the back of his right hand, but he didn't seem to notice.

Dashi didn't answer. Negan would have tried to take her from prison months ago, soon after she'd killed his brother. That meant the noble must have known about the statuette containing the golden needle...and planned to use her all along. It wasn't that she wanted to protect the noble—quite the opposite, in fact—but she doubted anything she said would make a difference. And she wasn't about to start groveling in front of Negan.

Dashi took a ragged breath. She hoped Sevlin had enough sense not to search for her at night. Once it was daylight he'd be able to spot the signs left by Negan's men and hopefully avoid them. If she'd had any doubt that Negan hated her enough to hurt her sister, she didn't any longer. Idree would be in danger if he ever found her.

"Why?" Negan asked.

Dashi's thoughts had been so firmly focused on Idree that she almost laughed in relief when Negan didn't ask where she was. He probably thought Dashi was riding alone.

"Why did you kill him?" Negan asked again, his voice tight.

He didn't look satisfied, the way she'd always imagined feeling if their positions were reversed. Instead, his face was contorted, twisted between anger and pain. Dashi recognized the expression. It was how she'd felt when she'd left the brothel. It was how she felt right now. Her friends were amazing: funny, sharp, and fierce. Even now, tainted though their memory was, she couldn't put into words how she felt about them. Negan's brother, on the other hand, was the type of person who not only killed people but stole the spoils from his comrades. How *dare* Negan look pained by his loss when he'd taken so much more from her?

"He took everything from me," she spat. "*You* took everything. You had them murdered in cold blood. Altan...Altan was one of the best people I've ever met. Your brother was nothing: a whoring, drunken murderer who deserved to die a lot slower than he did." The old flames were climbing, slowly but surely, heating her insides until she could barely feel the pain on the outside. "I'm *glad* I killed him. He died blubbering, telling me exactly how I could find you." It was a lie, but she wanted to make Negan feel the same pain she did.

Realization broke over Negan's face. Realization and a renewed loathing. "The spies?" he asked. "Onan died because of a bunch of *spies*?" He drew his sword and struck her in the ribs with the pommel. "Turning on your country for a few gold pieces. Faithless mongrel."

"Your brother...was...faithless...Told me exactly where to find you...Barely had to ask."

"Liar." His punch sent a jolt through her stomach and into her back. "My brother loved his country. He would never tell anything to a filthy spy. Who else in Karak City is working for the Tyvalarans? Is Captain Ese?"

Dashi shook her head.

"I want names. A list. I'll hunt them down the same way I hunted your friends."

"I don't know any," Dashi said, but it was hopeless. Negan wouldn't believe her; he didn't want to. She could see it in his eyes.

"You'll tell me something before you die," Negan sneered. "Then I'll return with the golden needle and a list of traitors. *I'll* have served my country well. No one will even know your name." He smiled slowly. "Take her to the other *captive*," he said to Aren.

Aren shoved her forward, jerking her arms when she fell to her knees. The ground was treacherous: loosely packed and crisscrossed by the deep fissures she'd already noticed. She couldn't see to the bottom of most of them.

Negan's men had camped at the edge of the trees, just out of sight of the rock that looked like a man's hand. She could see the light of their campfire as she ascended the slope, but the space around the fire was empty. Instead, a knot of people gathered a short distance away, leaning over one of the splits in the earth. Several of them glanced up at her approach, their expressions ranging from indifference to surprise, but they stayed where they were.

She wondered if the other racer who'd been captured had fallen into the crack or been thrown there, like she was about to be. Something about the predatory way that the men leaned over the pit made her feel cold. One of the men—no, it was a woman, Dashi saw, the same one who'd spoken with Negan at the start of the race—stuck a flaming branch into the pit, poking at whoever was inside. A high-pitched cry came from the hole. One of the men flinched, much to the amusement of the others.

The men and the lone woman who made up Negan's group parted as Aren shoved her forward. Dashi stumbled to a stop at the edge of the fissure. It was deep—at least twice her height—and one side had caved in, sending a tree to the bottom and half-burying it in a pile of soft soil. A creature stared up at her: a giant taiga ant. Negan's men had brutalized it. Burns blackened its coppery exoskeleton and the ant held two of its delicate legs off the ground, unable to put weight on them. It glared up at the humans with its fathomless bulging eyes, antennae waving fiendishly.

Dashi yanked at the rope that bound her hands, but it didn't yield. Negan's men were shifting in anticipation, elbowing each other and muttering like patrons waiting for a show. A slight movement made her look past them, but it was dark and one of her eyes was swollen shut, making it difficult to see. She thought she saw a dark shape, wriggling along the ground. The thing came closer, then stilled, becoming nearly invisible.

Dashi darted a glance at Negan, standing next to her, but he hadn't noticed anything. Blood and sweat were running down her face. She wiped her eyes on her shoulder as best she could and looked again. The flat shadow was still there. Had it gotten closer? There was movement again, slower this time. A thin, curved stick raised itself just above the grass. *No.* Dashi blinked again, this time because she didn't believe what she was seeing: a short recurve bow, just like hers but smaller.

Idree.

She scanned the dark tree line, trying to find Sevlin. He must be close. *Idree wouldn't have come without him...would she?*

The woman in Negan's group lashed a sword to a stout stick and stepped to the edge of the fissure. With swift stabbing motions, she drove the sword down at the ant. The first strike gouged a white line into the ant's back. The ant cringed and made the same high-pitched keening noise Dashi had heard before. The woman struck it again, by coincidence bringing the sword down next to the first gouge mark, so that the two cuts formed a perfect *V*. The wound remained white. Was the mark superficial, Dashi wondered, or were ants incapable of bleeding? It had to have hurt the creature though, or it wouldn't have cried out.

"Hit it again, Cari," someone called. "Take out one of those ugly eyes."

This time the ant was ready, however. When the sword came down, the creature reared up on its hind legs and caught the sword in its jaws. With a sound like cracking ice, the metal broke in two. There was a collective intake of breath from Negan's men, hardened though they were. In the pit, the ant snapped its jaws, daring them to come closer.

Dashi swallowed. The ant had broken a sword—tempered *steel*—as easily as a person would pinch a pine needle in half. What would happen to a human body in those jaws? *No, Idree is here.* She had to believe that Sevlin was nearby and that, against all odds, they had a plan.

"How many ways do you plan to split that purse?" Dashi asked in a raised voice, stalling for time. "Or do you plan to kill off some of your men on the return trip to make the division more favorable?"

The men didn't move, didn't even look concerned.

"What do you say?" Negan called to them. "Anyone want to listen to the mongrel whelp who killed Onan and Kapis?" There were head shakes and glares, jeers and insults. Negan laughed. To Dashi, he said, "My men have worked with me for years. They know they'll be compensated well."

Dashi blinked at the hard faces around her. These must be the same men who'd killed her friends.

"They're dedicated to Karakal," Negan said. He leaned closer. "Just like my brother was."

He put a hand on her shoulder and, without another word, shoved her into the fissure.

Chapter 22

Dashi toppled forward, landing hard on her shoulder and side. For a moment there was nothing but pain and the struggle to breathe. Then, groaning, she rolled to her knees. The ant was at the other end of the fissure, one antenna wobbling in her direction and the other pointing upward.

Cari, the woman, had affixed another sword to the end of a branch. She waved it in front of the ant's face and it snapped angrily, taking several steps toward Dashi.

"Think about the names of those other spies," Negan called from above. "But think quickly. I think the ant is agitated." His men snickered.

Suddenly, there was a scream from above, followed by another sound that made the hair on the back of Dashi's neck stand up: the snarl of a predator with prey in sight. Negan's men bolted away from the rim, shouting, but Dashi couldn't see why or where they were going.

The sword blade that the ant had broken lay in the center of the fissure. Dashi took a cautious step toward it, searching the ant's face for some sort of reaction. Its eyes were bulbous and uniform and, without irises or eyebrows to delineate its emotions, she could read nothing. She couldn't even tell exactly where it was looking. The jaws were motionless, as was the hard casing of its face. Only the antennae moved, but if something could be understood from their random waving, she didn't know what. She couldn't hear its breaths or smell the musk from its skin. The ant existed in her vision alone, a ghost to every sense but her eyes.

There was a spray of dirt from above and Dashi instinctively threw herself to one side as a giant taiga rat slid down the collapsed bank, dragging more dirt with it. The rat rolled to its feet, its square incisors already bared. Midnight fur, a hunched back, a pointed nose and a long, naked tail: it looked exactly like the one she'd seen in the blizzard. Its gait was sinuous and low to the ground, but whereas a city rat twitched and darted, the taiga rat was a different specimen. It was on the lookout for prey, not concerned about becoming it.

Dashi's breath hitched as the rat's eyes skipped over her and landed on the ant, which balanced awkwardly on its four good legs as the rat advanced. The rat circled the injured ant, snapping at one of its legs, then another. Dashi heard the jarring sound of teeth scraping against exoskeleton. The ant turned its head, following the rat's movements with its enormous jaws parted, but the rat stayed just out of reach, lunging and then dancing away again. White teeth marks glared from the ant's coppery exterior, marking the places where the rat had made contact.

Both beasts were directly in front of the collapsed bank, blocking the only part of the fissure Dashi had a chance of climbing. She glanced up at the rim, but Negan's men hadn't returned. She could hear more snarls, accompanied by the sound of men fighting. An entire pack of rats must have attacked. How long before another one tumbled into the fissure and focused on her instead of the ant? She had to get out. *Fast.*

Dashi darted to the center of the fissure, toward the broken sword. Squatting awkwardly, she managed to pick it up with her bound hands. The broken blade cut her as she sawed through the rope, but she didn't stop. She needed her hands free if she was to have any hope of defending herself. When the rope fell to the ground she picked it up and wound it around the broken sword and a branch that lay at the bottom of the fissure, creating a makeshift spear like the one Cari had used to torment the ant.

The rat had pushed the ant onto its side, pinning it against the wall of the fissure. It moved its head from side to side like a snake about to strike, waiting for a chance to get around the ant's jaws.

Dashi didn't know why the rat had attacked the ant and not her. Perhaps it was taking care of the bigger threat first. Perhaps, next to the ant, she was too small to seem like a good meal. She was certain about two things: the injured ant was losing and, when it did, she would be next.

Clenching her hastily made spear, she crept toward the beasts. She stayed next to the steep side of the fissure, trying to conceal her movement in shadows. Bedlam sounded from above, but inside the fissure, the soil was soft underfoot, masking the sound of her steps. If they heard her at all, the rat and the ant paid no attention. She was a gnat, buzzing languidly in the background, and they had a much bigger battle to fight.

The ant was still getting the worst of the conflict. With injured legs, it couldn't seem to right itself and, pinned on its back, the reach of its massive jaws was limited. The rat struck again and again, marring the exoskeleton with dozens of bites, searching for a killing blow.

Dashi crouched nearby, as close as she could get without leaving the shadows. Would her flimsy spear even hold up? She would have to be fast, she told herself, trying to take stock of her mobility after Negan's beating. *Really* fast. Adrenaline coursed through her, obscuring any pain from her injuries. She took a breath, repeatedly measuring the distance between herself and her target, trying to adjust to only seeing with one eye.

When the rat moved its head next, she struck, leaping across the intervening space and thrusting the spear between the animal's ribs. The rat made a loud noise—part hiss, part squeal—and turned toward her.

It was the only opening that the ant needed. Those massive jaws closed around the rat's head and Dashi heard the horrible crunching of bones. The ant shook its head, pulling the rat's skull in half. A shard of bone landed, soundless, in the soft dirt.

The ant righted itself and turned in her direction. Dashi was too close; one lunge and it would have her in those powerful jaws. But it stayed where it was, its antennae slowing. Dashi took a careful step backward, holding her weapon in front of her like it could save her if the ant became aggressive. Then she turned and fled, skirting the dead rat and pinwheeling her way up the collapsed bank. Her feet and hands sank into the soil, but the bank held as she climbed. She looked back only once. The ant had lowered its head over one of its injured legs, its jaws working rhythmically as it released a string of greenish saliva onto its wound.

By the time she pulled herself over the edge, the small clearing had dissolved into mayhem. Someone was screaming, his voice shrill with terror. When Dashi looked in the direction of the sound, she saw a taiga rat, tearing into a man's stomach with a flash of teeth. Another rat appeared out of the darkness, edging closer to the screaming man, but the first rat snarled, unwilling to share its meal.

The rats were everywhere. There had to be at least fifteen of them. They were eating men, eating horses, eating supplies. Another of Negan's men went down, screaming as a rat clawed at his back and another tore into his arm. She thought she saw Sevlin fighting with someone, but she couldn't be sure.

An arrow drove into the ground, nearly hitting her foot. Her gaze whipped around, seeking the source of the attack, but she saw only the slim dark shape of her sister, who'd retreated to where Spit and the packhorse were tied. Another arrow flew from her sister's bow and this time she saw where Idree had been aiming: at Negan, who was striding toward her, sword in hand.

Blood streamed from his nose, coating his beard in red, but he didn't seem to notice anything but her. She met his swing head-on, blocking with her spear. Splinters exploded in front of her face, but the branch held. *For now.* Dashi backpedaled, trying to find a better weapon without taking her eyes off Negan. Behind him, a man screamed for help as a giant rat bore down. Negan didn't turn. Her spear wouldn't survive another blow from his sword and she could tell from the gleam in his eye that he knew it.

He swung again and Dashi leaped back, avoiding a mortal wound by sheer agility. Negan raised his sword just as another arrow flew through the air, sticking into his calf like a pin cushion. He staggered a step and Dashi darted in with her spear, aiming at his ribs. He blocked at the last moment and her spear cut the inside of his arm instead. If the wound hurt, he didn't acknowledge it.

"You won't win," he growled. "Traitors never do."

Abruptly his gaze shifted to something over her shoulder. Dashi turned, just in time to see a taiga rat springing toward her. She brought the spear up at the last minute, but it hit the animal in the shoulder, a flesh wound only. She landed on her back with the beast looming over her, its coarse fur brushing where her pant leg had ridden up. It growled, low and menacing.

Dashi scrambled backward, but the rat pinned her in place with one foot. Sharp nails pierced her clothes, curling against her hip. Its breath was hot, chasing away the night air and filling her nostrils with the smell of meat and stomach acid. Those teeth...she couldn't pull her eyes away from them. They were nearly the size of her hand. Ancestors above, she didn't want to die like the man she'd just seen, screaming for mercy that would never come. Her fingers crawled across the ground, searching in vain for something to use against it.

Suddenly, the rat flattened itself against her feet, ducking as someone raced up to them. It was Idree, shouting and waving a flaming torch that had been dropped by one of Negan's men. She stood her ground when the rat hissed, her eyebrows drawing a fierce line across her round face. The rat lunged at her and Idree jumped back, hitting it squarely in the face with the flaming stick. Dashi rolled away and pushed to her feet, sprinting toward the first abandoned weapon she saw: a sword, several strides away.

When she turned around the rat was bearing down on Idree, who stumbled backward, nearly dropping her torch. With a shout, Dashi launched herself toward the rat's hunched back. It turned its head, ready to tear into her as she leaped through the air, but she brought the sword down on its muzzle in a spray of blood. The animal flinched away. Dashi's hand was already deep in its fur and she used its movement to pull herself onto its back, the same way she would leap onto a moving horse. Then, clinging with her knees, she buried the blade between its shoulder blades.

The rat staggered and Dashi leaped from its back, stumbling away so she didn't get pinned beneath it. When she looked back, the rat had flopped onto its side. Its toes twitched reflexively, their pink, fleshy underside a contrast to the dark fur that covered the top of the foot. On its side, the rat didn't appear so large, but she couldn't forget the animal crouched over her, its breath rank and warm.

Around them, the battle still raged. Dashi saw two rats fighting over a body, each pulling it in a different direction until one of the arms ripped free.

Dashi turned to her sister. "Let's go." Her body felt numb and she wasn't sure if it was from shock or relief or physical abuse. Probably a combination of all three. "Where's Sevlin?"

"Here." Spit's coat looked silver in the light of the dying torches. Sevlin's raised sword gleamed with blood. He'd looped around Spit's nose to make a halter, which was a good thing. Dashi doubted even she could ride him bareback and bridle-less this close to the taiga rats. He was trembling and tossing his head, showing the whites of his eyes.

Sevlin slid from his back, his eyes on Idree. "Are you alright?"

She nodded mutely.

"Good, get on the packhorse."

Idree obeyed, lurching toward the packhorse.

Spit's back seemed impossibly high, though by any standard he was a short horse. Just raising her arms to grab his mane made Dashi's ribs ache. Spit looked back at her with one baleful eye and snorted. Dashi wasn't sure if he was chastising her for thinking she could haul herself up to his back, or for putting him in the middle of such a mess in the first place

Wordlessly, Sevlin threaded his fingers together, making a place for her to put her boot.

Dashi shot him a grateful look that was probably hidden by the darkness. He mounted easily after her, his legs sliding against the back of hers and his arms reaching on either side to take the makeshift reins. They rode back to the ravine, the unstable ground forcing them to go slowly even though Dashi would have liked to leave at a gallop. It wasn't until the sounds of chaos receded behind them that she felt Sevlin's arms relax.

"How badly are you hurt?" he asked next to her ear.

"Ribs are bruised. My face..."

"Is a mess."

She snorted. "Thanks."

"I told you before: I dislike sugary assurances."

"There's a time and a place, Sevlin, and describing my face is one of them."

His chuckle was low.

"I didn't know you laughed," she said dryly.

"I don't when I'm surrounded by enemies."

"You must be a regular jester in Tyvalar."

"Something like that."

She could hear the amusement in his voice, but he didn't laugh again. "Did you see what happened to Negan?" she asked, unconsciously moving away from anything having to do with Tyvalar.

"The last time I saw him he was limping into the woods."

"Idree shot him in the leg," Dashi said, a small smile on her lips.

She stole a glance back at her sister. Gone was the girl who'd slithered through the grass to shoot at Negan and threatened a giant rat with nothing more than a flaming stick. This Idree sat hunched and frightened, perched uncomfortably between the packhorse's saddlebags. Negan's men hadn't gotten around to going through the packs, so they were still rounded with supplies and not at all suitable for a rider.

"I don't know if he'll make it far then," Sevlin said. "The rats seem drawn to blood. We could hear them all around us while we were looking for you. It seemed like they would attack any second, but when we got close to Negan, they stopped paying attention to us. I think they smelled your blood."

Dashi couldn't control her shiver.

They rode on in silence, Dashi leaning back against Sevlin's warm chest. It made her want to curl up, cat-like, against him. She was suddenly very cold. Her right eye was shooting lightning bolts of pain into the rest of her face.

"How did you know to come after me?" she asked.

"When you didn't come back, I knew something must have happened. We moved the horses closer, although Idree was all for rushing after you as fast as possible. Reminded me of someone else."

"I'm—Thank you for coming." The words were harder to get out than she'd anticipated. "I shouldn't have gone after the packhorse. You were right."

"Hearing you admit that is reward enough," he said lightly, but she sensed something else beneath his words.

"What?"

He swallowed, the sound loud against her ear. "I didn't mean to push you about Idree. I know the way my sister acts when she thinks she's being treated unfairly, but that doesn't mean it's the same for the two of you. It's none of my business anyway."

Spit picked his way through the dark, each stride moving Dashi's legs rhythmically against Sevlin's and swaying her back against his chest. The night was completely quiet now.

"I know," she said finally. "But you were right about that too."

The horses were still where Sevlin had picketed them, thankfully. Sevlin slid off Spit first, doing her the courtesy of neither trying to help her down, nor staying to watch her stiff dismount. Just as well. She couldn't look him in the eye anyway. Not after she'd gone in search of her packhorse because it would enable her to betray him, while he'd abandoned *his* packhorse to come to her assistance.

"Dashi," Idree gasped when Dashi turned toward her. "Your face!"

Sevlin's mouth hitched.

"Didn't you see it before?" Dashi asked.

"I don't know. I guess I did, but I couldn't pay attention to much besides the rats."

Dashi raised her fingers to the throbbing line of her cheekbone and eye socket. "I've gotten worse from a match of goathead," she said, but it was a lie.

"You should reevaluate your pastimes," Sevlin said, returning from the packhorse with water, a tin of salve and some bandages. He handed them to Idree. "Burn anything with blood on it. We don't want the rats following us. I think they're more of a concern tonight than having our fire spotted by the other racers. Agreed?"

"Yes," Idree said immediately. "I never want to see those things again."

"I'll get a fire going and tend to the horses then," he said and walked away without looking back at either of them.

Dashi felt a surge of gratitude toward him for not hovering—bad enough that Idree would—which was immediately followed by another stab of guilt.

Idree reached toward Dashi's cheek, but Dashi stepped away.

Her sister sighed. "I know you don't like someone taking care of you, but you're going to have to endure it this time. And sit down!"

Dashi suppressed a sigh of her own and did what she was told, seating herself on a log. "Since when did you learn to shoot?" she asked, watching Idree's hands as her sister wet the corner of a bandage.

Idree's fingers stilled for a moment, then resumed their activity. "When you were sent to prison, I didn't know what to do. Auntie Nima was fine with me staying, so it wasn't that. I just—I had no one, Dashi. I know we didn't spend much time together, but it was different knowing you were gone for good. Auntie Nima was great, but she—" Idree shrugged. "She is fond of me, but when it comes down to it, I'm an apprentice, not family. Altan and Zayaa and Baris were dead. Everyone I talked to said you were going to be executed any day. I felt so desperate and lonely and one day I just picked up the bow and started practicing behind the bakery. I wanted—" She looked sharply at Dashi. "Don't laugh."

"I won't."

"I wanted to rescue you. I thought maybe if I became as good as you were—" She shook her head. "But after a few weeks, I realized it would never work. I'd never become good enough in time and, even if I did..."

"The prison was crawling with guards. You'd have gotten caught in minutes—anyone would have."

"I know. After a few weeks, I realized I was being stupid."

"Being a good shot didn't keep me from getting caught," Dashi said quietly. Sevlin brought an armload of wood and began feeding the fire next to them. She waited until he left again before continuing. Admitting wrongdoing was like taking medicine. Best to take your dose all at once.

"You were right, Idree. It would have been stupid for you to come after me, just like *I* was stupid to go after the murderers. I should have listened to you that night, but I...well, like you said, I was feeling desperate too." Idree's fingers continued their tending, heedless of the difficulty Dashi was having in speaking. "But I should have thought about my chances and I should have thought about you." She shifted on the log, wanting to be up and moving. "It's hard for me to—I'm not good at being nurturing, Idree. I mean, I'm sure you've noticed. But I don't—when I snap at you, it's—well, I insist on treating you like a child and then I'm mad when you sometimes act like one," she said, trying to put it as eloquently as Sevlin had. "I'm sorry about that. I know you're growing up and...I'll try to do better," she finished, shrugging lamely.

She glanced up at Idree and saw with dismay that her sister's eyes were glassy with unshed tears. She'd been *trying* to apologize. *Leave it to me to upset her when I'm trying to make it better*, she thought. *I'm always awful at these things.*

But her sister only said, "I'm glad you're out of prison, Dashi."

"Without being carried out," Dashi quipped, cautiously. *Was that it? No outburst?*

"That too," Idree murmured.

For a few minutes, the only sound was the swipe of the clean bandage and the hushed *glug glug* of water as Idree poured more.

Finally, Dashi cleared her throat. "I'm surprised you kept that bow after my disastrous attempt at teaching you."

"It was from Father," Idree said simply. "I know he gave it to you, not me, but it's the only thing I have of theirs."

"He would be proud of you tonight," Dashi offered, thinking of her father appearing in the mist. "You hit Negan in the calf while he was moving. That's a hard shot to make."

Idree's mouth curved up. "I was aiming for his back."

Dashi laughed out loud. "Well, a lucky shot then." She reached out and, ever so briefly, touched Idree's arm. "Thank you for coming, when the rat had me. I mean that."

Idree rolled her eyes and reached down to uncork the wound salve. "As if I had a choice."

The salve stung when it touched Dashi's swollen cheek and lip, but it was a good kind of pain, holding the promise of future improvement.

Dashi smiled slowly at her sister's words, which sounded like they'd been taken from her own mouth. Sevlin had finished stoking the fire next to them and was now working to build a second fire closer to the horses as further insurance against the rats. The sight of him melted the smile from her face. They would reach the temple within the next day or two. She might not find another time to tell her sister about the pyrothrite belt, about why she had to return to Karak City no matter how wonderful Tyvalar sounded. It was a night for declarations of truth.

"Idree." She glanced toward Sevlin as she began to unwind her sash. He wasn't looking at them, but she turned her back anyway and edged closer to the crackling fire to cover the sound of her voice. "There's something else I need to tell you. Something I need to show you."

Chapter 23

By daylight, the place where Dashi had encountered Negan was marred with signs of conflict: blood, charred branches, and discarded weaponry. There were no bodies, however. Even the fissure was empty. She wondered if the ant had escaped or been dragged out by a rat.

Dashi stared at a brown stain next to her feet. It wasn't her blood that had watered the dirt, but it could have been.

"The rats got some of them anyway," Sevlin said. "At least half a dozen bodies were dragged into the forest." He was taking the opportunity to show Idree how to track. Dashi had even joined in with a few tips of her own.

"I wish it had been all of them," Dashi said, leaning over stiffly to pick up her knives, bow and quiver. They lay, forgotten, where Negan's men had dropped them.

"Negan was bleeding. Maybe one of the rats followed him," Idree said, but she didn't look like she relished the thought.

There was no sign of Negan or any of the other racers after that, but they moved cautiously anyway, making their way toward the foothills at the eastern end of the valley. The valley itself, once they'd descended the slope, was easy to navigate. Trees—willows and other deciduous species that Dashi didn't recognize—grew along the sides, shielding them from sight.

Idree, in particular, was subdued, and their passage was not marked by her usual chatter. She'd reacted to Dashi's revelation about the pyrothrite belt as Dashi had predicted: shock first, followed by emotion. Though, to her credit, Idree'd muted her response sufficiently that Sevlin hadn't noticed anything.

"I'm sorry," Dashi had said after she'd finished explaining the demands of the noble in Karak City. "You know what this means, right? I have to go back to Karak City."

"What about Sevlin?" Idree had whispered, her eyes darting over Dashi's shoulder to where Sevlin was hobbling the horses, his broad shoulders a contrast to the narrow foreleg before him. "You made a deal with him!"

"I know. I'm...I'm not proud of it, but what else could I do, Idree?" Dashi dropped her eyes, suddenly unsure of her sister's reaction. Idree could be stubborn when she wanted. What if she decided to tell Sevlin?

"And you're certain the belt will...?"

"Explode me into tiny pieces?" Dashi asked humorlessly. "Certain enough that I don't want to risk it."

"Well," Idree said. "I—well, of course you don't want to risk it. What are we doing to do?" She looked up suddenly. "You won't hurt him?"

"No," Dashi whispered quickly. "Of course not." She pointed to the small satchel that contained the medical supplies. "There are some herbs in there for pain relief. But if you take enough, you'll lose consciousness. I think the simplest way would be to slip him some and take the needle. That will give us a head start. We'll have to make sure we don't lose it."

"Somewhere safe though," Idree said firmly. "Out of sight of the other racers and safe from the rats. He won't be able to defend himself when he's..." She looked like she might start crying. "I...I can slip it to him. I always make our food." She breathed sharply through her nose, a sound that was part hiccup, part sniffle.

Dashi nodded.

"I really wanted to go to Tyvalar."

Dashi refrained from asking if her sister's desire to go to Tyvalar had anything to do with the soft expression that stole over her face every time she looked at Sevlin.

"I know," she said instead. "And I'm sorry, Idree. I really am. I'd still like to leave Karak City for, well, anywhere." Whatever happened, she couldn't imagine herself staying there. Not anymore.

"But we won't be able to see Sevlin again, even if we decide to go to Tyvalar eventually. I don't think he'll *want* to see us, not after this. We're going to *betray* him, Dashi," she said, barely breathing the words.

Dashi looked at her lap. "You're right. I don't think he'll want to see us. And we can't go to Tyvalar, since the queen sent him here. He won't be the only one we betrayed."

Her sister swallowed. "Alright. Somewhere else then. Somewhere *like* Tyvalar." She opened the jar of wound salve and pushed Dashi's deel open so she could begin applying it to Dashi's ribs. "Why didn't you tell me before?"

"I knew you'd ask that." Dashi picked up a pine needle and tossed it into the fire, which crackled cheerfully at the prospect of additional fuel. She was fairly certain the salve only worked on open wounds and wouldn't seep through to her aching ribcage, but she could tell Idree wanted to be doing something constructive so she let her continue. Anyway, as long as she was getting her bodily wounds tended, Sevlin would keep his distance and let them talk. By that reasoning, the salve wasn't being wasted.

Dashi stole a glance at her sister. "You said I didn't come to see you before the race, but I did. I watched you open up the bakery. I thought about telling you right then, and thought about it again when you found me on the steppe." She selected another pine needle to sacrifice.

"I told myself I didn't say anything because I didn't want to worry you. I was going to win the race and get the belt removed anyway, so what was the point of upsetting you for no reason? But the truth is, I was embarrassed."

"Why?" Idree looked up from her work, eyebrows rising. "It's not like that noble gave you a choice."

Dashi sighed again. "Because you were right about going after the murderers. You were right and I was wrong. That's why I ended up in prison and that's why," she gestured vaguely at the taiga around them, "all of this."

Idree wiped her finger on the hem of her deel and corked the wound salve, before giving Dashi a swift smile. "Just try listening to me in the future, alright?"

Now Idree was quiet, her posture tensing every time she looked at Sevlin. Inscrutable, she was not.

Dashi hoped that Sevlin, if he noticed, would chalk it up to Idree's nervousness about venturing into the temple. On second thought, Dashi conceded, that might indeed be contributing to her sister's tension. After some discussion, they'd decided that Idree would accompany Sevlin and Dashi inside. Though Dashi had originally planned to leave her sister with the mounts, their encounter with Negan and her pledge to stop treating Idree like a child seemed to dictate that they all stay together. Still, old habits died hard, and she found herself harping on all the dangers they might face within.

"And don't go ahead of us because there might be—"

"Traps that I might not notice," Idree interjected tightly. "I know, Dashi."

"Alright." Dashi agreed reluctantly. "Alright."

They made better time than she'd anticipated, reaching the outskirts of the ruins just before dusk. It was by far the largest ruin Dashi had been to—a city, really—with hundreds of buildings at evenly spaced intervals. In the fading light, it was easy to imagine them as they once were. Dashi longed to explore the entire place.

There seemed to be no rhyme or reason to the state of the structures: some buildings were fully intact, missing only a thatched roof, or the wooden doors and lintels. Others were little more than rectangular indentations in the ground. It was as if an enormous whip had snaked through the city, its tail decimating something each time it cracked: a large, wealthy house here, a tiny foundation on the outside of the city there. Which of the ancient Pureks had stood the best chance of escaping the city after the cataclysm? Rich or poor? Those who lived in the center of the city or those who lived on the outskirts?

Only the temple looked completely untouched. It sat on the lowest of the foothills so that it was elevated above the ruined city, presiding over the valley like a god staring down at its petitioners. The temple had four wings and Dashi knew without checking that each pointed in a cardinal direction. Its roof was a huge green dome—meant to represent the vitality of the earth—and the walls were made of light-colored stone.

From her current vantage point, inhibited though it was by twilight and the fact that one eye was mostly swollen shut, the temple appeared pristine. Dashi's heart started to beat faster. Besides the golden needle, what other secrets did such a well-preserved building hold? Paintings, scrolls, *history*. Her eyes lingered on its sturdy roof, its stalwart walls. How had the temple survived the intervening years so unscathed? And how had those fools the khan sent been able to turn their backs and return to Karak City without exploring such a trove of treasures? Even if she hadn't needed the golden needle, she would have gone inside.

The ruined city was laid out in a perfect half-moon, with twelve roads cutting like rays to the temple. Weather and age had rumpled the paving stones in some places, but they were, for the most part, intact. Dashi could almost imagine the spacious boulevards as they'd been, lined with businesses and teeming with ancient people dressed in the elaborate headdresses she'd seen in paintings. She was sure it had been nothing like the ill-planned tangles that passed for thoroughfares in Karak City.

By unspoken accord, they stopped at the base of the temple's hill.

"We need to eat something," Dashi said, "but I think we should go into the temple right after."

"Tonight?" Idree asked.

"We don't know which racers are left or where they are. And I don't want to repeat the mistake of assuming they're far away again." *And I don't have any time to waste.*

"If we went in tonight we could be out by morning," Sevlin said thoughtfully. "Before morning, maybe. We could be gone before anyone else gets here."

Dashi nodded, forcing herself to look him in the eye. "Exactly." She pointed to a small copse of trees growing halfway up the eastern slope of the valley. "We can picket the horses there, where they'll be out of sight."

Sevlin nodded. "I'm ready."

"Idree?" she asked.

"Alright," her sister said after a moment. "We do have lanterns," she added, almost to herself. "So it won't be too dark, right?"

Dashi flipped to her hands and crossed the floor of the ruined building they'd settled in for their meal. "Time to go."

"You're cheerful," Sevlin said suspiciously. "I thought the temple was going to be dangerous."

"It is."

"Aren't you going to eat anything?" he asked, still eying her warily.

"I'll eat on the way up the hill. I can't eat while I'm sitting still."

"Seems like the best time *to* eat."

"She means she can't sit still," Idree said, standing and brushing the crumbs from her deel.

They'd laid out all of their equipment before their meal, then carefully packed what they needed in three smaller bags, one for each of them. Now they picked up their weapons and packs and stepped through the doorway. They left the bedrolls and extra supplies with the horses, then—*finally, gloriously*, Dashi thought—they started up the hill to the temple.

The slope was steep but clear of obstacles, which made it easy to navigate by moonlight. They decided to save the lanterns for when they'd be needed most: inside the temple.

"Why aren't there any windows?" Idree asked as they ascended.

"The temple was sacred," Sevlin said. "It's located where the earth's geomagical influence was strongest."

"A vein," Idree said.

"Right. Only a few people, the seamstress chief among them, were supposed to access or even see the vein."

"No windows meant no one spying," Idree guessed.

"Spies can be anywhere," Sevlin said. "But a reduced possibility of spying, certainly."

"You think the seamstress was spied upon?" Dashi asked. She'd been about to protest that she'd never seen any proof of that in the Purek's records, but she caught herself. Perhaps Altan had sent that information to Tyvalar without her knowledge. "Do you know that for certain?"

Sevlin shrugged. "If the knowledge was valuable enough to be guarded, then it was valuable enough for others to try to uncover it."

"Kind of like what we're doing now," Idree said.

"Like your khan and my queen have been trying to do for years," he said.

Dashi looked up at the temple. What would happen to the golden needle after she'd brought it to Karak City? The noble had said he planned to give the artifact to the khan in exchange for influence, but she had no way of knowing if that was true. He hadn't even told her about the needle. And if the khan got ahold of the needle, what would *he* do with it? Would he really use it to start a war, like Sevlin said?

At least he can't do anything without someone to wield it. But the thought didn't give her much relief. The khagans of old hadn't had much trouble locating a seamstress. She thought briefly of Khagan Nuray, appearing out of the creeping mist, full of righteous anger at the khagan who'd mistreated her.

Dashi wasn't sure how much of that had been real and how much had been her imagination, but she didn't doubt that the seamstresses had been treated badly. *Would still be treated badly*, once the needle was found. The khan would probably launch a search for the seamstress as soon as he got his hands on the needle, and then some poor man or woman would have their life upended. Would the seamstress fare any better at the hands of the Tyvalaran queen? Sevlin seemed to think so, but he *would* say that about the queen he served. Protect the seamstress, Khagan Nuray had said in her dreams, but that wasn't her responsibility. *My problem is a pyrothrite belt. That's all.*

What had looked like the temple door from a distance was actually one of several relief carvings—decoy doorways—which decorated the temple's facade. Dashi walked next to the wall, trailing her fingers along the smooth, cold surface. It appeared to be made entirely from marble, something that seemed impossibly luxurious to someone who'd grown up in the leather circle. Finally, she found the real doorway: a narrow, arched aperture in the center of the front wall.

"Here," she called in a low voice.

She had a brief moment of disorientation as she stepped inside. The room was black as pitch and, judging by the way it swallowed the sound of her feet, quite large. Moonlight shone in from the open doorway and Dashi stopped at the edge of it, unwilling to step into the unknown spaces of the temple even though Sevlin and Idree crowded in behind her.

"I'll light the lanterns," Sevlin said and a moment later light flared from his cupped hands.

They stood in an antechamber of sorts, designed to protect the public from the elements as they waited to leave their offerings to the ancestors. The walls were covered with murals, surprisingly bright despite their age. One showed people feasting on the whole carcasses of stags and pigs. Another depicted the succession of ancient khagans. Khagan Nuray, Dashi was surprised to see, was shown holding a dagger in one hand and a platter of meat in the other. Her lips were pulled back in a snarl and her dagger dripped blood. It was the first piece of art Dashi had seen that depicted Nuray as less than serene.

In Dashi's mist-induced dreams, Khagan Nuray claimed to have finished building the temple herself. The thought of treading in the footsteps of the ancient Pureks had always given Dashi a certain thrill, but to know for sure that she was walking where Nuray had once walked...well, that was something else entirely. Her eyes roved the mural, searching for more clues. Yes, she thought with mounting certainty, Nuray must've had something to do with the mural's origins. For one thing, the lineage of khagans was shown in chronological order, from left to right, with no khagans shown after Nuray. Secondly, there was a red stain on the collar of the khagan who preceded Nuray. His left hand had also been severed—presumably by Nuray's dagger—and it lay on the ground, still holding a length of chain.

Did that mean her dream of Nuray had been entirely real? *Maybe I'm reading too much into it*, she thought. But the back of her neck prickled anyway.

"I thought you said no one was allowed in the temple," Idree said, interrupting her thoughts. "But it's open. There wasn't even a proper door."

"The public could access this room and probably the next one too," Dashi said, picking up her lantern. She pointed at another opening across from them. "I'd guess there's an altar in there. Come on, Sevlin," she called. He was examining the murals closely, his nose nearly touching the wall. "We haven't even gotten to the good stuff yet."

The next space was indeed a public altar room. The altar was colossal, stretching from one end of the room to the other. It held several fireplaces, since custom called for offerings to be incinerated after a certain period. Hundreds of tiny rounded shelves extended from the altar, cupped hands waiting to receive donations. Dashi stepped closer, curious about what had been left behind. A small collection of bones rested on the shelf closest to her, the offering of meat long gone. On another shelf a bracelet sparkled in the lantern light, its golden beads completely untarnished.

"It's said to be bad luck to covet someone else's offering," Sevlin remarked from just over her shoulder.

Dashi jumped. "What about *taking* another's offering?" she retorted. "What do you think the statuette is? It's probably made of melted jewelry and coins that were given to the temple."

"I'm not here for the statuette. And anyway I'm not taking it out of selfishness or greed; I'm taking it to prevent the evil that the khan will unleash. Motivation counts for something, I think."

"And taking that bracelet would be selfish?"

"The giver wanted to dedicate it to the ancestors. By taking it, you're saying your desire trumps the giver's wishes."

"The giver has gotten her wishes for hundreds of years. Maybe it's my turn now. I could be starving! That bracelet could be all that's standing between me and death."

"It's not."

"Well, if I *was* starving, I wouldn't leave a perfectly good bracelet lying around when it could buy me food," Dashi said, but she glanced down and for a moment saw, not the bracelet, but the golden needle on the offering shelf. She *was* greedy: greedy to keep on living. Greedy enough not to care who ended up with the needle, or what they did with it, as long as she survived.

"Were you really about to take the bracelet?" Sevlin asked, sounding amused. "Don't let me stop you. I'm sure breaking into the temple is bad luck too, and we'll be doing that."

"No," she said, turning her back on the offering shelves and walking toward the door that led to the next room. "I don't need a bracelet." *Ruthlessness and selflessness,* Khagan Nuray had said in her dream, but Dashi could find only ruthlessness inside her. She needed the golden needle. If she had to give it to someone who would abuse it so she could stay alive, she would.

The door was made from shiny black wood and every inch of its surface was covered with carvings. They were mostly nature motifs—flowers, rivers, trees, stars—with a line of script that cut through the middle. Dashi made out the words, "It is not for the commoner to pass," in ancient Purek. Or something to that effect. She'd never been very patient when it came to learning verb tenses. She shifted the light to see better but saw only her reflection in the smooth surface.

She dropped her gaze, looking instead to the handle. It was made from bronze and silver, fashioned to look like a tumbling waterfall issuing from the door. She knelt in front of it, removing the set of lock picks from the bag she carried. The lock was a complicated one, with a long cylinder, and she struggled to reach the tumblers while maintaining the correct tension. The minutes ticked by. She could hear Sevlin and Idree shifting behind her, but her attention remained focused on the black door. A cramp formed in the back of her neck, followed quickly by one in her hand. She wished that Zayaa, with her steady fingers and calm voice, was there to do the work instead, or at least coach her through the process.

Then, with a sudden series of clicks and a release of tension, it was done.

Dashi stood up and turned to face Sevlin and Idree. "We're about to enter the forbidden part of the temple." Her voice was serious, her restless excitement temporarily hidden. "From here on, we have to be very careful. No touching anything unless you have to, or unless you've made certain that it's not a trap. Relics, scrolls, artwork, even the floor. Anything."

Taking a deep breath, she turned the handle and stepped out of the way. Dashi held up the lantern, carefully scanning the floor on the other side for tripwires or anything else strange. The corridor was long and dark, with a floor of inlaid stone and walls made of the same black wood as the door. Tiles covered the ceiling, but they were painted in swirling blacks and grays that, taken together, resembled gathering clouds. The effect was decidedly ominous.

"There," she said, pointing to a stone with slightly rounded edges, set innocuously into the floor. "A pressure plate."

"What happens if you step on it?" Idree asked.

"Get something you don't mind ruining and we'll see."

"What about something from the temple? There was a sack of—well, I thought maybe it was grain, but I don't know. Anyway, it was left as an offering."

"That'll work," Dashi said. She wondered if Sevlin would protest Idree taking an offering, but he didn't. Perhaps his words had only been for argument's sake. She still hadn't moved from the doorway. Farther down the corridor she thought she saw something move, but when she looked again all she could see was darkness.

"Do you hear that?" she asked Sevlin. He was standing just behind her, peering over her shoulder, so that when she turned her head to ask the question, her cheek brushed the warm cloth of his deel.

He nodded, a slight frown making his scar pucker. "Sounds like water."

Idree returned a moment later, lugging something in both hands. "The sack practically disintegrated when I touched it, but I found this." She held up a thick rug.

"Perfect," Dashi said. She folded the rug into a square and, aiming carefully, tossed it onto the pressure plate. There was an immediate *whoosh* of air and, even though she'd been expecting it, Dashi stepped backward, her shoulders colliding with Sevlin's chest.

"Blessed ancestors," Idree breathed, staring at the corridor.

A spear, still shaking from impact, pierced the rug squarely through the middle.

"Interesting," Dashi said, retrieving the spear. "Usually they're arrows." She looked at the ceiling above the pressure plate. A piece of tile had swiveled to one side, revealing the empty cylinder that had launched the spear.

"Bigger temple, bigger weapons," Sevlin said. He looked regretfully at the rug. "That was in such good shape too."

"Better it than us."

She shook out the folds of the rug. The spear had punched a hole through each one. Dashi tossed it back into the public altar room but kept the spear. It would be useful if she needed to prod a trap.

She turned to face the corridor again and, taking a deep breath, stepped inside. Her lantern only illuminated a short distance in front of her, so she had to stop frequently to survey the floor and walls for anything that might be a warning sign.

"Another pressure plate," Dashi said, pointing to a second rounded stone. "Stick to one side, but don't touch the wall."

"Will you set that one off too?" Idree asked.

Dashi shook her head. "We'll be here all day if we set off every one. Best to leave them and proceed carefully." That had always been her friends' policy, anyway. Now she wondered if they'd had other reasons for leaving some of the traps in place. A paranoia that they were being followed by agents of the khan, for example?

"It's a pattern," Idree said a few minutes later. "Two in the center, one on the right, one on the left. Then it repeats."

Dashi nodded. She'd been concentrating too hard to notice the pattern, but she wasn't surprised. "The Pureks loved patterns. They thought symmetry was a natural occurrence—the balance of the food chain, the cycle of life and death, the rotation of the seasons and the stars—and they tried to emulate that."

"It probably didn't hurt when it came to avoiding the traps," Sevlin remarked. "Easier to remember where the pressure plates are when there's a pattern."

"You think they kept the traps rigged all the time?" Idree asked incredulously. "Even when the seamstress and the temple officials were going back and forth through this hall?"

"An unstrung bow isn't any use," Sevlin said. "The traps were made to deter thieves and usurpers. They never knew when an attack would come, so my guess is they were prepared at all times."

"That sounds like an awful way to live," Idree said. "Looking over your shoulder all the time."

"That's the dark side to power: you have to constantly look for the next threat."

I'm the next threat, Dashi thought, and had to force herself not to avert her eyes,

The sound of rushing water grew louder as they continued. By the time the corridor widened into a long room, Dashi had counted twenty-four pressure plates. The air was chillier and damper here and when Dashi raised her lantern she saw why: a river rushed through the center. Even though she'd heard the sound of rushing water, she was still surprised to find such a large river in front of her. It was wide—far too wide to jump across—with a swift current that sped across the circle of visibility cast by the lantern. It was impossible to tell how deep the dark waters ran.

"A river!" Idree said. "Did they...did they somehow divert it to make it flow through the temple?"

"I don't think we're in the main building anymore," Sevlin said after a moment. "I think we've gone underground."

Dashi looked around. The room smelled earthy and damp, though its appearance was no different from that of the corridor. The walls were paneled in identical dark wood and the ceiling, though higher, was covered in tiles that probably concealed more lethal surprises. The corridor *had* sloped gradually downward, though she hadn't put her finger on it until now. She glanced down, where the stone floor had transitioned to packed earth. If there were pressure plates here, they would be more difficult to spot.

"Now what?" Sevlin asked.

She grimaced. "I don't know. There must be some way to cross."

"Must've *been*," Sevlin corrected her. "It could be long gone by now."

"Then we'll find a new way," she said firmly. The river glittered darkly, taunting her. "Walk directly behind me and keep an eye out for anything that could be a trap. Maybe there is something along the bank that we can work with."

There was no need to work with anything, as it turned out. Instead, there was a delicately arched bridge, its wooden rails appearing out of the darkness before they'd taken more than a few steps. The river plunged back underground on the far side of the bridge.

"Well that was easy enough," Idree said, eying the bridge. "And it even looks like it's in good shape."

Dashi pursed her lips. The bridge *did* appear remarkably intact, but that didn't mean it was safe.

"Look at that." Dashi pointed to a spot directly in front of the bridge. The dirt had settled, creating a thin line around the pressure plate.

"What do you think that does?" Idree asked.

"I don't plan to find out." Dashi tapped the first plank of the bridge with the spear, fully prepared to throw herself to the ground, should she perceive a weapon flying at her. The board squeaked in protest when she put her full weight on it, but that was its only reaction.

"Don't touch the rails," she murmured, taking another step.

Halfway across, she halted abruptly. Idree slammed into her from behind and Dashi teetered briefly but managed not to break the tripwire she'd just spotted.

"Don't follow quite *that* close," she said, regaining her balance.

"Sorry."

"What is it?" Sevlin asked from behind Idree.

"A wire." Dashi dropped into a crouch, angling the lantern to make the wire gleam. "Actually, *two* wires." Both wires crossed the center of the bridge, before turning to run along either side. One spanned the length of the bridge in front of them; the other ran in the direction they'd just come.

She made sure Sevlin and Idree saw where the wires were before continuing. The forward wire ran parallel to the bridge railing, then veered right and climbed the wall on the other side. She could just make out its metallic shine in the lantern light. The walls on this side of the river were reddish. Art hung at regular intervals: huge panels of carved wood, tapestries, relief sculptures of people and animals, which jutted from the wall, stuck between two worlds. The wire led to one of the busts: a strange-looking man with what appeared to be horns growing from his head. The sculpture was large enough to conceal almost anything.

"Another spear?" Idree asked.

"Maybe." Dashi eyed the distance between the sculpture and the bridge. "But my guess would be an arrow. It's lighter and easier to launch."

"A smart place to do it," Sevlin said. "Everyone is all bunched together when they cross. One arrow for the first person who walks across, while that other wire probably triggers another arrow for the last man in line. The bridge is so narrow they can't even step out of the way."

"They could jump," Idree pointed out. "Maybe the river isn't too deep."

"They could, but they would only have a second before the current sucked them underground." He raised his fist and then brought it slowly down, like a stone sinking into the depths. "Intruder problem solved."

Dashi didn't join in the discussion. She'd discovered something in front of them: a line of silvery white tracing up the wall. It connected to a second line of white, then a third. They led into another corridor, which opened to the left of the bridge and disappeared into the gloom. Was the entire corridor strung with tripwires? They weren't very effective ones, she thought, her mind working with interest, not alarm. Each strand was as wide as her finger and she'd spotted their pale color right away. Plus, many of them lined the walls instead of the floor.

She took a step in that direction, fastidiously checking the floor. There was a second pressure plate at this end of the bridge, but it was easy enough to avoid now that she'd spotted its twin on the other side. She stepped over it with an absentminded warning to Idree, keeping her eyes on the strands. They glowed wherever the lantern light fell, reminding Dashi uncomfortably of the creeping taiga mist. Even as she had the thought, the strands vibrated, seeming to writhe toward her. Shadows moved in the depths of the corridor, the way the phantom shapes of her mother and father had emerged from the mist.

The strands trembled again. "Sevlin. Idree," she whispered. "What *is* that?"

Chapter 24

Idree's scream bounced off the walls as a spider shot from the dark corridor. Its body was as big as a shield and spade-shaped. It didn't scuttle like most spiders did but leaped from side to side, moving so fast that Dashi barely had time to draw her sword. Her lantern and spear crashed to the ground as her blade bit into the spider's body. A spray of pink-yellow liquid splashed onto her bare hands and wrists, tingling wherever it struck. She reversed her sword, sending it through the spider's center to make sure it was dead.

A second spider flung itself at her, then a third. They jumped erratically, sometimes diagonally, sometimes sideways, making it difficult to predict their trajectory. It required all of her concentration just to make contact. Their bodies, when her sword hit them, were soft and fleshy, not encased in armor like the taiga ants. That was some comfort, she thought clinically, because there were dozens of them, varying in size from the aforementioned shield to a dinner plate. She swung again, then pivoted, narrowly missing a bodily collision with another spider as it dodged past her.

Two smaller spiders, more agile than the first one she'd killed, raced across the floor, bouncing shadows with far too many legs. She swung low, cutting one of them clean in half. Its insides spilled out, nothing like the recognizable entrails of the animals she hunted or saw being quartered at the butcher's shop but a frothy stew of liquid and color.

The remaining spider launched itself at her leg, wrapping her calf in a tight embrace. Its mouth opened and she saw it bite the leather upper of her boot. Using the flat of her sword, she flicked it off of her, then sliced downward as it flew away from her.

Idree screamed again. Dashi turned to look for her sister and another spider hit her in the knees, knocking her to the ground. It was larger and far stronger than the one that had clung to her boot. It pinned her ankles together with its legs, preventing her from moving. Hair covered its body, legs and face, where eight eyes—two large center eyes and six smaller peripheral ones—focused unblinkingly on her. Its jaws moved spasmodically, opening to reveal two thick fangs each as long as her thumb. Dashi tried to raise her arm, intending to deliver a killing blow, but found her sword arm pinned by another bristly set of legs. A second spider crouched over her wrist. It lowered its abdomen and a stream of silvery white burst from its spinnerets, attaching her hand and the hilt of her sword to the floor with sticky silk.

With a cry that was a mixture of disgust and fear, Dashi lunged to the left. Her hand found the shaft of the dropped spear and she shoved it between the two largest eyes of the spider that held her legs. Jerking the spear free, she rolled to face the one pinning her right arm. It leaped at her, silk still flying from its spinnerets, but she met it with the spear. She shook its dead body off the end of her weapon with a flick of her wrist.

Her sword hand was still glued to the floor, held there by the spider silk. The stuff was surprisingly strong; she had to use her knife to extricate her hand and her sword. Using the side of the blade, she scraped the remaining silk from her palm, keeping the spear and sword within arm's reach for the next wave of spiders. She could hear more scratching along the corridor, hopping from one side to the other like some devilish species of toad.

"Dashi!"

Still crouching, Dashi spun around, her knife ready. But Sevlin wasn't warning her of another attack, only extolling her to hurry.

"Come on!" He was shouting, even though he stood nearby. A halo of dead spiders lay around his feet. Over his shoulder, she could see Idree sprinting for the bridge, her lantern bobbing with each stride.

Dashi had a sudden image of Idree, one arrow protruding from her chest and another from her back. "The tripwire, Idree," she screamed. "Watch out for the tripwire!"

Idree's steps didn't slow.

"She knows," Sevlin said. "I told her to get to the other side of the bridge and wait for us." As he spoke he jerked a tapestry off the wall, ripping it from end to end.

"What are you doing?"

"We have to keep them from following us." He moved to the opening of the spider's corridor, where Dashi had dropped her lantern. The glass had shattered, leaving the flame to hunker gluttonously over the puddle of fuel. Sevlin held the tapestry over the fire. It was so dry it ignited almost instantly.

"Buy me some time, will you?" he said, striding toward a second tapestry.

"Sure," she said, "but make sure they're not attached to a trap before you rip them down."

The next wave of spiders was upon them. The nearest one hopped out of reach as she swung, waiting for the arc of her sword to pass before springing forward again. She spun out of the way just in time. It feinted again and she was struck by the unsettling notion that it had been observing her fight, weighing her strengths and weaknesses before it approached. The spider lunged toward her. She sank to her knees and pulled her knife, letting the spider impale itself on her blade.

Sevlin's fire was going strong, its light illuminating the spiders' corridor. In the time it had taken Dashi to dispatch the spider, he'd added two more tapestries to the blaze. Now, he used her discarded spear to push the bodies of the dead spiders into the fire, adding them to the pile of fuel. He was slowly expanding the flames, creating a line that would stretch across the mouth of the corridor. A small opening remained, a breach several strides wide. Sheathing her sword and drawing her bow instead, Dashi began picking the spiders off as they came toward her, ricocheting off the corridor walls. After the first hail of arrows, none seemed inclined to get closer.

She glanced over her shoulder. Idree had nearly reached the other side of the bridge, having safely navigated the tripwires in the center. Sevlin was steadily adding fuel to his fire, slowly stripping the walls of their history. He approached a carving carefully, using his lantern, which was still intact, to inspect it for signs of a trap. Dashi felt a belated wave of relief; they were lucky they hadn't accidentally stumbled upon a trap and gotten impaled or shot while they were fighting the spiders.

Having deemed the carving safe, Sevlin lifted it from the wall and brought it back to the fire. The flames licked at the wood, making the surface ripple with heat. The opening to the corridor was almost closed now. Dashi backed up to give Sevlin room to work, this time remembering to check for traps before she took a step.

Spiders were collecting on the other side of the flames, their jumping shapes distorted by the smoke. Sevlin left and returned, lugging a huge carving. Dashi went to help him.

"Smells awful," she said as they laid the carving on the fire, completing the barrier.

"It's the spiders, not the wood." He gazed down as the flames bit hungrily into the carving. "These have lasted so long. I hate to burn them."

"I know," she said, "but no ideal is more sacred than survival. Everyone steals the bracelet when it comes down to it."

His mouth quirked a little.

"Where do we go now?" She'd seen how many spiders awaited them on the other side of the fire. They couldn't possibly fight off that many.

"I don't know." Sevlin started to run a hand over his hair but stopped when he caught sight of it. It was streaked with yellow-pink gore from the spiders. The skin beneath was red and irritated.

"I don't know," Sevlin said again. "I was thinking—"

There was a sudden shredding sound, followed by a mechanical roar, like enormous chains rattling or giant gears being forced into action. Dashi whirled, looking for the source of the noise, for a threat of some kind. The spiders hopped harmlessly on the other side of the fire. Everything else was still.

"*Idree!*" Sevlin shouted suddenly and the sound gripped Dashi's heart as surely as a vise.

Out of the darkness a wall slid past them, moving fluidly like a curtain being drawn across an open window. It slipped in front of the bridge, separating them from Idree with solid stone.

Chapter 25

"Idree!"

The wall stopped moving as suddenly as it had started.

"Idree! Can you hear me?" Dashi ran to the wall, pressing her hands against it while she shouted. "Idree?" *Please answer. Please be alive.* What was taking place on the other side? Had something else been triggered at the same time as the moving wall?

"Idree!"

"Dashi?" The voice was muffled.

"Are you alright?"

"Yes. Are you? Where's Sevlin?"

Sevlin leaned in beside Dashi. "I'm here, Idree. We're both fine."

"I thought it was safe so I started to come back and I...I stepped on the pressure plate at the end of the bridge. I felt it shift under my foot and then the wall started moving."

The breath went out of Dashi and she rested her forehead against the cold stone. "I'm just glad you're alive."

"Dashi, how will you get out?" Even through the wall, she could tell Idree was struggling not to panic.

"I don't know." *It could be worse,* she chanted to herself. The pressure plate could have released an arrow. "Just stay there, alright? We'll find a way to open the wall again."

They walked the length of the wall, searching for something—a switch, a pressure plate, anything—that would release it. With her lantern broken, Dashi was forced to stick close to Sevlin instead of splitting up to cover more ground. The delay grated on her. Together, they walked from one end of the wall to the other without finding a single hidden mechanism.

"Do you see that?" Sevlin asked, suddenly coming to a halt.

"What?" Dashi didn't look up from her inspection of the ground. There must be *something* here. The Pureks wouldn't block access to the rest of the temple without also having a way to restore it.

"That carving in the wall."

She glanced up hopefully, but the moveable wall looked as it had before.

"Not that wall, the other one." Sevlin was facing in the opposite direction.

She turned around, studying the relief sculptures carved into the reddish stone. They'd been designed to give the illusion of an outdoor view. A line of faux windows, separated by double columns, paraded down the wall in either direction. Each looked out onto a garden scene—flower beds, winding pathways, strolling couples, bushes trimmed until they resembled animals instead of plants—all carved shallowly into the wall.

"Which one?" she asked.

"Her." He pointed at a life-sized figure of a woman. This sculpture was done in high relief, so that the woman's head and shoulders were three-dimensional and independent of the supporting wall. She was turned away from the viewer, looking coyly back over one shoulder.

"What about her?"

"She's walking into the wall. And she's looking back over her shoulder like she wants us to follow."

Dashi took in the woman's suggestive smile, the way her deel fell to one side, exposing her shoulder. "Looks like she wants something else to me," she said, returning her attention to the floor.

"Look at the other carvings," Sevlin said. "They're all looking at her."

Dashi turned back to where he was pointing. A series of life-sized figures had been carved into the wall at regular intervals, alternating with the window scenes. There were people of all ages and descriptions, probably nobles or other important people from the time period. Each of the figures was looking toward the coy woman.

Sevlin didn't wait for her response, but went to the sculpture and began running his hands over it, poking and prodding with his fingertips.

"You should at least ask her name before you—" Dashi began, but broke off with a gasp. The statue had moved. "Did you see that?" she asked excitedly. "Whatever you just did, do it again!"

"Oh, you're interested now, are you?" Sevlin asked, but Dashi could hear the excitement under his dry tone.

He lined his fingers up with the woman's and pressed. The sculpture shifted once more, this time sinking into the wall and leaving a narrow passage in its wake. Sevlin held up his light, illuminating the area within. In contrast to seemingly everything else in the temple, it was devoid of decoration, aside from a few cobwebs drifting lazily in the air. Dashi eyed them suspiciously, but they were the normal variety, nothing unduly large or frightening. The passage turned to the right a little way down, blocking their view.

"This can't be right," Dashi said, turning back to the coy sculpture. She ran her own hands over it, searching for something Sevlin had missed. "There has to be a way to release the wall separating us from Idree."

Finding nothing, she turned to Sevlin. "We were focused on the floor and the moving wall. Maybe we missed something on one of the other sculptures."

Sevlin held the lantern as she checked the other relief sculptures, searching for something that would release the wall and allow Idree to join them again. There was nothing.

"Dashi," he said after nearly an hour. "We have to try something else."

"We can't just leave her out there!"

"Maybe the release mechanism isn't here. Maybe it's farther in."

She made a show of continuing to check the sculpture in front of her, but she knew he was right. They could spend all day here and they might never find a way out.

Reluctantly she returned to the moveable wall. Cupping her hands around her mouth she leaned against it. "Still there, Idree?"

"Well, I'm not leaving without you."

Dashi glanced at Sevlin. "You might have to. We can't find a way to move the wall, but we found a doorway that leads deeper into the temple."

"What?" Idree's voice rose. "Dashi, are you crazy? You can't go deeper into the temple! You don't have a way out. Sevlin! *You're* not crazy. Talk some sense into her."

Sevlin rested one shoulder against the wall, his face just above Dashi's. "She's right, Idree. Maybe the way to release the wall isn't here; maybe it's farther in. We've checked everything we could think of on this side and we didn't find anything."

There was a minute of silence.

"Idree?" Dashi prodded.

"I don't want to go."

"Is your lantern still lit?" Sevlin called.

"Yes."

"It won't last forever. You have to leave while you can still see the way. You know the pattern for the pressure plates and there's an extra bladder of fuel in one of the saddlebags. You can refill it and come back if we don't come out, but give us until noon, alright? And make sure to stay out of sight in case any of the other racers show up."

"Are you crazy?" Dashi whispered, looking up at Sevlin. "I don't want her coming back in here after us!"

He shrugged one shoulder. "Let's just concentrate on getting her out. She'll be safer outside and out of sight. Maybe we won't need rescuing."

"What if she gets hurt on her way out?"

"She could get hurt waiting for us too." He put a hand on her shoulder. "You have to trust her, Dashi. There's nothing else you can do."

Idree still hadn't answered.

"Idree?" Sevlin called. "Will you do that?"

"Alright," she said finally. "I'll leave." She paused again. "Try to find the needle while you're in there, Dashi."

Dashi smiled slightly. "I'll find it," she promised. "And Idree?"

"Yes?"

"Be careful."

The hidden passage didn't improve right away. It stayed narrow and musty-aired, while Dashi chafed over the thought of leaving Idree to exit the temple alone. What if one of the spiders had somehow gotten by them and followed her sister? What if Idree mixed up the pattern of the pressure plates? *You have to trust her*, Sevlin had said. She knew she'd promised Idree she'd do just that, but it was harder than it sounded. *Just concentrate on what's in front of you*, she told herself. *That's the quickest way to get out of here.*

"How long have we been walking, do you think?" she asked. Sevlin moved slowly, checking the floor and each wall before stepping forward.

"Mmm, fifteen minutes," he answered. "Tired?"

"Tired of staring at your back," she muttered. In truth she *was* tired, and her body ached from the beating Negan had given her. Her head and eye socket hurt enough that it was starting to affect her ability to concentrate, so she'd reluctantly agreed to let Sevlin take the lead in looking for traps.

"Is that what you're huffing about back there? You can be in charge if you like."

"I'm not worried about who's in charge! I'm just tired of not being able to see where I'm going."

"You want to be able to see where you're going because you don't trust me to do it for you. That's called wanting to be in charge."

"That's called wanting you to walk faster."

"Idree will be fine," he said after a moment. "The only things between her and the exit are the pressure plates in the floor and she knows the pattern. She'll be waiting for us when we get out of here."

Dashi cleared her throat. "Where do you think this leads? We're heading downward again."

"The information the queen received said the temple was built near a particularly strong vein of magic. I assume going down into the earth makes it easier to access."

She considered this. "That doesn't mean anything is there now."

"No."

"A vein hasn't been seen since the cataclysm. How do the queen and the khan intend to use the needle if there's no raw magic to work with?" She heard Khagan Nuray's husky voice in her mind. *The veins of magic are resurfacing.*

"The queen only intends to safeguard the needle against the khan. I have no idea what *he* intends."

"What makes you so sure your queen wouldn't use the needle if she could? All that power within reach and you think she'd just sit on it?"

Sevlin stopped abruptly. They'd reached the end of the passageway. A metal door waited in front of them.

"There's no lock," Sevlin said.

"That seems odd," she conceded. "Open it slowly."

Sevlin eased the door halfway open, then froze. She could see that they were standing at the edge of a room, but everything else was blocked by his shoulders and the door.

"What is it?" she asked, poking him in the side to make him move.

When he didn't answer she poked him again.

"Gold," he said finally, his voice hushed. "More gold than I've ever seen and I've been inside Tyvalar's royal vault." He turned sideways so Dashi could squeeze next to him.

When she did, she understood why he'd taken so long to respond. Gold, silver, gems, silk, brocade, lace, sculptures made of alabaster and bronze: the room was replete with every measure of riches of which Dashi could conceive. Even the air smelled of wealth: the scent of perfume and incense hung heavily about them.

"It's amazing," she said finally. "I've never seen—Why was there no lock on the door?"

"We're rich," Sevlin murmured, then barked an incredulous laugh. "Tyvalarans will want for nothing. They'll eat so much they'll have to be rolled down the street like barrels. They'll stable their horses on top of silk, and pave the roads with gold." He lifted her bag from her shoulder and thrust it toward her chest. "Fill it," he ordered. "As much as you can carry."

"Don't worry, I will," Dashi said. This much gold—*any* gold, really—would be useful wherever she and Idree decided to start over. "But we'd better find the needle first. Otherwise, carrying this much gold will make us drop from exhaustion." Dashi tore her eyes away from the gold, forcing herself to look at the pathway that wound between shimmering towers of riches, to a door on the other side. The needle had to be somewhere else. The Pureks would never just leave it buried among piles of coins. It would be someplace special, befitting its sacred status. Another altar, perhaps, or—

"Forget the needle," Sevlin said harshly. "We have what we need right here." They were crammed into the end of the passageway, standing almost chest to chest. He leaned forward, looking down at her with eyes that were suddenly glassy. "We'll send horsemen. Wagons. We can cart it back to Tyvalar in a few weeks."

He grabbed her by the shoulders, his breath falling softly on her face. His pulse was beating rapidly in his throat, fluttering unevenly the way a rabbit's did when the hunter pulled it from a snare, in the moments just before its neck was broken. In any other circumstance, she would have assumed he was about to kiss her. That's how close his lips were, how unsteady his breathing was. But there was something strange and fevered in his expression.

"This is going to change our lives," he said. "Are you ready, Dashi? To be wrapped in luxury for the rest of your life? To have your pick of the finest clothes, to be adorned with the rarest jewels?"

It was a testament to his state of mind, she thought, that he didn't support his argument with the prospect of good horses or saddles. Surely he knew her well enough by now to know that clothes and jewels would not be her weaknesses, even in wealth. He was gripping her shoulders so hard she could feel finger-shaped bruises forming. His other hand slid to the back of her neck, leaving a trail of alarm in its wake. This was a dangerous position.

"Dashi?" His tone was insistent, a mirror of his grip. He was waiting for agreement. Anything less would only enrage him. That's how the poison worked.

"Yes, Sevlin," she murmured, mimicking the coy expression of the sculpture that had led them to the passageway in the first place. At the same time, she shifted toward him, bringing their faces a hair's breadth apart and loosening his hold on the back of her neck.

Her elbow flew up with no warning, hitting Sevlin in the jaw and snapping his head back against the wall. Her fists followed in quick succession, raining blows as hard and as fast as she could. When his reflexes recovered enough to block her, she grabbed him by the shoulders, bringing her knee into his solar plexus at the same time. He grunted in pain, offering little resistance as she took the lantern from his hand and pushed him the rest of the way to the ground. Sevlin's legs were still in the doorway, preventing the door from closing fully. She'd need to move him, but first she had to do something about the breath she was holding.

She fumbled in her bag for the bandages she'd brought, her lungs screaming in protest all the while. Finding one, she wound it around her face, covering her nose and mouth and tying it tightly behind her head. *There*. Her breath rushed out and in again, bringing relief with it. Dashi grabbed a second bandage and, working quickly, began to wind it around Sevlin's face. He had a scarf somewhere—the same one he'd used to hide his scar at the beginning of the race—but she didn't know whether he'd packed it in the small bag he carried. Either way, she didn't have time to search for it.

Dashi was leaning over to secure the ends of the bandage when Sevlin roused himself. She blocked the punch intended for her face but not the one coming for her side. It wasn't the hardest she'd ever taken—he was laying flat on his back and didn't have much room to swing—but it knocked her sideways just enough that he could bring his knee up into her swollen cheekbone. Lightning flashed across her vision and she flew backward, hitting the wall with her shoulder. Dashi glanced at the still-open door. Now that Sevlin had moved, it could be closed. It *needed* to be closed if they were to survive.

She leaped toward it, but Sevlin thrust an arm across her chest. She dropped to the floor, sliding out from under his arm and pushing forward with her legs all in one movement so that she flew through the air. She landed in a squat, just close enough that her outstretched fingers brushed the door, pushing it closed. There was no time for self-congratulation, however. Sevlin was on top of her. Snarling, he pushed her to one side as easily as a doll. She hit him in the side of the head with her elbow, then uppercut him with her other fist. *Stupid, stupid, stupid*, she chided herself. *Should have tied his hands first, not covered his face.* At least he hadn't bothered to remove the bandage she'd wrapped around his nose and mouth—more evidence that he wasn't thinking clearly. That was good; with his airways protected, he'd come to his senses soon.

He was heavy—she remembered that from the first time she'd fought him—and she didn't want to get pinned beneath him. She rolled away before he could put his full weight on her and wrapped her legs around his waist, wrenching her hips sideways to throw him off balance. Her legs had trapped one of his arms, but his other arm remained free. He wrapped a hand around her throat, slamming her shoulders against the ground and cutting off her air at the same time. Dashi shifted her hips again, pivoting so she could aim a punch at his groin, but he backed up in time to avoid it.

His reflexes were recovering. She could see it in the way he'd ducked, in the way he was blinking normally once more. Mental capacity would follow swiftly, but she wasn't sure it would be quick enough. His grip on her throat was painful, so hard it made her head pound. Or maybe that was the lack of oxygen. She clawed at his fingers, but the pressure was still there, forcibly closing her windpipe.

Sevlin blinked rapidly, his eyes darting around without really settling on her. His expression looked clearer, less fervent. *He's close. He has to be*, she thought. The world was going dark at the edges. Her hand slid to her waist, feeling for her knife. Her eyes watered, making trails down her cheeks and into her hair.

"Sev...lin," she croaked as she drew the knife.

Abruptly the weight on her throat eased. Dashi rolled to her side, dragging in deep, wheezing mouthfuls of air through the bandages that covered her face.

"Dashi?" Sevlin leaned over her, his expression a mixture of confusion and worry. "Are you alright?"

She hacked a few more times for good measure, then nodded. Sevlin put his hand on her hip to help her sit up, then snatched it back like he didn't know whether it could be trusted.

"What happened?" He touched his jaw gingerly, seeming to realize for the first time that his face was covered. He started to pull off the bandages but stopped when Dashi grabbed his wrist.

"No, don't. The—" Her voice was barely intelligible. She fumbled for her water and lifted her mask a fraction to take a drink. "Do you smell that?" she asked once she could speak again. "Like dying flowers?"

"I thought it was an offering of incense."

"An offering to its victims, maybe." She smiled humorlessly behind her makeshift mask. "It's poison. A fungus bred by the Pureks. I didn't recognize it until you—" She broke off coughing and had to take another swallow of water. Sevlin waited beside her, staring at his hand as he flexed his fingers.

"The spores alter the way you feel things," she explained when she could speak again. "The Pureks originally used it in the bedroom. The mire of Passion, they called it. But too much of it, like there is in that room, makes everything you're feeling—good and bad—become warped."

His eye dropped to her cheekbone, which was still throbbing from where he'd kneed her. She could almost feel new bruises melding with the ones from her encounter with Negan. The results were certain to be ghastly.

"It can turn violent quickly," she said, answering his unspoken question.

"Dashi. I'm—"

She waved a hand. "It wasn't your fault. It does that to everyone if they breathe enough of it. Anyway, I hit you first."

He huffed in amusement. "I'm glad it affected you too. I would feel bad if the violence only went one way."

Dashi shook her head. "The spores float on the air, so the taller you are, the quicker you're affected. It would have gotten to me in another minute or so, but I figured out what was coming. There's no reasoning with someone drunk on it, so I had to get you down and cover your face."

"And you know about this...?"

"Through bad luck and experimentation. It was years ago—that's why I didn't recognize it at first—but my friends and I discovered it at another ruin. Luckily, it was Zayaa who'd gone into the room first. If it had been Baris..." She shook her head. It would have taken all three of them to contain Baris and even then it wouldn't have been a sure thing.

"What did she do?"

"Alternated between trying to make love with Altan and trying to kill him."

The lower half of Sevlin's face was hidden by the bandages, but his eyes crinkled with amusement. Had he smiled?

"I know. Altan didn't have a problem with the first one, but the second was a little disconcerting, I think. It wasn't funny at the time though. It took all of us to subdue her and get her out of there and by that time Altan had inhaled enough that he'd started to go a little crazy too."

"You said it was poison?"

"We only realized that later, when we found a trove of healer records. After your emotions, it impairs reflexes and coordination. Eventually, you pass out. If you don't get away from the spores, you'll die before you wake up."

His wary gaze shifted from his hands to the door that separated them from the treasure room. "Do you think this was done on purpose? Or did the fungus just breed out of control for all these years?"

She shrugged. "Both, probably. I doubt it's an accident that it's here, exactly where all the gold is, but the years have certainly added to its potency."

He glanced at her, then away again. "I know it was only a few minutes ago, but I don't even remember everything, just that I was trying to explain something and it felt like..." He stopped and rubbed at his scar. "Like I would do *anything* to convince you of my point. Any means would justify the end."

"You wanted to take the gold and leave the needle."

He gave a short laugh. "That sounds right. I don't want to be here. I guess, deep down, my mind is still grasping for any excuse not to come."

"You don't?" she asked, not bothering to conceal her surprise.

"No, but when the queen asks..." He spread his hands in a gesture of resignation.

Dashi nodded and began packing up the contents of her bag, which had spilled while she frantically rummaged for bandages. The Tyvalaran queen had *asked* him to come? As in, *personally*? In Karakal, the khan ordered you to go and then executed you if you failed. Tyvalar sounded like a much better place to live, she thought bitterly.

Sevlin got to his feet. "So we stay low?"

"And move fast. These bandages aren't that tight so they won't protect us forever."

The door swung open quietly, a sweeping arm welcoming them to the riches within. The gold caught the lantern light and held it, the reflection bouncing between piles of treasure until the room seemed abnormally bright. Dashi could still detect the sweet rot of the spores through her mask, but the stench was fainter now.

The floor was made of huge stones, each as long as she was, and she had to make do with smacking each one with the spear before she transferred her weight onto it. Still, she was able to move swiftly, keeping to a crouch. She tried to focus on the door at the end of the room, not the gleaming treasures on either side. There was no point in tempting herself to stop.

The door at the opposite side of the treasure room was locked. Dashi dropped her bag and withdrew her lock picks for a second time. She had to work quickly now; there was no time for mistakes. She could hear Sevlin's steps behind her—they'd agreed to cross the treasure room separately so that if she triggered a trap, he could try to help—but she didn't turn around. Instead, she closed her eyes, trying to channel all the lessons she'd been given. Altan, Zayaa and Baris would be half-circled around her, coaching her or, in the case of Baris, playfully disparaging her.

The lock was similar to the one at the entrance of the temple, but she opened it faster and cracked the door. Holding Sevlin's lantern high, she peered around the edge. The floor appeared to be made from a slab of solid stone, with no cracks or joints to denote pressure plates. Beyond that, she could see nothing.

Dashi took a step inside. The air was cool and free of the stench of spores. Beneath her makeshift mask, she smiled in relief. Once they'd closed the door to the spores, they could uncover their faces. Now that she was inside the room, she could see that it was empty. Four walls and a stone floor, all unremarkable except for the fact that they seemed to be made of seamless stone. The lantern cast flickering shadows on the wall opposite her and Dashi frowned. There was no doorway leading out. What had this room been—a quiet place for the seamstress to collect her thoughts? And where was the needle?

Sevlin's shout of alarm yanked her from her observations. "Dashi! The door!"

At the same moment, there was a loud rushing sound. Dashi nearly fell over as the floor lurched beneath her feet. She looked back over her shoulder. Sevlin was still halfway out of the room, pushing hard against the door, which seemed to be trying to close of its own accord.

"I can't...hold..." he panted. Suddenly he leaped forward, slipping past the end of the door just as it slammed shut, taking a piece of his pant leg with it.

Dashi stared at the closed door. This side had no lock for her to pick. It didn't even have a handle.

The slab of stone was still moving under her feet, bringing her closer to Sevlin as it slid *beneath* the wall. He was still trying to gain purchase on the closed door, looking as perplexed as she felt. Every few seconds he had to take a step backward to keep from being shoved against the wall by the retracting floor.

Dashi looked at the opposite side of the room and gasped. The floor was sliding away from the wall, leaving a yawning gap that grew with each passing moment.

"Can you see what's happening?" Sevlin yelled over the noise. "What's under the floor?"

Dashi staggered forward over the moving floor, arms out for balance. Orange light greeted her as she peered into the opening.

Chapter 26

Dashi jumped backward as if a fiery hand might somehow reach up and grab her. Indeed, the flames seemed to be trying to do just that, flaring and spitting erratically. Her eyes automatically turned away, attempting to shield her from the sight. *Flames spitting. Her mother burning.*

She forced herself to look at the space below the floor, to take in the way the blaze burned brightest along one side. She glimpsed a wet puddle of fuel beneath the flames and, in some strange inverse correlation, realized that her mouth had become dry. Extreme heat would detonate the pyrothrite, according to the noble in Karak City, but the blacksmith had acted like just being inside the smithy was dangerous. Which one of them was right?

Dashi turned and sprinted back to Sevlin, her strides unsteady because of the moving floor. He didn't need her to explain what awaited them. The heat and smoke had already made it obvious.

"What's burning?" He was still prying at the door with his fingertips.

"Oil, I think," she said, ripping the bandages from her face and using them to wipe her forehead. The room was heating rapidly, though it wasn't yet hot enough to make her sweat. The thought of what awaited them was the cause of that.

Sevlin cursed. "That's not going to burn out anytime soon and the floor is a third of the way gone."

Dashi glanced involuntarily over her shoulder at the approaching edge. He was right; they had, at most, five minutes before they fell into the inferno.

"Maybe it'll stop moving," she said without any real hope. She forced her hands to unclench so that she could begin running her fingers over the wall. The stone was smooth, almost polished feeling, and still cool to the touch. She wondered how it would feel after a few more minutes in the burning chamber. Sevlin began probing around the doorway, searching for a mechanism that would release the door.

"It won't matter if it does stop moving," he said. "The smoke and the heat will kill us soon enough, even if we don't fall into the fire."

Dashi grimaced as her palm hit more featureless wall. There wasn't anything she could use for a climbing handhold. No mortared seams, no decorative cornices, no carvings. The room was a giant oven and they were trapped inside. The thought made her lungs tighten. *An oven.* Like her family's rooms in Karak City.

Idree's small arms, wrapped around her leg. Her mother screaming from the burning room at their back. Altan shouting for her to jump.

Think, she ordered herself. To her right, Sevlin was cursing in an uninterrupted stream, which meant he hadn't had any luck either. This room was designed to prevent—no, *kill*—thieves, which meant they must have done something to trigger the retracting floor. But what? She'd seen no pressure plates. Perhaps the mere act of opening the door had caused it. *No,* she thought, *that couldn't be right.* The seamstress and temple acolytes needed to reach this part of the temple; they must have known of a way out.

Dashi turned in a full circle, keeping her eyes away from the pit of fire that was gaping steadily larger. What would the seamstress have done when he or she came in? Where would they have *gone*? There wasn't a doorway other than the one they'd come through. *No way out of the oven.*

She'd already checked the stretch of wall to the right of the door. Sevlin was working on the left. What remained? She tipped her head back, letting her eyes search the corners of the ceiling. The fire below was giving off so much light that she didn't even need a lantern. Rolling black clouds had begun to gather along the ceiling, but where the smoke was thin she glimpsed pure, unadorned stone. No balconies. No ladders. No escape.

Nearly half of the floor had disappeared. She swiped at the sweat running from her hairline. *Maybe there* is *no mechanism. Maybe there's no way out,* her mind whispered. *It's an execution chamber. The seamstress took another way to the needle, a different hidden door that you missed.*

Dashi put her hand on the wall. The stone was growing warm. *It's not an execution chamber,* she told herself. *It's a puzzle. Something to figure out—quickly.* She couldn't let herself think otherwise. That way led to acceptance, to death. There must be a way out.

From the other side of the room, Sevlin shouted that he hadn't found anything.

"Dashi!" he called again when she didn't move.

The alarm in his tone. The distinctly male voice shouting her name. She thought of Altan, waiting in the street below, his arms stretched up to the window of the room she'd shared with her mother and sister. *Jump, Dashi. I'll catch you.*

Jump. It was an expression she'd heard plenty of times before. *To get out of the oven you have to jump through the flames.*

Dashi ran toward the front edge of the floor. This time she made herself go all the way to the brink, until there was nothing under the tips of her boots but a maw of fire, nothing in front of her face but its hot breath, whispering in her hair. She forced herself to look at the fiery space below, squinting against the haze and the smoke that made her eyes tear.

There, barely protruding from the wall on her left, was a narrow walkway located just below the plane of the floor. It was constructed of the same stone as everything else in the room, with a solid stone rail that made it almost indistinguishable from the wall that supported it. It was just wide enough for one person and only a few strides long. Her eyes swept back to the right, to where the fire had begun. She'd been so horrified by the sight that she hadn't looked left, or at least hadn't looked left long enough to discern the way out.

The problem, however, wasn't the walkway's narrowness, but the fact that she'd seen it too late. If she'd walked through the door and gone directly to the opposite wall, she could have stepped easily onto the walkway as soon as it was uncovered by the moving floor. Doubtless, that's what the seamstresses had done, since they would have known to hurry. No such option was available to Dashi now. The floor had been retracting for several minutes and the walkway was too far away for her to reach, or even jump to.

"Dashi!" There was real panic in Sevlin's voice as he came up behind her. "Move back from the edge."

"I found the way out, Sevlin." She reached into her bag without turning around. If she looked away from the fire now, she might never be able to force her eyes there again. "But we're going to have to..." She trailed off, unable to finish the sentence.

Sevlin's eyes moved from her face to her hands, which held the rope and pronged hook she'd brought from Karak City, before finally sweeping down to the stone walkway hovering at the edge of the fire. He exhaled another stream of curses.

Dashi held the hook loosely in one hand. She'd only have one try. If she missed, the rope would be dragged through the fire below. There wasn't even time to take a practice swing. Each passing second took them farther from the walkway and her rope would barely be long enough as it was.

"We'll be swinging practically into the fire," Sevlin said, not taking his eyes off the walkway. He strapped the lantern to his pack.

Dashi nodded wordlessly. Her throat had dried shut. Sparks spit into the air, so large that fireballs would have been a more accurate term. It would only take one of those—

She threw the hook without any warning. It sailed through the air, suspended momentarily at the top of its arc before beginning to descend. The rope uncoiled steadily at Dashi's feet. With a clank that was barely audible above the crackle of the flames, the hook hit the edge of the walkway's railing. It teetered briefly on the lip, undecided as to whether it should fall forward or back. Every muscle in Dashi's body was taut, but she kept her hands loose, careful not to inadvertently dislodge it. The hook rocked forward, settling into place over the wall, and Dashi and Sevlin both let out a breath.

Dashi pulled the rope tight, testing to make sure the hook would hold fast. A piece of stone broke off the rail and tumbled into the fire below, where it sank without a sound, but the hook stayed put.

Sevlin ripped off his gauze mask and gave her a quick, desperate grin from one side of his mouth. "Now for the easy part." He grasped the rope as high up as he could, wrapping the trailing end once around the toe of his boot for extra purchase. He'd left his crossbow on the other side of the room during his search for an exit, but there was no time to retrieve it. "Ready?"

Dashi stood frozen, a contrast to the flames gyrating below.

The heat against her back. Idree's fingers biting into her leg. She couldn't go into the fire. And what about the pyrothrite? Would it detonate mid-swing?

Sevlin was stretched out over the edge. In another second he would either have to let go of the rope or be pulled over. He reached out a hand and grasped Dashi by the elbow, pulling her close. "Grab the rope, Dashi," he ordered in a quiet voice. "Good. Ready? One, two…"

In her head she could hear Altan again, audible even over her mother's screams. *Jump, Dashi. I'll catch you.*

Dashi closed her eyes and pushed off.

Chapter 27

Hot wind rushed past Dashi's cheeks, pulling at her hair and parching her eyes. The flames roared in her ears. Even the sound of her pulse was drowned by the fire's clamor to get to her skin, her clothes, her hair—whatever could be consumed.

Sevlin's and Dashi's combined weight snapped the rope tight, ending their brief free fall and turning it into a more controlled swing. The change in trajectory threw them apart, then banged them together again. Dashi's knees knocked into Sevlin's legs. Her cheek hit his chest.

The fire got closer and hotter. They were swinging so fast. *Too fast.* She blinked away her tears and kept her eyes open, estimating the distance, trying to judge whether they would escape being burned. They reached the bottom of the arc. Her boots were furnaces, scorching the soles of her feet. Then she was moving away from the fire's heat, coming so close to the underside of the walkway that her braid whipped the stone.

"Climb," Sevlin shouted in her ear as they began the return swing. Climbing was something that had always come easily to her, but on the moving rope, with Sevlin's hands and feet getting in the way of her own and the fire so close she couldn't concentrate, it was a different matter. She had the brief, grateful realization that Idree was safer on the other side of the temple, and then she looked down and fear blotted her thoughts away. Flames were climbing the end of the rope, moving toward them in steady pursuit.

"Faster," Dashi panted. "The rope."

Sevlin looked down and redoubled his efforts. They were close to the low wall that skirted the walkway. Metal scraped against stone as their weight rocked the hook. A ball of fire shot up from below, soaring through the air until it hit the stone wall in a shower of sparks. Dashi kept climbing. Sevlin's elbows hit hers. There was no place to put her hands; his body was everywhere, blocking her at each turn. The fire on the rope was closer now. It would reach her boots in another minute. With one final push, Sevlin looped an arm over the stone wall and pulled himself up.

He tumbled out of sight onto the walkway just as another ball of fire hurtled from below. It arched higher and higher, spinning toward her. Dashi ducked as the fiery mass hit the walkway, raining sparks onto her hair and hands. The rope above her head started burning. Strands broke free and curled away from the rest of the weave, blackening as they went. Dashi pushed upward with her legs. Her hand brushed the stone, but she wasn't high enough to get a solid grip. Between the fire and her weight, the rope was fraying rapidly. She had to get onto the walkway before it pulled apart completely.

Sevlin reappeared suddenly, grabbing her arm and pulling her up and over. They stumbled onto the walkway and fell through a narrow doorway recessed into the wall, landing in a heap.

Dashi blinked her stinging eyes. They were in a small, empty room. An engraved bronze door was right next to her, but she had no desire to open it. Compared to the heat of the oven room, the air in the small room was almost cool.

She'd landed face-down on top of Sevlin, her pack somehow tangled with the sword at his side. She could feel his chest rising and falling against her forehead as his heart beat out a frantic rhythm. Somehow that was comforting. It was good to know his pulse was racing as much as hers. She raised her head slowly, not quite if sure her body would still obey her brain. Perhaps it would revolt. She wouldn't blame it; her brain had put her in this dangerous situation and her body had nearly paid the price.

The smell of burning was everywhere, but for once it didn't conjure memories of childhood tragedy. Instead, Dashi stayed firmly rooted in the present. Focused on the cool air against her cheeks. On the sting in her hands and the blood rushing merrily through her veins. Of Sevlin's body beneath hers and his arms locked around her back. She looked up and her eyes met his pale ones and, for a split second, she thought about the treasure room—of his hand on the back of her neck and his breath on her face and of what that would feel like again.

She looked away as soon as the thought hit her. There was no point in it. No point in anything besides leaving this place with the needle in her hand.

"We made it," she said, sitting up. She winced as her bruised ribs complained. The pyrothrite belt felt warm. Then again, so did the rest of her. It hadn't exploded. That was the important part.

"So we did." Sevlin got to his feet.

She wondered if he even remembered how close they'd been in the treasure room.

Sevlin had dropped his pack on the narrow walkway back in the oven room. While he retrieved it, Dashi examined the bronze door. It had no locking mechanism that she could see. Cautiously, she pushed it with one finger. It drifted open, drawn by an invisible hand. She had her hand on her sword, just in case more spiders came pouring out, but there was no movement from inside.

Sevlin came back into the room, brandishing the lantern and wiping away the sweat that had immediately sprouted on his face.

"Fire's still going strong, but the lantern didn't break when I dropped my pack." He glanced at the open door and gave a cautious sniff, testing for the telltale scent of spores. "Think it's safe?"

Dashi shrugged one shoulder. "No way to know until you light that."

He did it quickly, then held the lantern aloft. Dashi sucked in a breath.

The room was lined with tiered platforms. On them, arrayed in neat rows, were hundreds upon hundreds of statuettes. They glinted invitingly: gold, silver, bronze. The rest of the room was decorated just as lavishly, a far cry from the bare oven room and the stone antechamber in which they now stood. Blue, white and gold tiles covered the walls. A few sections of wall had been left bare of tile and words had been chiseled into the marble instead. Dashi did a quick survey, but they were all verses and proverbs of one kind or another, nothing that screamed danger.

"Blessed ancestors, we found it," Sevlin muttered. He looked down at her, eyes bright.

She grinned, pushing aside the thought that, if they'd indeed found the statuette that held the needle, she would soon be wiping the elated expression from his face.

Sevlin squatted next to the threshold, holding the lantern while Dashi examined the flawless, white floor.

"I don't see anything," she said finally. "You?"

He shook his head. "Wouldn't you think if there was one place the Pureks would put a trap, it would be here?"

"Maybe they assumed that only a seamstress would get this far."

"Maybe," he said, unconvinced. "But every time I've thought something was safe in this place, it turned out to be deadly."

"I know what you mean." She studied the figures on the other side of the room, then stepped into the chamber. Nothing happened so she took another step, then another, her excitement growing, until she was standing directly in front of the platforms.

"Ah," she murmured.

"What?" Sevlin asked from behind her. He still held the lantern high, turning the statuettes into row after row of human-shaped sundials, their shadows flickering over the wall.

"I thought maybe it was another altar, that each statuette was a different ancestor, but that didn't make sense. Worship areas were accessible to the public." She pointed to the tiered platforms that held the statuettes. They were formed from plaster and the once-smooth topography was now marred with cracks and dust. "See how that crack completely encircles the base of this statuette?"

"Another trap," Sevlin muttered.

"I think we're relatively safe here, as long as we don't try to remove any of the statuettes. At least I think that's what *that*," Dashi nodded to a line of script etched into the wall just above the platform, "is trying to tell us. 'Stealing from the house of the ancestors is punishable by death,'" she translated. "I've seen that before. It was the first legal code to be made public. Khagan...Dharmek? I can't remember, but this is one of the laws, I think."

"So we're in a room full of statuettes and we can't take any?"

"We just can't take the wrong one."

Sevlin's mouth tilted. "Simple."

Dashi clasped her hands behind her and leaned closer to the statuettes. They were meticulously formed, each more lifelike than the next. Each figure had a unique expression, hair and clothes. Gems and pearls shone sporadically, winking at her from tiny eye sockets and glittering from the belts, scabbards and clothing of the small figures. Some of the statuettes were knee-height. Others were the length of her little finger.

There were hundreds of them. Outside, the rushing sound had finally ceased; the floor must have fully retracted by now. Did the ancient Pureks have some method of extinguishing the fire, she wondered, or would it continue to burn until it exhausted its fuel? Even if they selected the correct statuette, how would they get out of the temple?

"Here are two statuettes holding needles," Sevlin said. "How do we know which is the right one?"

Dashi peered around him. "Easy: neither."

"Why not?"

"Too obvious. They're holding *needles*, Sevlin."

"How about this one?" He pointed to a tall statuette of an old man. "He's holding a thimble. It could be a reference to the seamstress."

"Still too blatant. It's going to be obvious and hidden at the same time."

"That makes no sense."

"Sure it does. That's how the Pureks did everything. Like the pressure plates in the floor. They're right there in front of you, but they're disguised among the other stones. Or the passageway you found. The woman sculpture was completely visible, but her message was ambiguous."

"Well, the statuette is holding a thimble, which is obvious, but it's still hidden amongst all the other statuettes."

"I'm telling you, it doesn't feel right. It has to be something that grabs you."

"Grabs *you* or grabs me?"

Now that she'd put into words exactly what she was looking for, all the statuettes seemed completely unsuitable. They were either too obvious or too unremarkable. She began pacing in front of the platforms, pausing every few steps to examine them. Sevlin ignored her, letting her flow around him while he squinted down at the statuettes.

"Here's one with wings," he said. "Maybe it's a reference to stitching a particular kind of magic?"

Dashi pursed her lips, shaking her head. It would be foolish to select one based on such tenuous evidence. She needed to be *sure*. There had to be something she was missing, something that would help her decide.

She finished her circuit around the room nearly an hour later. Her neck hurt from staring down at the statuettes. Sevlin stood nearby, without a trace of the elation he'd shown when they first discovered the statuettes. They'd both been so excited; it had been like sharing an adventure with Altan or Baris or Zayaa. A frown slid over her face. She couldn't let herself think like that.

Dashi gave the statuettes one last look, then flipped onto her hands and executed a series of slow-motion backbends across the room, letting her thoughts wander. Something was bothering her, but she couldn't quite get her mind to pinpoint it. They were on the right track. They had to be. She didn't think the ancient Pureks would have wasted so much effort creating obstacles otherwise. A few pressure plates, maybe, but an entire room designed to throw its occupants into burning oil? That seemed excessive for a mere decoy trail.

The doorway loomed on her right and Dashi had a brief glimpse of the bare antechamber from which they'd come. Perhaps there was a clue to be had there. They'd tumbled inside from the oven, then gotten up and come into the statuettes' room without first checking to see if the antechamber contained any secrets. As she stared, the section of engraved script adjacent to the doorway caught her eye. She couldn't translate it at the moment—it was hard enough to translate ancient Purek when she was looking at the words right-side up—but it wasn't the words that piqued her interest. When she looked at the script upside-down, the straight parts of the letters looked like swords.

Dashi flipped back to her feet and stepped closer to the engraving. It was a small rectangle, positioned just to the left of the door so that she hadn't seen it until she'd turned her back on the legions of statuettes.

Purek was a harsh language, both in sound and in appearance, with few of the graceful arches or bubble-like curves used in present-day writing. Instead, each character was drawn with straight stems and hashes of varying angles and lengths. On this particular engraving, however, some of the characters had thicker lines. When she stood close, Dashi could see that the thick lines formed hidden pictures: swords, their hilts barely scratched into the surface; and needles, with sharp points and carefully crafted eyes.

Hadn't Nuray said she'd made her crest a crossed needle and sword? None of the swords and needles were crossed and the resulting engraving certainly didn't resemble a royal crest, but their presence seemed entirely too coincidental. She walked quickly around the room, noting the other engraved proverbs: none had hidden symbols.

She returned to the engraving she'd been studying and mentally tried out each of the words. *Lying...is easy. But...truth is only...swallowed on...hardness? No, swallowed with difficulty.* The words were familiar, but she hadn't read them in an old criminal code, she'd heard them from Khagan Nuray herself. *Deception is easy*, the dead khagan had said, punctuating her words with a poke in Dashi's forehead. *It is the truth that can be difficult to swallow.*

Dashi took a step back. It was unsettling, to discover things from her dreams in real life.

"What if the statuette isn't in this room?" she asked in a hushed voice. "What if it's somewhere else?"

"What do you mean?" Sevlin asked, not taking his eyes from the figures arrayed before them. "We're looking for a statuette and this room is full of them. Besides, there's nowhere else to go."

"Exactly," Dashi said, hopping lightly from one foot to the other. Now that the idea had taken hold, she couldn't shake it. "It just seems a little too straightforward, don't you think?"

"Straightforward?" He turned around fully to stare at her. "Nothing about this entire *place* has been straightforward. All you can tell me is that it will be obvious but hidden at the same time, and it has to be something that 'grabs' you."

"Yes! This?" She gestured at the room around them "It's too...conspicuous."

"What are you saying?"

"I'm saying it's a trick. The statuettes, the room, everything. It's a decoy, designed to make us carefully and painstakingly select the wrong statuette and probably die as a result."

"I take it you've thought of a way to avoid that outcome?"

"I have." She began rapidly tracing the engraving with her forefinger, depressing each of the tiny switches she'd seen in the letters, one after another. On the last letter, she turned and gave Sevlin a wicked grin. "Right *here.*"

The grinding of gears commenced at once. Only this time the sound came from in front of them as well as from behind them. The floor in the oven room must be moving back in place, readying itself for the next intruder. Sevlin reacted immediately, moving toward the exit, but Dashi grabbed his forearm and shook her head. "No, it's alright, Sevlin. Wait."

Slowly, like an unfurling flower, the middle shelf of statuettes began to shift, sliding toward the center of the room. The movement was so gentle that the statuettes remained completely still, silent witnesses to a rite that had been performed countless times before.

Once the platform had separated from the wall, it stopped moving, exposing a narrow doorway behind it.

Sevlin glanced down at Dashi. "You think this is it?"

"I know it is." She smiled broadly and, taking the lantern out of his hand, sidestepped the platform of false statuettes. The light flooded the small doorway, revealing a staircase that split around a stone pillar before continuing upward into the darkness. A niche had been hollowed into the pillar. In it, stood a golden statuette the size of Dashi's palm: a muscular woman with a strong face and a heavily jeweled headdress, holding a needle in one hand and a raised sword in the other.

Chapter 28

Dashi stepped into the stairwell and, without any hesitation, picked up the golden statuette of Khagan Nuray. Despite the statuette's small size, it was an incredible likeness, right down to the prominent nose. Of course the statuette that contained the needle would be in Nuray's image. Hadn't she boasted that she'd been the one to complete the temple?

"It's beautiful," Sevlin murmured. He reached out a finger and ran it over the tiny bejeweled headdress. "One of the khagans."

"Khagan Nuray."

"She's not holding a platter."

Dashi shrugged, unwilling to say how she knew for sure.

A fine seam delineated the place where the statuette's neck met its body. Dashi gently twisted until the head came off with a muted pop.

"Wait," Sevlin said, before she could dump the contents into her eager hand. "The needle is supposed to burn."

She raised an eyebrow. "Unless I'm the new seamstress."

He made a derisive noise in his throat. "And I'll be the next khagan."

The needle fell from the statuette like a heavy golden raindrop. It began to spin as soon as it touched her sash, which she'd used to overlay her palm. Sevlin took a step back, like he was afraid the needle would shoot through the air and impale him. Once, twice, three times it went around, revolving slowly and with a certainty that made Dashi's scalp tingle. So this was magic, the stuff of myth and legend, the endpoint of countless hints and veiled references in ancient Purek records. She'd imagined that finding the needle would be like uncovering any other piece of history, but this was at once more mundane and more frightening: an inanimate object that moved of its own accord, searching for someone to wield it.

On its third revolution, the needle stopped, its point indicating a direction somewhere to Sevlin's left. Now that the needle was still, she could feel how heavy it was. Heavier than it should have been. That, and its uncanny movement, were the only characteristics to mark it as unusual. It was the standard length of any needle, though perhaps a little wider, and the soft gold was scratched from heavy use.

"I guess neither of us is the seamstress," Dashi remarked after a moment.

"A good thing, that."

"You think your queen would be just like one of the khagans and use the seamstress as a slave?"

"The needle is of no use without a vein and she has a reputation for doing what's right but," Sevlin shrugged, "she's still young. One day she will be older. Political realities don't always allow for such luxuries as goodness and innocence." He paused, considering the needle. "Do you think it could be used to guide us out of here, or does it only point in the cardinal direction of the seamstress?"

"Cardinal direction, I think. Else it would be telling us to go up these stairs."

Sevlin gave the stairs an appraising glance. "I suppose that's the best choice, isn't it?"

"Anything is better than the oven. And we're in the seamstress' territory now. I think it should be fairly safe. Maybe this will bring us out on the other side of the wall and we won't have to figure out how to move it."

Dashi tipped the needle back into the statuette and returned the golden head to its body. She had the fleeting idea of putting Nuray's head on backward but decided against it. With the things of her dreams showing up in real life, it was probably better not to tempt the ancestors. Besides, she got the feeling that humor wasn't one of the dead khagan's strong points. Dashi tucked the statuette into an inner pocket of her deel. If Sevlin noticed that she didn't offer it to him, he kept it to himself.

The steps of the hidden chamber were wide enough for them to ascend side-by-side. A skeleton lay just up from the needle, its bones sprawling over the surface of four consecutive steps, like pools beneath a waterfall. Gold glinted among the yellowed white: a medallion, marking the remains as those of a priest. Dashi's fingers twitched, wanting to lift the golden chain from its resting place but something—the hush of the place, maybe, or the thought of Nuray's severe expression—stopped her.

They climbed for several minutes until they reached a hall lined with doors. The rooms were unlocked and, when Dashi poked her head inside one, she saw that it was mostly empty. Two narrow beds sat on opposite sides, empty and unremarkable except for the skeletons resting peacefully in each. The next room was identical, except for a mortar and pestle which sat on a rickety table next to one of the beds. The skeleton's fingers just brushed the edge of the mortar, cold bone meeting cold marble, reaching out for one last dose of whatever had been inside. Dashi peered over the edge, but the contents had long since turned to dust.

"The room across the hall is the same," Sevlin said, entering a moment later.

Dashi jumped. "Ancestors above, you startled me. Find anything?"

"More sick rooms. The skeleton in the other room still had bandages, or what was left of them, wrapped around his chest. This must be where the men and women who were stitched with magic recovered." He inclined his head toward the bed's occupant. "Or didn't."

Dashi's eyes wandered over the unadorned walls. "It doesn't look like a good way to go. Dying in an empty room after a failed magical experiment. Do you think they wanted to be here?"

He shrugged. "Some did. The records that Tyvalar received said that some people thought it was an honor, a chance at glory. Others did it to pay off debts. It's my understanding that just volunteering for the stitching came with a hefty reward. Afterward, if they survived, they received soldier's training and pay. I'm guessing this bunch was finished off by the cataclysm though, not the stitching."

She didn't reply. Is that what bringing the needle back to Karak City was going to do? Usher in another era of death and manipulation, of people subjecting themselves to stitching just for a chance out of poverty? She thought of the sun-tanned laborer entering the race to return his fortune. There were plenty more like him in the dirt circle. She still had no idea what the noble in Karak City actually wanted, but she could guess he wouldn't be a scrupulous master. The khan would probably be no better, but what was she supposed to do, send the needle to Tyvalar with Sevlin and wait for the pyrothrite to tick away the last minutes of her life?

Dashi and Sevlin checked the other rooms but found them to be the same. In total, the sick beds held the remains of twenty-four people. The last two rooms were different. The room on the left was larger and grander, with art on the walls and a canopied bed. It was empty. A door at the back of the room led to a small dressing area, which was lined with chests of drawers and rows of decayed clothes.

Dashi examined the cloth absently. Even mostly disintegrated, she could tell they'd been exquisite things, but for once she didn't mentally tally what they might have been worth. For some reason, the empty bed seemed worse than the beds with skeletal occupants, as if the seamstress had never found rest, even in death.

"I wonder where she died," Sevlin asked quietly. He ran a hand over the carved bedpost.

Dashi thought of the way Nuray had described her time as seamstress, of being a prisoner to the khagan and the needle. She turned away from the room. "Doesn't matter, I suppose."

The next room was worse. There was a workbench brimming with colored glass vials and rusting tools which looked vaguely medical, but Dashi noticed the wall art first: the strangest murals she'd seen in any of the ruins. The subjects were fantastical and horrible all at once: a sharp-toothed man covered in shaggy fur; another with what appeared to be beetles crawling all over him; a man with wings; a woman with horns.

Dashi turned to ask Sevlin's opinion, but her eyes caught on a bronze altar built next to the workbench. A skeleton was stretched across the center, its wrist and ankle bones still encircled by metal shackles. The skull had fallen onto the floor, but the spine lay in an arched line, straining against the manacles that held it in place.

"I'd guess this is where the actual stitching was done," Sevlin said, catching her shocked silence.

"I thought you said the people *wanted* to be stitched," Dashi whispered, not taking her eyes off the skeleton. "Why did they need to be restrained?"

Sevlin's lips pressed into a thin line. "For the pain, I think."

Dashi took a step toward the door. "I'm ready to leave," she announced, without looking back. "Idree is waiting for us and we still need to figure out how to reach her."

"No argument from me," Sevlin muttered, shutting the door behind them.

The stairs at this end of the hall were narrower and Dashi followed Sevlin's light, keeping one hand on the cold wall. After a few minutes, Sevlin stopped.

"It can't be a dead end," he said, surveying the wall in front of them.

Another inscription had been chiseled into the stone and Dashi translated hurriedly. She suddenly wanted to find Idree and be done with this temple. The verse was benign—something about the sky being a window for the ancestors—and she quickly traced the characters with her index finger, feeling the slender wire triggers as she did so. A section of the wall slid sideways to reveal a corridor made of stone and dark wood. Thick translucent strands covered the walls, stringing the hall in both directions.

"The spider's corridor," Dashi whispered. She drew her bow, scanning for movement.

"That way," Sevlin whispered, one hand on his sword. He pointed to the left, where the corridor sloped uphill. To the right, the hall continued downward, disappearing around a corner amid thickening strands of web.

Dashi turned left, moving quickly but cautiously. She breathed carefully, forcing her muscles to relax. There was no way of knowing how far they had left to go.

She received her answer a few minutes later. A jubilant laugh escaped her lips as she spotted the smoldering remains of the fire Sevlin had made to block the spider's corridor. The moving wall that had separated them from Idree was gone. The rushing underground river and the graceful bridge with its hidden tripwires were both visible now. And—Dashi's heart gave a leap—*Idree*! Her sister stood in a puddle of lantern light, waiting for them on the opposite side of the river. Dashi took a quick step forward, but something in her sister's expression made her stop, suddenly wary.

Something wasn't right. Idree hadn't moved at the sight of them, hadn't even smiled. She looked horrified, not happy. Dashi's eyes darted to either side of her sister, to the pool of shadows pushing toward her.

A glint of metal here, a dark shape there.

Idree wasn't alone.

"I knew you'd be the one to beat in this race," Negan said as he limped out from behind Idree. He was mud-spattered and bedraggled and one of his pant legs was torn at the knee, giving Dashi a brief glimpse of a bloody bandage. He held a knife. "I just didn't know you'd be stupid enough to bring a child with you."

Cari, the woman who'd stabbed at the ant, and three more men appeared, arraying themselves around Negan. All of them held crossbows.

Five against two. Even after the rats had done their worst, they were still outnumbered.

Negan eyed Idree almost hungrily. "You know I'd like nothing better than to kill her the way you killed my brother."

He jerked Idree's arm behind her back and raised the knife to her throat. Idree didn't so much as utter a sound, but her eyes bored into Dashi's.

"Unfortunately, I'd also like that statuette. Give it to me and you won't have to watch her die."

Chapter 29

Dashi's fingers trembled, demanding that she loose the arrow she'd trained on Negan. She could hit him in the eye from this distance, no question. Here he was—the same man who'd taken Altan, Zayaa and Baris from her—now threatening her sister. The only remaining family she had left.

She drew a breath and exhaled it steadily. Straight through the eye and into his fetid brain and she'd never have to look at him again. She'd have her revenge. But what about Idree? What would move faster, his knife or her arrow? Her eyes darted to Cari. Sensing her gaze, the woman raised her lip sneeringly and took a step toward Idree, aiming her crossbow at Idree's side.

Dashi's fingers stilled. No matter how good she was, she couldn't beat Negan's knife *and* Cari's bolt.

"Don't, Dashi," Sevlin murmured, echoing her thoughts.

Air hissed from between her teeth. "So what do we do?" she asked, but she lowered her bow before he answered. There was only one solution and she already knew what it was.

"What else can we do? Give him the statuette. We can catch up with him somewhere in the taiga."

Dashi nodded, but her mind was running as fast as the river in front of them, her thoughts tumbling over themselves as she played out different scenarios. Sevlin's suggestion was a decent one, but surely Negan would anticipate it. There was no way Negan would let them live if he thought they'd ambush him later. As long as they still had the statuette, they had a bargaining chip. Once that was gone, Negan would have nothing to lose in killing them.

Even if Negan *did* leave them alive and they managed to hunt him down later, how long would that take? At some point today, the twenty-first pyrothrite nodule would fall into the bottom of the disk. She had eight days to get back to Karak City. That would be hard enough to do if she left immediately, let alone if she had to find Negan first and *then* wrangle it from Sevlin. And if she failed to get the needle in time, if she exploded somewhere in the taiga, what would become of Idree?

"Alright," she called, raising her voice to be heard over the rush of the river. She held the bow and arrow loosely between the fingers of her left hand while she fumbled in her deel with her right, never taking her eyes off Negan. She raised the golden statuette over her head. "Bring Idree to the bridge and I'll give it to you there."

"It better have the needle inside," Negan yelled back, "or she'll die right in front of you."

And then you'll die too, Dashi wanted to shout, but she stayed silent and started toward the bridge. She'd known Negan was too canny to fall for a trick as simple as emptying the statuette of its contents.

Sevlin stepped in front of her. "I'll take it to him. You can cover me from here."

Dashi shook her head.

He frowned. "Then make them come to us. I can't help you from here. All I have left is my sword."

Negan would never agree to that. And if he did, Cari and the others would come too, negating the slight advantage the bridge gave them. She held out her bow.

He grasped the wood where she held it, covering her hand with his. "You know I can't use this like you can," he said, lips barely moving. "If I go with you, I can at least use my sword."

No, that wouldn't work. If Sevlin was behind her, everything would be ruined. She needed him alive; *Idree* needed him alive. "Just aim at Cari and do your best."

"Cari? What about Negan?"

"Don't worry about Negan."

"Just you," Negan yelled. "He stays where he is or she dies."

Dashi gave Sevlin a half-smile and forced her fingers to release the bow. She'd always thought she'd go down with it in her hands. It seemed unnatural to leave it behind now.

The planks of the bridge bounced slightly with each step she took. Negan had started up the other side, pushing Idree in front of him, and Dashi slowed her pace to match his. She didn't want to reach the center before he did.

She was close enough now that she could see Idree's eyes clearly. The fear in them was palpable, but Idree wasn't crying. Dashi stared hard at her sister, willing Idree to understand what needed to be done.

Idree's eyes moved from Dashi's face to her feet, moving inexorably forward. Her lips parted slightly. "*No,*" she mouthed.

Over Idree's shoulder, Negan's smile was twisted with unhappiness. "I told you I'd come for you."

"And I said I'd welcome it." Dashi stopped a finger's breadth from the center of the bridge. *One more step would do it. One more step would finish Negan.* She forced her attention away from Idree and onto him, trying not to think about herself, about what she was giving up: a good, cutthroat goathead match; warm *boortsog* on a cold day; the smack of air as she galloped over the steppe.

Negan's expression turned mocking. "And do you welcome it still, now that you're about to lose?"

Did she welcome the loss she was about to incur? *No.* Of course not. Who would? But she'd had a difficult hand from the beginning of the race, even more so since the pyrothrite had accelerated. It would end in defeat, despite all her efforts. That was bitter medicine to swallow, but at least she would be losing on her own terms.

Dashi lifted her chin, matching Negan's glare. "I do."

Her final stride was forceful, snapping the double tripwire that stood sentry at the center of the bridge. Even though she knew it was coming, Dashi flinched at the swish of the arrow cutting through the air. But she didn't duck. Ducking would mean that the arrow meant for her back would go into Idree's chest instead.

She heard Idree's scream and saw Negan's eyes bulge at the same time. The arm holding the knife jerked, but Idree had braced her hands against his wrist, and the blade only scratched a red line in her skin. She ducked under his arm, moving toward Dashi. Negan took a step, trying to chase after her, but he stumbled and nearly fell instead, giving Dashi a fleeting glimpse of the arrow that protruded from his back.

She wanted to laugh, to shower Negan with her triumph—her sister was still alive and he wouldn't get the statuette!—but somehow she couldn't. She caught the railing of the bridge, bracing herself against the conflagration that burned between her shoulder blades.

There was another hiss of air and a second arrow sprouted from Negan's back. He sagged against the side of the bridge next to her, gasping.

Belatedly, Dashi realized that if Negan had two arrows in his back that meant another was coming for her as well. When it came, a blink of an eye later, it didn't hurt as much as the first. She felt only the impact, like a small fist packing incredible force. The burning pain in her back widened, encompassing the new wound. There was a thump as Negan toppled face-first onto the bridge. She heard Cari's raised voice, but couldn't focus on what was being said.

"Take this...Tyvalar," Dashi managed, shoving the statuette toward her sister. Nuray's golden face gleamed back at her, unmoved. "The plate..." She was wheezing hard, each breath searing her chest. *Must have punctured a lung.* She tried to focus on freeing the words that were stuck in her throat, on making Idree understand. "Plate. The wall."

Instead of taking the statuette, Idree grabbed Dashi by both arms. "No! Dashi—" Her features were frozen in horror.

She's going to hesitate, Dashi thought. *She's got to run or it's going to be too late.*

There was movement over Idree's shoulder and with her last remaining strength, Dashi pushed her sister to the side and drew her sword. It was a clumsy movement since it had to be done with her left arm—her right had become suddenly immobile—but she moved out of habit, blocking the descending stroke that Cari had meant for Idree's back. The impact reverberated up her arm and into the wound in her back. She nearly dropped the sword.

"*Go*," Dashi coughed, raising the sword again. She managed a smile as she heard the pound of Idree's feet and then the growl of gears. Idree had stamped on the pressure plate. In a few moments, the sliding wall would be in place, protecting Sevlin and Idree from any pursuit by Cari and the remaining men.

Cari's sword sliced into Dashi's side, but she hardly felt the blow. Or rather, her whole body was consumed by pain, and one more drop in an already full cup went unnoticed. Dashi's hip crashed against the side of the bridge and she sank into it, leaning over the railing as the water called her from below. Her head was unwieldy, lolling to one side, then the other. *Take another breath*, she told herself. *Stay in this a little longer. The wall is almost in place. You only have to buy them a little more time.*

She saw the moment when Cari realized the wall was sliding closed: her eyes widened and she charged forward, spewing curses. There were more men behind her, the survivors who'd ridden with Negan, but the bridge was so narrow that they could only cross one at a time. If she could just hold them here for a moment or two, the wall would close—

Dashi pushed up from the railing, sword waving feebly.

"Out of the way," Cari spat.

There was a splash as Negan's body hit the water. His dark, lifeless eyes looked up at Dashi and then he was gone, sucked beneath the bridge and into the river's underground bed by the fast current. Dashi blinked, trying to clear her head. There was something she needed to do, a responsibility that couldn't be shirked—

Strong hands grabbed her, jostling her toward the railing, making her yelp as one of the arrow shafts in her back snapped. There was a moment of weightlessness as she fell, unmoored except for the throbbing pain in her back, and then the river closed over her head. Her thoughts dissipated in the freezing water. There was only pain and cold and the bite of something small and hard against her palm, as she followed Negan's body underground.

Chapter 30

The darkness held her tightly and Dashi didn't fight it. It felt good, the way everything was numbed. The pain in her back and side were quickly beaten back by the cold until all that remained was a dull ache. Even her worries over the belt and Negan and the needle were gone. All that remained were her senses, and those were innocuous enough; she saw only darkness and felt only the cold sensation of movement as the river pulled her farther into its lair.

Gradually, however, other things passed before her eyes. At least, she thought they did. She was too incoherent to judge whether they were really there or not. She saw Negan's lifeless gaze as his body hit the water. Nuray's face, hawkish and shrewd, first shrouded in white mist, then cast in bright gold. Altan, standing below her, yelling at her to jump. Then the dingy corners of her prison cell and Idree's round face, full of fear but not letting the tears fall. Nuray came again and this time her golden features were alive. Her lips moved sternly, trying to impart a message that Dashi was simply too tired to hear.

Go away, Dashi thought tiredly. *Let me rest.* Nuray disappeared, replaced by a swirl of leaves and light. Things pressed against Dashi's face: cold, hard, and smooth. She turned her head to the side so that the pebbles were no longer pushing against her lips and nose. Even that slight movement caused a groan to escape. Or rather, she meant to groan, but it came out as a cascade of coughing. Each cough felt like a branding iron was being pressed to her back.

Blissful darkness claimed her once more.

The light returned, more insistent this time, dragging her back into consciousness. Its very presence bothered her; it seemed to herald the return of feeling, the resurgence of a collection of agonies she'd rather forget. Where was the freezing darkness that had hugged her close, cushioning her from hurt? She was still cold—dimly, she could feel her body shaking with it—but it no longer blotted out the pain. And the pain was dreadful: a horrible fire that could not be put out and would not be content until it consumed her entire body. This must be what it felt like to burn alive. Perhaps she *was* burning, she thought. But no, that didn't make sense, she felt wet.

She groaned again and this time managed to roll to one side without coughing. Cheek resting against the cold pebbles, she opened her eyes. She was in a forest. The taiga. Maybe she was dreaming. Or maybe she was already dead and her spirit was only waiting for the mist to carry her to the spiritworld. But her body hurt so badly; surely, the ancestors didn't have to contend with that.

Dashi blinked and it took her a long time to reopen her eyes. When she did, she was still in the taiga. She was still cold, still in pain and the trees still looked down on her, their green boughs dancing indifferently in the breeze. A dark shape moved along the periphery of her vision.

How far had the river carried her? Not far if Sevlin had been able to find her already. He nudged her arm gently, but the movement jarred the sword wound in her side.

"Sev—ahh! *Stop!* Just leave me."

Sevlin pushed her again and she realized he was going to lift her from the ground.

"*No—*" she shrieked, but the pain severed her voice. She passed out again.

Dashi's head and arm dangled to one side, moving to the rhythm of Sevlin's strides. He was carrying her through the taiga—she could feel the occasional brush of leaves against her head. She wondered why he hadn't spoken yet. He probably didn't realize she was conscious. Hardly surprising, considering how frequently she was slipping in and out. That was fine. Let him think she was asleep; talking required far too much effort and she didn't think she could bear the pain if she started coughing again.

His chest was strangely hard. Not the way a sheet of muscle is hard. It was more like armor—

Her eyes flew open. She was draped over a rounded segment of body, her face pressed against the dark copper expanse. In front of her, she could see the back of a head: the same copper color, with two dexterous-looking antennae. She opened her mouth, but it worked soundlessly, gagging on her fear.

It wasn't Sevlin who was carrying her through the forest.

It was a giant taiga ant.

As if sensing her panic, one of the antennae waved in her direction, dipping backward over the creature's head. It was similar to the way Spit would flick an ear toward the sound of her voice, yet nothing could have been more different. Dashi tried to push herself up—maybe she could roll off of its back—but she was too weak. The movement did afford her a better view, however: more ants marched behind her. One of them trundled closer and Dashi couldn't help but flinch as she waited for the powerful jaws to descend. But when they closed around her arm and tugged her back to the center of the ant's back, the jaws were gentle. The second ant dropped back, lurking somewhere outside of her vision but close enough to correct her if she started to slide again.

Dashi thought of the ants they'd seen in the ravine, carrying away the bodies of the racers. That was to be her fate, she thought as she began to fade once more. Carried off to be eaten. *Like a breadcrumb from the kitchen*, Sevlin had said.

She'd lost too much blood. Was somehow still losing it, if the dampness along her side was to be believed. With any luck, she'd be unconscious when the ants decided to rip her apart.

This time when she awoke, it was dark. Not the star-slashed color of the night but the pure, pitch black of being underground. Dashi lifted her head. She was lying on her stomach and the arrow wounds in her back throbbed gently with each beat of her heart. She felt better. Not *well*, but better.

Very carefully, she stretched out her hand, exploring this dark world with her fingertips. The floor was dirt. Soft, not packed. The air was neither warm nor cold, which was probably why she hadn't immediately realized that she was naked from the waist up. Her deel was beneath her, cushioning her from the dirt. There was a dirt wall to her right and she could tell by the sound of her breathing that the ceiling was relatively low overhead.

Where am I? Underground, definitely. Her last memories were of the ants carrying her, but if they'd brought her here, then why hadn't they eaten her yet? She was struck with the horrible thought that perhaps they preferred their prey alive and she strained her ears for the sound of anything approaching. Their lair, if that was indeed where she was, remained silent.

Her fingers moved over the skin along her ribs, probing at the perimeter of the sword wound Cari had given her. It was covered with something fibrous and sticky. She poked a little harder and was rewarded with a jolt of pain. Her fingers moved farther, alighting on the pyrothrite belt. It was warm and this time she couldn't blame it on the oven room. The noble had said that would happen but only right before it exploded. Dashi squeezed her eyes shut, trying to think. On the night they entered the temple, there had been nineteen nodules of pyrothrite in the bottom of the disk. Another would have fallen while she was inside, making twenty. She didn't think she could have survived more than a few hours in the river. How much time had passed since the ants had found her? Suddenly, she wanted to be out of this dark tomb. She needed to look at the belt, to know if her death was imminent. Or, rather, *how* imminent.

Dashi pushed herself into an upright position, biting her lip against the pain that still coursed through her back and side. It hurt less than before, a development that seemed implausible, but it was still bad enough to make her carefully consider whether each movement was truly necessary. Her head spun and she reached blindly for the dirt wall she'd felt a few moments before. Her sash and undershirt were missing, so she wrapped the deel around her shoulders as best she could.

There was a breath of air from somewhere to her left. Keeping one hand on the dirt wall, she walked in that direction. The wall was rounded, bulging outward, and she followed it until she reached another opening. Dashi paused, her breathing labored. Where was she? It almost felt like being in prison again, but the uncertainty of her location and her physical weakness made it worse.

Ignoring the tightening in her side, she shuffled forward, one arm outstretched. Two tunnels branched in front of her. She couldn't be sure, but she thought the darkness to her left looked a shade lighter. Having no better options, she hobbled in that direction.

A sudden shifting of dirt made Dashi freeze. Something was coming. She groped for the small knife she usually kept in her boot, but it was gone, probably washed away by the river. So she did the only other thing she could think of: flattened herself against the wall, hardly daring to breathe. The noise approached quickly, until it was directly in front of her. Then it stopped. For a second there was no movement, not even the shifting of feet, though she was certain she'd heard many. Then, very softly, something moved over her face, brushing her cheek and nose with its bristly surface. Dashi pinched her lips together, trying not to cry out, but the thing was gone an instant later and the sound of movement over dirt resumed.

Dashi stayed still, listening to the ants pass in the opposite direction. Why hadn't they stopped her? Maybe they were already carrying something and needed to put their burden down before they caught her. Her steps quickened, breaking into a stumbling jog.

She couldn't keep it up for long, however. Her body was simply too weak. She slowed to a walk, senses sharpened for any indication that more ants were approaching. The tunnel was indeed getting lighter, the air around her slowly transitioning from black to dull gray.

The mouth of the tunnel was surrounded by a mound of soft dirt and Dashi scrambled out as best she could, holding her side with one arm and landing in an ungainly heap at the bottom. Her breath came in harsh rasps, but she pushed herself to her feet. Her deel flapped open, inviting her to look at the belt, but she kept moving.

It was early morning in the taiga and the thatch of needles and leaves sliced the sunlight a dozen different ways, so that it fell to the ground without warming her. The air was much cooler here than it had been inside the earth, but Dashi didn't care. There was no ignoring the heat from the pyrothrite belt now; the cool air made it all the more obvious. She hugged the deel around herself and kept moving, as far away from the ants as she could get.

The sound of water drew her and she didn't stop until she'd fallen to her knees on the rocky shore to drink her fill. Briefly, Dashi wondered if the river was the same one that had taken her from the temple. She was so disoriented that she didn't even know if it was flowing in the same direction. She leaned against a spruce tree with her eyes closed, trying to regain control of her breathing, then she tilted her head down and slowly opened her eyes.

The skin on her stomach and side was dark with dirt and old blood and whatever green substance now covered her wounds. But Dashi only had eyes for the disc of pyrothrite staring back at her. She squeezed the belt so hard that her fingers hurt.

More nodules had fallen to the bottom of the disc. A lot more. *One, two, three...*

When she finished counting, Dashi let her head fall back against the tree trunk. She suddenly felt tired. More tired than when she'd woken beside the river. She'd been wondering about her fate then, trying to figure out where she was and what had happened. But now she realized it didn't matter. Nothing she did would change anything. Twenty-nine nodules rested at the bottom of the disc. She'd been interred in the ants' nest for over a week. At some point today, the belt would become explosive.

She would die here. All she could do was pick the place.

The rustle of leaves made Dashi spin around, her hand automatically reaching for a sword that no longer hung at her side. Half a dozen ants had arrayed themselves in a semi-circle behind her. It was disconcerting, the way they could move so silently, and Dashi was suddenly reminded of the creeping mist, sliding through the trees.

The river still rushed at her back. She could dive in and hope to escape. But really, what was the use? Even if the ants didn't follow her, the pyrothrite belt would. It was always with her, dogging her steps.

One of the ants broke the stand-off first, moving toward her cautiously. It was horrible to look at—the inhuman eyes, slick and black, the whipping antennae, and those enormous jaws—but Dashi stood her ground. She had nowhere to go and she couldn't see the point in running further. She didn't know exactly where it was looking—its bulbous eyes could be peering at anything in the vicinity—but its antennae were pointed in her direction. It took one step, paused, then took another, until it had halved the distance between them. Then it lowered its head, dropping something on the ground in front of her.

That's when she saw the mark on its back: a whitish scar in the shape of a V. It was the same ant Negan's men had been torturing. The one she'd helped when she stabbed the rat.

Her eyes darted to the object the ant had dropped: her empty scabbard. She raised her eyes again, stunned. Not only had the ants refrained from eating her, but they were returning her belongings now?

The ant tilted its head and made a low noise, part clicking, part trilling. When she didn't move, it took a step closer, trilling again. This time, the noise ended on a high note, sounding distinctly curious.

Dashi swallowed. "Uh, thank you?"

The ant continued to stare in its enigmatic way, but one of its antennae jiggled from left to right and, like that was the cue they'd been waiting for, three more ants came forward. The first one opened its jaws and let a knife fall to the ground. It was the bone-handled one she'd kept in her sash. The sash itself came next, torn into several pieces. The scraps of fabric weren't much good to her, but she thanked the ant anyway.

The last gift rolled out of the ant's jaws and hit her boot in a flash of gold. Dashi choked on her breath. The statuette of Khagan Nuray lay at her feet, fixing her with a stern gaze. She remembered, as if from another lifetime, thrusting it at Idree and then, nearly simultaneously, pushing her sister away from Cari's sword. She must have held on to the statuette as she was swept downriver. It was too little, too late—there was no way she could get it to Karak City in time—but she murmured another thank you as she picked it up and unscrewed the head. She tilted the statuette carefully, so that the needle hovered at the lip but didn't fall out.

She looked up at the ants, but her voice, if the creatures could even understand it, had deserted her. She knew it couldn't be a coincidence that the ant she'd helped out of Negan's pit had returned the favor, but...well, frankly she hadn't credited the ants with that much intelligence. This required recognition. It required planning. It required the empathy to know what things *she*, a member of another *species*, valued and the ability to set them aside for her.

The places where Negan's men had cut the ant's legs were no longer visible. Instead, each injury was smothered in the same green, fibrous paste that covered the wound on Dashi's side and presumably the ones on her back as well. Only the V on its back was visible, the scar already looking old and hardened.

Dashi opened her deel again and examined the place along her ribs, where the skin was stretched tight around the green patch. *Healing.*

"You tended my wounds, just like you tended your own," she murmured, remembering the way the ant had drooled the greenish spittle onto its injured leg when it was in the pit. It felt silly to talk aloud to an ant, but it seemed equally important to say *something* to acknowledge what had been done. "You saved my life. For the time being, I mean. This'll still get me in the end," she smiled crookedly and rapped on the pyrothrite belt with her knuckles, "but I appreciate the effort just the same."

The ant's antennae wobbled back and forth. Its jaws didn't move, but Dashi remembered the way they'd snapped Cari's sword like it was a twig. Her lips twisted in thought. Anything could be broken with enough force and leverage, the blacksmith had said.

"See this?" She knocked on the pyrothrite belt again. Stupid, stupid hope. She could feel a bubble of it rising in her chest even as she told herself it was pointless. "Can you break it?"

The ant was silent. *Naturally.*

She picked up a stick and, holding it out for the ant to see, snapped it in half. "Break it? Like that?" She repeated the movements, tapping on the belt, then breaking the stick again.

The ant tilted its head but otherwise didn't move.

She stepped closer, until she could see the tiny bumps that covered the hard surface of its jaws. "Break it? Please? I've seen you break metal before." Her voice cracked a little, sounding an awful lot like Idree's. "Could you try?"

The ant stayed where it was, its antennae drooping over her head like the trailing leaves of a willow tree.

Heaving a sigh, Dashi turned away, crumbling the remaining piece of the stick between her hands. The statuette of Nuray was on the ground where she'd dropped it and she brought her foot back and kicked it into the trunk of a spruce tree. It bounced off with a reproachful clank. The ants might be more intelligent than she'd first imagined, but had she actually expected one to *understand* her?

A low sound, almost a purr, came from behind her and Dashi turned around. The ant with the V had come closer. Very slowly, almost as if it didn't want to alarm her, the ant brushed its antennae against her deel.

Dashi sucked in a breath, then pushed the deel open. The ant turned its head and ran the sharp tip of one jaw over the metal that encircled her waist.

"Yes!"

The creature jerked back.

"No, no. I mean, yes, that's exactly what I want and no, don't back up." She was babbling in a way that she rarely did, but she didn't stop herself, hoping that, by dint of sheer volume, the ant could gain some meaning from her words.

She'd lost weight over the past week. She could see it in the way her ribs and hip bones jutted out and feel it in the extra space between her abdomen and the belt, but the ant's jaws were still much too big to fit beneath the metal.

"Wait, try this." She lay gingerly on her back, her breath growing shallow as her wounds sang in protest. When the pain had waned somewhat, she sucked in her stomach, just the way she had when the blacksmith had tried—and failed—to help her. *Please be different this time.*

The ant watched her. Each of its eyes was nearly the size of her head. Other than its antennae, its face was completely immobile. It could be contemplating how to help her, or, just as easily, how to eat her. But Dashi remained where she was. *It's not like I have many other options*, she reminded herself. *It's this or nothing.*

She lay there for several minutes, wondering if she'd misinterpreted the ant's intentions. Perhaps her lack of movement convinced it because, when it moved again, it was more decisive. It turned its head, sliding the end of one mandible between the belt and her stomach. Dashi's heart sank. Only a small fraction of the ant's jaw would fit. *How can it possibly break the metal if it can't even get a hold of it?* But when the creature closed its jaws a moment later, her heart rose again, lodging somewhere in her throat. A dent had appeared in the blasted metal, a perfect imprint of the serrations along the inside of the ant's mandibles.

"That's right," she whispered encouragingly. "Good job."

The ant readjusted its hold on the belt and tried again. The dent widened incrementally.

It took half a dozen tries before Dashi began to think it might work. With each bite from the ant, the belt buckled and flattened, which in turn gave the ant—*V*, she thought, with a small measure of affection—more room to maneuver its mandibles and exert more pressure.

Dashi had no idea if V was male or female, but the way the ant tilted its head consideringly reminded her of Zayaa. V didn't seem to be in a hurry. Neither did the other ants waiting nearby.

Finally, when the belt was so thin that it resembled a metal fingernail, V snapped down hard on the metal, jaws quaking. Dashi squeezed a handful of pine needles, grinding them against her palm to mitigate, not pain, but hope. The metal flexed beneath the giant jaws until finally, with a creak, the belt broke.

Dashi gasped and tried to sit up, but V pushed her back down with one bristly foreleg. The ant continued working on the belt, pulling it this way and that, widening the break in the metal. The opening grew. It was as wide as a finger. Three fingers. A hand.

"I think that's enough," Dashi said, placing a hand on V.

The ant backed up while Dashi wriggled through the opening. It was barely wide enough for her shrunken stomach to pass through and the broken metal gouged a line in her skin, but she was out. *Free.*

Dashi got to her feet slowly, making sure to feel the ground against her knees. The pain in her back. She was awake, right? This hadn't been a dream?

She turned to the ant. "Thank you. You don't know—thank you." She tried to put all of her gratitude and relief into her voice, hoping the ant would understand the tone, if not the words.

V knelt in front of her, angling her body toward Dashi. Dashi glanced uncertainly at those inscrutable black eyes. "You want me to...get on?"

The creature continued waiting patiently.

"Just...one minute?" Dashi held a placating hand out to the ants while she scanned the river bank. Spying a washed-up log, she grabbed the pyrothrite belt and gingerly fit it over one end, then slid the log into the water. The river whisked it around a bend and out of sight.

Tucking the statuette into the pocket of her deel, Dashi approached V cautiously. The ant's height wasn't the problem—she could mount a horse easily enough—but its exoskeleton was slippery and she had to keep one hand pressed against her side to stop the pain. She tried twice to clamber up, both times sliding back to the ground with a thump. Before she knew what was happening, one of the other ants seized her, its jaws clamping on her arm. For a moment she dangled, kitten-like, face to face with those glossy eyes. Then, it deposited her on V's back. The other ants flowed past on either side, moving off beneath the trees.

It took her several minutes to realize they weren't headed in the direction of the ants' lair. They were going south by southwest. As if they were leaving the taiga. She was too awestruck to smile, but she touched the slight bulge in her pocket, then settled herself as comfortably as possible on the ant's rounded back.

Chapter 31

A boom split the hush of the taiga not thirty minutes later. Dashi startled, nearly sliding onto the ground. The ants froze, save for their antennae, which burst into a frenzy of twitching. More sounds followed: branches ripping through other branches, the muted crash of tree trunks hitting the ground. Dashi filled her lungs with air. Let it out. Filled them again.

She was free, not just of the belt, but also of the tension that had been her constant companion since the race started. Even Negan was gone. Once she found Idree, she was free to go...wherever. The thought stunned her. She need never return to Karak City. She would always carry memories of Altan and Zayaa and Baris wherever she went—and her ache for them as well—but with Negan dead, she might be able to move on. She and Idree could barter the needle in exchange for a new life in Tyvalar if that's what they wanted—and she was sure Idree *would*. The thought of putting the needle in the Tyvalaran queen's hands gave her pause, but not enough to change her mind. The needle would eventually be used by *someone*, after all, and they needed a place to go.

The ants started moving again, swiftly, always southward, while Dashi's tenuous strength ebbed slowly out of her. It was dusk by the time they stopped. A familiar smell—wood smoke—drew Dashi's attention. She slid to the ground, searching the shadowy forest until she found the source. A curl of smoke rose above the trees. Through the trunks, she glimpsed the switching tails of a string of horses. Two figures walked back and forth between the horses and a nascent fire: Sevlin and Idree.

Dashi's first impulse was to call out to them, to shout her joy at being delivered from the taiga and certain death. But she held off. She didn't think the ants would appreciate the sudden loud noise—they'd drawn back shyly the other times she'd exclaimed loudly—and she didn't want their presence to alarm Sevlin and Idree.

She glanced back at the ants and saw that all, but V had fallen back, melting silently into the taiga. She approached the ant slowly, her hand outstretched. V's antennae hovered over her palm, not quite touching.

"I don't know if you can understand me," Dashi said in a low voice, "but thank you. You've saved my life."

The huge ant was still for a second, the remaining sunlight dappling its hard back with splotches of orange. Then with a flicker of antennae, it turned and slipped back into the forest, leaving Dashi alone.

She watched it go, a little relieved to be away from the ants. They were strange creatures, at once alien and discerning. One of the horses snorted as it caught the scent, but Sevlin and Idree continued to set up their camp, oblivious to the proximity of the taiga's denizens. How many times had the ants—or something else, for that matter—observed them from the safety of the trees, she wondered.

Dashi turned back toward Sevlin and Idree, feeling alien herself as she watched them for a moment. Sevlin was feeding the fire, his face shrouded in white smoke. Idree was unpacking, taking out supplies for a meal. At first glance, everything seemed normal, unchanged by her disappearance. But Dashi knew better. Idree's steps dragged. Her lower lip was tucked between her teeth as she struggled to contain whatever emotions were roiling inside her. She stopped to pat Spit on the neck and to run her hand over the seat of Dashi's empty saddle.

Sevlin glanced at her, a worry line dividing his forehead. He'd made sure Idree made it out of the temple, and kept her safe from Cari and whatever other dangers lurked on the return trip. He would have done right by Idree if Dashi had died. Dashi felt certain of that. She wondered if any part of him would be relieved when she showed up and he was no longer responsible for Idree's wellbeing. Probably not. He was a better person than she was.

She didn't know if they would believe her story. With the ants gone, she almost didn't believe it herself. If it weren't for her proof—the green-covered wounds—she might have been tempted to keep it to herself, it was so incredible. She reached inside her deel to touch the patch over her wound and, from there, her fingers found the pocket that housed the statuette. It was her other insurance, not of credibility, but of a future. For herself and her sister.

She felt the strangeness in the statuette as soon as her fingers brushed its gold surface: a slight vibration, almost a buzz, as if a hornet was trapped inside. Puzzled, she pulled the statuette out and, covering her palm with the edge of her sleeve, poured the needle into her hand. It began to spin, just as it had in the temple. Dashi frowned down at it. Hadn't it moved slowly before? Now it whirred around her palm, completing its three revolutions in the space of a blink. When it stopped it was pointing due north, toward the unknown reaches of the taiga.

And toward Idree.

Dashi's frown deepened. Idree grabbed a kettle from the saddlebag and walked to the fire. The needle followed, its point moving just enough that Dashi couldn't help but notice it. Her sister continued to the small stream on the other side of the camp, squatting down to get water. The needle swiveled slightly to the west, stopping where Idree did.

No, Dashi thought, her fingers curling around the needle. The end of it was touching her hand directly, but it took her a moment to register the sensation of seared flesh. She unclenched her fingers, staring down at the red mark on her skin. Her thoughts moved backward to Nuray's stony face as she recounted the abuse she'd suffered as the seamstress.

Dashi had almost walked right into it. Almost handed over the needle *and* the seamstress in one fell swoop. Almost made Idree the pawn of the Tyvalaran crown. Blessed ancestors, if she'd taken the needle to Karak City she might have unknowingly done the same thing there, only *the khan* would have been Idree's master then, not the queen.

But now she knew what was at stake. By well-timed luck or the grace of the ancestors or whatever else was in this world, she *knew*. And she wouldn't allow it.

Sevlin's head whipped up at the sound of footsteps. His sword was already out, the reflection of the fire dancing over its blade, when Dashi limped into the camp.

"Wh—"

His question was cut off by a strangled cry and the sound of rushing feet. Idree collided with Dashi like a cart of bricks, nearly knocking her to the ground.

Dashi's groan wasn't feigned.

"Oh!" Idree released her. "I'm sorry! Are you alright?"

"Careful, Idree. She's supposed to be dead. You don't want to be what pushes her onto the pyre." Sevlin was smiling with both sides of his mouth, making his scar twist and bunch. The sight sent a pang through Dashi, but she was careful to keep her arm clutched to her injured side, shielding it—and the small bulge in her inner pocket—when Sevlin stepped toward her. She swore she could feel the burn of the needle through her clothes, but he didn't seem to notice anything amiss.

"Dashi," he said, gazing down at her. "I—" He shook his head. "I can't believe you're here." He held her by the shoulders, his grip gentle.

She flashed him a weary smile and took a step backward. "I can hardly believe it myself."

"What happened?" Idree asked, catching her hand and squeezing. "I saw the arrows. I thought you were..."

"I should be. The river swept me out of the temple and far into the forest. I don't remember anything about it. I don't know how I didn't drown. I woke up on the banks when," she blew out a breath, "when the ants found me."

"The ants?" Idree glanced at Sevlin and then back to Dashi. "The *giant taiga* ants?"

"The same."

Idree opened her mouth and closed it. Sevlin's eyebrows were so furrowed they nearly hid his eyes.

"They carried me into their lair," Dashi said, watching their faces. "I woke up days later and my wounds were healing and...patched."

"Patched?" Sevlin asked, noting her hesitation right away.

Dashi shrugged helplessly. "A mixture of grasses and...ant saliva? I saw it on one of the other ants."

Idree made a face

"Let me get this straight," Sevlin said. "You're saying the ants *saved* you? The same ones that have been hunting us for the past few days?"

Dashi raised her eyebrows.

"Their tracks have been everywhere."

"I think," she said slowly, "that they were following you so they knew where to return me."

Sevlin's expression turned incredulous. "*Return* you? What in this life or the next would make you think—"

"You can argue later," Idree interrupted. "Dashi, let me see where you're hurt." Without waiting for a reply, she tugged Dashi's deel open.

Dashi saw Sevlin's eyes take in the bare expanse of her stomach and then move up to her ribs and the side of her breast.

"*Idree,*" she protested, clutching her deel closed with both hands before Sevlin saw more than just her wound. "I don't have anything on underneath. The ants tore off my undershirt."

There was a moment of silence and she could see Idree processing the absence of the pyrothrite belt. "Really?" her sister asked, after a beat. "Modesty from the girl who once stripped naked and jumped in the slurry pit on a dare?" Idree rolled her eyes, but her voice was merry. "I want to see the wound with my own eyes. I need to make sure you're real...and that you don't need to be stitched up."

You're not getting anywhere near a needle. "Fine," Dashi said, casting a glance at Sevlin.

He held her gaze for a moment, then turned around.

He didn't see anything, she told herself. *Your hand was covering the statuette the whole time.* "Step behind the horses at least," she muttered to Idree. *Anything to get to the horses.*

Spit whickered a greeting and lipped her sleeve when Dashi approached.

"Hey, old man," Dashi murmured, running her hands over his speckled coat. "Thought you'd gotten rid of me for good, huh?" She touched the saddle the way Idree had, running her hand over the cantle and the hidden compartment inside. Had Idree and Sevlin saved the saddle because they hoped, somehow, that she'd make it back? She wanted to ask her sister, but her throat was suddenly too tight.

Idree grabbed Dashi by the arm, jerking her attention away. "What happened to the belt?"

"The ants chewed it off."

"*What?* What?" she repeated in a lower voice. "Why would they do that?"

Briefly, Dashi explained about seeing V again and how she'd pantomimed breaking the belt.

"And it *understood*?" Idree asked.

Dashi nodded.

"I almost can't believe that. It doesn't make any sense." Her sister was silent for a moment, then a smile spread across her face, sly at first, then radiant. "And I don't care." She twirled around Dashi. "I don't care why and I don't care how. All I care about is that you're safe and we don't have to go back to Karak City."

Dashi laughed. "That's the exact thought that keeps running through my mind."

Idree stopped twirling. "Now, let me see these wounds."

Dashi obligingly pulled back her deel, letting her sister fuss over the injuries and exclaim over the strange green patch and the healing that had already taken place. The mothering seemed to make Idree feel better, while Dashi wanted neither to mother nor be mothered. How could they be so different, she wondered. The thought came with a surge of affection this time. She needed to protect this girl, who was so different than herself. *Protect the seamstress.*

"I can see so much new skin already," Idree said, straightening. "And it's only been a week! It shouldn't have healed that quickly, should it?"

Dashi shrugged her deel over her shoulders. "Well, I can't see my back, but judging by the one on my side, no, I don't think so. I have a theory that it has something to do with their saliva. V's wounds from her run-in with Negan were nearly healed too."

Idree raised her eyebrows. "You're talking about them like they're people."

Dashi grinned. "I know. Let me get dressed. I'll tell you everything when I'm warming myself by the fire."

Her sister turned toward the saddlebags. "Where are your extra clothes?"

"I can find them." All she needed was a moment alone, away from Sevlin's sharp eyes and Idree's curiosity.

Idree leaned over a bag of supplies and peered in. "You did bring some, right?"

"I can do it." She wasn't sure if she could. She'd had a hard enough time putting on her deel when she woke up and she was even more tired now. But what she needed to do had to be done alone.

"Oh, here they are. Take that off and—"

"Stop hovering, Idree! I can blessed dress myself!"

Idree's hands froze, one holding the extra clothes, the other clutching the edge of Dashi's deel. Her face didn't look as round anymore. Dashi's eye flicked downward, to the deel hanging from her sister's shoulders. She looked sick and thin. Probably similar to the way Dashi herself looked, only Idree hadn't been wounded. She'd just been grieving.

"I'm fine," Dashi said, gentler this time. "Well, fine enough to get dressed by myself." She touched Idree's arm. "Really, Idree. I am. Just give me a moment and then you can fuss over me all you want while I'm laying by the fire."

Her sister nodded reluctantly, but before she turned to go, Dashi grabbed her in a tight hug. "I'm glad to be back too, Idree."

Idree smiled.

"Don't start crying now," Dashi said, giving her a push toward the fire.

Once Idree was gone, Dashi dressed as best she could, winding the extra breast band around her chest awkwardly and following it with a clean undershirt, deel and pants. Stealing a glance over her shoulder to make sure Sevlin's back was still turned, she slid the statuette out of her old deel and into the secret compartment of her saddle. It fit perfectly. Her fingers lingered briefly on Altan's pendant and then she snapped the compartment closed.

There, she thought, her shoulders sagging with fatigue. It was done. The statuette was safe.

The evening meal was brief, for Dashi anyway. She had no idea how long Idree and Sevlin stayed awake, but she dozed off mid-bite and didn't wake until late the next morning. The quiet *snick, snick, snick* of wood being splintered roused her first. She opened her eyes to see Sevlin sitting nearby, peeling bark from a stick and tossing it onto the coals of the morning's fire.

"Morning," she said, sitting up and rubbing her eyes. "Where's Idree?"

Sevlin jerked his head at a location behind her back. "Washing up."

Dashi sat up straight. "Is that safe?"

"Well, I can hardly supervise a twelve-year-old girl bathing, can I?" He leaned forward and offered Dashi some bread and dried meat. "We haven't seen any sign of the other racers since we found what was left of their camp."

"What was left of it?" she echoed.

Sevlin gave a terse nod. "More rats."

"No sign of survivors?"

"Not that I saw."

Dashi turned to look at the place where the stream disappeared into the woods and started to get to her feet. "Idree shouldn't be alone then. How long has she been gone?"

"There haven't been any rat tracks. Not since the ants started shadowing us around the same time."

"Oh." She settled herself back on the ground and took a bite of bread. It was old and hard but somehow still tasted delicious. "Well, that's good."

Sevlin didn't reply, just sat there watching her chew, peeling away at the bark until the stick was pale and naked. There was something different in his face this morning. Colder. He was no longer smiling with his whole mouth. He wasn't smiling at all.

He cleared his throat. "Idree told me about the belt."

Dashi swallowed the bread and took a sip of water, making it take longer than necessary. But when she answered all she could think of to say was, "And?" It came out sounding combative, even though she didn't mean it to be.

Sevlin's lips pulled tight on one side. "And it's a good thing I didn't expect an apology."

"It was my life, Sevlin. I'm not going to apologize for trying to save it."

"Were you planning to kill me in my sleep? Like you said in the temple: no ideal is more sacred to you than survival. Everyone steals the bracelet when it comes down to it, right? Is that what it would have been like with me?"

"No! Didn't Idree tell you that?"

"She did." He shrugged. "I didn't believe her."

Dashi took another bite of bread and chewed with deliberate slowness. "I wasn't planning to kill you, but believe what you want, Sevlin. I won't waste my breath trying to convince you when your mind is already made up."

"We had a deal. You gave me your word."

"You knew we were competitors. We were always competitors."

He ran a hand over his face, lingering on his scar. "There are enough people in Tyvalar who would stab me in the back if they could. I don't need one more. And neither does Queen Lyazzat. These are dangerous times for Tyvalar and we can't afford to take in dangerous people."

She gave a sharp nod. "Fine by me." If that's the way things were going to end, then so be it. She should probably keep Idree as far as possible from Sevlin and his queen anyway. He was only making things easier.

"What's that mean?"

"It means you offered us a place in Tyvalar in exchange for my help in getting the needle. I don't expect you to hold up your end for nothing. Idree and I will go elsewhere."

He sighed and dropped his hand from his scar. "I won't turn away two orphaned girls without offering other help."

"We're not *girls*—I'm grown and Idree is on her way, as you like to remind me. And we don't need your help."

"You have a lot of other offers?"

"I don't need any. It's a big world, and there are a lot of places besides Tyvalar."

He snorted. "None that are safe. Where are you going to go? Back to Karakal, where some madman strapped an explosive to you? Thracedon? They're one step away from anarchy. Yassar? They're peaceful, but they don't let in outsiders, so unless you have some Yassari relations, I don't think that's a viable refuge either."

"First you say we're not welcome in your country, and now you're worried about us?" She stood up and brushed the crumbs from the front of her deel. "Don't be, Sevlin. We'll go somewhere else and we'll be fine."

"Go where?" Idree asked from behind her.

Dashi glared at Sevlin. He shrugged one shoulder, as if to say he wasn't going to change the subject just because Idree was in earshot. Dashi turned to Idree. "Sevlin doesn't trust us and he doesn't want us to come to Tyvalar anymore. So we'll find somewhere else to go."

"But...where?"

Dashi pretended not to see Idree's stricken face. She'd known her sister's disappointment was coming. For a few brief hours she thought she could avoid it, but it had turned out to be inevitable. Sevlin had done her a favor, actually, by giving her an easy way out. A way to stay far from him that wouldn't raise suspicion.

"We'll find somewhere else," she said again.

She glanced back at Sevlin who, she noticed, hadn't contradicted her statement that he didn't want them in Tyvalar. "How far to the edge of the taiga?" she asked. The ants had traveled quickly yesterday, but she had no idea where their starting point had been.

"A day, maybe a day and a half? There was a storm and the ravine flooded. We've been paralleling it since we left the temple, but it's hard to gauge distance here."

She nodded. *Good.* There wasn't any point in lingering. The faster she got the needle and her sister away from Sevlin, the better she'd feel. "Start getting packed, Idree."

"Now?"

"Why not? There's no point in staying together. We're not going in the same direction anymore. Besides," she said, cutting her eyes at Sevlin, "our continued presence is probably making Sevlin nervous."

Again, Sevlin didn't protest and it bothered Dashi more than she cared to admit. Idree walked to the horses. Dashi followed.

"It's because of the belt, isn't it?" Idree asked. "I'm sorry," she said when Dashi didn't respond. "I was just so relieved and I wanted to tell—" She broke off, shaking her head. "You're right, I'm too trusting."

"It's not your fault, Idree. We'll be better off on our own."

"No, we're not."

"We *will* be. You'll see. Who knows where we'll end up or what we'll do." Dashi tried to make her voice excited. "We'll bribe our way onto a Yassari fishing boat. Or find a new city to explore."

Idree turned to her horse without responding.

Dashi led Spit a little distance away to saddle him. Using her body to shield her actions from view, she opened the hidden saddle compartment. The gleam of gold greeted her and, when she touched the statuette with her index finger, so did the buzz of the needle inside. She pulled her finger away, simultaneously reassured that the needle was still there, and distressed to find it still agitating to be united with Idree. Dashi closed the compartment and began removing Spit's hobbles, wondering if it was better to hide the statuette along the way, leaving it unguarded in the taiga, or to keep it close by so she could make sure it was safe.

Sevlin had been speaking quietly to Idree, but now she saw him walking toward her. She kept working. He leaned one shoulder against Spit's side, watching her silently. Dashi winced at the spasm of pain as she tightened the girth. Sevlin's fingers twitched, like he wanted to take the girth out of her hands and do it for her, but he stayed where he was. Over the top of Spit's back, she could see Idree pulling herself into the saddle. Her lower lip was tucked between her teeth.

Although she'd planned to ignore him, his presence was too grating. "What do you want, Sevlin?"

"You know I'm right about you being dangerous. Tyvalar might go to war with Karakal someday soon and we don't need people whose allegiance is compromised."

"I have no allegiance to the khan."

"I meant to yourself."

She rolled her eyes. "I guess I'm the only one not willing to fall on my sword for crown and country. If I'm that dangerous, maybe it was you who intended to double-cross me. Were you going to kill me along the way so I never made it to Tyvalar?"

"I would have made sure you and Idree had a safe place in Tyvalar," he said quietly. "Someone would have kept an eye on you, of course, but it would have been safe."

"I don't believe you." She did, though. She fit her boot in the stirrup and pulled herself onto Spit's back. Try as she might to keep the gasp of pain inside, it escaped anyway.

"Your reins are twisted," Sevlin remarked from the ground.

She ignored him. "Ready, Idree?"

Her sister nodded.

Sevlin was standing next to her knee, his hand brushing slowly over Spit's neck while his pale eyes watched her. "You never asked what happened to the statuette after you fell into the river."

Dashi calmly untwisted the reins. "Because I don't care." She settled the worn leather in her hands and looked down, forcing herself to meet his eyes. "You're the one with an allegiance to something bigger. My only allegiance is to myself, remember? As long as I'm safe, the statuette can stay in the temple as far as I'm concerned."

Sevlin stared at her for a long moment. "Good luck, Dashi."

"Good luck, Sevlin." Then, in a warmer tone, she added, "Thank you for making sure Idree was safe."

"Any time." His hand moved to her leg, squeezing once, just above the knee, before dropping away.

Dashi turned Spit southward, pulling back slightly on the reins so Idree could fall in beside her. The trees seemed better spaced here, not crowding into each other as they had deeper in the taiga. Sevlin was right; they were almost out.

Idree gave her a sideways glance. "I was thinking about what you said. These adventures, won't we need a lot of money for them?"

Dashi nodded. "Oh, yes. Definitely."

Idree waited a moment, then huffed impatiently. "Well? We don't *have* a lot of money! What are we doing to do?"

Dashi clucked to Spit and her extra mounts, guiding them beneath a low-hanging tree. "Have you ever heard of a man named Chertai? He's an artist."

Idree shook her head.

"He's very famous. One of his pieces can sell for its weight in gold. Now, granted, I don't have much experience actually *selling* art, only stealing it, but I distinctly remember Altan telling me that and, as we know, Altan never lied."

Idree snorted.

"I don't think he lied about Chertai though. At least, I can't think of a reason why he would."

"Why are you telling me this?"

"Because I want you to understand how important the vase is. We need to be certain—absolutely certain—that it makes it to wherever we're going in one piece."

"What vase?"

"The original Chertai that I stole from the noble who put the pyrothrite belt on me. You remember me saying he was a noble, right? Well, he was an art collector too. Beautiful stuff. Anyway, I stole it hoping I could use it to pay a blacksmith to take the belt off. When that failed, I hid it for you. I had a note sent a few days after the race, telling you where to find it. Of course, you decided to chase me down on the steppe, so you weren't there to receive it."

Idree was silent for a long moment. This time it was Dashi's turn to sneak a glance at her. She was staring straight ahead, her mouth set. But when she turned suddenly to look at Dashi, her eyes were dancing. "You're serious?"

"I never joke about taking other people's things."

Idree laughed, then grew immediately serious. "I'm sorry I ruined things with Sevlin."

Dashi shifted in her saddle. It felt uncomfortable all of the sudden. It could have been the guilt of keeping something from her sister, except that she'd never felt guilty for that before. Probably she was only stiff from her injuries.

"It's fine," she said.

"But—"

"Really, Idree. It's fine. Who wants to go to Tyvalar anyway? It's too staid. We'd end up as serious as Sevlin."

"So...where are we going?"

She wasn't sure if her sister believed her or not, but at least she changed the subject. "I don't know," Dashi admitted. "It'll be an adventure."

"But we'll have to decide something sooner or later."

"Well, first we have to sneak back into Karak City to get the vase. While we're there, we'll get a map. You can decide then."

"*I* can decide?"

Dashi nodded.

"Anywhere?"

"Why not?"

"No matter what country we end up in, we should find a larger town, so we won't stick out too much."

"I couldn't agree more."

"With lots of space for us to ride."

"You like riding now?" Dashi grinned. "Then absolutely."

Idree went on like that for a few minutes, listing attributes of their new home while Dashi let her mind wander. Where they ended up wasn't nearly as important as where they *weren't*: under the control of someone who knew about the needle and knew about her sister. If Sevlin had any reason to suspect she'd lied to him, he'd come looking for them. She had no doubts about that. The same was true for the noble in Karak City and the khan himself.

A rustle in the branches made Dashi glance over her shoulder, but there was nothing there, only the dark needles and darker trunks that made up the taiga. And the creeping mist, scudding along in the treetops, watching them leave. The sun broke through the clouds, turning the mist from silver to burnished gold, the exact color of the statuette hidden in her saddle. In the back of her mind, Dashi could hear Khagan Nuray's gravelly voice. *The veins of magic are resurfacing and they will either bring with them great good, or great pain...The key lies with the seamstress.*

Dashi turned her back on the mist. She didn't care about using the needle for good. She didn't care if the veins of magic were resurfacing. If she had anything to say about it, there would never be another seamstress again.

TO MY READERS...

After many long days (read: years) of writing, it's exciting to finally be able to share Dashi's adventures with you...so thank you for being here! Reviews really help drive sales for indie authors like me. If you enjoyed *The Golden Needle*, please consider leaving a review so other readers can connect with my work.

Want more Dashi? Get a FREE copy of *Treasure Chest*, a standalone short story that bridges books 1 and 2 of The Taiga series. Go to https://BookHip.com/TSJFKXD

ACKNOWLEDGMENTS

I am a firm believer that there are no self-made people in this world. I owe any success I have, in pursuits both literary and non-, to the wonderful people who have graced my life.

Mom and Dad, thank you for giving me the room to choose my own path and for teaching me how to set goals and work for them. Thank you also for the many hours you spent watching the kids so I could write. I would not be the person I am today without the two of you. Clay, Ty, Ross and Dan, thank you for reading, thank you for cheering, and thank you for only being a phone call away. You are each a blessing in my life.

Clare, you read the first mess I ever wrote (be honest: you skimmed, didn't you?) and, for some reason I'll never understand, you agreed to keep exchanging. You've helped me improve ever since. You're the editor-on-my-shoulder, asking me if I really need to include all that background information (I usually don't). You're a fount of knowledge when it comes to Scottish slang and you have a mean tablet recipe. A++ critique partner.

Books are created for an audience and my first readers are also my trusted friends, able to appreciate strong points and unafraid to point out weaknesses. Thank you to Katie, Sarah and Steph, for the three Rs: reading what I've written, rooting for me, and recommending good books. Oh yeah, and two decades of friendship. Nick, your knowledge about all things writing is unparalleled. I know my replies sometimes seem to travel via Pony Express, but I always appreciate your thoughtful responses and your willingness to tell me what I got both right and wrong. To Susan, Piper and Kelsey: my eternal gratitude for asking after my writing and for offering to read. Dave, you were there at the beginning of this thing. I like to think you visited for the diverting book discussions, but maybe it was the wings and bread. Arial & Matt, I appreciate not only your friendship and book-related advice but also your unfathomable willingness to take on my offspring. Kir, your enthusiasm always fills my flagging sails and your instincts are spot on. Thank you for your love and support.

C, G, and R: You are my absolute favorite people on this planet. Thanks for all the brainstorming help (a.k.a. D & D), for keeping me from taking things too seriously, and for putting up with me when I'm in another world.

Brad, I said this in the Dedication but it bears repeating: You've always believed I could do this. Thank you for the countless ways you have supported me on this years-long journey. With you beside me (clamoring to know what happens, demanding that I stop overusing certain words, bragging about me to coworkers and store clerks as I melt from mortification), I can always push on.

ALSO BY T.J. CARROLL

THE SILVER SEAMRIPPER--ORDER NOW!

A year has passed since Dashi narrowly escaped the khan's race with her life and reunited with her sister, Idree.

Now all Dashi wants is to lead a quiet life, but the revelation that her family is the stuff of Purek legend continues to bring dangerous attention.

When Idree goes missing, Dashi has no choice but to follow her sister's trail...even if it leads back to her homeland and a city rife with enemies. Balancing uncertain alliances and the dangers of discovery, she must infiltrate the khan's stronghold and free her sister.

Dashi's past is never far away, and as her misdeeds catch up with her, there is more at stake than Idree's freedom. With her life on the line, Dashi realizes that to free Idree she must once again brave the taiga and the traps left by the ancient Pureks. This time her goal is to find the seamripper, the mythical artifact that can counter the golden needle and stop the khan's growing power.

About the Author

T.J. Carroll has lived all over but now calls Earth home. When she's not writing, she enjoys hiking, saying she's going to establish a family game night, and lurking in bookstores. The Golden Needle is her debut novel and the first book in The Taiga series. She avoids social media but you can find her on Amazon's Author Central.